AIN'T NOTHIN' PERSONAL

CHRIS KELSEY

Black Rose Writing | Texas

The author grants the final approval for this literary material.

First printing

ISBN: 978-1-68433-702-6
PUBLISHED BY BLACK ROSE WRITING
www.blackrosewriting.com

Printed in the United States of America
Suggested Retail Price (SRP) $19.95

Ain't Nothin' Personal is printed in Chaparral Pro

*As a planet-friendly publisher, Black Rose Writing does its best to eliminate unnecessary waste to reduce paper usage and energy costs, while never compromising the reading experience. As a result, the final word count vs. page count may not meet common expectations.

To my wife, Lisa Kelsey, and my kids, Jasper and Meret.

ACKNOWLEDGEMENTS

As always, thanks to my intrepid beta readers,
Gisele Bryce, Lisa Kelsey and Judy Kelsey.

AIN'T NOTHIN'
PERSONAL

PROLOGUE

I reckon it's not news to anybody when I say the calendar flipping over from the 1920s to the 1930s was a cue for everything in this country to go straight to hell.

Do not pass go, do not collect $200.

I don't remember much about those days, being a small boy at the time, but the way my elders and John Steinbeck tell it, Oklahoma was hit especially hard. It made sense it would be, since the two primary drivers of our economy—petroleum and agriculture—went south at more or less the same time. In western Oklahoma, dust storms compounded our difficulties, turning day into night and making a simple trip to the outhouse as treacherous as Robert Falcon Scott's trek to the South Pole. I'm not religious, but I can understand why true believers might think the Lord was making us pay for living it up too much when the getting was good.

Personally, I don't think God had much if anything to do with it. Our problems were fairly cut and dried: too much oil coming up from under the ground, and not enough rain falling from the sky. The worst of our troubles did not abate until Mother Nature got herself back in adjustment, farmers learned to conserve the soil, and Franklin Roosevelt got elected President. Of course, a world war that blew the hell out of the planet also played a part.

If you want to thank God for making it rain again and inspiring the farmers to rotate their crops, be my guest. As for the election of FDR and WW II: I believe they're opposite sides of the same coin, attributable to both the wisdom and folly of the Lord's wayward children. God might work in mysterious ways, but I reckon when it comes to politics and war, he'd just as soon let us sort things out.

Families who'd once been well-off found themselves eating fried dough and whatever withered potatoes and turnips they could coax from out of the dust. Those who couldn't manage starved to death or headed west by jalopy or freight train, encountering various other hardships that are thankfully not relevant to this account.

Not everyone left. Plenty stayed. My folks stuck it out. So did most of their friends.

One way to identify a Dust Bowl survivor is to ask their opinion of the aforementioned Mr. Steinbeck. Younger people and latecomers to the state might tell you they think he's a fine writer, an American treasure; those of a certain age who weathered the '30s in place will probably cuss him.

Truthfully, I've never exactly understood why. I believe *The Grapes of Wrath* made us look resilient and kind to our neighbors, which are pretty fair attributes to have. My parents' generation takes a less sympathetic view, however. Even such a lover of literature as my mother, the late Marceline Hardy, thought Steinbeck's portrait of us was more unkind than need be, and she wasn't usually quick to take offense.

The pain and hopelessness inflicted by the Dust Bowl and Great Depression let loose an additional affliction: an outbreak of lawlessness that rivaled the bad old days before Oklahoma was a state, when it was refuge-of-first-resort for all manner of villains looking to evade justice. In the 1890s, the long arm of the law mysteriously came up short when it came time to reach into the twin territories.

In the '30s, things may have been even worse. When I was little, grownups talked about John Dillinger, Ma Barker, and Oklahoma's own Pretty Boy Floyd like they would baseball players or politicians. Banks were robbed and people were killed from Dallas to Kansas City and everyplace in-between, including plenty of small towns in Oklahoma. Every day, the newspaper ran a new story about this or that gang of thieves who held up a gas station or gunned down a lawman.

Some people even idolized those gangsters—considered them Robin Hood-like figures who stole from the rich and gave to the poor. I disagree. To my mind, they were a bunch of evil bastards, too lazy to work for a living. They didn't just take from rich folks. They robbed from whoever was handy—gas jockeys, bank clerks and the like, none of whom were millionaires. The cops they killed along the way sure as hell didn't make much money. Not the honest ones, at any rate.

The era's most infamous outlaws were a couple of murderous sociopaths named Bonnie and Clyde. Bonnie Elizabeth Parker Thornton was a high-school dropout and former-child-bride-turned-truck-stop-waitress from the slums of West Dallas. They say she had big dreams, but read some of the sorry-ass poems she wrote—the newspapers were full of them at the peak of her infamy—and you'll understand why she never achieved notoriety for anything except being a gunman's moll.

Her boyfriend Clyde Barrow was from West Dallas, too. As a kid, he learned to crack safes, steal cars, and hold up liquor stores. I don't know if his dreams were as big as Bonnie's, but if they involved becoming a mass-murdering piece of shit, you'd have to say he did what he set out to do.

There are plenty of books written about the pair, so I won't detail their short and sordid reign of terror. Suffice to say: They robbed and murdered for a few years, until in 1934 they themselves were shot to death in an ambush led by a legendary former Texas Ranger named Frank Hamer, who figured he'd bypass the legal system and just put them down like a pair of rabid dogs. It's hard to argue they deserved a better fate.

I only bring them up because of a crime they got accused of but didn't commit.

***

On the afternoon of October 11, 1932, a Pullman porter by the name of Ike Butler disembarked from a Santa Fe passenger train in Burr, Oklahoma, a small town located in the state's least-populated county, snug against the border of the Texas panhandle. Mr. Butler's intent was to jump off quick and buy a newspaper while they picked up or discharged a few passengers. For reasons unknown, the train left without him. A passerby found his body a few hours later on the side of a country road outside town, split nearly in half by what law enforcement at the time conjectured was a fireman's axe. Whatever it was, they never recovered it.

The next evening at an area watering hole, a certain local bigot was overheard by a sheriff's deputy bragging about having committed the crime. He even showed off the bloodstains on the clothes he'd been wearing and hadn't changed out of. The deputy arrested him on the spot.

The fella was proud of what he'd done. He confessed to anyone who asked until his lawyer eventually shut him up. It should've been an open-and-shut case, except at the trial, a few prominent citizens decided they didn't like the idea of convicting a local white man for killing a negro. They concocted a story about seeing a man and woman in a brown V8 Ford dump Mr. Butler's body. They identified the culprits as Bonnie and Clyde, whose names were just starting to be widely known. They were white, but they weren't local, and besides, the chance of them being arrested and put on trial in Tilghman County was practically nil.

The county attorney was ready for the Bonnie and Clyde excuse. He'd done his research and discovered the pair had killed a shopkeeper in Sherman, Texas at the same time they were supposed to have chopped up Ike Butler. He tried to submit evidence to that effect. The judge wouldn't allow it. The jury probably wouldn't have cared if he did. They found the defendant not guilty. The earthly remains of Ike Butler were taken home for burial to Chicago on the same train he'd ridden into town.

The killer faced some consequences. He was a chronic troublemaker. The townsfolk had gotten tired of it. Get the hell out of Dodge and don't come back, they said. He did. For over 30 years, few residents of Burr ever saw or heard from him.

That is, until one day in December 1966, when from behind the walls of the Oklahoma State Penitentiary, an old man suffering the last stages of lung cancer and wanting to make things right with his Lord claimed knowledge of an unsolved killing in Burr.

He told the warden he'd reveal what he knew to one man: Emmett Hardy.

That would be me. I'm Burr's chief of police. Or I was until I got suspended for being a drunk and spent two months in the hospital drying out. They tell me it's only a matter of time before I get my badge back. "Get your life back together," they said. "That's all you got to do."

Oh, is that all?

In that case, I should probably refrain from counting my chickens.

CHAPTER ONE

If a year ago you'd asked me to compile a list of experiences I hoped never to have, interrogating a 70-year-old convicted murderer dying of lung cancer in a prison infirmary would've been up there with finding a deep-fried mouse in my tater tots.

At least I've not been subjected to the latter.

The drive from Burr to the state prison in McAlester can take anywhere from four-and-a-half to six hours. The shortest way takes you through Oklahoma City. That used to mean negotiating a lot of local traffic, although I understand the new east-west thoroughfare called Interstate 40 bypasses a lot of that. I believe it's still under construction, however—I didn't want to find out, at any rate—so I took a more leisurely route. It was bad enough I was being asked to spend a lovely Indian summer afternoon in the company of a man who I wouldn't dump a cup of warm tobacco juice on if he was on fire. I didn't need the added aggravation of fighting city traffic.

Unless you've sinned against the State of Oklahoma, you'll likely never have reason to visit McAlester, which right there is about as good a reason to live a virtuous life as I can name. I'm sure the town is home to many fine people, but its reputation doesn't rest on them so much as the 1,200 killers, thieves, and rapists who are semi-permanent residents. When an Oklahoman mentions McAlester, they're usually talking about the Oklahoma State Penitentiary. That's the official name. Some call it Big Mac. Most just call it McAlester.

Essentially, the only reasons for a non-criminal to visit is if they work at the prison or have kin on the inside. Some—myself, for instance—are occasionally required by the rules of their profession to attend. Just driving by the place is enough to give you nightmares. If you can't avoid going, take your time getting there, do your business quick, and get out as fast as you can.

My last journey to McAlester was a few summers back, when I helped my buddy Keith Belcher, a Tilghman County sheriff's deputy, escort a recently convicted felon to his new home. I waited outside while Keith handed him off to the guards. I didn't have prior authorization to enter, and McAlester's surprisingly picky about who they'll let in, so I sat in the van and watched through a 20-foot-high chain-link fence as a group of convicts practiced for the prison's annual rodeo.

They threw ropes around each other's necks and took turns bouncing around on an oil drum suspended by inner tubes stretched between a couple of dead trees. Watching them strangle one another and nearly kill themselves falling off their makeshift bucking bronco wasn't the worst way to while away a half-hour. On our way home, Keith and I stopped at the only air-conditioned bar in town, drank 3.2 Pearl and listened to jailhouse stories of death and depravity told in flamboyant detail by off-duty prison guards doing their best to shock the shit out of us.

The warden called the Burr police station asking for me. Bernard Cousins, who's the acting chief until I get my job back, game him my home number. The warden said a prisoner wanted to confess to something big, and I was the only one he'd confess it to. I suggested he let Bernard handle it, but the warden was adamant I come. The prisoner wouldn't even tell him. It had to be me.

I asked the man's name. As soon as he told me, I knew what it was about. Or at least thought I did.

Rufus Kenworthy was the same redneck who got away with killing Ike Butler back in '32. I reasoned after all these years he was at last ready to own up to what he done.

The warden said he tends to take deathbed confessions pretty seriously, especially with someone like Rufus Kenworthy, who'd spent his golden years trying to get right with the Lord. He'd already confessed to several smaller, previously unsolved crimes. I asked the warden if Kenworthy had mentioned why it had to be me. Apparently Kenworthy told him, "Because he's his daddy's son."

I didn't like the sound of that.

I explained to the warden about my employment status, and how I might not be the best person to take this on. He was insistent. I made an appointment for the next day.

I figured I might, seeing as I had plenty of time on my hands.

On my way out of town, I stopped by my father's house. Dad's gotten so senile, sometimes he doesn't recognize me. Most often, he confuses me with his brother, Ernie. Sometimes he'll call out my mama's name and asks what's for supper. I say she's not there and ask him what he wants. He says fried chicken, which is all he'll eat and is about all I can cook.

I fried him up a batch the night before, which I left in his refrigerator. I told him I'd be getting back late and wouldn't see him until tomorrow. He seemed to barely realize I was there. He just stared at the TV and watched a load of ping-pong balls get dumped on Captain Kangaroo's head.

One thing about visiting Dad these days: Worrying about the shape he's in keeps me from worrying about the shape I'm in.

I drove out to Wes Harmon's Sinclair and filled up, even though it's in the opposite direction from where I was headed. If you can't say anything else good about me, at least I'm loyal.

I stopped for lunch at a drive-in outside Bugtussle, a little dot on the map near Lake Eufala, a few miles north of McAlester. My deputy Kenny Harjo is from the area and had recommended it highly. A carhop in white roller skates, blue ski pants and a tight green sweater brought me a charcoal-grilled hamburger the size of a baby moon hub cap. I'd rather have a good burger than filet mignon, and this one was better than good. Unfortunately, the fries were greasy and limp, which is about the worst thing you can say about a French fry. I ate a couple and stuffed the rest back in the bag, careful not to spill any on the dark-gray tweed sport coat and dress pants I'd donned for the occasion.

From the highway, the Oklahoma State Penitentiary looks like a cross between one of those huge grain elevators they got in Enid and a castle from an old Bela Lugosi movie. I reckon Dracula would fit in behind those bars just fine. Big Mac houses the worst of the worst. Oklahoma's bad guys are as bad as you'll find anywhere.

This time they had my name at the gate and let me in without a hitch. The first thing I noticed was how hot it was. Winter was taking its time getting here. The temperature when I left Burr that morning was in the high 60s. By the early afternoon when I arrived at the prison, it was in the 80s. Inside, it must've been ten degrees hotter. The State of Oklahoma must figure they have better use for taxpayers' money than providing air-conditioning to prisoners—especially on a December day when, by all rights, it should've been 40 degrees cooler.

A burly guard with a friendly grin and biceps as big around as watermelons escorted me through a series of checkpoints and locked gates to a large circular room lit up by dim incandescent bulbs and a skylight cut into the thirty-foot-high ceiling. The place smelled like a mix of sweat, cigarette smoke and urinal cakes. What I first thought were cracks in the plaster turned out to be, upon closer inspection, black ants crawling up and down the walls in single file.

Barred doors leading to cellblocks radiated out from the circular walls like spokes from a wheel. In the middle of the room was a ten-foot-high cage. Inside, a couple of guards with cigarettes drooping out of their mouths sat behind some kind of desk or console. On top of that cage was another one, in which a pair of armed guards surveyed the room.

The floor comprised bright red and white tiles waxed to a high gloss, with thick black parallel lines leading from one door to another. I asked my escort what the black lines were for. He gestured at the guards on top of the cage, and those on an elevated walkway running the perimeter of the room. "If an inmate walks outside those lines," he said, "those boys up there got permission to shoot 'em."

"How often does that happen?" I asked.

"Not too often." He grinned. "Sometimes."

I took care not to stray.

I followed the guard down a corridor to the warden's office. The gatekeeper was a tiny gray-haired woman in a brick-red woolen dress. She squinted over a pair of wireless spectacles and asked my name. The guard told her. She pressed a button on her intercom and announced my arrival. The warden told her to send me in.

His office wasn't much bigger than my own telephone-booth-sized accommodations in Burr. A metal desk took up almost half the room. A black file cabinet occupied one corner. On top of it was an underpowered fan, fighting a losing battle against the heat. Behind the desk, a bookshelf held a few legal volumes, and a trophy made out of a bowling pin. On the wall above the warden's head was a picture of Jesus mounted on a piece of lacquered wood with the inscription, "Get rid of all bitterness, rage and anger, brawling and slander, along with every form of malice. Be kind to one another, tenderhearted, forgiving one another, as God in Christ forgave you."

I thought that was a peculiarly nice sentiment, coming as it did from a man who runs a prison.

The warden was a chunky middle-aged man with a fringe of reddish-gray hair like a scrap of carpet wrapped around his pale bald scalp. Ashes flecked his blue pinstriped suit. The cigar set in the corner of his mouth was unlit. He stood to welcome me. We shook hands. "Thanks for coming, Sheriff Hardy," he said with a smile.

"Chief Hardy," I said. "Haven't gotten a promotion yet." Just the opposite, I thought. "Call me Emmett."

"Alright then, welcome, Emmett." He gestured toward a thickly upholstered brown chair. I took off the fedora I wear instead of a cowboy hat and laid it across my lap.

"Like I mentioned on the phone," I said, "it seems a little strange Mr. Kenworthy wants to confess to a crime everyone knows he did."

"Remind me what that was?" he said.

"He killed a negro fella in our town back in '32, but the jury was bought-off or intimidated. In any case, it didn't convict."

He nodded. "I guess it could be that, but I got the feeling this is about something else. Something he's kept to himself."

"I can't remember any cold cases of consequence, and I've lived in Burr almost my whole life. I guess it could be something that happened before I was born. Rufus must be getting up there."

"Nobody knows exactly how old he is. Not even him. We haven't been able to dig up a birth certificate. He claims to remember being in jail for drunk and disorderly the night they moved the state capitol from Guthrie to Oklahoma City."

I took a second to do the math in my head. "That puts him in his 70s or thereabouts."

"Sounds about right."

"Alright, then. Might as well see what he has to say."

He rocked back in his chair. "Rufus isn't looking for a 'Get Out of Jail Free' card. He understands he's almost done. If he wants to try for the Lord's forgiveness, I'm inclined to help him as much as I can. Who knows?" He shrugged. "He might have something helpful to say."

I had my doubts.

"What'd they finally get him for?" I asked.

"Murder," he said in a tone that implied: What else? "He and a buddy stabbed a colored gas station attendant to death in Langston back in '45."

Langston is mostly all-colored.

"They might've gotten away with it, except they ran over a broken ketchup bottle and got a flat tire. They tried to run for it on foot, but a group of townsfolk caught up with them. I wouldn't have blamed them if they'd beaten 'em to death, but they just took them to the town jail and held them for the highway patrol. Rufus got 25 years-to-life. Better than he deserved." He paused. "I always said the only way he'd be getting out of here is in a pine box."

"What happened to the other fella?"

"He hung himself in the county jail waiting for trial. Saved the state a few thousand a year."

He squirmed in his chair like he was itching to end our meeting and move on to the next thing. I'd driven a hell of a long way, however. I wanted to know everything there was to know.

"How much time does he have left?"

He fiddled with his cigar. I noticed he wore a big silver and gold Shriner's ring. "The doc says it's just a matter of days now," he said. "His mind still works, as well as it ever did, anyway. Oh, he looks bad, all right. He's on oxygen all the time, wasted away to almost nothing. But he still communicates. His voice gets raspy, but he makes himself understood."

We sat quietly for a moment.

"If what you say is true," he continued, "that he killed a negro on your town back in the day—well, that might explain what this is all about."

"How's that?"

He stuffed the cigar into his mouth and picked up a small silver-plated model of an airplane. "Wiley Post's Winnie Mae," he said with a wink. He flicked the airplane's tail section and a small flame burst from the nose.

"Anyway," he said, puffing hard to get it going. "You know about his history of hating negroes. He'd been here a long time before I got this job, but as I understand it, he used to be one of the worst Kluxers in the prison."

The cigar stunk like the two-for-a-nickel kind. "The fella who had this job before me decided he was going to teach Rufus a lesson. He put him in a cell with a negro prisoner just as prejudiced but from the other direction, if you get my meaning. I reckon he thought they'd finish each other off and he'd be rid of both. That's not what happened. They became friends. I believe they were both getting old. They realized carrying all that hate around was wearing them out. Both of them got saved and started witnessing for the Lord. A few months ago the colored boy died—"

"How old?" I asked.

"What's that?"

"How old was he when he died?"

"About Rufus's age."

Not a boy, then. "Sorry to interrupt," I said.

"Anyway, the colored boy dying just about broke Rufus's heart. Not long after, he got sick. He still went to chapel every Sunday, right up until he was too weak to get out of bed. When he asked me if I'd contact you ... well, knowing he had so little time and how he'd repented for a lot of his sins already, I couldn't refuse."

I'd heard enough. We both stood.

"Thanks for comin' in," he said extending his hand. We shook. "I probably won't be here when you finish, but call me in the next couple of days and let me know what he says."

He ushered me out with a pat on the back, good ol' boy-style.

Maybe I'm paranoid, but for some reason both he and his secretary seemed glad to see me go.

CHAPTER TWO

The guard with the big arms led me down a long narrow corridor. Closet-sized cells lined up opposite a row of barred windows looking out on the prison yard. A cataract of dirt, dust, and nicotine clouded the thick reinforced glass.

The inmates were crammed two-to-a-unit. Only three feet and a wall separated the bunks in one cell from the toilet in the next. Turkeys in a Butterball factory have more freedom of movement. A few clawed at us through the bars. The guard drew his nightstick and busted some outstretched hands. I had to wonder whether these men might be a little easier to deal with if given room to stand and stretch without banging their heads against the ceiling and skinning their knuckles on the walls.

The infirmary was long and low-ceilinged, with a dozen iron-framed beds lined up on each side of the room. Most were unoccupied. Judging by the stains on the bare mattresses, previous occupants might not have had working knowledge of a bedpan. Sickly sweet industrial-strength disinfectant battled the stench of urine. 60-watt bulbs on the ceiling were spaced so far apart, the nurses nearly disappeared in the darkness between beds. I've been in dive bars that were lit up brighter. The atmosphere was almost more sinister than the corridor of cells I'd just passed—from the moving shadows on the pale green floor, to the dour expressions on the faces of the handful of patients whose outlooks on life were assuredly worsened by the fact their feet were shackled to their beds.

A stone-faced orderly wearing light blue scrubs with *Property of O.S.P.* stencilled across the back took charge of me at the door. He directed me to a bed at the far end of the room next to the nurse's station. He moved the screen surrounding the bed so I could get in, then closed it behind me.

Rufus Kenworthy was as close to being dead as you can be and still have a pulse. His skin was as dry and thin as paper, drawn tight over his bones. A few scraggly threads of white hair stuck out wire-like from his bald head. His eyes were like dark holes burned deep into his face by a hot poker. A transparent oxygen mask covered his mouth. His chest rose and fell in spasms. A gauze bandage hung open on the inside of one forearm, attached by a single scrap of adhesive tape. Underneath was an angry rash he scratched absentmindedly. I wondered if it had something to do with the cancer or if it was an unrelated misery laid on top of everything else. His gown had bunched up, revealing a flaky, withered haunch. A wrinkled white bedsheet wove around and through his legs, tangled around a clear tube, yellow with the piss collecting in a plastic bag hanging on the side of his bed.

A squat, officious nurse did what she could to straighten the bed with the man still in it. She pulled the sheet from around one of his legs, causing him to wince. She put her face near his and informed him in a loud voice of my arrival. He nodded without opening his eyes. She pulled off the mask, leaving a red circle round his mouth.

"He wouldn't take his medication because he knew you were coming, and he wanted to talk and think clearly," she said. "I doubt he'll be able to take the pain for long, so you'd better say what you got to say."

She shook him by the shoulder. His eyes—yellowed and red-rimmed—opened. He blinked several times and licked chapped, bloody lips. The nurse secured the bandage on his arm with a couple more pieces of tape, then left us alone.

"Mr. Kenworthy."

"Emmett Hardy," he said in a choked voice. "Everett's boy."

"That's right."

It was all I could do to look at him. Not just because of his appearance, but because of what he'd done. I couldn't feel sorry for Rufus Kenworthy like I would an ordinary old man on his deathbed.

His mouth opened but only produced a bubble of spit. He tried again and made a sound I couldn't understand. I leaned in close.

"What was that, Mr. Kenworthy?"

"I remember you when you was little," he croaked.

"That right?" I didn't remember ever meeting him, but of course that was a long time ago.

I didn't drive all the way across the state to make small talk with a multiple murderer.

"I understand you have something to tell me, Mr. Kenworthy."

He nodded slightly. His bald head made a scratching sound like sandpaper rubbing against the pillow. He seemed to be having trouble saying what he had to say. I thought I'd help him along.

"Mr. Kenworthy, if you're looking to cleanse your soul about having killed that Pullman porter back in '32, I might as well tell you everyone in Burr knows you did it. They've always known it. If you're trying to make things right with Jesus, go ahead, but I don't need to hear it to know it's true."

His lips contorted into a jack-o-lantern smile. "Yeh, I did and I'm sorry for it, but I wanted to talk to you about something else."

He cleared his throat, but something went down the wrong way and he began coughing so hard I thought he might expel what was left of his lungs. It took him a minute to get it under control.

"You remember the Younger family?" he said.

I hadn't heard that name in a while.

"I do."

"I can tell you where they're buried."

I didn't know they were dead.

CHAPTER THREE

Except for a few Indians, Burr is an all-white town, and has been for a long time. It hasn't always been that way. When I was little, there were a few negro families living in Burr, and one or two in Butcherville. In the late '30s, however, a group of white folks decided to run them all off. By the time I was in junior high, most of our colored folks had relocated.

Except the Youngers.

Clarence Younger's skin wasn't much darker than mine. His son Gabe told me that was because Clarence's mother was a Seminole Indian. He still considered himself a tribal member—not that it mattered much when it came to how they were treated by the white community.

Back in the '20s, before I was born, Clarence Younger worked a piece of land outside of town for some old farmer whose name I don't remember. When he and his wife started having kids, they decided they wanted something better for themselves. I'm not sure I'd consider a life loading and unloading baggage for the Santa Fe Railroad as a step up from than sharecropping. Of course, what in hell do I know. I've never had to live in a one-room shack without plumbing or electricity, not to mention work 16 hours a day growing crops I didn't hardly get to keep or sell.

The dilapidated house in town where they lived wasn't any great shakes, but I reckon it was better than what they had before. It was located over on Jackson Corners, where Burr's colored folks had always lived.

They lived there happily for several years, or so it seemed to me. Of course, I was just a kid and pretty much unaware of the problems negroes had to face, although my mother did her best to educate me. All of us kids—colored and white—went to school together at a time when it was technically against the law in Oklahoma. As a kid, you don't always notice a lot of things you should. I vaguely knew about the Ike Butler killing, but that was before my time, and anyway, nobody ever talked about it.

I gradually became aware of conflict as I got older. Still, by the time I was 11 or 12 and relations between the races broke down completely, it took me by surprise. It probably shouldn't have, but it did.

I was never clear on the identities of the white folks involved, but beginning in the late '30s, Burr's negroes were bullied into leaving. One by one, negro families left town and moved God-knows-where, until finally Clarence Younger, his wife Eunice, and his kids Gabe and Ethyl were the last ones left.

Even while the other colored people got run off, Clarence stayed put. He figured he had most of the white people in town on his side. You couldn't blame him for thinking so. He was friendly and well-liked. He had a respectable job. Anyone taking the train in either direction had their luggage handled by Clarence. If you needed a ride to the station, you could always call the depot and Clarence would pick you up in his old Model T, free of charge. You could tip him if you were so inclined, but he didn't expect it.

Clarence's son Gabe was my age. We used to fish together from a tank on my father's property, serenaded by mooing cows and a squeaky windmill. We were friends. Not best friends, but pretty close.

Sadly, it was only a matter of time before the same people who ran off the other negroes turned against the Youngers. Clarence thought he had every right to stay, which he sure as hell did, but too many people were against him. Still, he hung on—even after having a cross burned in his front yard and his windows repeatedly broken—hoping "good" white folks would finally stand up for him.

They never did.

Not even the one person I would've expected to. My father, Everett Hardy.

I challenged Rufus Kenworthy with the truth as I knew it.

"The Youngers didn't die. They just got run out of town after a carload of rednecks burned down their house. Clarence told my daddy about it right after it happened."

Kenworthy closed his eyes and shook his head. "That ain't the whole story," he wheezed.

***

I knew the whole story, or thought I did. After the fire, Clarence paid a visit to my father—a man who'd always been civil to him and who he'd seen stand up to bullies and bigots before—and asked if his family could stay in our unoccupied bunkhouse until they could find someplace else to live.

Clarence had boulder-sized cojones. Even after all that had happened, he wanted to stay in Burr.

I'm sure he thought if anyone in town would stand up and help him get back on his feet, it'd be my daddy.

I would've thought the same thing.

My mama wasn't home that day, so when Clarence came calling, I answered the door. I looked past him and saw his family and what few belongings they had left loaded into his Model T. It didn't surprise us. We'd already heard what had happened.

Gabe waved glumly. I waved back.

Clarence was sweaty and covered in soot, but he still managed a polite smile when he asked for my father. Dad was out back cleaning the tool shed, the sort of thing he was born to do. He told me to go to my room, but I disobeyed and hid behind some curtains so I could listen to him and Clarence talk.

Clarence explained while my daddy listened. He'd scarcely finished when Dad made up some phony excuse why he couldn't help. I remember it sounded like he'd practiced it in front of a mirror, and it wouldn't have convinced a two-year-old. Dad's always been a rotten liar.

Clarence said nothing. I wished I could see his face, but I couldn't risk getting caught eavesdropping.

Finally he said, "Alright Everett, thank you for your time. You take care, now." I heard his boots clomp down the front steps and the sound of gravel under his feet as he walked to his car.

My father called after him, "I sure am sorry, Clarence." He meant it. I don't think I ever heard him sound sorrier. I finally took a chance and peeked out the window. Mr. Younger didn't look back, just started up that old bucket of bolts and drove away. That's the last I ever saw of the Youngers.

***

"Mr. Younger came by our house that day and asked my dad for help. He didn't get it. I saw him and his family drive away. They were fine when they left."

"Maybe so," Rufus wheezed, "but they never made it out of town."

"How would you know, anyway? You were gone a long time before this happened."

"Oh, I used to drive to Burr from time to time and go drinkin' with friends at one of them bars they had in Butcherville."

"I see, so one of your old buddies told you about it." He gave a labored nod. "How'd he know?"

"He was one of 'em who did it," he said. Before I could ask who it was, he told me: "Harold Prentiss."

I remembered Harold from when I was real little. He managed the Western Auto back when we had two hardware stores. I remember how most afternoons he'd take a break from selling tires, and camp out on a corner near Burr Elementary when school was getting out. He handed out lollipops—the old-fashioned kind, with a loop of waxed string instead of a stick—and smile and whisper to the little girls. I never knew what he said in those secret conversations, but I know when he died of a stroke around the time I left for the Marines, most women in town my age weren't sorry to see him go. I wouldn't be surprised at anything he might've done.

"Did anybody else back up Harold's story?"

"No one needed to," Kenworthy said. "The way he told me about it, all scared he was goin' to get caught, I knew he was telling the truth."

Rufus told how one night he met Prentiss and four other fellas at a bar. He'd driven to Butcherville straight from his job in Elk City. He'd been working overtime, so it was late when he got there. Harold Prentiss was there with some men Kenworthy didn't know.

I asked him how many and what were their names.

"Four," he said. "I was only familiar with Harold and one other fella. Harold called one of 'em Smiley, but I'd never seen him before." He coughed violently. I handed him a tissue.

He wiped his mouth and started back in. "They'd all gotten a head start on the drinking, but I caught up pretty quick. We was all pretty much three sheets to the wind. They was all acting funny, like they knew something I didn't. I tried to get them to tell me, but they'd only laugh and wink, or tell me I didn't want to know. I remember they were talkin' about how they'd run all the coloreds out of town. I couldn't keep up with what they were sayin', I was so drunk." He coughed some more—a harsh, dry sound, like radio static. "I was a terrible sinner back then."

"If you were so drunk you didn't know what they were saying, how can you be so sure Harold told you he'd killed the Youngers?"

He started scratching his arm through the gauze. "You don't forget something like that," he said. "It sticks with you. No matter how drunk you are. Harold offered to let me stay at his place so I wouldn't have to drive all the way back to Elk City. On the way home is when he told me the Youngers were dead."

"What exactly did he say?"

"I asked him why them boys at the bar had been actin' so strange. He wouldn't say and he wouldn't say until finally I got him to tell me if I promised never to tell nobody. He said they'd finally took care of their colored problem once and for all."

He paused to gather himself. I wanted him to hurry. He was fading fast.

"Meaning what?" I said.

"The night before, him and those boys from the bar had got to talking about how they'd gotten rid of all the negroes in town except for one family. That bothered 'em, I reckon, and they decided to do something about it. Harold and that Smiley character and a couple of others filled some empty bottles with gas from the pumps at the Butcherville Store. It was closed, but there's always a little gas left in the hose. They drove over to Jackson Corners, dipped rags in the bottles, lit 'em up and threw them through the windows. Burnt those coloreds' place to the ground."

The nurse looked in and asked if everything was ok. Rufus waved her away and continued his story.

"One of 'em seen Clarence Younger looking at them out a window. They was so drunk, they didn't worry about it. They reckoned Younger'd be so scared he'd just load his family up and leave town. But later, after they sobered up, they got word the Youngers had camped out at Burr Lake. They got worried Younger might go to the police or the sheriff so they'd better shut him up. Harold told me this Smiley fella and someone else went out there the next night and killed the whole family. Dumped their bodies in the lake."

He broke into another coughing fit. He motioned for a cup of water on his nightstand. I held it to his mouth. He spilled more than he drank.

"How do I know you didn't have something to do with it?" I asked.

"I reckon I understand why you'd think that, given my record," he said, then closed his eyes. He said nothing for a minute. I wondered if that was all I was going to get.

Suddenly he erupted in coughs. He opened his eyes. "Why would I lie?" he said after he'd calmed down. "I admitted everything else."

He had a point. His days were numbered. The one man whose name he knew he'd given was long dead. I tried to think who this Smiley could've been.

"You said besides Harold you knew another fella in the bar that night. Did you mean this Smiley character?"

He stared at me with those rheumy eyes. "Nah, I never met that Smiley before. This was someone else."

"Who?"

"I ain't too sure I want to say."

"Mr. Kenworthy, I appreciate how you're trying to get into heaven and all, but don't you think God would look more kindly on you if you told me who those other fellas were?"

"I've never snitched on nobody but myself, which is what I'm doing now. I ain't sure God likes snitches, anyway. I only told you about Harold because he's dead, and I told you about Smiley because I don't know who he was. You don't need to know who else."

"I do if I'm going to sort this out," I said.

He looked at me like I was the stupidest SOB on the planet. "I don't want you to sort this out. I called you here so you could find them folks' bodies and give them a proper Christian burial."

I'd started to sweat, and not just from the heat. "So you're saying you called me all the way out here just so I could track down some old bones buried in the bottom of Burr Lake? Just so I could bury them again in Burr Cemetery? That don't make a damned bit of sense."

"What other reason could there be?"

"To see justice done, goddammit."

"The Lord is the only judge I recognize."

"Yeh, well I got the feeling you're going to be knocking on his door in a couple of days and find out you've got the wrong address."

"His will be done."

I wanted to knock the pious look off his wasted face. "Can you at least tell me where in the lake they were dumped?"

He sank deeper into his pillow and continued scratching his arm. The bandage had fallen open again. The rash or eczema or whatever it was, was redder than ever. I'd have taped the bandage back in place, but I could bring myself to touch him. I know evil doesn't rub off, but I didn't feel like taking a chance.

"Harold just said they dumped them in the lake. He didn't say where."

"Did they use a boat?"

He shook his head.

"They didn't, or you don't know?"

"Don't know."

"You remember the bar where they were drinking?"

He shook his head.

"You know what they did with the Youngers' car?"

"Junked it, I reckon."

Probably still sitting out in some field. Butcherville's always had more than its share of abandoned machinery.

"You don't know anyone else involved except this Smiley fella?"

He shook his head.

I was mystified.

"Alright then," I said, unable to think of anything else to say. "I can see you're hurting and need your rest, so I'll leave you alone. Thank you for your time."

"Wait a second." A smile as foul as the sore on his arm spread across his ruined face. "I did kind of recognize one other fella. He didn't say much, but I was under the impression he was involved somehow."

"Anyone I'd know?" I asked.

He grinned his horrible grin and coughed and shuddered.

"No one you'd arrest," he said in between fits.

Want to bet?

"Alright, then. Who?"

"Your daddy."

Shit.

CHAPTER FOUR

I treat the memory of my father turning his back on Clarence Younger the same as this entire town does the Ike Butler killing. It's something I'd prefer to forget, but since I can't, I push it to the back of my mind and pretend it's not there.

Few residents of Burr are more respected than my father. Letting the Youngers stay with us would've been like the sheriff blocking the jailhouse door and facing down a lynch mob. I couldn't see the downside to it then, and I can't see it now. Living with the knowledge you could've saved someone but chose not to is like having your daily coffee spiked with arsenic. It might not kill you immediately, but it'll get you in the end.

Turning Clarence away didn't make my dad senile, but I can't believe it didn't have an effect on how he felt about himself. The last twenty-five years of his life haven't exactly been joyful. Most of his sadness had to do with my mother's passing. The first time I saw him after her death—I was a Marine in Korea at the time and couldn't make it home in time for her funeral—I realized a light had gone out of his eyes. I tried to help. Part of the reason I moved back to Burr was to watch over him. But nothing would ever rekindle that light.

Which is not to say he was ever the life of the party. Dad's always trudged through life like he was dragging his own coffin behind him. The situation with the Youngers made things worse, though. I knew he was ashamed of himself as soon as it happened, when he asked me not to tell my mother about it.

But never in a million years would he have taken part in anything like Kenworthy described. Rufus could say whatever he wanted in trying to buy his way into heaven. He might have seen my father in that bar, but if he thought daddy had anything to do with hurting the Youngers, he was as crazy as he was bad.

I remember daddy going out that night and not coming back until late. I figured it was because he couldn't face being around my mother, whose moral compass was as unerring as any human being I've ever known. At dinner that night she expressed concern for the Youngers. He squirmed and barely said a word. She knew something was wrong and asked what it was, but he wouldn't give a straight answer. Even in the best of times he was a man of few words, so she let it go. She was a little surprised when he went out that night—it's not something he often did—but I don't think she thought anything was seriously wrong. On the rare occasion daddy would go out with his friends, she and I would indulge our passion for music, something my father admired but could never make hide nor hair of.

Mama's little record player didn't get used that night, though. I went to bed early, stared at the ceiling and tried to reconcile the man who'd sent away Clarence Younger with the man I'd seen time and again in my childhood standing up for those who were cheated, abused and otherwise afflicted. I came to no conclusions then. I'm not sure I ever did.

***

I resisted the urge to throttle Rufus Kenworthy, nor did I wish him a pleasant trip to whatever circle of hell Satan had waiting for him. The interview, however, was over.

The guard led me out the way we'd come in. The warden was out. Thank God for small favors. I had no desire to rehash what I'd just been told.

I walked out to my truck in a daze. I'd driven halfway to Arkansas before I realized I was heading the wrong way. The road was too narrow to make a U-turn, but I did it anyway. The passenger-side tires left the road and my muffler scraped the asphalt. I'd damaged it a couple of months earlier and never got it fixed. I got out and looked. It wasn't any worse than before.

When I looked up, I saw a Black Angus on the other side of a wire fence bearing witness to my difficulties. "I'd still rather be me than you," I said. It stared and chewed its cud. I waved goodbye to old Bossie and drove away. Within a couple of minutes, I found a road I recognized and got back on track.

My mind was full of things I'd rather be rid of. I figured if I could separate what Kenworthy said about my daddy from the rest of the story, I might find a way forward. I was disinclined by nature to believe anything out of his filthy toilet of a mouth, but his claim the Youngers had been killed rang true.

My dad had nothing to do with it. I was sure of that. It was possible he'd been in the bar that night, but if he was, he wasn't with Harold Prentiss.

Everett Hardy might've been the last man to turn his back on Clarence Younger, but he wasn't the only one. The whole damn town bore responsibility for what befell the Youngers, not to mention the other negro families before them. What's worse is once they were gone, we almost never thought about them again. They might as well have never been there at all. I was as guilty as anyone. Gabe Younger was my friend. For a short time, I'd wonder where he and his family went. But after a while I just didn't anymore. No one else seemed to, either. The town hired a demolition company to erase from the face of the earth the wreckage of their home. By the time I joined the Marines a few short years later, the Youngers had mostly exited the stage of my memory.

I'd be lying if I said that my father turning his back on Mr. Younger didn't affect how I felt about him. He fell in my estimation, no two ways about it. After a while, the reason almost ceased to matter. The real-life Shane or Will Kane or Sam Spade I'd idolized as a kid became just another flawed human being—better than some, no worse than most.

**

It was almost midnight when I got home. My yellow Labrador retriever Dizzy bounced up and down, excited to see me as always. I rubbed her behind the ears a little longer than usual and filled her bowl with Gravy Train. She slurped it down before I could put the bag away. I settled into my La-Z-Boy. She conked out on the floor next to me. I thought about making a phone call or two but decided it was too late.

I watched the news and Johnny Carson's monologue, then leaned back in my recliner and closed my eyes. Sleep was elusive. I couldn't stop thinking about the Youngers lying somewhere at the bottom of Burr Lake, wondering if finding their remains was even possible after so long.

I'd have a better chance finding the killers—not great, but better than one-in-a-million. The key was tracking down this Smiley, whoever he was. My dad nothing to do with it. I knew that in my bones. However, he might know something helpful.

I almost hoped he didn't. It briefly occurred to me that in this case his encroaching senility might be a good thing. I felt ashamed for thinking it.

Ultimately, I'd just need to ask him if or what he knew. Let the chips fall where they may.

If he could help, fine.

If he couldn't, better.

CHAPTER FIVE

During the two months I spent in the drunk ward at the VA Hospital in Temple City, I got used to eating breakfast for the first time in my adult life. For years, I'd subsisted until lunch on black coffee and the occasional package of mini powdered doughnuts. The nurses at the VA brought me real food every morning. It took a while, but I got used to it.

My mama could talk me into eating about anything except oatmeal, so naturally that's what they tried first. After I sent it back untouched a few times, they started serving me bacon and sausage and English muffins. The best way to describe English muffins, they're like edible sponges. Break them apart, toast them and spread a little butter on the insides. Stuff some sausage and/or bacon between the two halves. Not bad.

I didn't check into the VA for the food, though. I did it because booze was killing me. I was ok with that until it became a real possibility and I realized I wasn't.

The folks there said I wasn't a drunk or a bum. I was an alcoholic. They were being nice. "Alcoholic" was too polite a word to describe what I'd become. I talked to a lot of therapists and doctors while I was there. In their professional opinion, self-hate was the biggest part of what was making me drink. They tried to convince me to be more forgiving and accepting of myself. I gave it a shot. I'm not sure how well it worked, but they meant well.

I stayed there from early September until the beginning of November, when I got tired of sitting around in my pyjamas playing Parcheesi all day and checked myself out. The doctors wanted me to stay, but I told them they were wasting their time, I wasn't ever going to get any better than I was.

I appeared before a meeting of the Burr town council and told them I was ready to return to work. I did a poor job of convincing them. They placed me on leave for the rest of the year. I don't blame them, inasmuch as I had—have—doubts of my own. The earliest I could return would be January 1st, 1967, and only if I could convince them I'd gotten my life in order. After everything that had happened, I reckoned that was more than fair.

The trip to the bottom was long and hard, and ended in tragedy.

A trio of lowlifes kidnapped a young boy in my jurisdiction by the name of Earl Collins, I suspect at the behest of a local businessman named Clyde Raymer.

Clyde pressured the boy's father, Merle Collins, to sell him the land their house stood on so he could expand his business, the WestOK natural gas processing plant. Merle refused. I believed but could not prove Raymer arranged to have Earl snatched to force the father's hand. The boy was killed by his captors—accidentally, but that didn't make him any less dead.

I discovered his body myself in an abandoned root cellar not far from his home. That and related events drove me over the edge.

It didn't help that in the months leading up to it I'd made a habit of drinking Old Grand Dad bourbon like water.

I drove away from the whole mess unsure whether I was going to ram my truck into a telephone pole or deal with my problems. I'm too much of a coward to kill myself, which is why I ended up in the hospital.

It's also why I found myself at loose ends for the final two months of the Year of Our Lord, 1966.

Being locked up gave me plenty of time to think. Too much, in fact. I tried to avoid dealing with my problems by watching a lot of television and listening to the radio. On Saturday afternoons they let us listen to University of Oklahoma football games understanding that denying a recovering Okie boozehound the right to follow the Sooners is the fastest way to drive him back to drink. Those games didn't always calm down the inmates. The nurses had to turn off the radio during the last minutes of the Notre Dame game when—with the Sooners losing by several touchdowns—my fellow patients started throwing deviled eggs and orange juice cartons at the speaker mounted on the wall.

***

Getting out of bed was a lot easier now that I'd cut my daily alcohol consumption from enough to kill a herd of elephants to zero. I'd even given up mouthwash.

The rest of the day is the hard part, in that it typically comprises situations that remind me why I drank in the first place.

A nightmare starring a younger, wickeder Rufus Kenworthy in his prime had me crying out in my sleep. My first conscious thought of the day featured the old, repentant Rufus, hours away from shedding this mortal coil, coughing and drooling and forcing a bunch of information on me I'd rather not be privy to.

The box of kitchen matches I'd been using to light the stove was empty. I found a Piggly Wiggly matchbook under the cushions of my couch along with 78 cents and a TV Guide from November 23, 1963, the day after Oswald shot Kennedy. I remember how I felt when JFK died. It wasn't much different from when I discovered Earl Collins' body. I don't think the country's ever gotten over Kennedy's death. I sure hadn't gotten over Earl's. Maybe I never will.

I fried up a load of bacon and toasted some Wonder Bread; Piggly Wiggly was out of English muffins. I promised my doctors I'd try to eat better, although I suspect their version of a healthy diet and mine are radically different. Theirs involves eating more vegetables. Mine involves eating what I like, which is not vegetables. I'm eating three squares a day instead of a pack of donuts here, an order of tater tots there, and a bottle of Old Grand Dad everywhere. They say eating like I do is likely to clog my arteries, but it gives me plenty of energy.

At least I'd cut out the bourbon.

Dizzy feels like it is her inalienable right to eat whenever I do, so I filled her bowl. She scarfed it down in about two gulps.

December had been notably hot. Winter was almost here, yet the weatherman had predicted a high temperature in the 70s. That's ok with me. Winter could take all the time it wanted. Unfortunately, since I wasn't wearing a uniform every day, I had to buy some clothes, and the clothes I bought—three new long-sleeved flannel shirts and a new pair of Levi's—

were not well-suited for warm weather. They were all I had, however, so I rolled up my sleeves and hoped for the best. I'd also splurged on plain, square-toed Acme boots. I had ruined my last pair during the solving of the aforementioned crime wave.

Out of habit, I opened the side-table drawer where I keep my Colt .45 semi-automatic, before remembering I wasn't presently a cop and had no official need to tote a gun. If you'd asked me a couple of years ago if there'd ever be a time when I'd feel it necessary to carry a gun every day—even on the job—I'd have said you were crazy. Burr didn't use to be that kind of town. After recent events, however, I felt naked without one. I checked to see if it was still there. It was. I left it in the drawer.

I put on my fedora and walked out the door. Dizzy slipped past me and jumped up and down on her hind legs, fishing for an invitation to ride along. I told her no. She pouted as I got in the truck and started the engine, but when I looked in the rear-view mirror as I drove away, I could see she'd already shrugged off any hurt feelings. She trotted off to pillage garbage cans and beg for kitchen scraps from housewives. Diz is the Blanche DuBois of dogs—she's always depended on the kindness of strangers.

I needed to visit Dad, but it was a little early, so I thought I'd make a quick trip out to Burr Lake. I didn't expect to all-of-a-sudden find evidence of the Youngers' fate after all these years. However, I wanted to go out and get the lay of the land. Now that I knew what I knew, I hoped being there might give me a sense of what had happened.

On my way out of town, I made a stop at the station to fill-in Bernard and Karen about what Kenworthy had said. Before he was Acting Chief, Bernard had been my Deputy Chief. I'm sure if I never came back to work he'd run our little department just fine, especially now that my former dispatcher and present girlfriend (or so I hoped; I was on probation with her, too) Karen Dean was now a full-time uniformed officer. Together, the two of them add up to a lot more than I'm worth, but they profess to be impatient for my return.

Ever since I got out of the hospital, people have walked on eggshells around me. Even Karen, with whom I frequently share a bed, seems concerned she might say something that'll cause me to return to my old habits. I dislike that I've given them cause to feel they need to treat me like

I'm always on the verge of collapse. I may be a slightly reformed drunk and a little crazy, but as long as I'm distracted from self-pity, I'm pretty tough.

I parked my truck down the street from the station. Bernard had parked his beloved Plymouth Fury police cruiser in my old "Reserved for Chief Hardy" parking spot, which is as it should be. Next to the Fury was the car I used to drive, a Ford Galaxie with a single, dome-shaped revolving red emergency light mounted on the roof. The Fury's light is blue and flat, which bothers Bernard, who thinks our cars should look uniform. I don't really mind one way or the other.

The door was locked. I could've used my keys but chose not to, given my current status. I put my face against the front window and tapped on the glass. Karen emerged from my office and let me in.

"Why's the door locked?"

"Well, good morning to you, too. I was in the little girl's room."

She presented her downy cheek. I gladly kissed it.

"Where's Bernard?" I asked. "The Fury's out front."

"It wouldn't start when he was ready to go home yesterday. I picked him up early this morning and gave him a ride out to Wes's place. He and Wes are on their way over to look at it. Or they will be as soon as Wes's help gets there." Wes Harmon runs the Sinclair station south of town.

"When's Bernard going to get around to buying his own car?"

Karen laughed. "The Fury is his own, or hadn't you noticed? Anyway, why should he? He's basically on-duty 24-hours a day."

True enough. "What's the problem? The starter again?"

"Bernard thinks it's just the solenoid this time." She sat down behind her desk—the same one she used when she was a dispatcher. She's still the dispatcher, but as a uniformed officer, she does other things, as well. "Of course, his mechanical knowledge is only slightly better than yours, so it could be anything. Don't you worry about it. It's not your problem."

It's not my problem. I'm getting sick of being treated like Humpty Dumpty all the time.

I poured myself a cup of coffee.

"I thought you'd come by last night when you got in," Karen said. "Or at least call me."

"I didn't want to interrupt your beauty sleep."

"Your truck took care of that. I heard you pull into your driveway all the way from my house. You need to get that muffler fixed."

"I'll talk to Wes when I get a chance."

She began sorting papers in her desk. "What did Rufus Kenworthy want?" she asked.

"To confess his sins. Except the sin he confessed to wasn't the one I'd expected."

"So it wasn't about that railroad porter?"

"He confessed to the Ike Butler killing when I brought it up, but he had something else on his mind."

"What was it?"

"You ever heard the story about the Younger family?"

She narrowed her eyes and thought about it. "No, I don't think so. Why?"

"It happened a few years before you moved to town." I related the story of the Youngers' house being burned down and about my daddy turning away Mr. Younger.

She stopped shuffling papers. "Number one, I can't believe I've lived in this town twenty years and never heard anyone speak a single word about that. And number two, that doesn't sound like your father."

I nodded. "He did it. I was there. I'm sure he's felt bad about it ever since, but it happened. As for the rest, it doesn't surprise me you never heard about it. Folks clammed up on the subject pretty much as soon as it happened."

"One of those dirty little small-town secrets," she said.

"Exactly. And apparently that wasn't the end of the story."

I told her the rest of what Kenworthy had told me, ending with the part about how the guy called Smiley and another fella killed the Youngers out at Burr Lake and dumped their bodies in the water.

She whistled silently. "You think he's telling the truth?"

"He has no reason to lie. The poor bastard's most of the way to hell already. I think he's telling the truth. Or at least believes he is."

"Any idea who this Smiley was?"

"He said he'd never seen him before or since. The only other name he gave up was Harold Prentiss, and he only did that because Harold's dead. Rufus may be reformed, but he still doesn't want to inform."

"He sure doesn't sound like he's in much of a hurry to get into heaven. I remember Harold Prentiss from back when we were in high school. He used to hang out at the candy store, drop pennies on the floor then bend over and pick them up so he could look up girls' dresses."

"Yeh, well, he's gone. Died fifteen years ago." I paused. "Rufus did say there was one other person he recognized in the bar that night."

"Who was that?"

I'd rather remove my eyeballs with a grapefruit spoon than confide that information, but I'd let the cat out of the bag and that was that. I reckon I brought it up because subconsciously I knew I needed to talk about it and Karen's the best listener I know.

"My dad."

She got a steely look on her face. "That's nothing more than a flat-out lie."

"I know. He was trying to wind me up. Under all that 'Praise the Lord' talk, Kenworthy's still as snake."

"Just as long as you don't believe it. I know you and your father two have rubbed each other raw over the years, but—"

"No, of course I don't. But he could've been in the bar that night. If he was, he might know who Smiley is, and who the other fellas with Harold were. He might even know and not realize he knows." I paused. "Hell, he might just have kept it to himself all these years. I could see him not telling anybody. Out of shame, if nothing else."

"Don't you think if he knew anything he would've gone to the sheriff?"

"I'm not so sure. He had to live here. Going to the law would have put him in an awkward position. In any case, I doubt whoever the sheriff was at the time would've done anything about it, being the Youngers were colored."

"Your vision of the world is mighty bleak, you know that?"

Only because the world's mighty bleak.

"Do you have any idea who might've done such a thing?" she asked.

"I haven't thought about anything else in the last 24 hours."

"The KKK?"

"By that time they'd mostly stopped flaunting themselves, although they dressed up in their robes and masks on special occasions. I know Clyde Raymer's daddy was a member because my father ripped off his hood at the Veterans' Day parade when I was little. I suspect other town fathers were, too, although I can't say for sure. Someone harassed all the black folks until they left town. Someone burned down the Youngers' house. Now it looks like someone killed the Youngers. I can only guess who, unless or until I find some evidence."

"Maybe your dad can help."

"I doubt it. Not in the shape he's in."

A burly fella wearing an unzipped green windbreaker over an orange Texas Longhorn sweatshirt stuck his head in the door, said he was passing through when his car broke down and asked if we could direct him to a good mechanic. I let him use our phone to call Wes Harmon. Wes told him the Burr police were keeping him hopping to, and he'd be here soon. I advised the fella to zip up his windbreaker all the way to the top before Wes got here, seeing that Wes is the world's biggest OU Sooner fan and he might not fix the man's car if he sees that orange sweatshirt. He thanked us, zipped up and said he'd wait outside.

When the fella had gone Karen said, "You know, I was just thinking; knowing your mother, I can't believe she didn't kick up a stink when those folks' house was burned down."

I chuckled. "Oh, she kicked up a stink, alright. Nothing came of it, as I recall, but she made some noise—went to Mayor Bixby and the town council and probably the sheriff, who I believe was Elton DeLong. Nothing got done, though. It all got swept under the rug. Folks just wanted to forget about it and move on."

She frowned in the particular way she does when she's disappointed in the human race.

"And no one ever came looking for those people?" she said. "No kin? I mean, if they were dead, like Kenworthy says, you'd think someone somewhere would've missed them and come looking."

"That's a good question. I don't remember hearing of anybody." I hung my head a little bit. "I don't know. I just don't know."

Her expression softened. "You been out to see Everett yet this morning?"

"No, I figured I'd let him sleep."

"I could go by when Bernard gets back."

Karen checks up on Dad almost as much as I do. He loves her. Always has, going all the way back to high school, when I was mooning over the first great love of my life, Denise Kinney. "That Karen's the one you should go after," he'd grumble whenever I was feeling mistreated by Denny. Karen's the daughter he never had.

"You're out there enough. I'll do it myself when I leave here. If you can drop on your way home this evening, though, that would be good. Make sure he eats. He's more likely to listen to you."

She nodded. "You remember Peggy Miller?" she asked.

"The funny little gal who helped us out on the Cheryl Foster case?"

"That's right. I was talking to her mama the other day. Peggy just graduated from nursing school with a specialty in geriatrics. That's a nurse who works with old—"

"I know what geriatrics means."

"Ok, well, she's looking for work and I thought it might not be a bad idea to talk to her about taking care of your father."

Hiring a helper for my dad had been on the table for some time.

"She was a nice kid," I said. "Couldn't hurt to talk to her."

"I'll call her."

I leaned across the desk to give her a kiss but the brim of my hat got in the way. She knocked it to the floor and completed the transaction.

"Thanks, Red." I'm the only person in town who gets to call her that. "You busy for lunch?"

"Is that an invitation?"

I picked up my hat. "Yeh, if you're willing to eat at Sonic. What would you say to a chili cheese burger?"

"I'd say 'Get thee back, Satan!' Lord, Emmett, you need to stop eating that junk."

"You can't expect me to give up all my vices at once."

"Your grace period is fixin' to run out."

"I'll try to be better."

"You'd better."

"I will."

"I've heard that before," she said. "Alright then, I'll see ya later, alligator."

"After a while, you sexy red-haired crocodile."

"That's Officer Sexy Red-Haired Crocodile to you."

"I'll try to remember."

CHAPTER SIX

My father isn't big and loud. He never brags about how tough he is. That said, he's never been someone you want to mess with. Dad has made a science out of turning the other cheek. But push him too far and you'll wish you hadn't.

He's always had a special dislike of bullies. Clarence Younger knew that, which is why he turned to him for help. I knew it, too, which is why I was surprised and disappointed when he didn't give Clarence what he needed.

The first indication I had that Dad was having mental troubles occurred a couple of years ago. I stopped by his place for a visit and found him digging a hole in his front yard. I asked him why. He said he was trying to dig up a map to a piece of property we'd once owned but had sold many years earlier. I hoped he was pulling my leg and put it out of my mind. I had other concerns at the moment.

Unfortunately, it didn't end there.

Before long, he started behaving strangely in ways I couldn't ignore. I'd go see him on Monday, come back on Tuesday, and he'd ask me where I'd been. I'd say I was just been there the day before. He'd say the hell I was, and we'd be off to the races. I thought he was just spoiling for a fight until I realized he really didn't remember.

What really set off alarms was when he stopped washing the dishes and making his bed and mowing the lawn and keeping his house clean. Except for feeding us (she was a great cook) my mama wasn't much of a housekeeper—which was ok, because Dad took up the slack. He didn't even seem to mind. In fact, I think he might've enjoyed it. He was always the neatest man you'd ever see.

These days he acts like it doesn't matter. For a while, I was asking him if he wanted me to mow the lawn. He'd cuss and say he'd do it himself, but he never would. Eventually I stopped asking and just did it. I'm not sure he knew or cared.

What bothers me more than anything, though, is how little he communicates. Dad was always a man of few words. Now he's a man of no words. And no interests. All he does is sit and stare at the television.

For a while, there were times when he seemed like his old self. Sadly, those days look to be about over. Karen visits on the weekends—cleans his clothes and washes his dishes and tries to get a conversation going with him. Outside of calling her 'Marceline'—my mama's name—and asking what's for dinner, sometimes he hardly even talks to her, and she's like a daughter to him.

Getting old ain't exactly a walk in the park.

I climbed his front steps, wondering if this might be the day he started getting back to normal—and if it was, whether I'd end up wishing it wasn't. I knocked, which I always do. We lived on a farm when I was a boy. Once we discovered natural gas on our property and the royalty checks started rolling in, Dad retired. They bought a place in town right after I left for the Marines. The idea was, he and my mama would get a head start on their golden years. They never came. Shortly after they moved into the new house, she died of ovarian cancer. I was in Korea. It came on so quick, I didn't learn about it until she was gone. I missed the funeral. I have no memories of my mother in this house. In my mind, it's always been his. That's why I always knock.

As per usual, he didn't answer. I let myself in. The house was neat and tidy, meaning Karen had recently visited. Dad sat in his old orange plaid armchair watching television. He wore his retirement uniform: dark yellow Carhartt coveralls and a pair of blue slip-on sneakers. It used to be the only TV he'd watch in the morning was the Today Show. Lately he's taken to watching Captain Kangaroo, a kid's show, which breaks my heart. I bought him a new color TV last summer. Maybe I shouldn't have, but I wanted to do something for him. Watching the tube was about all he did anymore.

"Dad, you should switch the channel to the Today Show," I said. "Hugh Downs has a new partner, Barbara something-or-other. She's real easy on the eyes."

He gnawed on his lower lip and stared at the screen.

I wandered out to the kitchen and saw no sign he'd eaten breakfast or had his morning coffee. "You mind if I make some coffee?" I asked. He didn't answer. I made an executive decision and started boiling water. He began drinking instant coffee just before his mind started to fail. It tastes like cigarette ashes but is less trouble to make.

I looked in the refrigerator. He'd eaten some of the chicken I brought over the day before. That heartened me some. I looked in the freezer and found a box of frozen waffles. "You want some breakfast, Dad?" He said something but I couldn't make it out. I walked to the living room.

"What was that, Dad? You want some breakfast?"

"No," he said in a husky voice.

I was glad to get even that much out of him. I asked if he wanted me to change the channel to the Today Show. He shook his head.

"Walters," I said, remembering the name of the new girl. "Barbara Walters. She's the gal working with Hugh Downs, Dad. You'd like her." He's always liked young women—not in a dirty-old-man way, understand. More fatherly-like. The way he likes Karen.

"She ain't new," he said. "She's been on the show a while."

"Huh. I guess I just never noticed. You want me to change it?"

"Nah."

I told him I'd gone to McAlester, but didn't say why. He refused to engage. A commercial for Fritos Corn Chips blared.

A lifetime of being terse had evolved into an old age of near total silence.

The kettle whistled. I fixed our coffees. I sat Dad's on the TV tray he keeps next to his easy chair. He didn't touch it. On the TV, a heavy-set man with boyish blond hair and a moustache read a book about a man and his steam shovel. His voice was kind and soothing. I wondered how much of the story was getting through to my dad.

"Drink your coffee, Dad."

"I didn't ask for no damn coffee," he grumped.

I should have known. Do something nice for him and he gets pissed off. Piss him off and he'll usually say something.

I sat on the couch catty-corner to his chair.

"Dad, you remember Clarence Younger?"

The fingers of his right hand tapped the arm of his chair in a faint, uneven rhythm. The Captain finished his story and was being assaulted by a rabbit puppet swinging a toy baseball bat. I thought about having a drink.

Stop it, I said to myself. It's been almost three months. One day at a time, like they told you at the VA.

"Clarence Younger, dad. You remember him. The last colored fella in Burr before they all got run off."

His fingers kept tapping.

"How about Rufus Kenworthy? Remember him?"

He closed his eyes.

"Harold Prentiss?"

The fingers slowed and stopped. "You remember those fellas, Dad? How 'bout someone named Smiley?"

His mouth drooped open. He started to snore.

I'd have to do this another time.

I turned off the television and draped a blanket over his chest, thinking: At least when he's asleep he can't hurt himself.

Not long before I got out of the hospital, he lit his stove to boil water then forgot about it. Luckily, Karen dropped by, by which time the water had all turned to steam and the kettle was glowing a bright orange. Dad sat in front of the TV, oblivious. She rushed out to her car and got a tire iron, hooked it through the kettle's handle, carried it outside and dropped it on the driveway. She sprayed the blackened blob of metal with the garden hose. It melted to the cement. Later, one of our part-time officers removed it with a hammer and chisel.

I made double and triple sure I'd turned-off the stove before I left.

***

My most vivid memory of Burr Lake involves the time I went parking with Denise Kinney and made one last stab at convincing her to marry me. That's when she told me she was engaged to my worst enemy—Edgar Bixby—and was more or less the moment I decided to join the Marines. Maybe if you asked her about it now, she'd admit she made a mistake, given that Edgar and their son are currently inmates at McAlester. On the other hand, maybe she wouldn't. She's always been the stubbornest woman you'd ever want to know. In any case, if you wanted to ask, you'd have to track her down. After her men went to jail, she moved away without leaving a forwarding address.

Considering it's the largest standing body of water within an hour's drive, it's amazing how little time I've spent at Burr Lake over the years. I guess we just take it for granted, like a New Yorker does the Statue of Liberty. On the other hand, there aren't a ton of reasons to go. It's ugly, and the fishing is bad. I've heard of a few crazies who dive into caves and ruts along the shore and try to catch oversized catfish with their bare hands. I've never seen it, so I don't know if it's true. If it is, I expect they have better luck than people who use a rod and reel.

The Tilghman County government created Burr Lake by damming up a trickle of water called Coyote Creek, a tributary of the North Canadian River so puny it wasn't on most maps until they stuck a cork in it. The idea was to attract tourists, but it didn't work out very well. The water from Coyote Creek flowed so slowly, it took ten years for it to fill up enough to justify calling it a lake. Eventually it got to be about 20-feet deep in the middle, which isn't bad by Oklahoma standards. The water itself is the consistency and color of chocolate milk. It's deep enough to swim in, but hardly anybody does. In fact, Burr Lake's primary function has always been as a place for horny teenagers to make out in their cars after dark.

A dirt road leads from US 14 to the lake. The drive can be treacherous, especially after it's rained, but it hadn't for God knows how long. Where the road meets the lake, there's a boat ramp and a bait shop owned by one of our city councilmen. It closes for the season in November. No one needs worms in the winter.

I parked near the spot where the old fishing pier once stood. I hadn't been to the lake since my breakdown. Not much had changed. I wouldn't have expected it to. The pier had rotted away decades ago, but you could still see pilings sticking out of the water. A few row boats lay overturned on the ground near the shore. The guy who runs the bait shop rents them out in the summer.

I walked along the water's edge. The wind had picked up, but it was a warm wind, not the kind of mid-winter gale that slices you in two. Brick-red waves slapped against the muddy shore. I'd started to sweat. I opened a second button on my flannel shirt.

I tried to visualize Clarence Younger and his family's dead bodies being taken out in a boat and dumped in the middle of the lake. I could believe it happened. What I couldn't believe was that we'd ever find their remains.

Twenty-six years had passed. Their bones had undoubtedly been picked clean. Anything left was likely to have sunk in the mud. I suppose some big-city police forces have personnel who handle tasks such as this, but we don't and likely never will. There's never been a need. I don't reckon even the State Bureau of Investigation or the Highway Patrol has much call to train scuba divers.

I got back in my truck, rolled down the windows all the way and headed back into town. I got to thinking of reasons to trust anything Rufus Kenworthy had to say. I couldn't come up with many.

Burr stopped thinking and talking about Rufus Kenworthy a long time ago. When they did occasionally use his name, it was as a synonym for notorious behavior. If my name was uttered only in the same breath as killers and thieves, I might tell a lie or two myself on my way out the door. Maybe I'd even make up stories to look like less of a son of a bitch than I was. On the other hand, some people just don't care. Just look at those Nazis. They didn't give a damn how they were remembered.

I was left wondering if, in fact, the Younger family was lying at the bottom of Burr Lake, and if my daddy—who was presently in the grips of senility and might never again be in a condition to recite the alphabet, never mind tell me salacious details of his life story—knew anything about how they'd gotten there. We'd all just taken for granted they'd made new lives for themselves somewhere else. A place where colored folks could live safely among their own kind.

Why should I trust a lying, scheming, murdering piece of shit like Rufus Kenworthy when he told me otherwise, and, in the bargain, dragged my daddy's name into it?

Once again, I thought a swallow or two of bourbon sure would hit the spot.

Once again, I said to myself: Stop it, Emmett. Stop it right now.

CHAPTER SEVEN

Jerry Fuller and my dad have been best friends since they were kids. Both were born to parents who staked claims near Burr during the land rush of 1891. They were original Okies—that is, if you disregard the Indians who were here already and the Quakers from upstate New York who tried to civilize them.

Jerry grew up on a farm, like my dad. Unlike my dad, he had non-farmer-like ambitions. Jerry couldn't care less about agriculture or ranching or the oil business. If he'd been born back east, he might've gone to an Ivy League college and become a scientist. As it was, he grew up in rural Oklahoma and the best he could do was go to optometry school in Wichita. There's nothing wrong with that, but I always got the feeling he'd have preferred something more challenging than fitting middle-aged accountants with bifocals.

Jerry was married to a lovely woman by the name of Nadine. They lived in Wichita for many years before moving back to Burr in the late '30s. After Pearl Harbor, Jerry joined the military at an advanced age, was commissioned a First Lieutenant and served as an Army optometrist for the war's duration. After the war, he came home to continue his civilian practice. Sadly, like my mother, Jerry's wife passed well before her time, dying of breast cancer not long after he retired, seven or eight years ago. They'd never had children, so Jerry was left all alone.

The loss of Nadine nearly killed him, but, somehow, he managed to pull himself together. He bought himself a house in Alva. His friends were afraid he'd gone there to die, but things turned out better than expected. Jerry hired a housekeeper a few years younger than him. Her charms were sufficiently potent to eventually inspire a marriage proposal. Dad was Jerry's best man. He and Becky have been together for almost four years, happy as a sack of kittens. I do not expect that to change. Becky's a sweet gal and Jerry's as fine a man as they come.

Jerry being so far away took a toll on his friendship with my father. They're still close, but they don't see each other as much as they used to. It hasn't affected Jerry so much, since he has a wife. But Dad's been mostly alone for a long time. Karen and I try to fill the void, but it's not the same as when Jerry was around. With Dad's mind going, we all feel Jerry's absence even stronger.

Jerry's still sharp as a tack. I reckon if anyone could tell me things about Dad that Dad himself has forgotten, it would be Jerry.

It took about 45 minutes to drive to Alva. Jerry's house is in one of those housing developments that started popping up after World War II. Houses on his street look more or less the same—wide, deep and low-slung, with small concrete porches and flimsy wood columns framing the entrances. The primary difference is the color of the bricks. Jerry's are various shades of red and brown. The fake shutters around the windows are yellowish-green. The roof slants just enough for rain to roll off. Jerry's cranberry-colored Oldsmobile Toronado wasn't in the carport, so I assumed he'd gone out. I reckoned he'd be back soon. Jerry's as much a homebody as my dad.

Becky saw me coming and greeted me at the door.

"Emmett, I am so glad to see you! We've been expecting a visit."

I hadn't seen her and Jerry since before I went into the hospital.

"I know, Becky. I'm a little overdue. Karen's been after me to come over, but you know me. I get to thinking about one thing and it pushes everything else out of my mind."

"Well, you're here now, aren't you? Come on in."

She walked me back to the kitchen. The living room was decorated with macramé hangings and vases of artificial flowers and bright art prints of rural scenes. Becky does the decorating. I don't know many men who have style except when it comes to cars. That Toronado of Jerry's has style.

"Where's the old man?"

"He just ran to Safeway for me. Should be back any minute. Could I get you a cup of coffee?"

"That sounds good."

"Black with two sugars?"

"Just black. I gave up sugar for lent."

"Alright then," she said with a smile. "I just made a fresh pot."

I sat down at the kitchen table and watched her pour from a big chrome percolator. We made small talk about the weather and the latest happenings in the news and such. After a few minutes Jerry walked in through the kitchen door, a big smile on his face.

"Boy, there's no mistaking that old Ford pickup of yours," he said. I got up out of my chair. We shook hands. "It's about time you showed up. Where the hell you been, young man?"

"Right now I'm flirting with your wife."

He fake growled. "Watch it, boy."

"You're the one who'd better watch it. Someone's liable to snatch this pretty lady out from under your nose."

He laughed and sat down across the table from me. Becky sat a cup of coffee in front of him then busied herself washing dishes.

Jerry is upwards of 70 but looks 20 years younger. He's kept active, intellectually and physically. He reads science magazines and keeps up with world events as well as anyone I know. He bowls on a team once a week and plays golf when the weather allows. Jerry didn't treat retirement as an excuse to wind his life down. If anything, he's gotten more vigorous since he closed his practice.

He asked about my dad. I gave him a not very positive update. It made him sad, and he promised to take a trip to Burr soon. We talked a bit about what was wrong and what could be done, before I got to the meat of the matter and told him all about my meeting with Rufus Kenworthy.

After I'd finished, Jerry stared at the floor and drummed his fingers on the table. "I can tell you this. Everett never forgave himself for turning away Clarence Younger. In some ways he was never the same man after that. I can't speak to them being killed. He never said anything to me about them being killed and I doubt he knows. But he was ashamed of himself for sending them away. I think ... I know it bothers him to this day."

"When did he tell you about it?"

"Oh, heck, that very day. He came over to our place afterwards." Jerry and Nadine were living in Burr by that time. "He wanted me to help him track down Clarence and tell him he'd changed his mind. We drove around looking, but couldn't find him. We figured he was gone for good." He shook his head. "We didn't check the lake."

That fit with how I remembered it. Dad was gone most of the afternoon. Mama came home while he was out. He got back while she was cooking supper. We ate. She wanted to talk about the Youngers' being burned out of their house. He didn't.

"Did you go out with him that night?" I asked.

"I didn't. I dropped him off just before supper time. You say he went out?"

"He did. I remember it clearly."

He thought. "Hmmm. If he did, it was without me."

"Kenworthy made it sound like Dad was drinking with those boys who killed Clarence, and that maybe he knew something about it."

"Well, that's ridiculous. I don't need to have been there to know that."

"I agree," I said, "but it's possible he could've heard those fellas talking about it."

"Maybe. But don't you think he would've gone to Frank Ickes if he'd heard them talking about something like that?"

Frank was the police chief back then. Now he's the editor of our local newspaper.

"I don't know, Jerry. Maybe. Maybe not. He could've felt threatened. He had a family to consider."

"True. He'd have done anything to keep you and your mama safe. But Everett couldn't have lived in the same house as Marceline knowing a crime like that had been committed. No one lied to your mama and got away with it."

He was right about that. My mama was a flesh-and-blood polygraph machine.

"I suppose it's possible he was too embarrassed to tell me about it," he mused. "Sometimes I thought there was another Everett underneath the one I saw. Someone so ashamed of his mistakes, he'd wouldn't even talk about them with his best friend."

That's what kept Dad from confiding to anyone but my mother, and I couldn't swear he was always totally open with her.

"You say he never forgave himself," I said. "Couldn't that be because he knew the Youngers were killed?"

Jerry shook his head. "I never got any indication of that. I'd bet my life otherwise, in fact. He was just disappointed in himself for the way he acted." He leaned forward and clasped his hands. "I know Everett was hard on you, Emmett, but he was even harder on himself. I believe a big part of why he felt so bad was the poor example he set for you. If I remember correctly, he asked you not to mention that incident to your mama."

"You're right, and I never did. I don't believe she ever knew."

"He didn't tell her, I can tell you that. Anyway, he felt like he'd compounded his mistake by asking you to lie."

"Him not telling her was its own kind of lie."

"I'm sure he knew that. It must've eaten him up inside."

Becky had finished the last of the dishes and asked if wanted a bite to eat. I said thanks but no. Jerry asked her to steam him some cauliflower. He looked sheepish and explained, "My doctor's got me on a vegetarian diet." We took our coffees into the living room. He sat on the couch. I sat in the easy chair where Becky does her crocheting.

"I always kept clear of Harold Prentiss," he said. "So did Everett, although he had to buy supplies from him on occasion. He sure as heck didn't socialize with him, although I suppose it's possible he socialized with someone who did." He paused. "He could've been on the fringes of something, I guess."

"On the fringes of what?"

"I could see him hanging around on the edge of a group of men talking in a bar. Everett was antisocial, but he didn't exactly want to be. He would've liked to have fit in, but just didn't know how. It's conceivable he could've listened in on a conversation about something like that. If he did, though, he would've done something about it. Gone to the police or the sheriff."

He gave me a rueful smile. "I don't know if you're old enough to remember but at one time Burr was pretty accepting of negroes. You know the story of the Quaker boarding school?"

"I know there used to be one outside of town, but that was way before my time."

He leaned back, crossed his legs and told me about a group of New York Quakers who, a few years after the end of the Civil War, got permission from the government to build a boarding school for the Cheyenne and Arapahos. I'd heard most of it before, but I figured if I could hear out a scoundrel like Rufus Kenworthy, I could listen to the reminiscences of a nice old guy like Jerry.

"The building was just southeast from where Jackson Corners ends, where the dump is now," he said expansively. "They called it Akin School." Jackson Corners is an unpaved street that juts out from the town like a sixth toe. The Youngers lived on Jackson Corners.

"Quakers don't believe in violence and are in general pretty liberal in their views. They built these schools all across the West, thinking they'd educate and civilize the savages. They'd dress 'em up in white man's clothes and told 'em about George Washington chopping down the cherry tree and all that. I'm not sure how well it worked, but they tried."

He sipped his coffee. "The Quakers were dead set against slavery. Before the Civil War, some of the biggest abolitionists were Quakers. After the land run in '91 that opened up this area up to whites, a handful of colored settlers staked claims in what's now called Jackson Corners. The Akin School folks welcomed them with open arms. It set a pattern, I guess. Other places in Oklahoma negroes harassed and worse, but in those early years they were more or less welcome around here."

"So what happened?"

"You're probably too young to have seen that movie, *The Birth of a Nation.*"

"I've heard of it, but I never saw it."

"You know what it's about?"

"Isn't it about the Klan?"

"That's right. It was about how the KKK saved the south after the war. They showed it at a theater in Watie Junction when your daddy and I were in high school. We went together. Heck, everyone went who could afford to. Best movie I ever saw, I guess, even if most of it was a lie. Made the Klan look like heroes. They weren't, of course. By then the Klan didn't even exist, but once that movie came out, it started up again. That's when things started to get bad between whites and coloreds around here. At first there were a few cross burnings. Nothing really bad. No lynchings or anything like that, at least not in Tilghman County, although they did happen in other places. Anyway, it flared up and was gone in a few years. I don't remember the negroes in Burr getting bothered too much until later on."

"What brought that about?"

He scratched his forehead. "You know, Emmett, I can't tell you for sure. I had only been back in Burr a short time when the Youngers' house was burned down. I remember when we moved back they were the only colored family left in town."

"Any idea who burned down their house?"

He fiddled with his watch. "My memory's not as sharp as it used to be," he said, "but if I think about it a while, I might remember something. Give me a day or two." He took another sip of coffee and made a face. "I hate drinking it black, but the doctor won't let me have cream and sugar." He sat the cup on a coaster that had a picture of a mustachioed cowboy. "What are you expecting to do, anyway? Even if Kenworthy was telling the truth, I don't imagine you'll find the guilty parties, even if they're still around."

"I'm suspended until January 1st, so I got a lot of time on my hands," I said. "This'll give me something to do."

He nodded and smiled. "Well, good luck, young man. I'll be rooting for you."

I got up to leave.

We shook hands. "You're your parents' child, I'll say that for you," he said. "I'll put my mind to it and see what I can remember."

"I'd appreciate that, Jerry."

He walked me to the front door. "You know what you should do is talk to Frank Ickes," he said, then called to Becky that I was leaving. She gave me a hug and kiss. We said our goodbyes.

On the way back to Burr, I thought how nice it would've been if things had turned out for my dad like they did for Jerry. These days, about the best I could hope for was for Dad to come out of the darkness long enough to make things right.

CHAPTER EIGHT

Oklahoma was once full of characters like Frank Ickes—men who came here because it was new and uncharted territory, a place they could reinvent themselves. Those land runs weren't populated by rich business tycoons but common people looking to make a new start. Doing what they did was hard. Sure, the land was free, but they had to build on it, farm it, make it productive, or give it back and let someone else try. They made themselves into farmers, ranchers, builders. They published newspapers and opened general stores and worked at every type of job under the sun. Most were law abiding. Some were not, which is why Oklahoma needed men like Frank.

Like Rufus Kenworthy, Frank isn't sure how old he is, but remembers riding on the back of a buckboard driven by his daddy during Oklahoma's first—and most famous—land run in 1889. Frank's daddy worked as a deputy under Bill Tilghman in Dodge City. Bill decided to take part in the Run of '89. He convinced Frank's dad to join him. Within a few years both were Deputy U.S. Marshals working out of Guthrie.

Frank went into the family business at a young age, landing a job as one of Heck Thomas's deputies in Lawton during the first decade of this century. His career highlight came in 1908 when he played a posse member in a one-reel film called *The Bank Robbery*, directed by none other than his boss's friend and colleague, Bill Tilghman himself. Frank claims the famed Comanche warrior Quanah Parker also took part in the production. I've always suspected that to be one of his embellishments.

Frank's movie career began and ended with that single role. Thereafter he worked in and out of law enforcement across the state, before settling down as Burr's police chief in the late '20s. He stayed for almost a quarter-century. He seemed to like the job, and the town was glad to have him, so it was a surprise when one day in 1953 he bought the local newspaper, *The Burr Gazette*, and submitted his resignation to the Town Council—an action that launched the series of events which led to my hiring.

What made it even stranger was the fact that Frank was a serial fabulist. His tall tales put Uncle Remus to shame. Give the devil his due, however. Upon taking on the responsibility of reporting the news, Frank cut down on his fabrications. As a newsman, he's as honest as they come. He even writes editorials critical of me when I deserve it.

The *Gazette* office is on the same side of Main Street as the police station, at the northern end of a line of mostly interconnected buildings that make up Burr's business district. Unlike the police station—a charmless cube constructed on the cheap out of cinder blocks—The Gazette Building was built to look good and withstand the ravages of time. It's a two-story structure, about twenty feet wide and twice as deep, constructed out of red bricks, with a white awning running across the front. The supporting columns are layered with a century of painting and repainting. To see the intricate designs carved into the wood you have use your imagination. To one side of the orange door is a display window. The words BURR GAZETTE are painted on the glass. On the sidewalk out front is a green park bench that, on weekends, handles the overflow of chatty geezers from the barber shop next door. The number "1893" inlaid in concrete over the front door indicates the year of its construction, although some people confuse it for an address. *The Gazette*'s founder built it to be a newspaper office. That's what it's always been.

A bell rung over the door when I walked into the office, empty but for a few unoccupied desks. I could hear a repetitive clanking from behind the wall separating the newsroom from the back where the printing press is. Frank prints the paper on Sundays. During the week he takes in random printing jobs—advertising and the like. I once used his services to print out "Wanted" posters.

Frank stuck his head through a curtain hanging in the doorway connecting the two rooms. His bottom lip was loaded with snuff. His right hand held a Dixie cup to spit into. "I thought I heard the bell," he said with a tobacco-flecked smile. "Where y'all been keeping yourself, Chief? Haven't seen you in ages."

"Oh, I've been doing what needs doing, I guess you could say." I tossed my hat onto the nearest empty desk. A cloud of dust swirled, illuminated by a thin sunbeam poking through a side window. "You all by yourself today?"

"I'm always by myself. Except for Junior, of course."

Over the years, Frank laid off almost all of his employees. These days, he writes the stories and editorials, takes the pictures and even sells ads. The only thing he doesn't do is run the printing press. That's handled by Junior Belle, his lone employee.

Junior's been running *The Gazette* printing press since he was a teenager. He's now pushing 80, probably making him a few years older than Frank, although that's a guess. I reckon Junior Belle's the only person alive who knows how to run that machine. If he ever retires, Frank'll be up a certain malodorous creek with no apparent means of locomotion. It's the only printing press *The Gazette*'s ever had. It was already old when the paper started up in 1893. The man who trained Junior got drafted into the army and was killed in the Argonne Forest during the Great War. Frank often talks about having Junior train his successor, but he always procrastinates and forgets.

"How is Junior these days?" I asked.

"Bitching and moaning as usual. Keeps talking about retiring. He's full of shit. He's not going anywhere, and we both know it. That machine back there is the only family he knows."

I wanted to point out that Junior might be a tough old bird but had to give up the ghost eventually. But I refrained.

I asked Frank if he had a minute. He said he did, so we sat down at what looked to be the only desk currently in use. He sat in an old green swivel chair. I sat in a threadbare armchair that smelled like a wet dog.

When Frank quit as Police Chief, he washed his hands of it completely. When I first got to be chief, I'd ask him questions about one thing or the other. He'd just smile and tell me he'd left that all behind and was sure I'd figure things out for myself. I eventually quit asking. This time was different.

"There's something I wanted to talk to you about from when you had my job," I began. He started to make the same old objections. I talked over him. "Hold on, Frank. I'm not asking for advice. I need information."

He grinned crookedly and spit into his cup. I related my Rufus Kenworthy story in as much detail as I could almost without taking a breath, lest he try to cut me off. I did not include part about my dad turning the Youngers away. That's not a story I wanted widely known.

At first his wrinkled burlap bag of a face registered stubborn resistance. The deeper I got, however, the more concerned he appeared. Halfway through he crossed his arms and closed his eyes. At some point the noise in the back stopped, and the only sounds were my voice and Frank's labored breathing.

I finished. Frank frowned and the saggy skin under his chin jiggled.

"Alright," he said glumly. "What do you want to know?"

"What do you remember about the Youngers and how they were run out of town?"

He spit in the cup. "I try not to remember anything from those times."

"C'mon now, Frank. You ain't that old. What did you do about it?" I paused. "Anything?"

He sighed. "Come on, Emmett, times were different back then. I wasn't like now, with that King fella rousing the coloreds and rioting in the streets and such. Coloreds were treated different in those days. I ain't saying it's right and I ain't saying it's wrong. It's just the way it was. If I'd tried to put a white man in jail for burning down a colored man's house, I'd have been strung up myself."

Sadly, that might've been true. I like to think I'd have done something if I'd been in charge, but walk a mile in another man's shoes, if you know what I mean.

"I tried to ask my dad, but he's in no condition to remember. I need to hear from someone who was there."

"Huh. And I'm the lucky fella?"

He traced a game of tic-tac-toe in the dust on his desktop. "You know how it is," he said. "You bear only as much as authority as the people give you. When you sent Edgar Bixby and his boy to McAlester a couple of years ago for killing that colored girl, I thought, 'Good for you.' I'd have liked to have done that when the Youngers was run out of town, but folks just wouldn't've stood for it." He drew a line through a row of X's then wiped it all away.

"I get that," I said. "I'm not here to blame you. I'm just trying to understand. At the moment I don't have the authority to do a damn thing about it even if I wanted to. I'm mostly looking into this for myself. For one thing, I need to satisfy myself that my daddy didn't have anything to do with it."

"C'mon now, Emmett. You know better."

I nodded resignedly. "I guess I do, but I sure didn't like hearing his name come up in relation to this."

Frank frowned. "I only know what I know myself, of course. I knew about the Youngers' house getting burned down. Everybody who was here at the time knows that."

"How 'bout them being killed?"

"This is the first I ever heard about that," he said, too earnestly.

"Alright then," I said. "Who burned down their house? If Kenworthy's right, at least one of the men who burned down the house—this Smiley fella—had a hand in killing them. Who was Smiley, and who helped him? You must know, Frank. Or at least have some idea."

He shifted in his chair, leaned forward and spit his wad of snuff into the paper cup. His gut strained against the buttons of the yellowed, ink-stained white dress shirt he wore. He opened the side drawer of his desk, pulled out a pint bottle of Jack Daniels, and took a swig. He wiped the bottle with his shirt and offered it to me. I waved it away. He tried to screw the cap back on, but couldn't make his fingers work properly, so he slammed the bottle down on his desk. He then shook his head and said something I expect he'd been waiting a long time to say.

"I know who did it, Emmett. I know."

CHAPTER NINE

Last night, instead of counting sheep, I calculated the days, hours and minutes since my last drink. 89 days, six hours and twenty-three minutes. Charlie Parker, my all-time favorite saxophone player, was a heroin addict all his adult life, but it's the booze that got him. He died of cirrhosis of the liver at age 35.

Frank offering me that drink made me think of that.

"I know who did it, Emmett," he said, his voice flat and defeated. "I know."

"Who?"

He took another gulp of Jack and belched.

"Tom Bixby and Harold Prentiss."

The town's mayor and its resident pervert.

"You're telling me the two of them burned down the Youngers' house and killed the family?"

"I don't know about them being killed, but I've always been convinced it was those two who burned down the house. Tom was the head mucky-muck for this secret club here in town. I guess it was some sort of social club, like the Moose or Elks Lodge, but everyone knew it was basically just an excuse to run off all the negroes."

"I don't reckon Harold and Tom were the only members," I said.

He shook his head. His jowls quivered. "No, they weren't, but Tom was the president and Harold did all Tom's dirty work."

"Who else was in this club?"

"I can't tell you."

"Can't or won't?"

He caressed the bottle as if were a lover.

"Can't," he said. "It was secret. Like the Masons. No one knew. I only knew about Tom because he was the one who asked me to join."

"How'd you know about Harold, then?"

"I just assumed. Everybody knew Harold did Tom's dirty work."

"You didn't join?"

"Nah. I didn't want to spend any more time around Tom than necessary. I had to put up with enough of his bullshit when he was mayor."

"But you knew it was Tom and this group who burned down that house. And you didn't do anything?"

"What could I do?" he pleaded. "There weren't any witnesses. No evidence except for a couple of scorched whiskey bottles. No fingerprints, or else they all got burned off. The only thing we had were suspicions."

"What about the sheriff? Did he do anything?"

He shrugged. "He sent a deputy to look things over. I reckon he figured the same as I did. There wasn't any evidence."

"Did you knock on any doors?"

"I talked to some people, if that's what you're asking. Didn't come up with anything. Of course, there wasn't a white person in this town who would've admitted to knowing who did it."

I didn't enjoy leaning on Frank. I'd always liked him well enough, and anyway, he was an old man. But listening to him make excuses rubbed me raw.

"Dammit, you were the law, Frank. It was your job to track down whoever it was did that."

His eyes were moist. "You're not wrong, Emmett, you're not wrong," he said. "I should've done more. But, like I said, if I'd pushed too hard, I've been out of a job. Maybe you'd have done it different. I'm sure you would've, in fact. But I did what I did." He wiped his eyes with the loose cuff of his shirt. "There's nothing I can do about it now."

"That's not true. You could help me find who did it."

"Ain't that what I'm doing?" He swept his hand across his desk and the bottle overturned, spilling what was left of the whiskey. "I'm telling you all I know! It ain't much, but it's all I got."

I reckoned he was telling the truth. He didn't know much, most likely because he didn't want to. Playing dumb was less trouble. Knowing can be dangerous.

The thing is, Frank was too good at his job. You could never make me believe he didn't know who burned down that house. He gave me Harold, because I already knew about Harold. He gave me Tom Bixby because, as mayor and president of that club, his name was bound to come up sooner or later. As for fingering anyone else, he wasn't about to go down that road.

I gave it one last try.

"You remember anyone back then named Smiley?"

He looked genuinely puzzled. "Smiley? Nah, I don't recall anyone called that."

"I doubt it was his real name. Probably just a nickname."

"Sorry, I can't remember anyone named Smiley. Except Smiley Burnette, and he was in the movies."

"Was it something they might've called Tom Bixby?"

He laughed humorlessly. "No one was ever going to call Tom Bixby Smiley, I'll tell you that. Only time he smiled was when he got the best of someone in a business deal."

I listened to the wind blow in through the gap under the office's front door. Frank should get that fixed, I thought.

I shook my head sorrowfully. "I always thought better of you than that. You never struck me as being too prejudiced. You sure as heck didn't seem like someone who let someone like Tom Bixby tell him what to do."

His face reddened. "Emmett, you wanted to know who burned down the Younger place," he said angrily. "I told you. Don't make me go through the whole list of things that went on back then. I'm not up to it. I quit that job because for too many years men like the Bixbys and the Raymers did nothing but piss all over me. I'm finished with that."

The Raymers.

"The Raymers were part of it, too?"

"I never said ... what I mean is, the Raymers, well ... yeh, I forgot about them. I reckon Vernon Raymer—Clyde Raymer's daddy—was probably involved in that club. I can't say for sure, but I'd say chances are good he was part of that group."

He looked like he'd been worked over with a bag of doorknobs. "I've said all I'm going to say about it, Emmett. I need to get back to work."

We both stood.

"One last thing," he said. "I don't want you leaving here thinking there's a chance in hell your daddy had something to do with any of this. I know for a fact, he didn't care for any of those fellas. He wouldn't've had anything to do with them. You can set your mind at ease about that."

"Alright, Frank. I appreciate that. While I'm here, though, one more thing: Would you mind if I went through some of your back issues?"

He got a puzzled look. "Back issues are over to the library," he said. "I gave them to Kate Hennessey a while back. She put them on microfilm." His body swayed and I reckoned the Jack was having its effect. "Any other queshuns?" he slurred.

"Just one," I said. "Did Clarence come to you after his house burned down?"

He looked ten years older and a lot more helpless than when I'd walked in the door.

"Clarence came knockin' on my door in the middle o' the night," he said, trying to enunciate clearly and mostly failing. "I wrote down his statement. He said he couldn't identify the men, and he didn't recognize what kind of the car they 'uz driving. He did say it was kind of unusual, but couldn't say exactly how."

I'd never seen a statement like that in our files. "What did you do with it?"

"Tried to give it to the sheriff. He didn't want it. The County Attorney didn't want it. I asked Tom Bixby what I should do with it. He told me to throw it away." He hiccupped. "So that's what I did."

He turned and walked unsteadily to the back of the room. As he disappeared behind the curtain, he said, "Say hi to your daddy for me."

CHAPTER TEN

Tom Bixby liked people to think he was one of those tough men of the soil whose wealth came as a result of hard work and gumption.

That was 100% unadulterated U.S. Grade A bullshit.

Some folks around Burr remember him as someone who made his fortune when one of the biggest natural gas plays in the southwest was found on his land.

That story's not quite as misbegotten, but it still doesn't come anywhere near the truth.

Tom did raise corn as a young farmer and for a while he did pretty well for himself, until prices dropped so low he couldn't give his crop away. Fortunately, he sensed the way the wind blew without so much as wetting a finger and putting it up in the air. Tom realized corn could be used for something besides food if you had no compunctions about following the letter of the law, so he built a still in his barn, made large quantities of sour mash, and sold it all over the state.

Prohibition never had much of an effect in Oklahoma. The state had been officially dry since it had been admitted to the union in 1907, anyway. Manufacture and consumption of alcohol had always been criminal.

Booze being illegal didn't stop anybody from drinking it, however, and Tom Bixby was happy to give the people what they want. For the better part of a decade, Tom went through the motions of being a farmer when in fact he was a bootlegger. How he managed to keep the fraud going, I can't say.

Most of this happened before I was born. I reckon he just paid off whoever he needed to pay off. It wasn't very long ago that I discovered my own very first drink had been a product of Tom Bixby's still.

As if I needed another reason to hate the men in that family.

In the '30s, an ocean of natural gas was found on the Bixby spread. Soon, the income from his mineral rights dwarfed the not inconsiderable sum he made peddling booze. In the '30s he left the bootlegging business, got himself elected mayor and accrued whatever power there was to be had in our town.

For years, Tom Bixby ruled Burr like a poor man's Huey Long, until he got skin cancer at a relatively young age and was forced to hand things over to his sons. The disease literally ate away his nose and lips, to the point that he eventually he stopped appearing in public, except for Burr High School Patriot football games where he sat on the 50-yard line wrapped in an old-fashioned raccoon coat with the hood pulled over his head. By the end of his life, just a glimpse of Tom Bixby's face caused children to flee in terror.

One might wonder why nobody ever talks about Tom Bixby's outlaw past. As in the cases of Ike Butler and Clarence Younger, I attribute it to my fellow Oklahomans' propensity for avoiding unpleasant truths.

***

Just as I exited the newspaper office, the noon whistle blasted and about gave me a heart attack. I remembered I was supposed to eat lunch with Karen. I walked to the station. She wasn't there, but Kenny was. She'd told him to tell me something had come up and that she'd see me tonight.

I took that as permission to eat whatever I wanted. Hello, chili cheese burger.

The Sonic on the edge of town was packed with high school kids. I managed to pull into the last vacant stall ahead of a kid in an old black Nash Rambler with no hubcaps and a missing front bumper. He started to flip me the bird before realizing who I was, whereupon he scratched his forehead with his middle finger like that was what he'd meant to do all along. I ordered and a few minutes later a cute little apple-cheeked blond on roller skates who I thought should've been in school herself brought me a chili-cheese burger with tater tots and a Coca Cola. I let her hook the tray to my window and tried to enjoy the unseasonably warm weather while I ate.

My talk with Frank had cause my mood to take a turn, however, and I lapsed into brooding, something my doctors at the V.A. explicitly told me not to do. "Excessive self-reflection is a good way to get depressed," one of them said, like he'd just discovered the cure to cancer. Hell, he hadn't even discovered the cure for depression.

These days, since I'm not going to work, I end up spending most of my time alone. I could hang around the barber shop and shoot the shit with the old farts, or drive out to Wes Harmon's Sinclair and let him talk my ear off about college football while he's working on cars. But that's not me. If I want to talk, with only a few exceptions, I save it for Karen, or else I talk to my dog. She's a good listener and seldom argues.

I once heard someone refer to booze as a social lubricant. If that means what I think it means, I reckon it's true. When I'm around a group of people I get so uncomfortable, a few squirts here and there are desirable, if not essential. Sometimes when I'm around a lot of people, I get distracted and forget about wanting a drink, but not too often.

It's something I need to work on, especially now that I can't grease my gears with bourbon.

***

After lunch, I drove to the library. Kate Hennessey, our town librarian, is one of the exceptions to my rule about not liking to talk talking to people. She loves to read as much as I do, so we always have something to talk about. When business is slow, I'll pop in the library and we'll talk books. We share similar tastes. Both of us like mysteries and crime stories and biographies of famous people. We liked *Tom Sawyer* but loved *Huckleberry Finn*. We share an affinity for southern literature, however, neither of us cared for *Gone With the Wind*. On the other hand, we both thought *All the King's Men* was terrific. Neither one of us has ever made much headway into William Faulkner.

There was no shortage of parking along Main Street. I found a space right in front of the library. Kate was sitting at the circulation desk when I walked in. The remains of a ham sandwich and a half-eaten Granny Smith apple lay on a crumpled sheet of wax paper in front of her. She held a book on her lap below desk level, like a kid trying to read a comic book while her teacher's yammering on about geography. She didn't notice me come in.

"Whatcha reading there, Kate?"

She like to have jumped out of her shoes. "Oh, hello Chief," she said, startled. "I didn't see you there." She moved to shove the book in a drawer but it wouldn't fit, so she finally just sat on it. "What was that you said?"

"I said, what're you reading?"

"Oh, that," said with a wave of dismissal. "Just something a friend recommended, that's all." She began rearranging the tape dispenser and stapler and the other things on her desk like it was the most important thing she'd do all day.

"What's it called?"

She blushed like she'd been caught stealing from petty cash. "Alright," she said, understanding I'd blocked all avenues of retreat. "If you must know—"

She looked around. The only other person in the library was her assistant, Melba Jones, shelving books in the back. Once satisfied no one was paying attention, she pulled the book out from underneath her and handed it to me.

The cover was a crude painting of a man in a brown suit sitting at a plain wooden table. A bottle of whiskey sat in front of him. A pretty woman in a yellow dress lay at his feet, a pool of blood spreading beneath her head.

"*The Killer Inside Me*, by Jim Thompson," I said. "That's a heck of a book."

"I think so, too," she admitted with an embarrassed grin, "but isn't it awful?"

"It's not Dame Agatha Christie, that's for sure. D'you know the writer is from Oklahoma?"

She took off her glasses and let them hang from a silver chain around her neck. "My uncle worked with him on the Federal Writer's Project back in the '30s," she said. "Thompson was his boss. I'd always wanted to read his stuff, but they're hard to find. I'm not even going to tell you where I found this one."

"I've got several of his books at home, if you want to borrow any. I never brought him up because I didn't think you'd be much interested, since they're so racy."

"Don't worry about me. I'm a big girl."

I sure didn't want to take *that* any further.

She asked if there was something she could help me with.

"I hope so," I said. "I should warn you, though. It might turn out to be pretty gruesome."

"I told you. I'm a big girl."

"Alright," I said, and began the telling of Kenworthy's grisly tale. I didn't pull any punches. True to her word, she didn't bat an eye.

"So what can I do to help?"

"Frank Ickes over at *The Gazette* tells me you have back issues the paper on microfilm."

"We do. Not all of them, but at least a few from every year it's been published."

"He mentioned a group named after Aaron Burr from back in the '40s—"

"The Sons of Aaron Burr Society," she said. "It was a men's club. Very secretive. Like the Masons."

"More like the Klan, if Frank is to be believed."

I explained how the group's primary concern was to run the negroes living here at the time out of town. "The thing is, Frank either doesn't remember or doesn't want to tell me who all was involved, except for the leader, Tom Bixby, and Bixby's lackey, Harold Prentiss. Both have been dead for years."

"Hmmm. Deke and Edgar Bixby are his sons, right?" I nodded. "Maybe they were involved."

"Edgar's my age, and I was only 12 or 13. Deke was a few years younger than that."

"Not old enough, then?"

"I doubt it. I'm pretty sure Clyde Raymer's daddy would've been a part of it, though. Clyde's about ten years older than me, so he was old enough for something like that."

"Have you asked him?"

"Not yet. I thought I'd do some research, which is why I want to look over any back issues of *The Gazette* from that time."

"Let's go see what we can find."

She led me to a back room the size of a large walk-in closet. Against one wall were a couple of private microfilm viewers, standing face to face. Along the opposite wall were rows of shelving containing small square boxes of microfilm. Kate ran her fingers lightly along the labels until she found what she was looking for.

"Do you remember the date this happened?" she asked.

"July 31st, 1941."

She pulled out two boxes and handed me one. It was labeled: *Burr Gazette: January-June 1940.*

"I would imagine it's best to start early in the year then work up to it," she said. "You take this one. I'll look through July through December." She offered to show me how to use the machine, but I already knew.

Scrolling through those old newspapers was like going back in time. I meant to focus on what I was looking forward but I couldn't resist reading one unrelated article: "Burr Man Finds Possums in Car." Apparently, a fella left his car parked in a barn for 20 years, then out of the blue decided to drive it, only to find an angry mama possum and her babies living in the front seat. I thought I vaguely remembered the incident although the man's name did not ring a bell.

That was the extent of my self-indulgence.

I scrolled through slowly, not wanting to miss any mention of The Sons of Aaron Burr. A photograph of Tom Bixby and his henchmen standing in front of the Younger place, Molotov cocktails in hand, was probably too much to wish for.

Tom's name did pop up frequently—in stories about him presiding over Town Council meetings, for instance, or serving as spokesman for the Chamber of Commerce and Rotary Club. There was a small article congratulating him on donating 20 dollars to the Burr Athletic Booster Club. But nothing about The Sons of Aaron Burr.

I finally discovered something relevant, if not especially useful, toward the end. An unsigned editorial bemoaned how the houses on Jackson Corners were a blight on the town and should be razed. It said if the people living there wouldn't vacate voluntarily, plenty of God-loving folks here in town were willing to give them a nudge.

I'm somewhat familiar with the neighborhood from around that time, since that's where Gabe and I used to meet when we went fishing. Jackson Corners itself was never a garden spot, but the Younger home was neat and well-kept, even though it was made mostly out of tar paper and corrugated metal.

What I remember best about that house was a small, octagonal, silver-plated badge nailed next to the front door. Written on it was "101 Ranch Season 1907," and the name "Pickett." I asked Gabe about it. "My daddy's good luck charm," he said. "It belonged to Bill Pickett, the man who invented bulldogging. He's a negro. My dad says he's the greatest rodeo cowboy who ever lived. That was his badge from when he starred in the 101 Ranch Wild West Show over by Ponca City. Mr. Pickett gave it to him as a souvenir when dad was a little boy."

I'd never seen nor heard of colored cowboys. I guess as much as my folks tried to teach me, there was stuff they missed.

I didn't really know any of the other colored families who lived in Burr, but I always thought the Youngers did their best with what little they had. Apparently, their best wasn't enough. The editorial had to have been referring to the Youngers. By that time, they were the only ones still residing on Jackson Corners.

I finished the reel without finding any mention of The Sons of Aaron Burr. I walked over to Kate's machine and if she'd found anything.

"Take a look at this," she said.

Newly Constituted Sons of Burr Society Lead July 4th Revel

Mayor Thomas Bixby presided over Burr's annual Independence celebration by calling for citizens to come together and support the values handed down by great Americans like Robert E. Lee and our state's own Governor William Murray.

Mayor Bixby's speech began: "Since Christopher Columbus landed on the shores of Plymouth Rock, America has been a country devoted to the idea that all men are created equal and that we owe it to ourselves and those toiling beneath us to take care of the less fortunate. That means we must make our fair town a place where women and children live without fear of being defiled. Thank the Lord I've been blessed with the moral strength and courage to do what is righteous ..."

I read it all the way to the end (no easy task, since I expect my dog Dizzy knows her American history better than Tom Bixby), hoping it would provide more names. It did not. To read it, you'd think Tom Bixby was the only man standing against the alleged depravity of the single remaining negro family in town.

I wish he had been the only one, but I knew better. He had help. There was a fella named Smiley out there who was happy to give him a hand.

CHAPTER ELEVEN

Most of the old coots who hang out at Bill Haygood's barber shop are lifelong Burr-ites, and therefore can remember when Tom Bixby was king of all he surveyed. I reckoned it stood to reason they'd have memories of any secret societies he might've run.

Bill has three barber chairs, but he's done all the barbering himself for years, so only one is ever in use. The other two are invariably occupied by whoever among a rotating group of retired farmers gets first dibs. The rest are consigned to a row of red plastic chairs along the wall, except on weekends when the weather's especially nice, when the overflow has to sit outside. I don't believe I've ever set foot in the joint when there weren't at least three or four old men talking hogwash. During football season there's a lot of conversations about the Oklahoma Sooners and bitching about the local high school team. Other times they tell of youthful adventures in which apparently every last one of them was irresistible to members of the opposite sex.

Bill's pitiful excuse for a barber pole looks like a piano leg that's been painted red, white, and blue by an elephant or some other animal that lacks sufficient digital dexterity to manipulate a paintbrush. As usual, I prepared to rib him about it when I walked in the door.

"Bill, when in hell are you going to get yourself a decent—"

My jaw about hit the floor. Someone besides Bill was cutting Les Renfield's hair. Someone wearing a dress.

Bill spun around in one of the other chairs and grinned. "Emmett, you know Cathy, don't you?"

"I do. Hey, Cathy." Cathy Stallcup has been cutting my hair off-and-on for five years. Not at Bill's, but at the Jesus is Lord Hair Salon here in town, a place that caters to women. I'm their only male customer—or client, as the girls call it.

Cathy smiled. "Chief Hardy, you look like you just seen a ghost."

"I guess I never thought I'd see the day when a woman would willingly come inside this place."

She snipped a few stray hairs around Les's ears. "Since Bill owns the beauty salon now, he figures it's ok to borrow one of us girls once in a while."

"When I'm feeling lazy," said Bill. The old coots laughed.

Bill purchased the Jesus is Lord Beauty Salon a while back, thereby securing a monopoly on hair-cutting in Burr. Until now, the only sign of women in his shop were the scantily clad models on the covers of the detective magazines he scattered about to entertain the clientele. Today they were conspicuously missing.

"What do all you dirty old men think about this?"

"She's easier on the eyes than Bill, that's for sure," said Les. "Thank you, Les," she said primly, then rolled her eyes and added, "I guess," to laughs from the peanut gallery. I always thought Cathy was a cute Shirley Temple-type, but in this context, she was a regular Brigitte Bardot.

Clay Archer—a sharp-nosed old fella as old as Moses and a long-time friend of my father—sat with his legs crossed in one of the chairs along the wall. "Heck, Emmett," he said, "it's almost 1967. Got to change with the times."

This was notable, in that Clay is 90 years-old if he's a day and still rolls his own cigarettes because he doesn't trust those new-fangled packaged kind.

"Now you don't got any reason not to come here," said Bill. He's harbored a good-natured grudge against me since I stopped letting him butcher my hair as a teenager. The last straw was when I asked him to give me a Cary Grant-style cut and I ended up looking like Moe Howard. From then on until the Marine Corps barbers got hold of me, my mama cut my hair. Now the girls at the salon do it.

"Is that why you brought in Cathy? You wanted my trade that bad?"

"I brought in Cathy because I needed help, and she's a darn good hair cutter."

"I thought you said it was because she was always getting in cat fights with them other gals," snickered George Hammacker. Hammy was wearing what he does every time I see him—a red-and-green flannel shirt and raggedy blue jeans held up by a pair of olive drab Carhartt suspenders.

"Hammy, the only fight goin' on is between that big ol' belly of yours and the buttons on that ugly shirt," said Cathy, resulting in hoots all around.

I stood in the middle of the room, waiting for the laughter to die down. "As much as I'd love to contribute to the sophisticated reparteé for which you gentlemen are widely known and admired, I was wondering if you could help me with a bit of Burr history."

"Sophisticated ree-par-tay?" muttered Hammy under his breath. "What in hell is that?"

"That's French for 'you're a dumb ass'," said Les, to more laughs.

"What're you lookin' to know, Emmett?" asked Clay.

"Any you boys remember a club back in the '40s called The Sons of Aaron Burr?"

The room got so quiet, all I could hear was the tinny sound of Buck Owens singing "I got the hu-u-u-ngries for your love and I'm waiting in your welfare line," coming from an unseen transistor radio.

Cathy broke the silence. "What's the matter, y'all?" she said as she brushed Les with talcum powder and took off his smock. "Don't tell me this another one of those things around here nobody's supposed to talk about."

"Cathy, why don't you go back to the salon and see if they need some help," Bill said.

"I can just call 'em on the phone—"

"No, I want you to go over there."

She frowned. "I don't know why I should have to walk all the way over there in the rain when I could just as easy call on the phone," she said, "but you're the boss." She dunked her scissors into a jar of greenish-blue liquid and headed for the exit. "I swear, this town has more secrets," she said, slamming the door behind her.

"She's a wildcat, that one," chuckled Les. The others uh-huh'd their agreement.

"So none of y'all has anything to say about The Sons of Aaron Burr?"

"What about 'em?" said Clay.

"What kind of club was it? Who belonged? What did they do? I know Tom Bixby ran it, just like he ran everything else around town back then, but that's about it."

"It was a secret society," said Hammy. "Like the Masons."

Bill gave him a steely look. "That's not something we talk about, Emmett," he said, turning to me. "That was Tom Bixby's thing. It died with him. It's best for everyone if it stays dead."

"Bill, dammit, making it sound so mysterious just makes me want to know more about it."

No one responded.

"I'll tell you why I'm asking," I said, then gave them an abridged version of what I knew, regarding the destruction of the Youngers' house and their subsequent disappearance. "All I've found about the Sons of Burr is an old story in *The Gazette* that made them sound a lot like a polite offshoot of the Klan, which makes me suspect they might have had something to do with running off not only the Youngers, but all the rest of the colored families who lived here back in those days."

Clay snorted. "Hell, Emmett, where you been? Every white man in town wanted the coloreds gone. Them people just stunk up the town. We had to get rid of them."

I felt my face redden. "Are you telling me you burned down their house, Clay? Did you kill that family and dump their bodies in the lake?"

He smirked. "I didn't have nothin' to do with burnin' down their house, and I don't know nothin' about them bein' dead. But I'll say this: I wouldn't tell you even if I did. Hell, I'd give whoever done it a medal if I could."

Not one of them would look me in the eye. "You boys agree with Clay?" I said. "You think burning down that family's house and shooting them to death was the right thing to do? One of them a ten-year-old girl, another a thirteen-year-old boy?"

Hammy spit into a cup. Bill lit a cigarette. No one said anything.

I'd known these men and others like them my whole life. They were friends and neighbors. They looked out for each other's kids and grandkids when our parents weren't around. That's what folks did in those days. Everyone helped raise everyone else's children. Those old boys can be a pain in the ass, but they were kind to me when I was young and supportive after

I became police chief. I'd probably heard these particular men express similar vile sentiments before, but not in a long time. I guess I'd forgotten how ugly it sounded.

My parents taught me people can be good in some ways and bad in others, and that people in this town were generally the kind and generous type, except when it came to colored folks and Indians. Hate the sin but love the sinner, my mama said, although that didn't stop her from putting them in their place when she reckoned they deserved it.

I wasn't as outspoken. I mostly kept quiet when I heard such things. Maybe I shouldn't have. No *maybe* about it, I guess. I chose to believe people who talked that way did it out of habit, and that with the passage of time they'd see the error of their ways and put aside their hate.

I used to think there was hope for folks like that. Now, I'm not so sure.

"So you're all saying you're not going to tell me what you know about The Sons of Aaron Burr or the Youngers and what happened to them?"

Bill rose slowly out of his chair and punched a key on the cash register. A bell rang and the drawer snapped open. Les handed him some folding money. Bill gave him change, thanked him for his patronage, and turned to me.

"Leave it alone, Emmett," he said. "It was a long time ago. Nobody cares."

"You got that right," snorted Clay. "Nobody gives a good goddam."

CHAPTER TWELVE

I left feeling like I'd just gone swimming in a pool filled with human excrement laced with battery acid. If the men in the barbershop didn't have a hand in killing the Youngers, there was a chance they knew who did. Multiply those four idiots by a few hundred, and you have a whole town unwilling to see that justice is done. They'd hidden the truth for 26 years. Why stop now?

Clay's always been like a big brother to my father. I couldn't help but wonder how they'd managed to be friends all these years, especially while my mother was alive. When it came to writing-off bigots, she had an itchy trigger finger.

Kate was at the circulation desk when I got back to the library.

"Find anything?" I asked.

"Let me show you something." She led me back to the microfilm viewer. "Look at this." She switched on the machine. "What date did you say was the last time you saw Clarence Younger?"

"July 31st," I said. "The day before my mother's birthday."

"This is the August 5th issue. The first one to come out after the Youngers' place was burned."

She showed me the front page. There were stories about a significant natural gas find in the area, a horse that got his tail caught in a thresher, and a local pastor who was leaving his flock for a church in Muskogee. "What am I looking for?" I asked.

"Scroll down."

Toward the bottom was a blank space. Somebody had carefully cut out whatever had been there.

"Now look at this." She scrolled to another page in the back of paper. Another empty space. "In every issue, there's a section called 'Legal Notes' here. It's where they write up any crime committed or court proceedings in town that week. There usually isn't much, but for some reason this week someone thought it needed to be removed. Not only that—"

She scrolled to the next week. A hunk of the front page had been cut out. "It's missing 'Legal Notes,' too. The same thing happens in every paper from August to September. Articles cut out, as well as 'Legal Notes.' What do you want to bet, they're all about the Youngers?"

"That'd be a good bet, I reckon. Would you mind calling Frank? See if he knows anything about those things being cut?"

She called. Frank said he had no idea. Whether that was the truth is anybody's guess

She hung up and said, "There's no way whoever transferred those papers to microfilm would've done this."

"Someone did it beforehand, then."

She nodded. "Someone trying to erase history. Who had a reason to do such a thing?"

"I could think of a few off the top of my head," I said, sounding more sarcastic than I'd intended.

Kate shook her head. "Why did no one come looking for those people?" she said. "I mean, if they'd been killed, you'd think someone somewhere would've missed them and come looking for them."

"Karen made the same point. I guess that's an argument against believing Rufus Kenworthy. If all they did was move to another town, there would've been no reason for anyone to look for them. On the other hand, if they were dead, you'd think someone would've missed them and come looking. As far as I know, no one ever did."

"Maybe he was lying," she said hesitantly.

"Maybe he was."

The sun was set, and I needed to get over to Dad's before it got too late. On my way out, Kate mentioned she had a sizable collection of historical materials she intended to go through, looking for something that might help. Most of it hadn't been cataloged, she said, but she'd dig around and see what she could find. I thanked her and said I owed her a meal. She demurred, but judging by her smile, I think she liked the idea. I hoped she understood I'm a one-woman man.

When I got to Dad's, he was in his chair, same as when I'd left him that morning. There were signs—an open newspaper on the kitchen table, dishes in the sink—that he'd been up and around. I tried asking questions about The Sons of Aaron Burr Society, but he was his typical uncommunicative self, so we just sat in front of the television and watched a soap opera.

Karen arrived in the middle, sat down on the couch next to me and tried to explain to us what was happening in the show. I pretended to pay attention. Dad didn't even try. She gave up and puttered around the house making sure it was neat and clean.

I asked Dad if he'd like to have supper with us. His answered was a firm "no." I washed the few dishes in the sink and checked to make sure there was still some leftover chicken in case he got hungry. Karen told him, "Just so you know, Everett, I've boiled you some water to make coffee." He said, "Thank you, sweetheart," then looked up at me with the barest hint of a smile. "That little ol' gal's too good for you."

I winked at him and said, "Tell me something I don't know." Karen gave Dad a hug and asked if there was anything else he needed. He said no. We told him we'd see him tomorrow.

Since we'd come in separate cars, we agreed to meet at her place after I went home to clean up and feed Dizzy.

I fed Diz her Gravy Train, then took a shower. Diz barged in with an old tennis ball while I was drying myself, hoping I'd chase her. I wasn't up to that, but I felt bad I hadn't spent time with her in the last couple of days and asked if she wanted to go to Karen's. She raced around the house, which I took to be a yes. I put on a fresh shirt and pair of jeans and we headed out. I locked the door behind me. I didn't use to do that, but Burr didn't use to have kidnappings and murders, either.

Karen doesn't like me to park my truck in front of her house when I stay the night, so Diz and I walked to her place. She lives around the corner from the First Baptist Church, where she worships on Sundays. The Reverend Hankins' parsonage is within view of her driveway. We're close to being married as it is, but in this part of the world, marriage ain't like horseshoes. Close doesn't count.

It took us about five minutes to get there. The temperature had cooled to the point where it had gotten nippy, but it was still warmer than usual for this time of year.

Karen had changed out of her uniform and into a pair of blue stretch pants with the stirrups that go underneath her feet, a short-sleeved pullover with rainbow stripes, and white slippers that looked like ballet shoes. Someone ought to give the fella who invented stretch pants some kind of award.

She was stirring a pot of something on the stove, which frankly isn't a positive sign. Dizzy ran up to her, looking for some affection. Karen obliged. I shooed Diz away and wrapped my arms around her waist. "What's that new shampoo you're using?" I nuzzled her. "Your hair smells great."

She turned to allow me a peck on her cheek while she continued stirring. "I believe it's called Head and Shoulders," she said. "It's supposed to get rid of dandruff." She tweaked my nose with her wooden spoon. "Real sexy, huh?"

Red was cooking her specialty. She calls it "goop." It consists of boiled potatoes, a pound or so of fried hamburger meat, and a can of Campbell's Cream of Mushroom Soup. With enough salt and pepper, I can just about get it down.

Karen's the spitting image of Susan Hayward, red hair and all. She's also the smartest, kindest, funniest, most talented woman I've ever met. It's for those qualities—and more—that I love her.

But not her cooking.

Of course, I'd never tell her that.

I set the table. She ladled out goop, and I pretended to like it, like I always do.

"Sorry I stood you up this afternoon," she said. "Bernard asked me to take a box of groceries out to Hannah Granger and make her some lunch. He'd have done it himself, but he had some luncheon he had to attend in Temple City. Rotary Club, I think."

Mrs. Granger is Bernard's aunt. She and her husband Hiram raised Bernard after his folks died. Hiram passed away in October while I was still in the VA. Hannah's now living all by herself in a house way out in the country.

"He's a good nephew," I said.

"He is. When's Bernard going to have you do some real police work? By the way, where's the salt and pepper?"

"Real police work seems to only come around when you're in charge," she said on her way out to the kitchen. She returned with the salt and pepper shakers.

"It was nice to hear Everett laugh," she said.

I nodded while I salted my goop.

"I talked to Peggy Miller about helping with your dad."

I nodded while I peppered my goop. "What'd she say?"

"She said she'd love to do it. She'd rather be a personal caregiver than work in a hospital or nursing home."

"You trust her? I remember she seemed a little flaky."

"She showed me her grades and letters of recommendation. Straight-A's and rave reviews. I say we hire her."

"Alright. Let's find a time to talk to her about it."

She smiled. "I'll call her."

I put down my fork, pushed away my plate and patted my belly like I'd enjoyed the meal.

"So what did you do today?" she asked, her voice cheerier.

I told her of my adventures and discoveries.

"I guess I shouldn't be surprised, since my whole family was like that," she said after I'd told her about the filth spewed by Clay during my barbershop visit. "But they got better over the years, at least a little bit. I guess not everyone has."

"I guess not."

"Who would've cut those articles out of the paper?" she said. "Frank Ickes?"

"Frank says he doesn't know anything about it. He reckons it happened before he bought the paper. Clancy Bengston was the publisher back then. I guess I could make a trip out to the cemetery and ask him."

"Let me know what he says," she said sarcastically. "You know what you should do is talk to Burt Murray." Burt is the Tilghman County sheriff. "Wasn't he a deputy back then?"

"I believe he was. That's a good idea. I'll give him a call."

"You got anything else planned?"

"Kate's going to go through some historical material she's got stowed away, looking for mention of that Sons of Aaron Burr Society."

"Too bad you didn't know about this when you went to McAlester. You could've asked Edgar Bixby about it. Maybe he knows who this Smiley is. Heck, maybe it's him."

"Nah, he would've been too young. I doubt he'd be willing to say much to me, since I'm the reason he's in there."

"He's in there because he broke the law."

"Still."

"I hate to mention this—you've probably already thought of it yourself—but you should probably go out and ask Clyde Raymer what he knows. He could be Smiley. He's old enough. How many years is he older than you? Ten?"

I plucked a stray bit of potato from my plate and popped it in my mouth. I was hungrier that I realized. "Something like that," I said.

She pushed her plate away and asked, "What was his daddy's business?"

"Vernon Raymer was a fertilizer salesman."

She laughed.

"I'm not kidding," I said. "He worked for one of the companies that first started manufacturing chemical fertilizers. In fact, now that I think about it, Tom Bixby was one of the first farmers around here to use it. Not many could afford it. That's probably what kept him growing corn when no one else could."

"He used the corn to make whiskey, right?"

"People say that for a while he was the biggest bootlegger in Oklahoma. Before he got respectable, that is."

"What'd he do *after* he got respectable?"

I shrugged. "Bossed people around."

We stood and began clearing the table. Karen said, "Looks like you've got an appointment with Clyde Raymer tomorrow.'

I'd rather have all my teeth pulled with a rusty crescent wrench.

CHAPTER THIRTEEN

Karen rolling out of bed at the crack of dawn woke me up. I tried to go back to sleep, but Dizzy sensed an opportunity and licked my face until I finally capitulated. I wiped off the dog spit, got dressed, kissed the girl, and escorted Diz out the back door.

Red's yard is enclosed by a stockade fence on two sides and a six-foot-high hedge that separates her house from an alley in back. After Dizzy did her business, we slipped through a gap in the hedge to lessen the chance of being seen by her neighbors, especially the aforementioned Reverend Hankins. We snuck down the alley and came out on the street where we were free and clear. Anyone who saw us would've surmised I was simply an early riser out walking my dog and not some reprobate slinking home after a night of sin.

No sooner were we home, than Diz made it apparent she needed to be somewhere else. I let her wander off to play with her friends and beg food and whatever else she else does during the day. In Burr, leash laws are considered an unconstitutional infringement on our dogs' right to life, liberty and the pursuit of table scraps. Our dogcatcher, Kenny Harjo—the same Kenny who's one of my part-time officers—has the easiest job in town.

I let myself in the house and kicked off my boots before I realized I'd forgotten to bring in the morning paper. I tiptoed across my unpaved driveway in stockinged feet and looked around for my copy of *The Temple*

City Pioneer. It ended up being under my truck, courtesy of my scatter-armed paperboy.

The Pioneer is the only daily newspaper in Tilghman County. It apparently gets its marching orders from The John Birch Society. According to its editorial writers, any damn thing the government does to help people is a communist plot. I shouldn't be giving them my money, but I need a paper in the morning.

I was already starting to fume over an opinion piece calling LBJ a traitor to his country, when the telephone rang and startled me into spilling my coffee all over the paper. I stuffed the soggy remains in the trash and answered the phone.

"Chief Hardy, this is Kate down at the library."

"You owe me a newspaper, Kate down at the library."

"I'm sorry, what was that?"

"Nothin'. I'm just having one of those mornings. What's up?"

"Well, I've found a couple things I think you should see."

"It's not even eight o'clock."

"I could hardly sleep last night, thinking about this, so I came in early. I dug through some boxes of documents and came across a photograph and a book of bylaws for The Sons of Aaron Burr."

"Sounds like you hit the jackpot. You at work?"

"I am."

"I'll be there in a few minutes."

***

I sat down at a long table. Kate pulled a slender white paper-bound booklet from a cardboard box full of documents. On the cover in bold capital letters was the word ZABURR. Beneath was a woodcut of two grown men in knickers shooting it out with black-powder pistols (presumably Aaron Burr and the doomed Alexander Hamilton). Below that was *The Sons of Aaron Burr Society* in gothic letters. At the bottom of the page, in tiny print, it read: *The Holy Scriptures of The Sons of Aaron Burr Society, Copyright 1940 by The Sons of Aaron Burr Society, Burr Oklahoma.*

"This looks like quite a find, book lady. Any idea what 'Zaburr' means?"

"Before I answer that, I want you to see this," she handed me another booklet, the same size and shape as the first. "I found this in the same box."

The printing styles were almost identical, except the second one read: KLORAN, *Knights of the Ku Klux Klan, K-UNO, Karacter, Honor, Duty.*

"That was printed in 1916," she said. "That's when the Klan was reformed, after having been dead for a long time. It started in Georgia, then spread all over."

"Including Oklahoma."

"For a while. It had a heyday for a few years, then started to fade away. By 1940 it was mostly gone."

"But not forgotten."

"I guess not." She pointed at the Zaburr. "The date on that one is 1940. The Kloran was published in 1916. They're both rule books."

"Which one should I read first?"

"Doesn't matter. They're practically the same. The Zaburr is clearly modeled on the Kloran. In some places it's copied almost word-for-word."

"You were going to tell me what those two words mean: Kloran and Zaburr."

"I had to look them up, myself. They're bastardizations of the names of two holy books: the Koran and the Zabur. The Koran is like the Moslem bible. I'm not completely sure about the Zabur—spelled with one 'r', by the way. I think it's the holy book of David, written before the Koran. Don't quote me on that, though."

I opened the Zaburr:

"We solemnly declare to the World that The Aaron Burr Society is duly incorporated in the year 1939 under the laws of Oklahoma and the town of Burr as a Ritualistic, Fraternal, and Patriotic Society dedicated to spiritual and material growth to all lovers of Courage, Justice, and Manhood; protection and happiness in the homes of our people; and honorable peace among all men and nations."

Sounded reasonable enough. The following paragraphs extolled virtue in flowery and incomprehensible language. I was starting to think maybe these boys meant well, until I got to the passage that, in my mind, made members of The Sons of Aaron Burr Society number one on the hit parade when it came to looking for whoever killed the Younger family.

"*... to share with us in performing the sacred duty of protecting the God-given supremacy of the white race.*"

The rest was fifty pounds of horse-shit in a five-pound bag—hateful garbage about how the white man had a duty to rid the United States of Negroes, Catholics, Jews, Indians, and Mexicans. I threw it down on the table in disgust.

"It only gets worse," Kate said.

"Maybe you can give me the gist of it sometime." Kate picked up the pamphlet using the tips of her fingers like tweezers and placed it back in the box.

"There was a picture?" I said.

She placed a photograph face-down in front of me. On the back were words scrawled in faded pencil. I had to pick it up and hold it up to the light at a certain angle just to read it: "*The Sons of Aaron Burr Society, Miller's Drug, May 31st, 1940.*"

"Bingo."

"Don't count your chickens, Chief."

I turned it over.

It was an old black & white photograph, about eight by ten inches, of a group of men posing around the soda fountain at Miller's. On the wall behind the counter was the same huge, elaborately framed mirror that's still there and has been since before I was born. Soda glasses were stacked in a pyramid on a shelf in front of the mirror. An oblong sign about six feet long by two feet wide hung overhead: "Try Our Creamy Thick Malted Milks—20 cents." A smaller green and yellow sign offered fresh-squeezed lemonade for a nickel.

Some of the men wore a coat and tie, but most wore shirt-sleeves, which made sense, since it starts getting hot around here around Memorial Day. Those at the lunch counter spun their stools around halfway, so they faced the camera. Those at tables sat with their hands clasped or stretched flat on the tablecloth. Some grinned. Some laughed. In the center was a man standing with his legs shoulders-width apart and his arms crossed, head thrown slightly back and a self-satisfied look on his face.

Names were printed under faces in thin black ink. Tom Bixby was the man in the middle. Most of the others were only vaguely familiar, but I remembered them by name. Harold Prentiss was there, of course, and long dead. Also, Warner LaPeer, who was reported missing in action during the Battle of the Bulge and never heard from again. Russell Longbaugh died of lung cancer, like Rufus Kenworthy was about to; as I recall, Russ was just as mean. Joe Gassaway was the oldest man in the picture, but outlived many of them, having died of a stroke just short of his 99th birthday on the day LBJ beat Goldwater. I couldn't remember how Billy Ray Crabtree and Eldon Tuck passed, but I knew they'd been dead for years. Harl Bird got stung by a mud dauber while plowing. He fainted, fell off and got run over by his own tractor. He hadn't known he was allergic to mud daubers.

Three of the men I knew by sight. Two sat side-by-side at a table on the left, arms draped around each other's shoulders. Their hair was styled the same way, combed straight back from their forehead and shiny with Vitalis. One's was gray, the other's was black. The older man was Vernon Raymer. The younger was his son Clyde.

The last man had wavy dark hair and wore a shit-eating grin. His teeth were so blindingly white, you'd think they belonged to some Hollywood star and not some shady redneck who liked to associate with cut-rate Klansmen. I was reasonably confident this fella was still alive, although I had only the foggiest idea where he could be found. His was the only name not written under his face.

It didn't matter. I knew who it was.

That shady redneck was Ernest Hardy. My dad's big brother.

CHAPTER FOURTEEN

When I was growing up, I read every book I could find about World War I—or, as they called it before the sequel outshone it in terms of global mayhem: The Great War. Like most boys, I was fascinated by derring-do, so when I found out I had a close relative who'd fought under General Black Jack Pershing, I was enthralled.

Ernest Hardy was a real-life war hero. Uncle Ernie was seven years older than my dad, which made him barely old enough to serve in the Army during World War I. My grandfather expected him to eventually take over the farm, but Ernie wanted nothing to do with farming or Burr or Oklahoma for that matter, so you could say the war came at an opportune time for him.

Uncle Ernie craved more adventure than could be had driving a plow horse. When Woodrow Wilson decided sacrificing many thousands of young American lives would be a small price to pay for making the world safe for democracy, Uncle Ernie was at the head of the line to sign up.

My grandfather wasn't happy to see his oldest son go off to war, thereby forsaking the family business. My father liked it even less. He was too young to join the service and he knew if he stayed home he'd get stuck with the farm. By the time he was old enough, the war was over and the script was written. When Grandpa Hardy died, the farm would go to his youngest son. My dad didn't like it, but he was too loyal to rebel.

Ernie, on the other hand, got sent overseas with the first batch of doughboys in 1918. As luck would have it, his first job was as the driver of a mule team carting artillery batteries over the French countryside. He showed me a picture of him and one of his mules wearing gas masks one time, which I thought was uproariously funny. I had to take his word for it that it was him. Whoever it was looked more like a giant blue-bottle fly than a human being.

Ernie's mule-driving career lasted only as long as it took to be accepted by the U.S. Army Air Service. He got his pilot's wings and flew a Sopwith Camel on loan from the Royal Naval Air Force, shooting down four German planes in only a few months. The war ended before he could shoot down a fifth, which would've qualified him as an "ace." He led me to understand that was a big deal.

1927 was the year of my birth. Babe Ruth hit 60 homers for the Yankees that year, and Charles Lindbergh flew solo across the Atlantic. 1927 was also the year Uncle Ernie retired from the newly renamed U.S. Army Air Corps.

He was stationed at Pearl Harbor at the time. Family lore has it—Ernie was cagey on the subject—he married and divorced a young Hawaiian woman, then moved to Utah, where he got a job flying a mail transport from Salt Lake City to Los Angeles. On what turned out to be his final flight, engine failure impelled him to ditch his Douglas M-2 in the middle of Lake Tahoe. He swam five miles to the California shore and hitched a ride to San Francisco with a car full of college boys. That was the end of his postal career.

In San Francisco, he worked as an engineer for a small railroad along the coast. Something mysterious happened to him about that time—mama always suspected trouble with the law—which caused him to move back to Tilghman County. For a couple of years in the '30s, he lived over a bar he bought in Butcherville. On Monday nights he'd eat dinner at our house and regale us with tales of his adventures.

I always only half-believed Ernie's stories. I'm sure there was much he left out. After I went to bed my folks would quietly discuss his skirmishes with the law—events he'd hint at with a wink and a smile but never totally reveal.

Ernie's saloon burned down under suspicious circumstances, so he moved in with us for a while. My folks thought he was a bad influence. Maybe he would've been, if I didn't strongly suspect he was full of shit.

I can understand how my dad might've resented my spending so much time with Ernie, feeling like he'd been relegated to being a supporting player in his son's life. If he did, he was wrong. I idolized my dad. Ernie was trouble. I always knew that. I just enjoyed his company. Dad was hard-working, self-denying, and devoted to his family. Uncle Ernie never loved anyone nearly as much as he loved himself. But damn, he was entertaining.

My mama couldn't stand Ernie, principally because—among his other faults—he was racially prejudiced, something my mama had no patience for. He'd make fun of how dark-complexioned I was, calling me Buckwheat, after the little colored boy in the "Our Gang" films. I guess I didn't understand what that meant. She knew, though, and didn't like it one bit.

I was never sure why Uncle Ernie moved away. For years, I half-thought my mama had kicked him out. All I knew was, one day he packed his bags, told us he'd gotten a job in Tulsa as a pilot for some rich oilman, and drove off in the same 1937 Frazer Nash BMW he'd come to town in. My Lord, what a slick little car.

Anyway, that was the last time I saw him—no more than a couple of days after the Youngers disappeared.

It's funny how I never made that connection.

***

I told Kate which men in the photograph were dead and which were still alive. The latter list was short: Clyde Raymer and Uncle Ernie.

"I was going to say, that fella looks a lot like you."

"He looks like my father, is who he looks like."

"Well, you must feel relieved."

"How's that?"

"Mr. Kenworthy probably got confused. He thought it was your father, when it really was your uncle."

Suddenly, the weight of the world floated off my shoulders and flew around looking for somewhere else to land. That explained everything—well, not everything, but it explained why Kenworthy thought it was Dad in the bar that night. It was perfectly in character for Ernie to be drinking with Harold Prentiss. I wasn't exactly delighted to discover a member of my family might've been this Smiley, or one of his partners in crime. But if true, I'd much rather it be Ernie than my dad.

I thanked her heartily and once again told her I owed her a fancy meal, careful to add, "I'm sure Karen would love to come along." She blushed and waved it off. I asked to borrow the photo. "Take it for as long as you need it," she said. I rushed over to the station to show it to Red.

Bernard was in the back when I got there, sitting at what used to be my desk in what used to be my office. Karen sat at a desk behind a four-foot-high Formica counter, along with her police radio and typewriter. Bernard came out to say hello. I showed them the picture and explained its significance.

Karen blurted, "Lord, Emmett, is that Everett?"

"Nah. It's his older brother."

"So that's the famous Uncle Ernie," Bernard said. "I'll be danged."

Both of them had heard stories about my uncle. Neither had ever known him. Karen moved here long after Ernie left town, and Bernard was just a twinkle in his daddy's eye.

"He looks exactly like Everett did when I first met him," said Karen.

"He looks exactly like you, if you ask me," Bernard said with a grin. He wore braces on his teeth for a long time. He had them removed when I was in the VA. Now, he smiles every chance he gets.

"I don't know about that," I said, "but I think that's why Rufus Kenworthy thought it was my dad in the bar. Ernie couldn't stay out of trouble if he tried. And he never could be bothered to try."

I asked Karen if she'd brought Bernard up to speed. She'd told him everything.

I pushed my hat to the back of my head. "I can't believe I never made the connection between the Youngers getting run off, and Ernie leaving town a couple of days later."

"That's suspicious timing," said Bernard. "I never knew him, but from what I've heard, it sounds like he was more likely to be part of something like that than Everett."

"Ernie was a prejudiced son of a gun and he wasn't scared to mix it up. I don't believe he'd ever kill anyone, but he was a hell-raiser, for sure."

"Where is he now?" asked Bernard.

"That's a good question. Last I knew, he was in New York, but that was way back in '52. I'd been discharged from the Marines and decided to live there a while. Dad wanted me get in touch with him. He told me Ernie had gotten a job flying a private plane for some rich Wall Street banker and was living somewhere in the city, but he didn't know where. Dad gave me a phone number, but it had been disconnected. I looked around a little bit, but my heart wasn't in it. I never did get in touch."

"I bet now you wish you had," said Karen.

I shrugged. "I don't know. In 1952 being a cop investigating a murder was the furthest thing from my mind."

"So what about these other men?" she asked. "You going to try to track them down?"

"They're all dead. Except for Clyde Raymer—and as far as I know, Uncle Ernie."

"Then you'll have to talk to Clyde," she said.

"I guess I will," I said, "if I want to get to the bottom of this. Of course, the Bixbys probably know about it. Tom Bixby ran everything in town Vernon Raymer didn't, including this Sons of Aaron Burr Society. I doubt Edgar or Deke will talk to me, but I guess I should give it a shot. I'll try Clyde, too, although I expect I might as well interrogate a dead skunk for all he's liable to give me. I'd ask Ernie, but I don't know where he is, or if he's even still alive. Wouldn't surprise me if he wasn't, given how he's lived."

I thought back to the stories Ernie told. They always had a punchline. Somehow, I think he would've had a hard time thinking up a funny ending to the Youngers' story.

"Red, would you mind double-checking the other men in this picture and make sure I'm right, that they're all dead?"

She raised an eyebrow. "I don't know," she said and swiveled to face Bernard. "Boss, am I allowed to do jobs for civilians?"

"I reckon just this once," he said, smiling again.

It occurred to me that, without his braces, Bernard looks a little like that fella who played his own mother in that Alfred Hitchcock film.

What was that movie called again?

CHAPTER FIFTEEN

Time never seems to move as fast or slow as you want it to. When you want it to fly, it crawls. When you want it to creep, it scoots along like Willie Mays running down Vic Wertz's fly in the '54 World Series.

I wouldn't be surprised if H.G. Wells invented time travel as a 14-year-old sitting in algebra class.

On the other hand, good things can go by so quick, you're left wondering if they ever really happened.

In some ways, the weeks after my breakdown limped along like a three-legged turtle crossing a four-lane highway. Every day spent getting my head shrunk and my body weaned off alcohol seemed like a year. Things didn't get much better after my release into the wild. As much as I would've liked to put distance between myself and the events that drove me over the edge, physical laws governing space and time wouldn't allow it.

It seemed like forever since Clyde Raymer and I had last met, but of course only three months had passed since I'd questioned him in relation to the disappearance of Earl Collins. Soon after, I found myself locked in a ward at the VA hospital and being subjected to the blood-curdling screams of drunks suffering from delirium tremens 24 hours a day. Meanwhile, Clyde got what he wanted: Earl's father, Merle Collins, was so devastated by the death of his son, he sold his land to Clyde and moved away.

Not only did Clyde stay out of jail, his plans to expand his natural gas processing plant would go forward as planned.

Life can be a real bastard, can't it?

Western Oklahoma doesn't have a Beverly Hills or an Upper East Side, so a rich fella like Clyde has to live amongst us peasants, even if he does have a gigantic house with gates and fences that make sure none of us get too close without permission. The drive to stately Raymer manor only took about seven minutes. As much as I dislike him, I did look forward to seeing his wife, Clara. She's as nice as Clyde is mean and deserves better than him. That mansion of theirs is so enormous, I reckon she probably only runs into him once in a while.

There was a strong possibility he'd be at the worksite overseeing construction of his new baby. Maybe he'd flat-out refuse to see me, in which case I would've wasted a trip. On the other hand, Clara likes me. I reckoned she'd show me in to see him whether Clyde liked it or not.

As I was approaching the road leading to his house, Clyde's black Mercedes came from the other direction and turned onto the highway right in front of me. I fell in behind, but his car had a lot more get-up-and-go than my old F-1 pickup. I quickly lost sight of him. It didn't matter. I had a pretty good idea where he was headed.

Clyde needed Merle Collins' land in order to build his cherished plant expansion. Merle was the last holdout among a slew of local landowners whose property Clyde coveted. Clyde offered to make him rich. Merle said no.

The other landowners were eager to sell, but Clyde made it clear: If he didn't get all the land he wanted, he wouldn't buy any of it. Merle's refusal pissed-off a lot of people. He thought he was standing up for principle. The others said: To hell with principle, we want our money. They pressured Merle to capitulate.

Merle declined. Not only that, as Butcherville's interim mayor, he had the power to deny the zoning changes needed to expand the plant, which he did, causing a town-wide uproar.

Not that Butcherville's much of a town, but it hurt to have his friends and neighbors curse him on the street and make threatening anonymous phone calls night after night. Ultimately, several men angry over his intransigence kidnapped his son, Earl—at the direction of Clyde Raymer, I suspected but was unable to prove—with the idea they'd hold him until

Merle agreed to sell. Their hare-brained scheme went horrifically south, and they accidentally killed the boy.

Earl's death took all the starch out of Merle. He and his wife sold their home and land to Clyde, packed up and moved away. As with the Younger place many years before, bulldozers erased all evidence of the Collins house's existence. Construction of Phase Two of the WestOK Natural Gas Processing Plant got under way.

Since my release from the VA, I'd consciously avoided Butcherville. I did not desire to witness the expansion going forward, knowing what it had cost in human lives. I was afraid it might give me the urge to start drinking again—which was silly, since almost every situation triggered that desire. Going to the bathroom triggered it. Eating powdered mini doughnuts triggered it. Mowing the lawn triggered it.

The fact is, I'm a booze addict. That urge will always be there. I have to fight it off as best as I can and not let it get in the way of doing what needs to be done.

The original WestOK plant is a collection of pipes, tunnels, towers and tanks covering a few dozen acres. Presumably, it was assembled in some sort of logical order, but as far as I'm concerned, it might as well have been made out of an enormous erector set by a giant baby with a vivid imagination.

The old plant was considerably run down. Components were speckled with rust. Weeds sprouted through cracks in the concrete paths between structures. In contrast, the expansion looked like a just-unwrapped Christmas present. Everything was high-gloss. The sidewalks were as smooth as glass. When you look at the two sections side-by-side, the expansion resembles a brand-new battleship towing a garbage barge.

The county installed a temporary traffic light where the plant entrance meets the road. It was red when I got there. In front of me, a Peterbilt hauling a trailer loaded with huge metal pipes was angling to make the turn. It required much creative maneuvering on the part of the driver to avoid knocking over the ten-foot-high chain-link fence surrounding the installation. I sat there watching for several minutes before the truck finally cleared the gate. The driver pumped his fist and honked his horn. I snuck in behind him before anyone could close the gate.

Dozens of hard-hatted men moved about, carrying pipes, operating forklifts and driving trucks. The roar of diesel and the clashing and screeching of metal on metal was deafening. Workers shouted to make themselves heard across distances of only a few feet. Wind whipped up dust everywhere, making it difficult to see what was right in front of your face.

Clyde's Mercedes was parked near a small trailer that served as the construction office. I saw him talking to a tough-looking fella with the name "Mathis" written in magic marker across the front of his hard hat. He was showing Clyde a set of blueprints. Clyde was trying to boss the man. The man wasn't having any of it. Clyde's back was to me. The man saw me walking toward them. He lowered the blueprints and nodded curtly in my direction.

Clyde turned around. Seeing it was me, he made a face like a toddler being told to eat his spinach.

"Hardy," he yelled over the caterwauling, "get the hell out of here. This is a hard hat area."

"That's alright, I got a hard head."

Clyde started to snap back at me, but a sudden gust of wind blew dirt in his mouth. He spit out a brown glob and motioned for me to join him in the trailer. A hugely pregnant young woman with turquoise-blue eye shadow and tightly curled bleach blonde hair sat at a desk entering figures into an adding machine. She saw Clyde and stood awkwardly, causing her stomach to knock over a paper cup of something that looked like either tobacco juice or coffee. Probably coffee. She didn't seem the snuff-dipping type.

"I'm sorry, Mr. Raymer, I'll clean this right up," she said, her eyes darting side to side, probably looking for a cloth or towel. Not finding one, she mopped the spill with the tail of her white blouse.

"Just leave it, Darla. I'm going to need the office to myself for a few minutes."

She squeezed out from behind the desk and managed to lug her belly out of the trailer without causing any more damage. Clyde sat in her chair.

"I won't ask you to have a seat," he said. "You won't be here long enough to get comfortable."

I sat anyway. "Why, I'm doing peachy, Clyde. Thanks for asking."

He scowled. "Don't make me call security, asshole. Whatever pissant authority you might've had is long gone."

"Now, now. Just calm down, Clyde. There's no need to get your back up. This isn't about the Collins case."

That was partly true, but mostly a lie. When it comes to Clyde Raymer, until the day I put him behind bars for good, it will always be about what happened to Earl Collins.

"I wanted to ask you a question or two about some ancient history. Burr history."

He glared but didn't respond.

"You remember a club called The Sons of Aaron Burr Society?"

"Why do you want to know?" All that moved was his lips, and not very much.

"Oh, just curious, is all," I said. "I've got a lot of time on my hands these days, so I've been killing time looking at old copies of the Burr Gazette at the library. I found mentions of The Sons of Aaron Burr Society from back in the '40s and was wondering what it was about. It looks like a pretty elite club, and I figured since your late daddy was a big deal back then, he might've been a member."

His eyes narrowed. "I wouldn't know," he said. "I was away at college. I didn't keep up with what was going on here."

I thought about the picture in my shirt pocket, featuring the beaming mugs of Clyde and his father.

Of course he'd lie.

"Hmmm," I said. "You don't recall Vernon ever mentioning it?"

"My dad and I didn't always get along too well in those days," he said carefully. "I went off to college to get away from him, then joined the Army. Whatever clubs he belonged to, I can't tell you."

As someone who once upon a time couldn't wait to get away from Burr himself, I might have believed him. But I knew better.

I moved to his side of the desk and pulled out the photograph. He tensed up like he thought I was going to hit him. Clyde's as soft as a roasted marshmallow.

"Calm down," I said. "I want to show you something."

I held it for him to see, keeping hold of it in case he tried to snatch it out of my hand and tear it up.

"Recognize anyone?"

He shrugged. "Some men at Miller's. That's my daddy with his arm around me. So what?"

I flipped over the photo and showed him the inscription. "See that?"

He squinted. "I can't read without my glasses."

"Let me help. 'The Sons of Aaron Burr Society, Miller's Drug, May 31st, 1940.' Ring any bells?"

He affected nonchalance. He's a lousy actor.

"So what? Me and my father at Miller's. It doesn't prove anything. I can't imagine why it matters, anyway."

"It matters because exactly two months after that picture was taken, a group of men burned down the house of a black family here in Burr. You might remember them." I paused. "The Youngers?"

"Again I say: So the hell what?"

I changed tack. "You ever know a fella nicknamed Smiley back in those days?"

He shook his head slowly.

I rested my hands on the desk and leaned close. "That wasn't what folks called you, was it? Or your daddy?"

"Smiley? What in hell is this? Those doctors at the VA must've let you out too soon. You're not making any sense. Only Smiley I know is Smiley Burnette."

I was getting to the point where I couldn't be held responsible for my actions, which is a bad place for me to be, especially when I'm in close proximity to the object of my ire. "Smiley's one of them who burnt down the Youngers house and killed them. I'm starting to think I might be looking at him right now."

He stuck a stubby finger about an inch from my nose. "You'd better not be accusing me of anything in public, or you'll have a lawsuit on your hands."

"Well, how am I ever going to sleep tonight?" I pointed out Harold Prentiss. "You know Harold confessed, don't you?"

That wasn't strictly true, but Clyde didn't need to know.

"Harold? The only crime that stupid SOB ever committed was looking up little girls' dresses."

"On the night of July 31st, 1940, he and three other men burned down the Younger house. The next night he killed the whole family. Not all by himself, of course. He had help ... by some or all of the men in this picture, I'm betting."

His jaw worked and his eyes flitted. After a few seconds, he said with surprising calm, "You know, every time I see you, Hardy, you're accusing me of some goddam crime. I don't know what I ever did to you, but I'll tell you: I'm about sick to death of it. All you got is a photograph of a group of men who belonged to some secret club I don't know anything about. Maybe my dad did belong to it. I don't know, and I don't care. I don't know why I'm in that picture. Maybe my daddy took me along that day to get a root beer float. It was a long time ago and I don't remember. I do know I'm not going to stand still and listen to you accuse me or my father of being an arsonist and a murderer. Now, you'd best get out of here right now before I call security and have you thrown out."

I lowered my voice to match his. "That's just the sort of gutless thing you'd do, isn't it, Clyde? Have someone else take me on, just like you had your thugs take on Merle Collins and his 12-year-old son."

I was close enough to smell the bourbon on his breath. I hadn't realized we had that in common.

"I know you were behind the abduction of Earl Collins," I continued. "You wanted Merle's land, and you'd have done about anything to get it. I'm not saying you wanted the boy dead, although I expect you didn't care much one way or the other. But you planned and set in motion events that caused the deaths of six people. Merle wouldn't sell, so you had his son snatched and told him if he didn't play ball he wouldn't get him back." I stood up straight and took a deep breath. "All those folks would still be alive if you weren't so greedy." I wagged a finger at him. "I know you did it, Clyde. It's just a matter of time before I find the evidence."

He picked up the phone. "Tony, get over here right now. And bring a gun." He slammed it down and glared at me.

"The last refuge of a chickenshit, Clyde. Not that I'd expect anything better." I shook my head. "My Lord," I said, largely to myself. "Six people dead. Just so you could add a goddam front porch to your eyesore of a gas processing plant."

A heavy-set fella burst into the room. His hand rested on a .45 automatic. "What's up, boss?" he said.

"This gentleman is trespassing."

Tony reached for my elbow. I jerked it away and gave him a look saying he'd best back off. "I'll be leaving under my own power, thanks," I said, then turned to Clyde. "I'll get you one of these days, Clyde. If not for Earl Collins, for this Younger thing." Tony stepped aside and held the door open. I stepped outside, turned and said, "I'll just say one last thing, Clyde. When they ship you to McAlester and strap you into Old Sparky, I want a front-row seat."

He smiled. "You're too much. It's hard to believe they let you run free, never mind work as a cop. You're not going to find anything, but have fun looking."

I don't know if "fun" was the right word for it, but I'd keep looking, alright. The evidence was out there. I just hadn't found it yet. Until I did, there wasn't much I could do but walk away.

"I'll be seeing you, Clyde."

"You'd better hope not."

I reckon if I had more regard for my personal safety, I'd have taken that as a warning.

CHAPTER SIXTEEN

I'm not sure what woke me up first the next morning: Karen's elbow in my ribs or an overextended bladder. Either way, I was awake.

I stumbled to the bathroom, stood there for what seemed like half an hour, returned to bed and burrowed under the covers, thinking irrationally that I might sleep for another hour or two.

Karen took care of that.

"So are you going to New York or not?" she asked.

I poked my head out from under the covers. "What in hell are you talking about?"

"To find your uncle."

It took a few seconds for the cobwebs to clear before I understood she was picking up our conversation from the night before, about my uncle being in that Sons of Aaron Burr picture. Karen thought since he was the only whose name wasn't written down, he might not have been an actual member. Maybe he just happened to be there when they took the photograph. I said, 'We won't know until we ask him,' or words to that effect, and that's where we left it.

"I doubt it," I said. "There're still things around here I haven't done. I haven't talked to Burt Murray, for one thing. I was thinking about taking another trip to McAlester so I could show that picture to Rufus Kenworthy. Hopefully being a couple of days closer to the Great Beyond might make him more cooperative."

She sat up. She as wearing a long flannel nightgown that was about as sexy as a repurposed feed bag. I made a mental note to replace it with something more attractive one of these days.

"You can do those things, too," she said, "but if you ask me, you're going to need to track down your uncle."

I folded my hands behind my head and examined the ceiling for cracks. There were two.

"You're probably right," I said. "But even so, I can't believe Uncle Ernie would've been a part of that. I don't care how big an outlaw he is."

Karen swung herself over the side of the bed. The nightgown dropped just as she went through the bathroom door. She has this amazing ability to get dressed every morning without revealing an inch more skin than absolutely necessary. I consider this a personal affront, since seeing her clad in next-to-nothing is typically the highlight of my day.

She couldn't see me pout. "It's worth talking to him, though," she said as she brushed her teeth. "You never know about people. Not many folks would've thought Darryl Martin capable of doing what he did."

Most days I try to make it through breakfast before I think of Darryl Martin and what he did.

"I'd rather call him," I said. "I'll call directory assistance or look around Dad's house and see if he has the number written down. Maybe this'll be one of his good days and he'll remember it."

I didn't expect it to be, but I guess I'll never stop hoping and wishing.

"Whatever you do today, you're going to have to do it without me." She stood in the doorway for an instant, giving me the briefest glimpse of what I'd hoped to see, bless her gorgeous little heart. "I've got a lot of work today," she said, "and I'm late already." She closed the door.

My breakdown was partly the reason Karen was elevated from dispatcher to full-time uniformed member of the force. The other, more-important-but-related-part, was that she showed up in the nick of time and blew a bad guy's head off before he could do the same to me. She already deserved a promotion. She's always put in longer hours for shorter pay than any of us.

"What if I need help?" I said. "I'm accustomed to having an entire force at my disposal." In truth, the entire Burr police department consists of Karen, Bernard, and me, plus two part-timers, Kenny Harjo and Jeff Starns.

Jeff can't police worth a damn. Kenny can and does, but he has to divide his working hours between us, the local Oklahoma Tire and Supply where he's the assistant manager, and his job as town dog catcher.

"That's not my fault," she said. "Why don't you ask your little librarian friend? What's her name—"

Karen knows Kate Hennessey's name. She's just a little territorial where I'm involved.

"I'd be a fool not to. A lot of what I know about this is because of her."

The water in the shower was running full blast and Karen couldn't hear me, or at least pretended she couldn't. "Uh-huh, you do that," she said.

"I think Kate has a crush on me."

"I can't hear a word you're saying, Emmett."

That was probably for the best. Kate's nearly young enough to be my daughter. I don't have designs on her. To pretend otherwise, even in fun, could cause Red to sulk, and her sulking does not usually work to my benefit.

I got dressed while she showered. She had someplace she needed to be. I didn't.

Least of all New York City. I have ghosts there. I have ghosts everywhere, but the ghosts in New York are far enough away to ignore. Long-distance phone service between here and there works fine. I just needed to find his number. Should be simple enough, I thought.

Dizzy and I made our usual escape through the alley. Despite everything going on in my life, I felt reasonably good. For one thing, I'd been up for an hour and I hadn't thought about having a drink. The weather was sunny— cooler than the day before, but still warmer than usual for December. I probably didn't need the blue denim jacket I was wearing, but I'd rather be too warm than too cold.

Reverend Hankins was out front of the First Baptist, changing the marquee in a University of Oklahoma sweatshirt and pyjama bottoms with little cartoon giraffes. He puts up a new message every day in the weeks leading to Christmas, which was just around the corner.

"What's today's lesson, Reverend?" I said from the sidewalk.

He turned and saw it was me. "The stories are different, but the lesson's always the same, Emmett. God loved us so much, he gave his only son." He smiled. "You're out-and-about early."

Reverend Hankins used to intimidate me, given my natural inclination to sin. However, I've come to learn that, except for Sunday—when he girds his loins for battle against the Prince of Darkness—he's pretty easy going.

"Ol' Dizzy here insisted on her walk," I said, hoping he wouldn't notice or remember that I ordinarily let Dizzy run all over town unattended. I could hardly have said, "Oh, I'm sneaking home from Karen Dean's, where I stayed last night. We slept in the same bed and all, and I got to see her naked for a couple of seconds this morning. Diz and I snuck out the back door hoping you wouldn't catch us. Oh well." Giving the roly-poly minister a stroke would've laid heavier on my conscience than a white lie about my dog. Sometimes you have to choose between the lesser of two evils.

The Diz took the reverend's hello as an invitation to jump and slobber all over him. He was a good sport about it, laughing and rubbing behind her ears. I wished him well, and we continued on our travels. I detoured to Dad's house instead of going straight home. He used to love throwing a tennis ball around with Diz in the backyard, but those days are mostly past. Diz can fetch maybe two or three times before aching knees shut her down. As for Dad, it's hard enough to get him up out of that chair to eat. Still, he likes seeing her, and I hadn't taken her for a visit in a while.

Diz squeezed through the door ahead of me, skidded across the kitchen floor and into the living room, where Dad sat in front of the TV. "There's my girl!" She did her little dance around his chair, hoisting her front legs up to his lap and trying to get close enough to lick his face. He was glad to let her do it.

"How're you doin' today, Dad?"

"Oh, pretty good." His smile faded, and he leaned back in his chair. I went out to the kitchen and filled a bowl with water. Diz heard me and scampered out to drink.

"Dad, you heard from Uncle Ernie lately?"

"No," he said. "I ain't been out to see him."

"I wouldn't expect you to, Dad, since the last we knew he was living in New York City."

He looked confused. "New York?" he said weakly. "Ernie lives in Butcherville."

"Nah, Dad, don't you remember? Ernie moved to New York a long time ago. Got himself a job working for some rich fella."

He scowled. "What in hell'd he do that for?"

I couldn't answer in a way that would've meant anything to him. Instead I asked him if I could get him anything.

"Nah," he grunted, and turned back to the TV.

"Alright then, I'm going to look for some socks I think I left in your laundry room."

I slipped into his bedroom instead. He keeps a list of important phone numbers in an ancient Big Chief pad in the drawer of his nightstand. Only one page was filled. Three numbers were listed next to Ernie's name. Two were scratched out. I tried the third. Disconnected. So much for that.

I walked back to the living room. Dad was smiling. "Ernie, you remember that time you drove the tractor to school? Daddy 'bout skinned you alive."

It hurt to do, but I smiled back. "I remember that story Dad, but Ernie's not here. I'm Emmett."

His smile thinned. "Oh, yeh. I meant to say Emmett." He's not so far gone that he doesn't sometimes get embarrassed when he makes a mistake like that. "I was thinking about your uncle."

I sat down and read him some jokes out of an old Reader's Digest he had lying around, trying to get a chuckle out of him. Failing that, we sat quietly for a while until he fell asleep. I turned off the TV, left a glass of water on the TV tray next to his chair, and left.

Outside Dad's house, Diz kindly asked my permission to go do her socializing. I dismissed her with a "Go on, you dumb dog." She trotted down the alley behind the house, jumped up and peeked inside the barrel one of Dad's neighbors uses to burn his trash. There must not have been anything uncharred or edible. She got down and continued on her way.

I didn't want to be an accessory to her crimes, so I walked in the opposite direction.

When I got home, I made myself a cup of coffee and surveyed the unholy disaster area that was my house. Karen wouldn't set foot in the place, it was such a mess. I couldn't blame her. I'm not much of a housekeeper, but Jiminy Christmas, I'm almost 40 years old. It's time to grow up.

I put on one of my favorite records, Miles Davis's *Someday My Prince Will Come*. The first song had only been on for a minute when, without thinking, I dropped my broom and kicked-back in my La-Z-Boy. I instantly realized what I'd done and gave myself a mental ass-kicking. I took off Miles and put on a Count Basie and Lester Young LP instead. The Count's music isn't the kind you have to sit down to enjoy.

For the rest of the morning, I washed dishes, scrubbed the floors, did laundry and cooked up a batch of fried chicken to take to Dad later in the day.

Once the house was in reasonable shape, I rewarded myself by listening to the Miles album. I lost myself in the music, experiencing the usual pleasures. John Coltrane's tenor saxophone solo came up. I was struck by a cherished memory from my time in New York.

The year was '52 or '53. A buddy of mine from the service—he was a saxophone player, too, only he was a lot better than me—told me about this bar in New Jersey where he'd gone to listen to music the night before. I had to hear the saxophonist, he said, and wouldn't take 'no' for an answer. I hadn't lived in the city long, but I knew that going anywhere outside of Manhattan without a car can be a major hassle. I let him talk me into it, anyway.

That evening we took a train to Newark, where we caught a taxi. The cab driver wouldn't take us to the club unless we paid double. It was in a dicey neighborhood, he said. There weren't any other cabs around, so we reluctantly agreed. On the ride there, I bitched and moaned about having to risk my life to listen to a sax player I'd never heard of. My buddy gave me a dirty look and said, we'd survived the Korean War so we could probably handle Newark. When we got there, he handed the cabbie the price on the meter and not a penny more. The cabbie complained. My buddy reached through the open window and grabbed him by the collar. The cabbie suggested my friend screw himself. My friend dragged the cabbie's upper body through the window. The cabbie extricated himself and drove off, cussing a blue streak. My friend was shaking as we walked into the club. "There's nothing wrong with this neighborhood," he said. "That asshole just doesn't like negroes."

Suffice it to say, I quit my bitching and moaning.

The alto saxophonist in question was a colored fella about my age. He played a little like Charlie Parker, but with a passion and originality all his own. He was raw, but he had something special. My friend and I wanted to talk to him, but he disappeared backstage after every set. On his break, we could hear him practicing over the sound of the jukebox.

We finally caught up with him after the last set. He told us he was from Philadelphia and had recently completed a tour with Dizzy Gillespie's band, which impressed the hell out of both of us. He was staying in the city at the time, so we shared a cab with him back to Manhattan. We talked about jazz and—since we were all sax players—about our horns. He mentioned that he was considering switching from alto sax to tenor sax. Looking back, I reckon if all the musicians in New York had been as nice as that fella, I might never have come back to Burr.

Anyway, to make a long story short, his name was John Coltrane, and within a few years, people in the know considered him the greatest tenor saxophonist in the world.

The reason that story came to mind had less to do with Mr. Coltrane than it did my buddy who dragged me out to New Jersey.

For a couple of years in the Marines and during my stay in New York, Hary Loyd ("One R, one L," he always used to say) was my best friend. After I left the city, we drifted apart. I hadn't seen nor heard from him in years. Unlike me, he stuck it out in New York. Also unlike me, Hary had talent. He's played with a lot of well-known musicians, people I listen to on records. He's even made a few of his own. The jazz business being what it is, Hary's always needed a sideline to make ends meet. Hary parlayed his experience as an MP into becoming a private detective.

One thing private detectives do is find people.

I had someone who needed finding.

Maybe I should take that trip to New York.

CHAPTER SEVENTEEN

One thing Burr could really use is decent diner. Our only sit-down restaurant is The Piazza, which has delusions of grandeur and prices its food accordingly. We've also got a couple of drive-ins. Burger Mart has been around since I was a kid, and of course there's the new Sonic, but there's no place you can go to sit down and have a decent home-style meal at a reasonable price. Lately I've been driving 20 miles to a greasy spoon in the town square in Temple City called Cup O'Joe's. Not every day, but at least once a week. Its specialty is biscuits and gravy, which I love. Today I had another reason to go.

Cup O'Joe's is where Burt Murray, the Tilghman County sheriff, eats lunch.

In fact, I ran into him last time I was there. We made some random chit-chat but sat at separate booths. Burt's usually there with one or more of his deputies, none of whom—with the exception of Keith Belcher, who's a friend of mine—I have any use for. Today I hoped to corner him in the hope he could help me with the Younger case.

Burt's eager to please, but if you want to talk to him, you've got to get to him outside the courthouse. Getting in to see him in his office is like trying to sack Bart Starr; first, you got to deal with the Green Bay Packers' offensive line. Edith Percival, Burt's secretary, is an impenetrable block of granite. I've found getting past her to see Burt or even getting him on the phone are nearly impossible.

Face-to-face, however, my chances were pretty good.

I got there a little before noon. I settled in a booth and opened a day-old newspaper, reading with one eye and watching out for Burt with the other. A waitress with platinum-blond hair teased into a helmet that nearly scraped the ceiling handed me a menu and filled my water glass. She called me 'sweetheart' and her wink implied that more than lunch was on the menu if I played my cards right.

The newspaper was *The Daily Oklahoman*. It had its usual mix of these-are-the-end-times Cold War horror stories and aw-shucks bullshit. The United States and Russia agreed to a treaty designed to make it less likely they'll blow each other up. A snowstorm in the panhandle inspired the usual number of panicky motorists to drive their cars into ditches. I wondered how we managed to dodge that bullet; around here it had been almost like spring. The top of the front page was dominated by a blurry photograph of three tow-headed youngsters playing tubas. The caption read: *All-School Chorus Plans Christmas Program Here*. What kind of chorus uses tubas? I thought. The All-School kind, I reckon.

The tall-haired waitress was walking toward me when the bell over the door rang. A man of medium height and built like a sack of potatoes with sawed-off broomsticks for legs walked in. With him were a couple of muscle-bound Charles Atlas lookalikes in gray deputy sheriff outfits. The sack-of-potatoes fella's uniform was tan with gold epaulettes on the shoulders. He wore a badge and a name tag reading "Sheriff Murray." Miss Tall-hair squealed like a teeny bopper, minced over and smothered Burt in hugs and kisses. One of his deputies made a slight move to get in between her and the sheriff, but not before Burt patted her on the rump and called her Blondie, which may or may not have been her real name.

Like the gifted politician he is, Burt looked over the place in a princely manner. He saw me and waved. I gave him and his entourage time to settle into a circular corner booth. Burt contracted his stomach just enough to squeeze in, although a lumpy slab of belly fat swelled over the edge of the table. I walked over to pay my respects.

"Hey there, Emmett, buddy, how you doin'?" He offered his hand, treating me like a potential voter. I vote, but not for him.

"Fair to middlin'," I said in the Okie drawl I unconsciously adopt when I'm in certain company.

We made the usual small talk while the deputies read their menus. Burt asked about my daddy. I gave him a more positive report than was merited. He mentioned how glad he'd be to see me back on the job. I thanked him but said Bernard was doing fine in my absence.

"So what could I do you for, Emmett?"

"I just wanted to know when might be a good time for you and me to have a talk."

"How 'bout right now?"

"This is something I'd like to discuss in private." I said. "No offense to you boys," I added for the sake of the deputies, who showed no sign they heard or cared.

Burt folded his hands behind his chubby neck and said, "I got a lot on my plate right now."

I'd anticipated token resistance. The reason Burt has Vince Lombardi for a secretary is because he doesn't like to get pinned down by anyone who might ask him to do actual work.

"It won't take long, Sheriff," I said. "I'm looking for information about something that happened in my town about 25 years ago. I thought you might be able to help."

He nodded sagely. "Well, I reckon I got some time right after lunch. How 'bout you drop by the office when we're finished here, and we'll talk?"

"As long as you let Edith know I'm coming."

He laughed. "Don't worry, I'll tell her to let you in."

I thanked him and nodded to the deputies. One of them might've nodded back, or he could've been flexing his ear muscles. Hard to tell.

I returned to my table. Blondie expressed less interest in me now that the sheriff was in the joint, but politely took my order. When my biscuits and gravy was ready, another waitress brought it over. I enjoyed every bite. I left a quarter on the table and settled up at the register. On my way out, I called over to Burt that I'd see him in a few minutes. He smiled and nodded.

Whatever it was he was eating, Burt was likely to take his time. There's no telling which men and women of influence might come through the doors of Cup O'Joe's wanting to bend his ear about this or that project that might benefit from his endorsement or cooperation or willingness to look the other way.

In other words, I figured I had some time to kill.

It was a beautiful day—temperature in the 50s or 60s, nary a cloud in the sky. I took a leisurely walk around the square, breathing in the fresh air, peeking into store windows, looking for something to give Karen for Christmas. Every year she pretends to get mad and says, "Emmett, I told you not to give me anything." I reckon she does it to hide her reaction, in case she's disappointed, which is most of the time.

Every year I screw up in a new and innovative way. Last year it was because I paid too much attention to TV commercials. Like a dummy, I drove all the way to the Sears in Enid and bought her the latest Hoover vacuum cleaner with all the special attachments and accessories. When she said "Emmett, I told you not to get me anything," she wasn't kidding. I took the vacuum back the first chance I got, and exchanged it for a gift certificate. I subsequently learned there's not a damn thing at Sears Karen wanted—not clothes or shoes or vacuum cleaners or socks or bras or underpants. "I didn't know you hated Sears," I said. "Now you do," she replied. Live and learn.

This year, I wasn't about to make the same mistake. I might make a mistake, but it would be a *different* mistake.

After peeking through a few shop windows, I came upon a shop specializing in fancy ladies' underthings—the kind of place you go to get the silky pyjamas and whatnot that I'd like Karen to wear. I walked by it a few times, trying to overcome my shyness. Once I was confident no one was watching, and after taking a lot of deep breaths to calm myself, I ventured inside.

As soon as I did, I wished I hadn't. The young woman who waited on me was a cute little brunette who'd gone to school in Burr and just the previous spring graduated from Burr High. I remembered her from when she was a girl playing jacks on the sidewalk. Now she was a grown woman working in a lingerie store. I couldn't remember her name. Unfortunately, she knew mine.

"Hello, Chief Hardy!" she said in a sing-song voice. "You must be looking for something for Miss Dean."

"Uh, hi, do you have a restroom I could use?"

"Why, sure. Right this way." She showed me where to go.

I was too embarrassed to pee into a strange toilet, so I counted to fifty, flushed, washed my hands, and came out.

"Can I help you find something?"

"No thank you, I just needed to use the restroom."

I beat it out of there as fast as I could.

Naturally—because this is me we're talking about—Burt and his deputies came walking down the sidewalk at that precise moment. "Stocking up on frilly things, Emmett?" Burt said. His sidekicks found it hilarious.

"Don't knock it 'til you try it," I said.

Burt chuckled. The deputies looked at me like I'd farted in church.

The courthouse was on the other side of the square, so I walked alongside Burt until we got there. The deputies loaded themselves into a radio car and drove away in search of hippies to harass. Burt pointed at a bench on the grass across from the courthouse and suggested we sit outside. "Too nice a day to spend cooped up in an office," he said. I had to agree.

He extended his arm along the top of the backrest and took up two-thirds of the bench. I sat with one cheek hanging off the edge.

He dug a bag of sunflower seeds out of his shirt pocket and popped a handful into his mouth. "So what's this about, Emmett?"

"You know Burr pretty well, don't you, Burt? Being that it's your wife's hometown."

He nodded. "You could say that."

"How is Kath, by the way?"

Burt's wife Katharina was a couple of years ahead of me at Burr High.

He chuckled. "Well, you know Kath. She's always got something wrong. The latest thing is her lungs. They've been giving her trouble. She's staying with a cousin of hers in Arizona. Doc hopes the dry air will help."

I barely knew Kath in school. Even now, I see her maybe once every two or three years. She's quiet and mousy and gives the impression that she'd be content to disappear into the background wherever she is. "Give her my best next time you talk to her," I said.

He spit out shells and loaded up some more. "Yup, I will," he said. "So, what can I do you for?"

"I recently heard of an organization in my town back in the '40s called The Sons of Aaron Burr Society."

He held the bag of seeds out in front of him and peered at it like he was seeing it for the first time. "Been chewing these instead of tobacco," he said, shaking it between his thumb and forefinger. "Kath said I had to choose between her and Red Man. I reckon I'll choose her." He spit out more shells. "For now, at least."

"So does that ring a bell, Burt?"

"What was that? Sons of what?"

"Sons of Aaron Burr Society. I believe it was meant to be some kind of Shriners or Masons type of thing. Tom Bixby ran it. You remember Tom Bixby?'

He threw back his head and bellowed. "Oh hell yes, you better believe I remember Tom Bixby!"

A small brown bird swooped down, sniffed a couple of the spent shells and flew off. "You know what," he said with a flash of recognition so phony you'd think he was auditioning for a TV commercial, "I remember that club of old Tom's. It was a chamber-of-commerce-type thing, if I remember correctly."

"My impression is that it was more secretive than that."

He shook his head. "You could be right, Emmett. I don't really know. That was a Burr organization, and I was living here in Temple City."

"But you went to visit Kath's folks sometimes, right?"

"Yeh, I did. But it's not like I was following local events too close."

"Ok, I understand. Do you remember hearing about anyone else who belonged to the Sons of Burr besides Tom?"

"Nah." He spit out some shells. "Like I said—"

"It was a Burr thing."

"That's right."

"And you lived in Temple City."

He nodded again. "Correct."

It was clear he was avoiding eye contact, which I took to mean he was uncomfortable with the subject. If I was interrogating him as a suspect, I'd circle around, let him stew on it, then come back to it later. Since he was in a position to cut me off, however, I kept firing questions.

"The reason I ask, is that I'm looking into an arson committed in Burr back in the summer of 1940. I don't know if you remember, but around that time a certain contingent of white folks was trying to run off all the colored folks in town. They managed to scare off all of them, except one family. You remember the Youngers?"

His loaded up on seeds. "Can't say I do."

"Clarence Younger was the fella who used to handle baggage at the Burr train station."

He didn't respond, but instead watched folks climb the stairs to the courthouse and waved at passers-by. A big mixed-breed dog ran up to him. He scratched it behind the ears. He seemed willing to pay attention to anything and everything except me.

"So how about it, Burt?"

"How about what?"

"Clarence Younger. You remember him?"

He smiled again. "Oh, I'm sorry, Emmett, I got distracted. You know, come to think of it, I remember that fella at the train station. Clarence Younger was his name, you say?"

"That's right." The bird came back. Burt flicked a shell at it. The bird stood its ground. "Oh, yeh, yeh, uh-huh. Clarence Younger. I remember him. Sure."

"Well, I reckon you remember his house got burned down, then."

"I seem to remember something along those lines, yeh. An electrical fire, wasn't it?"

"No, the way I understand it, someone threw Molotov cocktails through the windows. In fact, I don't see how it could've been an electrical fire, since I'm pretty sure they didn't have electricity."

"How would you know that?"

"I was friends with the son, Gabe. I remember going inside at least once. They used oil for light and a wood stove for heat. No electricity."

He made a skeptical sound. "Is that so? I'm pretty sure that's what the sheriff at the time decided. An electrical fire." He spit another shell. "Maybe they got wired up after your visit."

That didn't happen but there was no sense in arguing.

"So the sheriff did work the case?" I asked.

"Well, I started as a deputy in '41, so that was before my time, but I seem to recall hearing something about it."

"Elton DeLong was sheriff back then, right?"

He smiled at the mention of the name. "That he was. Old Elton had been in office almost since territory days."

"Was he the one who hired you?

He nodded. "That's right. I owe that man my career."

"When exactly did you start with the county?" I asked.

He squinted like he was trying to remember. "I reckon it must've been 1941," he said, then turned to look at me for the first time since we'd sat down. "What's all this about, Emmett?" His good ol' boy face was starting to slide a little bit. "What do you care about some house fire that happened 25 years ago?"

Sometimes it's hard to know where you stand with Burt. He plays the part of the glad-handing politician well, but like most politicians, there's something hard and calculating underneath. I like him, but I've never exactly trusted him. I wondered if I could now.

I decided I probably could *not*, but since he was one of the few people in a position to help, I told him Rufus Kenworthy's story anyway.

"Hmmm," he said when I finished. "That's all news to me. And you think Tom Bixby and this Aaron Burr Society—"

"Sons of Aaron Burr Society."

"Gol' dang, that's a mouthful, ain't it?" He chuckled. "Alright, this Sons of Aaron Burr Society burned down this house, got scared they'd been recognized, went out the next night and killed the whole family? Is that it?"

I nodded.

He frowned and shook his head. "Nope. I ain't buying that for a second. I'm not going to take the word of someone like that over the reputations of men like Tom Bixby and Vernon Raymer."

He pushed the sunflower seed bag back into his shirt pocket. "I guess those folks' house did get burned down," he said, "and that's a shame. Maybe it wasn't an electrical fire. For all we know they could've gotten drunk and knocked over a candle or something and tried to blame it on someone else. But Tom and Vernon committing murder? Never would've happened."

I started to respond but he stopped me before I could. "I'd leave this one alone if I were you, Emmett. Nothing can come of it other than soiling the names of honorable men. There ain't a crumb of evidence except what this piece of trash told you, and that ain't near good enough for me. It shouldn't be for you."

He stood slowly. His knees were giving him trouble and he moaned. "Oh, my goodness, I ain't as young as I was, I'll tell you that much. You think being 50 is old, Emmett?"

I shrugged. "Ask me in ten years." If I live that long.

He laughed. "You still got a while, don't you?"

"Be here before I know it," I said.

The look he gave me wasn't friendly. "Whatever happened to those folks was their own damn fault," he said in a hard voice. "They burned down their house and left town the next day. That's all there is to it. You need to listen to me on this and let it go."

Given that I was on probation with the world, I held on to my emotions. Barely.

"Alright, Burt," I said. "Thank you for your time."

We shook hands. "Nice talking to you, Emmett." He started to cross the street, got halfway, then turned back around.

"Did I tell you the Burr Town Council wants me to advise them on whether you're ready to go back to work?"

"That's the first I've heard of it."

A car wanted to get by. Burt held out his hand like a school crossing guard. "Yeh, they asked my advice. Right now, I don't see why you shouldn't."

"Glad to hear it."

He grinned amiably. "Don't give me a reason to change my mind."

CHAPTER EIGHTEEN

I told Karen about my conversation with Burt.

"Well, I'm not surprised," she said. "Burt Murray was never one to rock the boat. I'd bet you anything he knows more than he's letting on."

"Probably. He wasn't with the department when it happened, though. He signed on in '41."

"He's got ears. He could've heard things."

"I reckon. He did seem uneasy talking about it."

"Did you ask him if remembered anyone named Smiley?"

I could've kicked myself. "No, I forgot," I said.

She was alone in the office. Bernard was out doing his rounds. Kenny was due to come in when he got off at the hardware store around five. I had no idea where Jeff was. No matter. Karen's who I wanted to talk to.

"Clyde's not going to tell me anything," I said. "If Burt knows something, he's keeping I to himself. I guess I'll go after Deke Bixby. Maybe I'll get lucky"

"Maybe I'll win the Miss Oklahoma pageant."

"There's a lot better chance of that happening," I said. "I also could drive back to McAlester, see if I can get in to talk to Edgar, although I doubt I'd get anything out of him, either."

"I like what you said about talking to Kenworthy again."

"Yeh, that's worth a try, I suppose. You mind giving the warden a call?"

She ripped the top sheet off a notepad and slapped it down on her desk. "There's the number," she said, pushing the phone to where I could reach it. "Warden's direct line."

The secretary answered after one ring. The operator announced it as a person-to-person call. The secretary asked me to hold. The warden picked up after a few seconds.

"Sheriff Hardy, I was just about to call you."

"I appreciate the promotion, warden, but that's Chief Hardy."

"That's right, dang it. Sorry about that, Chief," he said. "Anyway, I wanted to tell you Rufus Kenworthy passed away this morning."

So much for that. "Well, that's inconsiderate of him. I had a picture I wanted him to look at."

"I'm sure he would've loved to hang on a couple more days, but the Lord had other plans."

It was just as likely he died to piss me off.

"Who am I to question the Lord?" I said.

"His will be done."

I wished the warden well and hung up.

"So much for Rufus Kenworthy, huh?" said Karen.

"Yeh. Wish I'd had that picture when I talked to him."

"Too bad you can't see into the future."

"I can barely see into the present."

"Speaking of presents, you get me anything yet?"

"No."

"Don't."

"I haven't had a chance to go to Sears."

"Very funny," she said. "I'm telling you, boyfriend, your best bet night be going to New York City and hunting down your uncle."

"Believe it or not, I've been thinking the same thing."

"Why wouldn't I believe it?"

"Did I ever tell you about my friend Harry Loyd?"

"That saxophone player you knew in the Marines?"

"Yeh. He became a private detective after we got out of the service. As far as I know, he's still living there, doing whatever a big-city private eye does."

"I wonder if one of those things is help hicks from the sticks track down their kin?"

"You calling me a hick?"

"If the shoe fits."

"What does that make you?"

"Oh, I know I'm a hick. Never claimed otherwise. Of course, I never lived in New Yawk City."

"I think I still got Hary's phone number somewhere."

"He still live in that little apartment you shared with him? What was that neighborhood called? The lower depths, or something?"

"The Lower East Side. Last I heard he did. But it's been years since I talked to him."

"Maybe he struck it rich and moved to one of those penthouse apartments like at the beginning of Green Acres."

"If I know Hary, he's still playing jazz, and if he's still playing jazz, he hasn't struck it rich."

"You don't have to be back at work for another couple of weeks," she said. "You should do it. Go to New York and find your uncle. It'd be good for you to see him, anyway."

"I probably should tell him about Dad's condition."

"So you have no idea where to find him?"

"None whatsoever. Dad had a couple of old numbers for him but they've been disconnected. I called directory assistance for New York City. They had so many E Hardys and Ernest Hardys and Ernie Hardys. They couldn't nail it down because I don't know his address."

"Maybe you could track down a New York telephone book."

The Manhattan phone book is about a foot-and-a-half thick and weighs a ton. The same goes for the Brooklyn, Staten Island, and Bronx directories.

"I could try, I guess, but I expect it would be a waste of time. Anyway, I'd rather eat broccoli for dinner seven days a week than try to call every Hardy in New York City. It's like finding a needle in a haystack." I thought for a second. "Maybe I'll just buy a plane ticket and go."

She nodded. "I think you should," she said. "You got the money?"

"I do."

Back when he had all his faculties, Dad signed half his natural gas royalties over to me. I've got plenty of problems, but money's not one.

"Then go," she said. "Maybe while you're there, you can find someplace better than Sears to shop for my Christmas present."

"I thought you didn't want me to buy you anything."

"That was before I knew you were going to New York," she said. She fluttered her eyelashes. "Ever heard of Tiffany's?"

"I don't believe I have. Do they sell vacuum cleaners?"

***

The first thing Hary Loyd ever said to me when he found out I was from Oklahoma: "The problem with Oklahoma is that it has a giant chip on its shoulder. It's called Texas."

Guess where Hary's from.

Okies and Texans are supposed to be deadly enemies. Truth be told, I'm sure we think a lot more about them than they do about us.

That's what Hary's joke was getting at.

The University of Texas Longhorns and the University of Oklahoma Sooners play an annual football game that's about as close to mortal combat as a sporting event can get. The Sooners win more than they lose. In every other arena of human endeavour—from politics to the arts to education to the excellence of their Mexican food—Texas beats us like a rented mule. When they deign to so much as recognize our existence, they treat us like an annoying little brother.

Texas was once its own independent country. They act like they still are.

It drives Okies crazy.

Hary Loyd is smarter, tougher and more ambitious than me. He's also as nice a fella as you'd ever want to meet. Except when you get him mad, like that cabdriver did. At such times he can be meaner than me, too.

On top of everything, he's a better saxophone player than I am. A lot better.

Dammit.

The only area I have him beat is size. I'm a head taller and 50 pounds heavier. Hary can't be over five-four in a pair of platform shoes. It doesn't matter. He carries himself like someone who knows he can whip nine-tenths of the human race. He's strong for being so small, but more than that, he's the most determined man I've ever known. When we were in the Marines, he won every fight he got into—there were plenty—by sheer force of will. I've seen Hary shake off punches that would've dropped me like a stone.

One time I asked him how he was able to keep going against guys bigger and stronger than him.

He laughed like the answer was obvious. "Hate, man. I hate bullies more than anything. When someone tries me, it's usually because they expect me to be an easy mark. To hell with that, is what I say. My life's work is to prove those assholes wrong. Beyond any doubt."

Hary grew up just outside Ft. Worth, the son of a rich Republican lawyer. He and his dad didn't get along, which is about all I know of his life before the Marines. He seldom talked about either of his parents and in general had little interest in discussing his past.

He would occasionally open up about his musical background. Once he told me he started on the tenor saxophone in sixth grade. By high school, he was playing jazz in Ft. Worth's colored night clubs. His was usually the only white face in the joint.

I asked him one time why he joined the Marines. "I heard they had a great band," he said. How he ended up in the MPs? "I can't read music." It worked out in the long run. "I realized knocking drunk sailors on their ass is probably more fun than playing 'Hail to the Chief' whenever the president takes a shit." As for how he managed to make it into the Corps even though he's several inches shorter than the minimum height required: "That's my old man at work. Pulling strings is about all he's good at."

We served in the same unit in Korea, fought alongside one another in the field and in the shadier neighbourhoods of Seoul, where much of the aforementioned "knocking drunk sailors on their asses" took place. That part of the job appealed to Hary. He wasn't crazy enough to enjoy combat, but no one fought harder. When we went up against the Red Chinese, I wanted him by my side.

You might think being from the same general region of the country is what brought us together. If you're from Oklahoma or Texas, however, you know that it probably would've had the opposite effect. Our love for music—

especially jazz and specifically the saxophone—formed the basis of our friendship.

Both of us were self-taught. Evidently Hary taught himself better than I did. When I met him he was 19 and already playing as well as all but a very few of the best negro musicians twice his age. Whenever we got leave we'd fly to Tokyo and go to jam sessions. Hary always brought the house down. The Japanese jazz fans treated him like visiting royalty. We'd make a circuit of all the clubs, sometimes hitting them all the same night. The young girls loved Hary. He was surprisingly humble about it. "Man, in the land of the blind, the one-eyed man is king," he'd say. I don't think he gave himself enough credit.

Hary got his discharge before I did. He decided to move straight to New York, the jazz capitol of the world, and convinced me join him as soon as I got out. He rented a shabby one-bedroom apartment in a tenement building on the Lower East Side. I was discharged shortly after the armistice in the summer of '53. My flight to the states landed in San Francisco, where I exchanged my ticket to Oklahoma City and got one that took me to New York. I telephoned Hary from a booth at the San Francisco airport and told him I was on my way. I flew into LaGuardia on a hot August night, carrying my Marine duffle bag and the Conn Wonder alto sax my mama bought for me in 1938. I knew I was in the big city when I got off the plane and heard Mel Allen describing a Yankees game on a skycap's little transistor radio.

Hary was there at the gate waiting for me. He didn't have a car but figured I'd have trouble finding my way to his apartment. I understood how kind that was, when it took us the better part of two hours and I don't know how many bus and subway transfers to finally get to his apartment. No sooner did I drop off my bags when he tried to get me to go out and hear some music. I begged off. It wasn't until the next night that I had my first musical adventure, and started down the path to understanding not all dreams are meant to come true.

That's a fact Hary never had to face. When it came to playing jazz, he was the real deal. That's not to say he got rich—few if any jazz musicians do—or even famous. But he earned the respect of every musician on every bandstand he ever played on. For Hary, the respect of his peers was the main thing. That's not to say he never made any money playing music. He made some, but not enough to live on.

For times when music jobs were scarce he needed another way to make a buck. Besides jazz, the thing he did best was being a cop. NYPD doesn't hire officers to work part-time between jazz gigs, so Hary settled on being a private detective, which is how he's made his living for going on 13 years.

At least it was the last time I talked to him. It's been a while.

CHAPTER NINETEEN

Hary's phone number was mine, too, back when we were roommates. It's faded from memory over the years, however, along with other things I once could recall at the drop of a hat, like the name of my kindergarten teacher or the words to all six verses of "This Land is Your Land."

I'd need to dig out my old address book.

Kenny came through the station door as I was on my way out. He asked me when I'd be resuming my duties. I told him January 1st, 1967, the Burr Town Council willing.

He said with a wink, "Can't wait. Bernard's running us ragged."

"As hard as that boy works," I said on my way out, "I'm surprised there's anything left for the rest of y'all to do."

I found Dizzy lying on the front porch when I got home. It was early for her to call it a day, but sometimes she gets tired and comes home to recharge her batteries. For a dog, the old girl is on the far side of middle-age. I'd been feeling that way myself. She lumbered inside without even begging for food—just conked out in her spot next to the La-Z-Boy where she's worn a spot in the carpet.

I didn't want to tear the house apart looking for the address book and undo all the cleaning I'd done, but the more I searched, the more frustrated I got, and pretty soon I stopped being careful and dumped the contents of drawers on the bed and pulled things off shelves onto the floor without bothering to pick them up.

I kept getting madder and madder, until, after a sudden flash of recall, I checked the glove compartment in my truck. There it was, lying under a greasy pair of pliers.

I went back inside, cleaned up my mess, then sat down in my chair and thumbed through the book. Some of the people I barely remembered. Some I didn't recognize at all. Some had been kind enough to help me, like a fella by the name of Billy Bauer, who looked like a high school English teacher but played a mean jazz guitar. I got to talking to Mr. Bauer one night at a nightclub called Birdland. He gave me the phone number of the great saxophonist Lee Konitz, who I ended up taking a few lessons from. Mr. Konitz wouldn't let me depart too far from the melody of the song when I improvised, which sounds easy but something I found unusually hard to do.

Hary's number was written in blue ink inside the book's back cover. I had butterflies in my stomach just thinking about calling him—knowing that if I did I'd be opening myself up for God knows what. What if Hary couldn't help? Hell, what if he could? I was almost more scared to find Uncle Ernie than not.

"What's it going to be, Diz?" I said speculatively. She tilted her head and gave a breathy "woof," which I took it as a vote in the affirmative. I seldom argue with Dizzy.

I gave the operator the number and said I wanted to make a person-to-person call to Hary Loyd. It was around six o'clock in New York, as good a time to call him as any. Earlier, he'd have been at work. Later, he'd probably be out playing music. The operator placed the call. Someone picked up. A familiar voice said, "Yeh?" A nasal voice said she had a call for Hary Loyd from Emmett Hardy in Oklahoma. Through a curtain of static, I heard someone say, "Emmett Hardy?" The operator said, yes, Emmett Hardy. "Goddam! Yeh, of course this is Hary Loyd. No one here but us chickens, man." The operator clicked off. "Emmett, man, what's going on, my brother? When you comin' back to the Apple?"

"How about this week?"

"Sounds good, man. Bring your horn. I'll book us a gig."

***

Hary and I didn't talk long. There'd be plenty of time for catching up when I got to New York, which, after talking to him, had gone from being a crazy suggestion to a foregone conclusion.

First, however, I had to take care of a few things.

I called Karen and told her about my conversation with Hary. She was about to go off duty. We made plans to meet at Dad's. She pulled up in front of his house at the same time as Diz and I did. I reckon I won't ever get used to seeing Red driving the Galaxie squad car that was mine up until a few months ago.

Diz ran up to the front door and did her kangaroo hop, anxious to get in.

We humans took our time.

"Don't say anything in front of Dad about me going to New York."

"What kind of idiot do you think I am?"

"Just the regular kind."

That earned me a punch on the arm.

Diz forced her way in ahead of us and went straight over to Dad. Karen followed her over and gave him a hug. Dad stood and tossed an old rubber ball around the living room for Dizzy to chase.

After a few throws, he sat down in his chair. I served him some of the chicken I brought.

"That's good," he said. "Tastes like your mama's."

He's said that before, but not in a long time.

He started to nod off. Red tried to get him to go to bed, but he wasn't having it. I told him I had things to do and asked if he'd mind if we hit the road.

"Oh hell, Emmett, I ain't six years-old," which I took as permission for us to head out, which was probably safe to do. He's been mostly good about going to bed on his own and dressing himself in the morning, although he doesn't do much in-between except watch TV.

We were almost out the door when I remembered Peggy Miller. "Dad, Karen and I are going to talk to a girl about coming over here during the day and giving you a hand with things. Her name's Peggy. Is that ok with you?"

I expected an argument but all he said was "fine." Karen went over and gave him a kiss on the forehead. Diz licked his hand and got a rub behind the ears in return.

We stepped onto the porch. It was dark already, and the sky was overcast. I looked through the picture window and saw Dad, his face lit up by the TV, sitting just like we'd left him.

"I'll give Peggy a call first thing in the morning," Karen said. "I was going to do it earlier today, and I forgot."

"Yeh, we need to get on that. How does he seem to you? Better? Worse? To me, he seems about the same as he has been, but I'm not sure if that's because the change is so gradual, I'm not seeing it."

"I don't think he's any worse. I could be missing it, too. I'll be interested in what a trained geriatric nurse has to say."

It took me a second before I realized she was talking about Peggy Miller. It was hard to imagine the silly young girl I'd met a couple of years earlier working as a trained medic. People grow up, I guess. I might not, but some people do.

"You might have to do the interviewing if I have to leave early," I said as we walked to our cars. "While I'm gone, it would be good if you looked in during the day. Make sure she doesn't have him dancing around the house to some of that teeny-bopper music she listens to." I'd sampled Miss Miller's musical tastes during our first encounter.

"She won't do that, but of course I'll check on him. You know I'll do anything to help that dear man. He's the closest thing to a daddy I have left."

We met at Karen's place, with me parking in the alley to avoid detection. She cooked us some hamburgers, which is one of the few things she does well, food-wise. We watched Walter Cronkite as we ate, then did the dishes. I washed, she dried. Afterwards, we sat down on the couch and half-watched some silly western on television, while making plans for what to do next in terms of my investigation.

"Did you show Frank Ickes that picture?" she asked.

"I didn't have it yet when I talked to him."

"You should show him."

"I'll do it tomorrow."

"You should also go and talk to Deke. I don't expect he'll have anything interesting to say, but it can't hurt to try."

Asking a Bixby for help with anything hurts my pride, but I couldn't let that stop me. I tried to think of anything else I was forgetting, if anything. "Let me go over this and you tell me what you think," I said. "I'm going to explain it like I'm telling it to you for the first time, ok? If I skip over something, let me know."

"Will do. Shoot."

"Ok, here we go. Rufus Kenworthy calls y'all up at the station—"

"Rufus didn't call. The warden at McAlester called."

"Right. The warden calls y'all at the station asking for me. He doesn't know I'm on leave, and you don't tell him—"

"Bernard. He was talking to Bernard."

"Bernard then," I said. "Bernard doesn't tell him but says he'll take a message and have me call back. Bernard gave me the message—"

"I gave you the message."

"Alright, you gave me the message. Now, do you mind if I talk?"

She smiled mischievously and gestured for me to continue.

For the next half-hour I outlined what I knew, beginning with Kenworthy's story of how he learned about the arson of the Youngers' house, and the family's death at the hands of someone called Smiley.

At one point, I made reference to the Youngers being colored.

Karen held up her hand. "Hon, let's stop for a minute. You got to quit calling folks 'negro' and 'colored.' They want to be called 'black' these days. I've been meaning to tell you for a while, but I didn't want to hurt your feelings."

I'd heard Walter Cronkite use the word 'black' in talking about Martin Luther King, but I thought it was interchangeable with those other words.

"I guess I'm behind the times in that regard."

"That's alright, hon. Just so you know."

I talked some more. I got riled at the part about Vernon and Clyde Raymer possibly being involved, and she had to calm me down. I got a little choked-up remembering how my daddy turned away Clarence.

"As far as I can tell," I said, "he and I were the last to see them alive, except for whoever killed them."

"If they were killed."

"They're dead. I'm convinced of it. That Smiley character killed them, probably with help from someone else. I'd bet my last dollar Clyde Raymer had something to do with it."

She sighed. "Emmett, don't take this wrong, but just because Clyde got away with his involvement with Earl Collins' death doesn't mean he was guilty of this."

"You don't think it could've been him?"

"I'm not saying that, but just because he took a picture with a bunch of men—"

"A bunch of pieces of shit."

She held out her hand and said, calmly: "Whatever. Just because he took a picture with that group of men, it doesn't mean he killed that family."

"It doesn't mean he didn't, either."

"No, it doesn't, but if you're going to get him, you're going to need hard evidence."

"Which is why I'm going to New York to find my uncle."

Left unsaid was the possibility my uncle could have been involved. He was in that picture, too.

We turned off the TV and sat quietly for a while, listening to the night sounds float in from outside.

Karen broke the silence. "You spin a good yarn, boyfriend."

"You're a pretty good audience. Would you be so kind as to get me a glass of water?"

She went to the kitchen and brought back ice water in a green metal cup. I downed it in one swallow. It gave me a massive headache, but I almost didn't mind, I was so parched.

We watched the late news and Carson's monologue, then went to bed. Karen rolled over and closed her eyes. I tried to read but was too wound up. I turned off the light and counted the same cracks in the ceiling as last time.

Something popped into my mind. I switched the light back on and shook Karen awake.

"I just realized something. The town keeps records, right?"

"Mmmm-hmmm."

"We should check them out, don't you think?"

"Mmmm-hmmm."

I thought some more.

"I got a lot to do, getting ready to go to New York and all."

She put a pillow over her head. "Mmmm-hmmm."

"Would you mind going to Town Hall tomorrow and look at their files?"

She ripped the pillow off, raised up on her elbows and fixed me with fiery eyes. "I will, if you let me go to sleep! Now turn that dang light off!"

"Alright, sorry."

I turned off the light and kissed the back of her head.

"You want to have lunch tomorrow?"

"GO TO SLEEP!"

***

I lay awake most of the night. I had a lot to think about. Not just the Younger case. Going back to New York again weighed heavy on my mind, as well.

I'd moved to New York to play music. I wasn't there very long before discovered I wasn't cut out for it. It was a hard life. The best players had to compete for lousy-paying gigs. Many paid the rent by delivering groceries or selling shoes or something equally disappointing if not downright degrading. What chance did I have? Even if I could cut it, I wasn't sure I wanted to.

I don't mean to say it a waste of time. I loved New York the short time I lived there. I heard terrific music, went to museums, learned what it was like to live in a city full of people of different races and religions from every country on the planet. Living in New York made me a better person.

I quit the city because it and me weren't a good fit in the long term. I experienced as much of it as I could stand before boarding a Greyhound back to Burr and accepting the job I have now. All I brought were a few paperback novels and a Conn Wonder alto saxophone. I left everything else behind.

Including a wife.

***

Sofie Boucher played drums. That might not sound like a big deal, if you don't understand how poorly female jazz musicians are treated by their male counterparts.

Jazz is as male-dominated an endeavour there is outside of professional football or garbage collection. Women singers are tolerated, mostly because a band with an attractive woman on stage has a leg up on finding paying gigs (no pun intended). That said, they're seldom considered full-fledged musicians by her male colleagues, unless their name is Ella Fitzgerald or Sarah Vaughan—in other words, someone so great, not even the biggest male-chauvinist jazz musician can deny it.

Women instrumentalists have it even worse. They're treated by the men with skepticism at best and hostility at worst. To survive, a woman in that situation has to be tougher than boot leather.

Sofie was tough. She could also play. In fact, she was a hell of a lot better musician than I was. Not that it mattered to her. I learned damn quick that male musicians tend to judge you as a person by how well you play your instrument. Women aren't like that, or at least Sofie wasn't. We became fast friends.

It didn't take long for us to become something more than that.

We started going out. We were the same age and enjoyed each other's company. She was from France, I was from Oklahoma: a pair of outsiders who came to New York to play jazz. We loved each other's accents. I loved her talent. Lord knows what she liked about me. Other than my looks, of course.

In contrast to Hary, who only cared about music (and the private detective agency he was trying to get off the ground), Sofie had a wide range of interests. She took me to the Metropolitan Museum of Art and Carnegie Hall. She introduced me to things I never dreamed of, growing up in little old Burr, Oklahoma. I loved her for that, too.

At the time we met, there was no question of me getting seriously involved with a woman. I still fantasized about prying Denise Kinney away from Edgar Bixby, although I never acted on it.

Still, we had what I guess you could call an affair. We slept together a few times, but our strongest bond wasn't romantic. It was musical. I loved playing with her and, for all my faults, she loved playing with me. We became friends and creative partners and would've been satisfied to keep it that way.

Perhaps we would have, if Sophie's immigration status hadn't become an issue.

Sofie wasn't an American citizen, so when someone from the Immigration and Naturalization Service came knocking on her door, she was thrown into a panic. The INS man told her she'd overstayed her visa and had to go back to France. She didn't want that, but she didn't want to play hide-and-seek with the federal government, either.

Someone who didn't know Sofie might think she trapped me into marriage so she could get her green card. Nothing could be farther from the truth. For one thing, the first several times I proposed, she turned me down.

I didn't want her to leave, so I kept after her. Meanwhile, she moved from one sublet apartment from another, trying to stay one step ahead of the authorities.

One night we were sitting on a bench in Tompkins Square Park when I took out the crumpled application for a marriage license I'd been carrying around and said, "I'm not taking no for an answer."

The next day we got our blood test, then took the subway downtown to City Hall and had a clerk perform the ceremony. Hary and his girlfriend were our witnesses. Afterward we went to an Automat for sandwiches. There was no honeymoon. Nothing changed between us. We lived in separate apartments, slept together when we felt like it, and remained close friends and musical colleagues right up until I moved back to Oklahoma.

Now—as I lay beside the woman I was in love with and wanted to marry—I realized that besides hunting down my uncle, there was another thing I needed to do on my trip.

Get a divorce.

CHAPTER TWENTY

For the first time since my release from the hospital, I got out of bed before Karen. I didn't want to wake her up, so I fumbled around for my clothes and got dressed in the dark. I had no idea of the time. I whispered for Dizzy and we tip-toed out the back door. All my care went for naught when I started my truck, which in the early morning silence sounded like a bomb going off. When we got home, I refused to let Diz go on her daily rounds, figuring it was too early to be getting in people's garbage. She sulked, but I held my ground.

The clock on the stove said 5:15. There wasn't much I could do at that hour except eat breakfast, and I wasn't hungry. The only thing on TV was static. I sat in the La-Z-Boy and picked up a book called *The Getaway* by that Jim Thompson fella Kate Hennessey and I were talking about. I'd bought it in the Greyhound terminal in New York City just before I'd gotten on the bus that brought me back to Burr.

I relented and let Diz out around 7:00, made bacon and toast, and read the paper. On the front page was a picture of a young woman in knee-high boots, all bundled up, hopping and skipping across a snow-covered city street. It reminded me I'd better buy a pair of shoes with a tread. I learned from experience the first time I went to New York how unsuitable cowboy boots are for walking on ice.

I drove over to Dad's around 8:00. Karen was there already. She said she'd call Peggy Miller as soon as she got to work. I asked if she remembered the promise she'd made in the middle of the night about looking through the town archives for me. She said of course she did, but she could only do one thing at a time. I thanked her.

She snapped, "You're welcome, dang it, now let me go, so I can do the 1000 things you and everybody else in town is asking me to do."

I did the gentlemanly thing and held the door. I saw to it that Dad had what he needed, and made my exit.

The warm temperatures of a few days earlier had gradually dipped over the course of the week. It was now downright cold. The sky had the overcast quality that usually means snow. With a drive to Oklahoma City and a plane trip in my immediate future, icy roads were the last things I wanted to deal with.

My first task for the day was to buttonhole Deke Bixby, but the bank didn't open until nine, so I'd have to wait.

I killed time by driving out to the lake, hoping again that the sight of it might shake loose some ideas about the Youngers' fate.

A thin crust of ice had settled over the water. I thought about a wintry Saturday when I was a kid. We'd had a week's worth of sub-freezing temperatures and the lake had frozen hard and deep enough for ice skating. Of course, no one in town owned a pair of ice skates, so the kids slid around in their sticking feet, pretending to be Sonja Henie or whoever the male version of Sonja Henie was. My mama wouldn't let me go, to my great disappointment. Late in the afternoon a 12-year-old boy and his dog fell through the ice. The dog died and the boy almost did. After that, when mama wouldn't let me do something, I didn't argue.

Alas, the sight of muddy old Burr Lake did not inspire any new revelations. I walked over to where the old fishing pier use to be and briefly considered wading out to look for human remains. That was ridiculous, of course. Any bones that close to shore would've been found long ago.

I reminisced once again about my fateful encounter with Denny Kinney. The memory made me sad. Being sad made me crave a drink. I mentally beat myself up, started the truck and headed back to town.

When I parked, the clock outside the bank said 9:07. Inside, I was greeted by the security guard, a fella by the name of Ron something-or-other, I don't recall his last name. The uniform the bank gives him to wear has so many bells and whistles, it puts mine to shame. He's licensed to carry a firearm, which for the time being put him one up on me.

He greeted me and asked, "You fellas in the market for another officer?" like he does pretty much every time I go to the bank—which is one more reason I try to avoid going to the bank.

"Let's see if they want me back, first," I said.

"Ah hell, Chief, you'll be back. You're a legend."

I felt like saying, "I believe the word you're looking for is 'infamous'," but I let it go. Instead, I slapped him on the shoulder and asked if the boss was in.

"If you mean Mr. Bixby, he sure is. Came in about a half hour ago."

I thanked him and made my way toward the back, where Deke's office is.

The walnut door had a gold name plate engraved with the words, "Deke Bixby, President." His secretary's desk was vacant, which worked in my favor. I'm not sure I'd have gotten in if she'd been around to intercept me.

Deke sat in a swivel chair talking on the phone. His back was to me, and his face to the wall. I knocked lightly. He spun lazily. I could tell he'd gained weight since I'd last seen him. His neck bulged over his collar and his blue pinstriped suit jacket stretched too tight over his shoulders. Instead of his usual buzz cut, he'd grown his hair and waxed it into a flattop. He saw it was me and spun back to face the wall. After a few seconds, he checked over his shoulder and saw I was still there. He winced and brought his conversation to a close. He slammed the phone down and glared, hostility radiating from him like stink off Pepe Le Pew.

"What do you want?"

"Well hello to you too, Deke. How's every little thing?"

"Some of us have work to do. If you've got something to say, say it and get out."

Deke's dislike for me dates back to when I joined the Marines and fought in Korea. Later, when the town fathers—over the Bixbys' objections—brought me back as Chief of Police, folks treated me like a conquering hero. The Bixby brothers, on the other hand, were widely suspected of dodging the draft so they could stay home and tend to the family business of making more money than anyone would ever need.

Deke and Edgar didn't like the disparity in how we were perceived and thereafter made it their mission to undermine me.

I always felt like I should be the one doing all the hating. After all, Edgar stole my girl. In his capacity of Town Council president, Deke had tried to have me fired on multiple occasions—most recently as a way to prevent me from investigating Edgar's son EJ for murder and later Edgar for trying to cover it up. I wouldn't be surprised if Deke himself was involved, although I must confess, there's no evidence to that effect.

Furthermore, I expected Deke do everything in his power to ensure I wasn't reinstated on January 1st. Fortunately, the rest of the council tends to side with me. I reckoned as long as I didn't antagonize them between now and then, I should be fine. Of course, I still had to worry about Burt Murray's recommendation, but I'd cross that bridge later.

"You heard from Edgar or EJ recently?" I asked.

"If that's what you're here to ask, you can go to hell."

I wished I could enjoy sticking pins in Deke more than I was, but mostly all I felt was uncomfortable. I wanted this over with.

"Alright Deke, don't piss yourself. I just had a question or two about your daddy."

He glared at me with bullfrog eyes. "How' bout I call Burt Murray and have him send out a deputy? You wouldn't be so smart then." His voice shook out of fear or loathing. Probably both. "You have no authority. Maybe I'll just have Ron throw you out."

The idea of Ron trying to manhandle me was laugh-out-loud funny. "That's not going to happen," I said. "I won't be here long enough to make it an issue. I just wanted to ask if you could tell me anything about an organization your Dad ran in the '40s called The Sons of Aaron Burr Society."

"Yeh," he said warily. "I was told you'd been asking around about something like that."

Frank or Burt must've told him.

"Never heard of any such thing," he said dismissively. He sat his hands flat on his desk and I noticed that on one finger he wore a diamond ring surely worth more than all my worldly possessions combined.

"It was some kind of secret club your dad ran in the early '40s," I said by way of perking up his memory.

He affected boredom. "How would I know about that? I was just a little kid."

"I was hoping you might remember hearing Tom talk about it, is all."

He shrugged. "Doesn't sound familiar. Is that all?"

"You're sure?"

He laced his hands behind his head and rocked back. The fancy ring clicked as it hit the wall. "You railroaded my brother and seduced his wife," he said. "You bullied some retarded teenager into framing my nephew for murder. To be honest, nothing would please me more than if you were to curl up and drink yourself to death, like I fully expect you to do someday. You're bad for my family and you're bad for this town. For all I know, The Sons of Aaron Burr might as well be a group of left-handed badminton players. Even if I did know something—which I don't—I wouldn't tell you anyway, so why are you wasting my time?"

That badminton crack was pretty clever. Also, the possibility of me drinking myself to death should never be taken off the table.

Of course, the rest was a crock. I didn't frame anyone, I didn't railroad anyone. While I did try for the better part of a decade to seduce Denise Kinney, I never had a lick of success. Once she was married, I gave up, notwithstanding fantasies to the contrary.

Yet, for all that, I half-believed him when he said he didn't remember the Sons of Burr. Oh, I expect the name was familiar to him, but it was possible he didn't know what the group was up to. His ignorance certainly seemed genuine. He and Edgar were always easy to read. A good liar has to be a good actor or else he has to able to con himself into believing the bullshit he's peddling. Neither Bixby brother will ever be confused for Marlon Brando, nor are they any good at fooling themselves. Edgar knows his face looks like something rotten the dog keeps under the house. That's why he treated Denny so nice while treating everyone else so bad. Deke knows he's ugly and mean, and he knows the world knows he's ugly and mean. I'm no Sigmund Freud, but if I were to guess, I'd say neither Edgar nor Deke likes himself very much.

"Ok, Deke," I said, "if something pops into your mind—"

"It won't," he snapped.

"Well, if something does," I continued, "I'd appreciate it if you'd let me know. Or better yet, call Karen Dean and tell her, since I'm going to be out of town in a few days."

"How 'bout you do us all a favor and just stay away?"

Part of me would've been glad to do just that.

CHAPTER TWENTY ONE

The last time I'd been on an airplane was when I got discharged from the Marines, 12 or 13 years ago. The government took care of the planning, at least until I got to the states.

This time I'd have to book the flight myself. I didn't have a clear idea how to go about it. I thought I'd try TWA, only because they used to fly planes in and out of an airfield up in Waynoka back in the early days of coast-to-coast air travel, and I figured they probably still had Oklahoma connections. Turns out they did, but they don't fly to New York. The lady on the phone suggested I contact a travel agent. A travel agent is something Burr does not have and probably does not need, so I looked in the Temple City yellow pages. There was one listed. I spent the rest of the morning driving to Temple City and making the necessary arrangements.

I stopped by the station when I got back to Burr. Bernard was drinking coffee in the back office and jawing with a prisoner in the holding cell. He showed me an old yellowed APB from '65 for a white male wanted for a filling station robbery in Watie Junction. The guy in the cell was a white male. "You sure this is the guy?" I asked Bernard. Before he could answer, the guy in the cell chirped, "Oh, I done it."

"He's glad he got caught," said Bernard.

"My conscience has been bothering me something fierce," the guy said.

"We're just talking about cars," said Bernard.

"That Fury of y'all's is awful slick," he said. I guess Wes Harmon must've fixed that busted solenoid.

Bernard said Karen had run to the drug store and would be right back. I hung around outside on the sidewalk and watched her walk out the door of Miller's and cross the street. She looked like she was in a hurry. We went back inside the station. I asked how the document search went.

She tossed her purse onto her desk and hung her flight jacket on the coat rack by the door. "There wasn't a doggone thing we can use," she said. "Whoever was in charge of keeping records back then did a terrible job. They've got nothing to show from 1940 through 1948. They must've hired someone competent in '49, because after that, the records are mostly complete. But for the time you're looking at, there wasn't a single relevant picture or document or letter or anything. Sorry."

"I hadn't expected much. Thanks for trying."

"What've you been up to?"

I described my encounter with Deke Bixby.

"Looks we uncovered exactly the same amount of information," she said.

"Zilch," I said. "I guess I'm off to New York."

Her face tightened. "I'm going to worry about you going up in an airplane."

"Oh, it's not just one airplane. It's two. Oklahoma City to Chicago, and Chicago to New York."

"Oh, Lord."

"And I'll have to do the same thing over again on the way back."

"Ok, you can stop now."

I laughed. "You're the one who thought I should go."

"I know," she said.

"Did you worry when I was in Korea?"

"I didn't even realize you'd gone."

"Alright, then. Just pretend we had a fight and you're disgusted with me and we're keeping our distance for a few days."

She smiled sarcastically. "Oh, that's a brilliant plan. When do you leave?"

"Tomorrow."

"I guess that means you're done looking around here."

"For the time being, anyway."

"Any idea where to find your uncle?"

"Nope. Somewhere in New York, I hope."

"That's not encouraging."

"Keep your expectations low and you'll never be disappointed, is what I always say."

"I don't remember ever hearing you say that."

"I say it quietly to myself."

"I understand."

I asked if she'd called Peggy Miller. She said she'd arranged to interview her tomorrow.

"What would us Hardy men do without you, Red?"

"I shudder to think."

***

As sometimes happens, out of nowhere I was struck with an urge to drink as I walked out the station door. I decided to fight it off with a late lunch of tater tots, a chili-cheese dog and a Coca-Cola at the Sonic. It was delicious, but made me feel like a naughty ten-year-old who'd eaten a carton of ice cream behind his mother's back. I tried to imagine my Coke was infused with bourbon, but that didn't help. You can't acquire a buzz from Coca-Cola no matter how hard you try. The carhop retrieved my tray, and I paid my bill.

I started the truck. The broken muffler boomed and everyone in the driveway looked my way. I pretended not to notice. I circled around to the exit and waited for a few cars to go by so I could turn onto Main Street.

I saw a highway patrol car was parked on the shoulder directly across from the drive-in. I'm like anyone else; when I see a cop, I drive extra-careful. I don't have to worry about it when I'm driving an official vehicle, but in my old Ford pickup I'm just another redneck in a beat-up truck. Of course, on the odd occasion I am stopped, I identify myself as police and get off with a warning. Cops tend to give each other leeway as a professional courtesy. It may not be ethical, but that's the way it is.

The trooper stared at me through dark glasses, like he was daring me to pull out. There was nothing else I could do. I eased onto the road, slowly and carefully.

The trooper immediately hit his lights and pulled up behind me—so close I had to slow-down gradually just to avoid getting rear-ended. I parked on the shoulder and wondered why I was being stopped. Probably that muffler.

Usually when you get stopped by a state trooper, you look in your mirror and see him talking on his radio, running a check on your license plate. This fella just sat and stared at the back of my head.

After a couple of minutes, he put on his Smokey the Bear hat, slanted it as far forward as it would go, and walked toward my pickup with his right hand resting on his gun.

I rolled down the window as he approached and gave him an ingratiating smile. "Sorry about that muffler, officer, I've been meaning to get that fixed."

He was smooth-faced and chubby, in his early 20s and apparently in a very foul mood. "Face forward and place your hands on the steering wheel," he barked.

I acceded to his request. I tried to look at him out of the corner of my eye to see if he looked familiar. With the dark glasses he had on, it was hard to tell. He wasn't wearing a nameplate, which I found strange. Stranger still was the fact he'd covered his badge number with a strip of black electrical tape. The hairs on the back of my neck stood at attention.

This wasn't your average traffic stop.

"Son, my name's Emmett Hardy. I'm the police chief in this town—"

"I know who you are, asshole, and you're not the police chief anywhere."

"Well, maybe not now, but—" I reached for my wallet.

He shoved a gun in my face. I recognized it as a Charter Arms Undercover .38 Special; I'd recently priced one as as an off-duty weapon. It's a double-action revolver, five-shot instead of the usual six—a back-up or off-duty gun, not something a highway patrolman would normally carry as a service weapon.

It could still put a big hole in my forehead, however, so when he yelled, "Put those hands where I can see them!" I complied without hesitation.

"Sorry officer. I thought you'd want to see my license."

"I don't need your goddam license," he said, leveling the gun at me. "I know who you are."

He looked around the truck's interior.

"Any firearms in the vehicle?" he asked.

"No," I said. I haven't carried a gun since I got suspended.

"Alright. Get out of the vehicle, lean forward with your hands on the hood."

"Is this a joke?" I said. "Did Kenny put you up to this?" Kenny can be a prankster.

"Get out of the vehicle and place your hands on the hood," he said in a tone that did not betray a hint of humor.

I did as I was told. He held the gun to my back with one hand and frisked me with the other. Cars slowed to rubberneck. Someone yelled, "Hey, why're you arresting Chief Hardy?" My back was turned. I couldn't see who it was.

"Get back in your car and clear the area!" the cop shouted.

From behind me, I heard a man ask, "You want me to tell Miss Dean, Chief?"

"You do that," I said while trooper jerked my arms behind my back and squeezed my wrists together. He slapped on a pair of handcuffs, making sure they dug into my wrists. He yanked me away from my truck and dragged me to his cruiser.

Just then, the Fury skidded to a stop across from the highway patrol vehicle. Bernard jumped out almost before he'd put it into park.

"What's going on?" he said angrily. "Where do you think you're taking him?"

The trooper pushed my head down to clear the door frame and shoved me into his back seat.

"Get back in your car, boy," he told Bernard. "I got this under control."

"Don't tell me to get back in my car, darn it. My name is Bernard Cousins and I'm the deputy police chief around here. That man's my boss and I want to know what this is all about."

The trooper slammed the door, turned, and pointed his weapon at Bernard. "I got a warrant for this man's arrest. Unless you want to join him, I suggest you get back in that piece of shit and drive the hell back to Mayberry."

I have no doubt Bernard could've beaten the hell out of the S.O.B., but the trooper had a gun pointed at him and I didn't want him getting shot.

"Let it go, Bernard," I yelled to make myself heard through the closed door. "Make some calls, find out what this is about."

He nodded and walked around to the rear of the car. The trooper got in the cruiser and started the engine. I turned around and saw Bernard was looking at the bumper. "Where's your license plate?" he shouted. The trooper didn't answer but left the scene at great speed.

Within thirty seconds we'd cleared the city limits.

"I assume this is about more than just my busted muffler."

He didn't respond.

A couple of miles out of town, he pulled over, got out and started rummaging around in the trunk. I looked around car's interior for some identifying information, but didn't see anything.

He opened my door and pointed the gun at me. "Out," he said.

Apparently, I moved too slow. He jammed the gun to my head, reached behind me, and dragged me out by the handcuffs. My hands were slippery with blood from the cuffs digging into my flesh. He dragged me to the rear of the car and tried to shove me into the trunk. I resisted. "Get in," he said, pointing the gun at my head, "or you're dead." I weighed my options, realized I had none, and crawled in, laughing as I did.

My numb nuts captor said, "I wouldn't be laughing if I were you."

"Nah, I reckon you wouldn't, would you? I was thinking how it was a good thing I called off my deputy or he'd have shoved his foot so far up your ass, you'd be tying his shoes with your teeth."

"That so?" he grunted. "I'd wipe the floor with that skinny little freak."

"How 'bout when this is all over, I set something up between you two?"

"Anytime, anywhere, old man," he sneered, and slammed the trunk shut.

"I'd pay to see that," I yelled, but I'm not sure he heard.

CHAPTER TWENTY TWO

As I lay in the dark—inhaling exhaust fumes and trying not to pass out—I thought of that scene in *White Heat* when Jimmy Cagney forces a whiny henchman into the trunk of his car. The guy complains he can't breathe. Cagney shoots the trunk full of holes.

I didn't want to be that guy.

So I kept my mouth shut.

But it was damned uncomfortable, being crammed in such a small space with no light, no air, and—I was starting to believe—no hope. Unless I'd royally pissed someone off about something else and forgotten about it, this had to be about my fishing expedition regarding the Youngers. I'd only been looking for a couple of days, but in that time, I'd angered the two richest, most powerful men in Tilghman County, even going so far as to accuse one of them of arson and murder.

Yeh, this was about that.

Given my predicament, I was starting to wish I'd been a bit subtler in my inquiries. I tried to run my manacled hands over my butt so I could pull my legs between my arms and my hands would be in front, but that was a fool's errand. It also cranked the pain up several notches.

I lost track of how long I was back there. I slipped in and out of consciousness.

I'd been out for a while, when I was awakened with a jolt. Numb Nuts had evidently turned onto a deeply rutted road, causing my bruised body to bang against every surface of the trunk's interior. At first my knees ached, until, mercifully, they became numb. The same cannot be said of my wrists, which felt like they'd been whittled to the bone with a hacksaw. I tried to position myself so my weight didn't rest on my hands, but every time we hit a bump I became slightly airborne and landed on my back, sending jolts of electric pain up my arms. In Korea, I was briefly a prisoner of a small group of Chinese soldiers, who stabbed me several times in the leg with a hot bamboo stick. This hurt almost as bad.

I reckoned eventually we'd stop and Numb Nuts would open the trunk. I thought about what to do when that happened. I reached around in the dark searching for a tire iron or something else heavy, but couldn't find anything. Not that it would've mattered. With my hands bound behind my back, there wasn't much I could do in the way of bashing him over the head.

I reckoned I had two options: Attack him as soon as he opened the trunk, trying to catch him unawares, or pretend I was in worse shape than I was, lull him into a false sense of security, then pounce when he let his guard down. Whether I had any pounce left in me was doubtful, but not so doubtful as the idea I could instantly eject myself from the trunk like a lethal jack-in-a-box and strangle the bastard with my thighs.

Playing possum was the better choice.

We drove on that bumpy-ass road for what seemed like forever. Country roads in western Oklahoma are bad-to-horrible. The county's getting around to paving some, but most are still made of dirt, or if you're lucky, gravel. Of course, we could be in Kansas or Texas. No way to know.

Wherever it led, the path we were on was worse than even your average county road, leading me to believe we were driving on private land.

The car finally stopped. Numb Nuts left the engine running and got out. I heard footsteps slapping on hard ground, then Numb Nuts cursing as he strained against something heavy—a large door of some kind, I conjectured. It opened with a huge creaking sound. He got back in the car and slowly pulled ahead for a few seconds, before shutting off the engine.

In the sudden near-silence I heard the sound of crickets and the hoot of a barred owl. Nighttime sounds. I'd been in that trunk long enough to travel as far as Oklahoma City or the middle of the Texas panhandle, or even central Kansas, depending on which direction we'd gone. I was pretty sure he had not transported me to a jail. Not the official kind, at least.

My mind was blurred by pain. I forced myself to focus. Knowing where we'd gone wasn't nearly as important as planning what to do when he lifted the lid.

Keys jangled. I heard one inserted into the lock. The trunk lid opened. I saw Numb Nuts outlined against the faint glow of an overcast night sky. "Get out," he said and stepped to one side with his hands on his hips.

I didn't have to pretend to be in pain. I saw a report on the news not long ago about a machine used by junkyards to crush an entire automobile into a cube the size of a small cardboard box. I felt like I'd gone through something like that.

The worst part was where the cuffs had cut into my wrists, but my knees were no treat, either. They've been bad dating back to my high school football days. Now, they felt like they'd been run over by a Sherman tank.

Under my own power, the best I could manage was to extend and hook my legs over the edge of the trunk. That didn't suit Numb Nuts' timeline. He reached around my back, grabbed the cuffs again and dragged me the rest of the way out. I let loose a string of curses and fell to the floor. I smelled hay, felt dirt under my fingers, and saw the wheels of another car parked alongside the OSHP cruiser. Apparently, we were in a barn doing duty as a garage.

Numb Nuts jammed his hand under my left armpit and tried to pull me to my feet. My legs wouldn't cooperate and I flopped back down. "Just give me a minute," I said, sitting spread-eagled on the ground. He lit a cigarette. "We ain't got all night," he said.

"Just let me get some feeling back in my legs."

I eyed Numb Nuts. His uniform shirt was untucked. The top few buttons were undone. I could smell alcohol on his person. For a second I experienced a sense of outrage, then I remembered how often I'd driven under the influence over the years. It made me laugh.

He looked at me like I was a crippled dog he couldn't wait to put down.

"You got a strange sense of humor," he said.

I chuckled some more. "So I've been told."

I was starting to get feeling back in my legs. They hurt, but I figured I could straighten them and stand. I didn't want him to know that.

He opened the trunk of the other car and said, "Alright, asshole, it's time. Get in."

He'd have to kill me first.

I rose deliberately to a half-standing position, remaining bent at the waist. I thought if I could blot out the pain in my wrists, I might make some sort of last stand.

I moved too slow to suit him. "Let's go," he said, reaching behind my back to grab me by his favorite handle, the handcuffs.

Enough of his bullshit.

I raised the top half of my body suddenly and with all my strength, slammed my head backwards to where I hoped his face would be. I heard a surprised grunt and felt soft tissue—nose cartilage, probably—give way. Blood spurted onto the back of my head. While he was stunned and with my hands still cuffed behind my back, I grabbed him by the belt and turned him so our positions were reversed. I shoved him hard backwards against the second car, forcing him ass-first into the open trunk, where he landed on his back. He came to his senses, pulled his gun, and tried to sit upright, but was insufficiently careful and knocked himself silly on the trunk lid. I gave him head-butt for good luck, then plowed into him with my shoulder so he fell back into the trunk. As he tried to gather himself, I stood on my tip-toes, hooked the trunk lid under my chin, and pulled it down as hard as I could. Before it closed, he stuck his hand out of the trunk, holding the Charter Arms Undercover .38 Special. It discharged wildly without coming close to hitting me. I jumped up and sat down hard on the trunk lid. It shut on his forearm. Bones cracked. He squealed like stuck pig, which, I got to say, did not exactly break my heart. The gun dropped to the floor. I kicked it away, used my knee to shove his forearm—now bent unnaturally and bleeding from a latch-shaped gash—back inside the trunk. I sat on the lid, slamming it shut.

I took a second to catch my breath, then asked, "How you doing in there?"

He cussed and whimpered something unintelligible.

"You breathing ok? How 'bout some air holes?" I asked.

"Oh God, no, hell no!"

I reckon he must've seen *White Heat* a time or two, himself.

CHAPTER TWENTY THREE

I could've left that squirrelly piece of shit where he was and wouldn't have lost a minute of sleep over it, but I'm better than that.

Part of me is, anyway.

There's also a part of me that's a whole lot worse—a compost heap made up of everything rotten that's ever happened to me. That part of me would have liked nothing better than to leave the son of a bitch locked in that trunk alone out in the middle of nowhere and let him piss himself to death.

There had to be a middle ground. I wasn't going to leave him to suffocate or die of dehydration. However, letting him out would give him a chance at regaining the upper hand. I couldn't have that.

First thing I needed to do was get out of those handcuffs. If this guy kept his key in his duty belt, I'd be screwed. Fortunately, I found one on his key chain, which had fallen to the ground in the course of our fight. Unlocking them with my hands behind my back and my wrists gouged to pieces was a challenge I hope never to have to repeat, but I got them off.

I found his flashlight and looked around outside. In the barnyard there was a pump with a rusty bucket under the spout. I worked the handle up and down a few times. Nothing came out. Maybe it needed to be primed. The bucket held a little water, enough to wash my mangled wrists or drink, but not both. I hoped there'd enough to prime the pump. I'm not much of a gambler, but this time I won. After a few pulls, I could soak my wrists and drink my fill.

Next, I had to determine where I was. It was the middle of nowhere—that much was obvious—but I couldn't be more specific than that. The surrounding land was endless pasture as far as I could see, which admittedly wasn't very far. Other than the moon shining faintly behind the curtain of clouds, there wasn't a light to be seen.

The barn was built out of wood. Over time it had probably been painted and repainted a dozen times. Now it was the dingy brownish-gray color of a wasp's nest.

I climbed a rickety ladder up to the loft. It was empty except for some scattered pieces of hay. No tools or farm implements were to be found anywhere. The OHP cruiser and the second car were all there was.

I shone the flashlight on the rear bumper. The car had a Texas plate—black letters and numbers with a plain white background. Along the bottom was the word "EXEMPT" stamped in capital letters. In Texas, exempt plates are used by law enforcement entities, especially the Rangers and the Highway Patrol. The car was the same model of Plymouth Fury that Bernard drives, only instead of being black-and-white, it was greenish silver.

I got behind the wheel. On the dash was a framed certificate with a photo of a fella in a cowboy hat. Underneath was the name "Frank Sallee." Above were the words, "Texas Department of Public Safety—Ranger Division."

I got out again and pounded the trunk. "Hey in there, can you hear me?"

He answered with a muffled "Yeh."

"You and me are going to have a talk."

"Let me out of here!"

"I'm sure you'll understand why, given your actions toward me, I am disinclined to accommodate your request."

"LET ME OUT! I GOT CLUSTERPHOBIA!"

"Well, I guess you should've thought about that before you kidnapped me and locked those handcuffs so tight and drove me all over creation for the apparent purpose of doing me bodily harm."

He was quiet for a second, then said, "C'mon Hardy, can you please talk regular?"

"Alright, if you want me to let you out, you're going to tell me where we are."

Silence.

"Did you hear me? Where are we?"

"Texas. We're in Texas."

"Where in Texas?"

"Outside Borger," he said. "Some place outside Borger. Don't know exactly."

Borger is northeast of Amarillo in the Texas panhandle, some 150 miles from Burr.

"Why are we here?"

"I was supposed to change cars and hand you off to someone."

I assume that would've been this Frank Sallee. "Was his name Sallee?" I asked.

"I don't know. They didn't tell me his name."

"I guess you were supposed to meet him here? Is that right?"

He hesitated, then said in a panicky voice: "Nah, I was going to drive you somewhere else."

I suspect that was a load of crap. He didn't want me to know reinforcements were on the way.

I got back in the car. The key was in the ignition, on a ring with another one that I assumed fit the trunk.

I started the car.

"Hey, you said you was going to let me out," he whined.

"You are misremembering something that only happened 30 seconds ago," I said. "Maybe you should see a doctor about that."

He started kicking the trunk lid. "Wait!" he said. "Where are we going? I didn't mean ... no one's coming, I promise. Please let me out of here." He paused. "If you do, I promise I'll let you go."

"I don't need you to let me go. I'm free as a bird. It's you who needs letting go, and that's not going to happen." At least not for a while, I whispered to myself.

I started to back out, then remembered the .38. I might need that. I braked, got out, and shined the flashlight over the floor. The gun wasn't in plain sight, so I got down on my aching knees and looked under the OHP cruiser. There it was, right where I'd kicked it. I brushed it off and placed it on the seat beside me.

The road we'd come in on was a narrow, weed-grown path, extending to the horizon in both directions. Without being able to see the stars, I couldn't tell north from south, or east from west. I couldn't remember which way

Numb Nuts had turned to pull into the barn. I didn't bother to ask, figuring he'd be pretty hard to trust. I turned right and hoped for the best.

The road was so potholed, I couldn't drive any faster than 10 miles per hour. Numb Nuts cussed a blue streak every time we hit a bump. I knew how he felt.

After a couple of minutes, I spied the glow of headlights coming over the rise. Numb Nuts' partner in crime, I assumed.

I cut my lights and slowed to a crawl. The land along the road was flat and as hard as concrete. I turned off and drove a couple hundred yards deep into the adjacent pasture.

I cut my engine and waited. After a couple of minutes, the car drove past. The driver didn't show any signs of having seen us. I couldn't see his face, but I could see the type of car he was driving.

A Texas Highway Patrol cruiser.

Goddam, I thought. I must've been a real bastard in a previous life.

On the bright side, I seemed to be headed in the right direction. I waited until its lights were out of sight, then got going again—a little quicker now, meaning Numb Nuts experienced an even rougher ride. "Sorry buddy, but we've got to make better time," I yelled. He hollered back something I couldn't understand.

I finally reached the main road. I had to turn in one direction or the other, so I flipped a coin in my mind and turned right. Before long, I passed a couple of billboards I recognized from my many trips to Amarillo. I knew more or less where I was.

I switched on the unit's police band radio. Within seconds came a BOLO for a Texas Ranger slicktop—an unmarked car—with the license plate number of the car I was currently driving.

I needed to get the hell out of Texas. That "EXEMPT" license plate might as well have been a neon sign flashing: "Here's that poor simple bastard y'all are looking for!"

I was on the main highway connecting Borger and Amarillo, so it would be only a matter of time before I came upon a THP car. I needed to find a road that would let me cross into Oklahoma unnoticed, so my people could come to my rescue.

Fortunately, I know the roads between Burr and Amarillo almost as well as the roads in Tilghman County. In fact, I knew exactly where I wanted to go and how to get there.

I passed through a couple of little no-horse towns, far away from anyplace the state cops were likely to patrol. Within an hour, I'd reached my destination—a diner straddling the border of Texas and Oklahoma.

Strictly speaking, it's the parking lot that straddles the border. The restaurant itself lies in Oklahoma. At the end of the lot extending into Texas, there's a sickly-green house trailer that serves as the home office for a gaggle of prostitutes who cater to long-haul truckers. Cheryl Foster—the young black girl who'd been killed by EJ Bixby—had worked out of it before her death. One of her co-workers had given me critical information that led to me solving the crime. I hoped she was on duty tonight. I could use her help again. She's a sweet gal and I still come out here once in a while to make sure she's ok. These girls are independent contractors and their clientele tends to be unsavory. I reckon they can use all the help they can get.

The parking lot was lit by a single streetlamp off to one side that turned everything an otherworldly orange. Three trucks were parked out in front when I drove up. A girl jumping down from one saw my car approach and began yelling something I couldn't make out.

Suddenly, all hell broke loose. Girls jumped down from the other two trucks, zipping-up this and that, arranging different articles of clothing and running for the trailer. They got inside and turned off the neon "Welcome" sign in the window, which was a new addition since I'd last visited. Meanwhile, the trucks got in each other's way as they all tried to pull out at the same time. It would've been comical to watch if my situation had been less dire.

I gave the trucks a wide berth to leave. When things had calmed somewhat, I knocked on the door to the trailer and called out for my friend.

"Yvette, you working tonight?"

I heard confused voices coming from inside. A familiar face pulled aside a curtain and peered out. "Chief Hardy!" she said, then turned around and said with a laugh, "Don't worry, it's just Chief Hardy." Yvette unlocked and opened the door. "What in the world are you doin' driving a Texas Ranger slicktop?" she asked.

That explained the ruckus; these girls know their police cars better than I do. "Yvette, honey, you wouldn't believe me if I told you and I don't have time to try. I'm in a hurry and I need a favor."

She rubbed her hands together and grinned lasciviously. "Oh, Emmett Hardy, you *devil*, you! I've been waiting for this since the first time I set eyes on you!"

She stepped aside and motioned for me to come in. She was wearing a red-and-white-checked halter top, unbuttoned and tied at her midriff. Her Levi's were cut short so the pockets wagged from under the denim. I was too gentlemanly to stare.

"You come in and make yourself comfortable," she said. "Let Miss Yvette take care of all your lovin' needs. Tonight's special is two for one, and the first one's free!"

Giggling, she tried to lead me in by the elbow. I resisted. She tugged again then noticed my bloodied wrists. Her smile disappeared. "Oh my, what happened to you?"

I stepped inside and closed the door halfway, so my friend in the trunk couldn't hear. "It's a long story sweetheart, and like I said, I'm in a hurry. I need to borrow your car. Some folks are looking for this one, and I'd rather they not find it in my possession."

She pushed aside a long strand of bleach blond hair that had fallen across her face. Yvette's really a pretty gal when you look past all that face paint.

"Sure, hon," she said softly, all fun fading from her voice. "Whatever you want."

She grabbed a set of keys from a hook beside the door and handed it to me. "It's that light blue Volkswagen over there," she said and pointed across the parking lot. "I'd appreciate it if you didn't leave that Ranger-mobile parked out front. It's bad for business."

"Well, the thing is, Yvette, there's a fella in the trunk who's got it in for me. I reckon he's got some friends who are, too. I can't leave him in locked-up forever, so I figured I'd park that thing over by the phone booth and handcuff him to the steering wheel before I make my escape. He won't be going anywhere and you don't need to do anything, but I figure there will be a law enforcement convention out here before the night is through. You might want to close up shop for the night."

She sighed. "Alright, then, if it's a matter of life or death."

"In a way, it is."

She winked and smiled mischievously. "Why, Emmett Hardy, I always knew you were a bad boy at heart. Sure, babe, do what you need to do. We'll take the rest of the night off."

I reached into my wallet and took out what cash I had. "For your trouble," I said.

She pushed it away. "Your money ain't no good here, Chief." I tried to insist, but she wouldn't have it.

I nodded toward the 'Welcome' sign. "Where'd that come from?"

"Oh, that's right. You haven't been here since we added that," she said. "We reckon it pays to advertise."

"What's wrong with a red light?"

"Oh, c'mon, Chief," she scoffed. "Join the 20th century!"

I shrugged. "I guess I'm just old-fashioned."

She smiled and pecked me on the cheek. I told her I'd return her car as soon as I could. She said there was no hurry, she could always borrow one of the other girls'. We said our goodbyes.

The phone booth was located on Oklahoma side, out by the road at the extreme opposite end of the parking lot. I parked the slicktop next to it, got out and felt around in my pants pockets for some change. I didn't have any.

I called out to Numb Nuts that I'd be back in a minute. His reply sounded pitiful. I'd mostly stopped being mad at him. I'd even started to feel mean for leaving him confined so long, and for how I'd slammed the trunk on his arm.

I trotted over to the diner. It was empty except for a waitress and cook. A cooler full of Coca-Colas and some small bags of Fritos corn chips stood by the cash register. I bought two of each and got change for the phone.

I tossed the brown paper bag with the Cokes and chips in the back seat. I went inside the phone booth, pulled the door shut and dialed Karen's home number. No answer. I tried the station. She picked up on the first ring. "Burr Police Department."

"It's me."

"It's him!" she cried out. I could hear a couple of voices cheering in the background. "Where've you been?" she asked. "We've called everybody— Burt Murray, the OSBI, Rex McKinnis, the highway patrol, every local police station within a hundred miles—"

I had to cut her off. "Alright, Red, I'm fine, but I can't talk right now. I need you to go to my house and find my black satchel. It's on the floor of my bedroom closet. Pack me a couple shirts, a pair of blue jeans, some underwear and socks, then meet me at the old Tastee Freeze in Otisville as soon as you can. Take your own car and wear civilian clothes. Don't tell anyone except Bernard where you're going. No one. Understand?" I paused. "Oh, and while you're at it, feed Dizzy."

"Got it," she said. "I fed Dizzy already. He's at your dad's, keeping him company."

"Ok now, listen. This is important. First of all, who's there with you?"

"The whole crew. Bernard, Kenny, and Jeff."

"Good. When you get off the phone, you need to act casual and pretend everything's ok. Don't tell them you're coming to meet me. Just say there's nothing to worry about, that I'm staying in a motel in Amarillo or something, and will be home in a couple of days. Tell them I said you should all go home and get some sleep. Tomorrow you can tell Bernard and only Bernard, but right now you're the only one I want to know about this. Is that clear?"

"Yes," she said worriedly.

"Alright, I'll see you in about half an hour," I said. "By the way, I'll be driving a light blue Volkswagen.

"Where'd you get—"

"All will be revealed," I interrupted. "Don't worry. Sell those boys on your story and get there as fast as you can."

"Will do," she said. We said our goodbyes.

I took stock. Neither of the people in the diner had expressed any interest in me. The brothel was shut tight, and the lights were turned off. The highway was clear. No one had driven by since I scared the truckers away.

I got the .38 from the car and made sure it was loaded. I bashed the police radio with a billy club so Numb Nuts couldn't call for help, threw the billy club and the car keys into the weeds across the road.

"Ok," I said to Numb Nuts. "I'm going to let you out now. But first we got to set some things straight. I'm holding your gun in my hand. It's a nice little piece. I figure since you seem to know something about me, you probably know I'm a pretty good shot. I'd advise you not to try anything when I open the trunk."

"I won't," he said. "My arm's probably broke, anyway."

"Ok, sorry about your arm, but that'll be the least of your problems if you try anything. I'll shoot you in the knee, and if that doesn't do the trick, I'll put one in your forehead. You got that?"

Silence. "Got that?" I yelled, louder. "Yes!" he shouted back.

I unlocked the trunk, stepped back and let the lid rise on its own. Numb Nuts squinted and rose slowly to a sitting position. He was in rough shape. His right arm was a bloody, crooked mess, there was a gash on his forehead where the lid had knocked him senseless, and his nose looked like a squashed tomato. Still, he'd live.

"Catch," I said, and tossed him the handcuffs. He let them bang against his chest and gingerly picked them up with his uninjured hand.

"Crawl out of there," I said, "nice and easy."

He did as he was told. I opened the driver's side front door and told him to get behind the wheel. He squeezed in, careful not to knock his arm against anything. I locked one cuff over his good wrist, and the other on the wheel. I'd have preferred to have given him less freedom of movement, but it was the best I could do under the circumstances. His right arm was so damaged, I didn't think he presented much of an escape risk.

I left the car door open and stood over him. "Comfortable?" I asked.

"No."

"Too bad," I said. "Now you're going to answer a couple more questions."

"I already told you all I'm going to."

I twirled the gun on my forefinger and said, "You'll answer if you know what's good for you."

He stared blank-faced.

"I'm terrible with names," I said, "but I never forget a face. I don't remember yours, so I reckon this isn't something personal between you and me. Someone else must've put you up to this. Who was it?"

"Nobody," he said dully. "I did it all myself."

"Son, I have a very low tolerance for nonsense at the best of times, and this is not the best of times. Don't make me hurt you any more than I have."

He rested his forehead on the wheel and moaned.

"I ain't talkin'," he said resignedly. "Go ahead and shoot me if that's what you want to do."

I reckoned I should take him seriously on that count, considering how much pain he must be in already. He might not be all that bright, but he was tough.

I reached into the car, tore the badge off his chest and peeled off the black tape covering the number.

"Is this real or did you get it at the five-and-dime?"

"It's real."

"What's your name?"

He looked at me tiredly. "Leander McNelly."

I slipped the badge in my shirt pocket. "What're you going to do for a job now, Leander? After this, I figure your law enforcement career is over."

He almost smiled. "You don't know what you're talkin' about, old man." He tried to lick his lips but his mouth was too dry.

"Hey," he said, "are you going to get me something to drink? I'm dying of thirst."

I reached into the back seat and grabbed one of the Cokes. I didn't have a church key, so I had to open the bottle with my teeth. It's not as hard as it sounds.

"There you go," I said, and stuck the bottle in his non-broken hand.

He tried to grab it but couldn't manage. "C'mon, man, at least hold it up to my mouth."

"Why should I help you after what you did to me? Tell what I want to know and maybe I'll help you."

He frowned. "I've told you my name. If it ain't enough you can go ahead and kill me."

He'd said that enough times, I reckon he was pretty sure I wouldn't do it. He was right. Sometimes I wish I was meaner than I am.

"Alright, forget about the 'who.' Tell me why."

He shook his head wearily. "You got to be kidding? You don't know?"

"The Younger deal?" I said.

"Give the man a cigar. Let's just say you've pissed-off some very powerful people."

I didn't have to think too hard to guess who they were.

"See? You told me something," I said. "Was that so hard? I reckon that's worth a swallow of Coke." I held the bottle up to his mouth, not meaning to give him the whole thing, but before I knew it, he'd drained it.

"Thanks," he said

"You're welcome." I opened one of the bags of Fritos and put it his hand. He managed to guide a few into his mouth.

"Don't eat too many" I said. "They'll just make you thirsty again." He spilled most of them, anyway.

Given that it was unlikely I'd learn any more from Leander McNelly—and that it was probable his buddies were hot on my tail—I decided to bring the interrogation to a close. "Alright," I said, "today's your lucky day. I'm going to let you keep your knee. Any parting advice before I make my getaway?"

He let his head fall back against the seat. "Get out of town or you're a dead man."

"That right?" I put my hand on my heart. "Hmmm. Still beatin'."

I turned and walked toward where Yvette's car was parked.

"Hey," he yelled after me. "Could you light me a cigarette?"

I called back, "You're too young to smoke."

"You're a dead man," he yelled, in case I hadn't heard him the first time.

I gave him one last wave. "See you in the funny papers, Leander."

"Not if I see you first."

I wedged myself into the VW and drove into the good night, confident Leander McNelly was one son of a bitch I'd never see again.

CHAPTER TWENTY FOUR

These days it's a ghost town, but at one time Otisville was the literary capitol of Oklahoma.

In the early years of the century, Otisville was home to no fewer than five published authors—not too shabby for a town of fewer than 1000 people. All five were woman. They were all close friends. Two were poets. One wrote cookbooks. One wrote children's stories. One wrote novels.

The novelist's name was Myrtle Perkins. She was the most famous, having authored a series of dime novels featuring a Texas Ranger character named Terry "Two-Guns" McIntyre. Old "Two-Guns" never met a man he didn't like—that is, unless they were Mexican or Indian (Myrtle's villains always were), in which case he'd shoot them down, kiss the girl, and ride off into the sunset.

Otisville was proud of its literary heritage, but it was wheat that kept its small economy going. Back in 1909, the Katy railroad built a line out of Otisville for the purpose of transporting grain to the co-op elevators in Temple City. They shut it down about ten years ago after years of declining business.

The death of the railroad was the final nail in the town's coffin. The Tastee Freeze was the last business to go belly up. Now, Otisville's population consists of a few possums and squirrels, and a guy name Pete, who drinks medicinal turpentine and lives in the attic of an abandoned house with a pet armadillo he calls Silent Cal.

In other words, there's no place in western Oklahoma I'd be less likely to run into a state trooper.

Yvette's VW sounded and handled more like a riding lawn mower than an automobile, but I'll say one thing for it; the heater cranked out hot air like a blast furnace. Unfortunately, there seemed no way to turn it off, or control it in any way. I opened my window and let in cold air, hoping it would mix with the hot and make things tolerable. Sadly, that's not how it worked. I spent the 20-minute drive to Otisville rolling the window up and down, alternately sweating my ass off, and shivering like a shaved chihuahua.

The Tastee Freeze sign looked ready to light up at the flip of a switch. The rest of the place was collapsing in on itself. I parked to one side so I couldn't be seen by passing cars, just in case there were any.

I finished off the remaining bag of corn chips and a bottle of Coke while I waited for Red. I hadn't realized how hungry I was. Lunch at the Burr Sonic seemed a very long time ago.

The Fritos corn chip jingle went through my mind: Ay, yi, yi-yi. I am the Frito Bandito. Watch your ass, Frito Bandito. This is Terry "Two-Guns" McIntyre's town.

Before long, I heard the clattering whine of Karen's Ford Falcon. It sounds like a sewing machine with a couple of missing gears. I've been meaning to take it out to Wes Harmon's garage to have the engine looked at, but haven't gotten around to it.

As a boyfriend, I lack in certain areas.

Just as I was hidden from the road, the road was equally hidden from me. I couldn't see her, but I could hear her slow down. I reckoned she was casing the joint before committing herself. Her headlights cast shadows across the building's roof. I considered getting out and flagging her down before she came around the corner, stopped right in front of me and got out of the car.

She held me like I was the only thing standing between her and eternal damnation.

"You stupid idiot," she said, laughing and crying in equal amounts. "Are you hurt? What did they do to you?"

"Nothing that can't be fixed," I said and without thinking looked at my wrists. The bleeding had stopped and the wounds had started to crust over.

Karen drew a sharp breath. "My Lord, you need to have a doctor look at that."

"Oh, it looks worse than it is. I don't have time, anyway. I got a plane to catch in a few hours."

"You're not telling me, after this—"

"I know it sounds crazy, but let me tell you what I've just been through." I related my story in shorthand. She listened, wide-eyed.

"What are you going to do?" she asked.

"Go to New York as planned. The ticket's in my wallet. Hary knows I'm coming. With any luck, I'll track down my uncle and get the names of whoever besides the Raymers and Bixbys were members of this Sons of Burr thing. Maybe even find out who Smiley is."

"Whoever's behind this will still be here when you get back."

"Yeh, but hopefully I'll have some ammunition against them. I wish I could tell you I had this all figured out, Red, but I just don't. I do feel like I have an unpaid debt, though. My father could've helped the Youngers. He didn't. It would've been bad enough if they were just forced to leave town. If it turns out they were murdered—" I trailed off. "I'll say this: If Clyde Raymer and Deke Bixby and whoever else is so worried about this that they're willing to have me killed, I must be on the right track."

"What do you want me to do?"

"Well, for one thing, you can switch cars with me." I explained how circumstances had conspired to have me borrow my friend Yvette's car, and how Leander McNelly had seen me driving it and would assuredly tell his friends, which might very well result in a BOLO for a blue VW. I told her to hide it somewhere until I got back.

"I'll ask Bernard if I can leave it in his Aunt Hannah's barn," she said.

"That's good, just make sure he doesn't tell anybody anything about any of this. You and him are the only ones who can know."

She zipped her lip and threw away the key.

"It might be nice if you took a trip out to Yvette's trailer and tell her we're going to need to hide her car for a few days." I smiled. "I'd like you two to meet. I've always thought you'd get along."

She made a face. "I'm not sure how to take that."

"Take what?"

"The fact that my boyfriend seems to think I could be buddies with a truck stop hooker."

"Hey, there but for the grace of God ..."

"I *will* smack you," she said. I doubted her sincerity.

"One more thing," I said. "I expect folks will come sniffing around asking questions. If they do, just tell them the same thing you tell the boys—that I'm staying in Amarillo and you don't know how to contact me but I should be back in a few days."

"I will, if you promise me you'll see a doctor about those wrists when you get to New York."

"They have doctors in New York? I thought they only had Joe Namath and juvenile delinquents."

"Hilarious," she said. "I'm serious. Promise."

I shrugged. "I promise. If I have time."

She sighed. "I guess that'll have to do."

We exchanged car keys. "Satchel's in the back seat," she said.

"The Beetle's just a little three-speed stick," I said. "It won't hardly break 50, but take it easy, anyway. You don't want to attract attention. The heater won't go anything but full blast, but that won't kill you. Wake up Bernard up as soon as you get back so you can hide this thing."

"I'm sure he'll be up," she replied.

"Alright then, let's get going."

We kissed one last time.

"You drive safe," I said.

"You fly safe," she said.

"I'll tell the pilot if he doesn't, he'll have to answer to you."

CHAPTER TWENTY FIVE

It was a little after midnight when I got underway. The straightest shot to Oklahoma City would've taken three hours. It also would have led to maximum scrutiny by state law enforcement, which I had reason to avoid. Since my plane didn't take off until 7:00, I decided the safest plan of attack would involve utilizing the skills I had developed over the years for avoiding the highway patrol while driving under the influence, and take all the back roads I knew between Otisville and Oklahoma City.

Speaking of drinking, all that fighting for my life had given me a powerful thirst. I'm not talking booze, I'm talking water. The Coke just made my mouth sticky. Those Fritos hadn't exactly sated my appetite, either. I knew of a diner near Arnett that stayed open late, but it was shut tight when I got there. The rest of the towns I drove through had likewise rolled up their sidewalks, so I had to settle for taking a few sips of rusty water from a drinking fountain I found under a street lamp at a school playground in Vici.

Karen's car squeaked and clattered but showed no particular sign of conking out. It did ride rough enough to make me feel bad about not having taken better care of it for her. In my defense, she hadn't mentioned it in months. Now that she has access to the department's official vehicles, she hardly drives it. Anyhow, I only cared the Falcon would get me where I wanted to go.

I pulled into the parking lot at Will Rogers World Airport around three o'clock. It was dark and quiet, with no planes taking off or landing. I got my first look at the shiny new terminal, which I'd heard about but never seen. Unfortunately it was closed. I stayed in the car and tried to catch some z's, trusting I wouldn't fall so deeply asleep that I'd miss my plane.

I was awakened with a start by a low-flying jet. I became aware of the bitter cold. My jeans jacket is fine for running between my truck and a heated building, but it doesn't stand up to extended exposure. The sun was peeking over the eastern horizon. I looked at my wrist but my watch wasn't there. I found it in a pants pocket. It was almost six-thirty. I grabbed my satchel, scrambled out of the car and sprinted to the terminal.

I flashed my ticket to an official-looking gentleman and asked where I should go. He was smiled calmly, told me I had plenty of time and directed me to the proper gate. The plane had almost finished loading when I got there. A lady in a blue wool uniform told me where to sit. I stuffed my satchel under the seat in front of me, watched the stewardess put on a little show about what to do if the plane crashes—putting your head between your knees and kissing your ass goodbye was not one of the options—and five minutes later we were up in the air. I didn't even have time to get nervous.

I repeated more or less the same process in Chicago. On the second plane, we were served lunch and told we could purchase alcoholic drinks. I reckon people who do a lot of flying have ample reason to drink so early in the day. I had my own reasons but resisted the urge.

From above, the island of Manhattan looks like an ironing board covered haphazardly by stacks of blocks. The first time I flew there more than a decade ago it was night time. The view was almost inviting—like the midway at the state fair after dark. Seeing it during the day, on the other hand, almost made me want to ask the pilot if he'd mind turning around and taking me home. That more than a million and a half of people live stacked and jammed together on a slender tongue of land about one-third the size of Enid, Oklahoma—population 41,682—was equal parts amazing and terrifying. I'd lived there myself for a while. Maybe if I'd flown over during the day that first time, I'd have been scared into leaving a lot sooner.

The plane flew into John F. Kennedy International Airport, a step up from LaGuardia, where I'd landed on my first trip. LaGuardia was more like a particularly disreputable subway station than an airport that serves millions of people from all over the world. Kennedy, on the other hand, was bright and clean and modern and provided a more attractive welcome to a city not exactly known for its hospitality.

I was standing in the aisle of the plane waiting to get off when I realized I hadn't told Hary when my plane was supposed to land. I'd told him I was coming, but I hadn't given him my time of arrival. I had some hope he might divine it himself and be waiting when I got off the plane, but that was not to be the case. Unlike the last time, when he escorted me to our new home, this time I'd have to find the way myself.

Thankfully, I hadn't checked my bag, so I didn't have to worry about picking up any luggage. I followed signs that were supposed to tell me how to get into the city—JFK is about as far away from where Hary lives as Burr is from Temple City. I eventually got frustrated and approached one of the folks whose job it is to help rubes like me. A loud but friendly black gentleman with what I believe was a Brooklyn accent (there are about as many New York accents as there are fish in Burr Lake; more than five but less than 100) directed me to a bus that would take me to Grand Central Terminal, where I could catch a subway that would take me to the Lower East Side, and the tenement building where I'd lived with Hary 12 years ago.

Looking out the window of the bus while driving through Queens into Manhattan was like watching a documentary about traffic jams. It had recently snowed, so the roads were slick and covered in oily black slush. The only signs of life were the faces of drivers caught in their slow-motion race to wherever. Angry faces mouthed silent curses. Welcome to New York. Enjoy your stay.

After a two-hour bus ride that in decent weather would've taken only 45 minutes, I was discharged on the corner of Park Avenue and East 42nd Street, directly across from Grand Central Terminal. I bought a few subway tokens in Grand Central and rode the IRT down to the Astor Place station. A jazz trio—tenor sax, bass, and drums—was set up on the platform, playing a Charlie Parker song. I dropped whatever change I had on me into a coffee can they'd set out in lieu of a hat. The group could easily have been playing the Village Vanguard instead of a crummy downtown subway station. It's amazing and sad. Musicians of that caliber playing for nickels. It's one reason I left New York.

Above ground, I realized my jean jacket wasn't going to be nearly warm enough. I'd forgotten how biting the wind could be on a cold winter's day as it blows across the island. I'd left my overcoat in New York when I moved back to Burr. I'd need another one if I was going to survive the next few days, I could tell that already.

From the subway station, I crossed diagonally Astor Place and Cooper Square and stood in front of Carl Fischer's Music, one of my favorite places in the world. Carl Fischer's is huge and has musical merchandise of every kind. I couldn't resist going in. I'm not too good at reading music, but I browsed through the sheet music anyway for a half hour, reminiscing about my life in the city. I could've spent the whole day but I had business to attend to.

The faces of the drunks passed out on the benches in the park next to Cooper Union seemed unchanged from when I'd last seen them, 12 years before. It's possible that had I stayed in New York, I might have taken up permanent residence there myself.

Every step I took led me past a dive bar I'd once frequented or someplace I used to go to hear music. I couldn't help but associate all of it with booze. I'd just started getting used to abstinence. Now, I'd only just stuck my head up from underground and was already being tempted anew.

Hary's office was in a storefront on East 3rd Street between Avenues A and B—the same block as the apartment we used to share, and where he still lives. Some call the neighborhood Alphabet City. I always called it the Lower East Side, although I've been told by people who should know that the Lower East Side begins south of Houston Street.

Whatever it's called, a lot of poor people of every creed and color live there. A lot of musicians do, too, which is why Hary settled there, and not someplace nicer in Brooklyn or Queens. I always liked the neighborhood, myself. The food was tasty and cheap, and you could get just about anything you wanted, any time of the day or night. Hary and I spent many an early morning in a 24-hour Ukrainian restaurant on 2nd Avenue talking about music, and how one of these days we'd be up there on the bandstand instead of in the audience. It happened for Hary.

Snowplows had mostly cleared the narrow crosstown streets, but in the process had buried cars parked by the curb underneath big, sooty mountains of packed ice. A narrow path had been cleared on the sidewalk. Rock salt was scattered everywhere. My boots made navigating treacherous; I almost fell on my ass multiple times. I cursed myself for not buying shoes with treads before I left Oklahoma.

Hary shared his office with a bicycle messenger service. I hadn't written down the address, but he told me to look for a bunch of bikes chained to a short iron fence. Unfortunately, with all the snow, the bicycle messengers must've stayed home. There wasn't one to be seen anywhere, so I just peeked into windows until I found the right place.

Above the sidewalk, a faded blue and white sign reading "KRYSACKI'S CANDIES" hung by a pair of chains from a bracket jutting out of the front of the building. "SILVERQUICK BICYCLE MESSENGERS" was painted in bright red, purple and orange letters on the shop window. On the glass door was a neatly printed cardboard sign: "Hary Loyd and Associates, Private Investigators." Taped below that was a flyer for a performance that evening by the Hary Loyd Quartet at a place called "Slugs' in the Far East."

Stepping into the office from the cold was like going from a deep freeze to a sauna. Most New York buildings have steam heat, which works like the heater in Yvette's Volkswagen. It has two settings: 'On' means hotter than the hinges; 'Off' means it's summer and you need to go outside.

A depressed-looking bald fella with droopy eyes sat at a messy desk, his sleeves rolled up, a tie loosely knotted under his unbuttoned collar, and a cigarette hanging out the side of his mouth. "Help ya?" he said. "I'm here to see Hary," I said. "There," he said, hooking his thumb and pointing to the back of the long narrow room.

Hary sat with his back to me in a battered old office chair, his feet propped up on his desk, his eyes closed and a pair of huge headphones covering his ears. The headphones were connected to a large reel-to-reel tape recorder.

When Hary listens to music, he's on another planet. I tapped his shoulder. He jumped like he'd been jabbed with a cattle prod. "Shit!" he said, barely able to keep himself from falling over. "What the—?"

He looked up at me, irritated but not surprised, like it had only been yesterday and not 12 years since we'd last seen each other. "Hey Emmett," he said. "Where's your horn?"

***

"Man, you spent a couple of winters here," Hary said as we walked up Avenue A—heads down, collars up around our ears—on our way to get something to eat. "Why'd you show up dressed like Roy Rogers?"

I caught my hat before it went flying and jammed it over my ears. I glanced at my reflection in a store window. I looked more like Smiley

Burnette than Roy Rogers. There I go with Smiley again, I thought. "I didn't have much time to pack," I said. "In fact, I didn't have *any* time to pack."

"Yeh, well, you'll have to tell me about it. At least you're wearin' a hip lid. I'm not sure how long you would've lasted around here if you'd shown up in a cowboy hat." He took a look at me and laughed. "Doesn't look too hip now, though."

We came to a diner called Odessa. Hary held the door.

"What happened to our old joint?" I asked.

"It's too cold to walk all the way to 2nd Avenue," he said. "Besides, that place is getting too cool for school, full of cats from Jersey taking a walk on the wild side with their little debutante girlfriends. This place opened about a year ago. The tourists haven't found it yet. The food here's just as good, and it's cheaper. You'll dig it, I promise."

We sat at a booth. A middle-aged waitress with a hairnet and a set of varicose veins that looked like a map of the New York subway system handed us menus. "How's it goin', Roberta?" said Hary. "Eh, you know," she said with a shrug. "My feet hurt, my hemorrhoids are screaming, my deadbeat ex-husband's marrying an 18-year-old baton twirler from Muncie. On the bright side, I'll be dead soon and all you'll have left are beautiful memories."

"Yeh, that's too bad, sweetheart," he said, "but I wanted to introduce you to my friend Emmett. He's from Oklahoma."

She looked at me with suspicion. "Yeh? Say something in Oklahoman."

"Pleased to meet you, ma'am."

"Huh. I guess you are from Oklahoma. You can lose the 'ma'am,' though. Call me Roberta."

"I'll do that, Roberta."

"What can I get you two cowboys?"

We ordered. She trudged back to the kitchen.

"That's pretty harsh, don't you think?" I said when she was out of earshot.

"What? You mean the whole, 'I'll be dead soon' thing?"

"You didn't seem too sympathetic."

He grinned. "That's just her schtick. I've been coming here since it opened, and every time she talks about how she's about to kick the bucket. She'll outlive us all, man. Of that I have no doubt."

"So you got a gig tonight?" I said. "Slug's in the Far East? What's that, a Chinese restaurant?"

He laughed. "No, man, it's a bar on East 3rd down the street from our place. They book only the hippest cats."

"Which is why they booked the Hary Loyd Quartet."

He slapped the table and howled. "Oh man! I haven't heard an accent like that in so long!"

"Yours used to be similar, as I recall."

"Yeh, I guess," he said wistfully. "Anyway, man, it's great to see you. Too bad you didn't bring a horn, but you can borrow my alto. I'm using a metal mouthpiece these days. You might not like it. It's not for everyone, but the music I'm playing now calls for something loud, and man, that baby will peel paint."

For the next few minutes Hary talked and I listened. He told me about a new type of jazz he was playing these days ("Cats call it 'free jazz'. It started with a saxophone player from my old stomping ground in Texas, a cat named Ornette Coleman ..."), his assistant in the private investigator business ("... a little chick named Sally, although she likes to be called Florine ... she also plays a very mean guitar ..."), the war in Viet Nam ("That shit is sick and has got to be stopped ..."), and how painful it is to a New York Mets fan ("Why couldn't I have picked the Yankees?").

He's always been a talker, but it seemed like he'd gotten even mouthier with the passage of time. I enjoyed listening but eventually started looking for a chance to tell him why I'd flown 2,000 miles in the middle of winter to visit a city I'd said good riddance to a long time ago.

I found my opening when Roberta served our meal.

"Hary," I said, "about my uncle—"

"Oh, your uncle," he said manner-of-factly. "I found him."

"You found him?"

"Well, I know where to find him. We'll go see him tomorrow. So, you're coming to Slugs', right?"

I couldn't believe my ears. "Wait. What? You know where he is? I expected this to take some time."

"Yeh, well, it's a funny story, really. You know that name you gave me— the guy you said your uncle was flying a plane for?"

"Yeh. Neil Dellacroce, I think it was."

"Neil Dellacroce, alias Aniello Dellacroce, sometimes called John, sometimes called 'the Polack' when he's out of earshot. Turns out your uncle's boss is a big shot in the mafia."

If he'd said the guy was president of General Motors, I wouldn't have been more surprised.

"The mafia?"

"Yup. La Cosa Nostra. Not just a member, either, my country mouse friend. Former capo and newly promoted to underboss by Carlo Gambino, who's head of his own motherf***ing crime family. Dellacroce is his second-in-command. Apparently, your uncle is his personal chauffeur-slash-pilot. Has been for years."

CHAPTER TWENTY SIX

We finished our food and headed back to Hary's, stopping on the way at a drug store so I could buy some gauze and ointment for my wrists. Hary's building was like I remembered it, except now the concrete façade was painted blue instead of crimson. When he rented the place, the landlord had described the tenement as "pre-war," but, as Hary said at the time: "She didn't say which war."

My money's on the French and Indian.

East 3rd Street was recognizable, although it had taken on a more sinister cast. Shady-looking characters lurked on every corner—drug dealers, according to Hary, not fellas to mess with. The light fixture in the building's small entrance way was encased in a small metal cage, which hadn't prevented someone from breaking the bulb. "Hookers need a place to bring their customers," said Hary while he looked for the right key. "Drug fiends need a place to shoot up." Judging by the not-so-delicate aroma, winos also need a place to pee.

The five-story tenement had been pretty run-down back in the '50s. Things had only gotten worse. "The building is on a rent strike," said Hary, "so at least I'm not paying for this dump."

His apartment was neat and clean. The first thing I did was use the tiny bathroom on the left as soon as you come in the front door. I used to bang my knees on the bathtub every time I sat on the toilet. At least the bathtub wasn't in the kitchen like it is in some New York apartments. In that kitchen you'd have a hard time fitting anything larger than a washtub.

The living room was similarly cramped, although not as much as in the old days when my mattress took up two-thirds of the floor. Hary's bedroom was a small room separated from the rest of the apartment by an open doorway.

The most expensive item in the apartment was a hi-fi system that appeared to have been designed by NASA scientists. Hary saw me admiring it. "Oh man, I got to listen to my Coltrane. You remember when we went out to Jersey to hear him?"

"I was just thinking about that the other day."

"He's playing 'out' these days, too—that music I was telling you about. He might show up tonight. You never know. Almost every time I go to Slugs' I meet someone famous." He looked concerned. "Trane hasn't looked too healthy the last few times I've seen him, though. Cats are worried he's sick."

It was 7:00. "Why don't you use my bed, get some sleep?" he said. "We go on at 9:30, but we play until at least 2:00, maybe later. I'll give you my spare key and you can lock up when you leave. Slugs' is over on the next block, so you shouldn't have any problem. You're a big SOB. Nobody's going mess with you."

I cleaned and bandaged my wrists, applying the ointment the pharmacist had recommended. They still hurt, if not quite as bad. A belt of bourbon would've helped.

Hary got what he needed out of his bedroom and left it for me. I fell asleep immediately. I had terrible dreams, but I couldn't say what they were. As soon as I woke up, they scattered from my mind like a cloud of bats.

Hary's little electric clock said it was 12:15, which meant I'd been out for five hours. For me, that's a full night's sleep.

The street outside was so noisy, I wondered how I'd managed. I showered and changed into a fresh set of clothes. Hary left a note on the refrigerator: "Do me a favor and bring my alto!" I knew he had an ulterior motive, but I grabbed it anyway.

Thankfully, when I got downstairs, the entryway was empty of hookers and heroin addicts and winos. I expected there to be a lot of people out, given how noisy it sounded inside, but the sidewalk was mostly deserted, although a fairly steady stream of cars drove through the slush. I felt seriously out of place.

Hary was right. I was a country mouse, even if I had lived here for a short while, a long time ago.

I pulled my hat down over my ears again, ready to swing Hary's alto case like a bludgeon if need be. I stepped carefully on the icy sidewalk and made the three-minute walk to the club.

A wood sign shaped like some kind of heraldic shield, with the word *Slugs'* painted in Gothic letters. The storefront was modeled after an old English pub. Two rustic wooden doors with heavy metal hinges were set between two large picture windows. Music came from inside, but it was a Charlie Parker record, which told me the band must be between sets. A couple of young black men in suits and ties stood outside, smoking a reefer. They nodded. I nodded back.

The club smelled like cigarettes and beer and male body odor. On the left was a bar. On the right were tables. The bandstand was in the back. In the center was a drum set so small, it might have been a toy. A double bass lay on its side. A hollow-bodied electric guitar sat on a stand. A battered upright piano was pushed to one side. On top was Hary's tenor sax.

The crowd was about the size you'd expect on a Thursday night a couple of days after a record-setting blizzard with a little-known band on the bill. It was almost empty.

Hary was sitting at a small table, talking to a woman and a short, skinny guy with a bleach-blond crew cut. The woman wore a black turtle-neck sweater and a green camouflage billed cap with a red hammer and sickle sewn on the front. She was very young. The skinny fella's back was to me, so I couldn't get a look at him.

Hary saw me and waved. "There he is!" The woman in the hat barely gave me a glance. The fella with the blond crew cut turned and smiled.

It wasn't a fella. It was Sophie.

***

I've had a few short-term romances over the years, but when it comes right down to it, I've loved only three women. Denise Kinney was the first—the woman who, out of self-destructive obsession more than anything else, I remain in some sort of twisted secret love to this very day. The third was Karen Dean, who was my buddy long before I ever fell in love with her. She knows me better and cares more about me than anyone, and is the one person alive I cannot imagine living without.

In between, there was Sophie.

Sophie and I were lovers, although not how Karen and I are, or the way I wished Denise and I could've been. Sophie wasn't the one-man-woman type. She was what I guess they call nowadays, a free spirit. I loved her the way I love music—I was just grateful she was in the world.

When we first met, I was just a kid just out of the Marines with no clear idea where I was headed. I only knew the trip was going to be fueled by a hell of a lot of bourbon. You'd have to ask her what it was she saw in me.

Sophie never said anything about my drinking. It's not that she didn't care. She just didn't feel like it was her place to say. The way she figured, people are entitled to make their own choices. If I chose to drink myself to death before I was 30, that was my business.

Sophie lived in the moment and expected everyone around her to do the same. If during the time we were together we could learn from and enjoy each other, well, what's wrong with that?

I don't talk much about Sophie with other people, because nothing I say can do her justice. In the telling, it might sound like she was selfish, but I don't think she was. If anything, she was naïve, like kids are. I can't help but think I got a lot more out of our relationship than she did. She introduced me to so many wonderful things I might never have found if not for her.

On top of everything, we shared a love for playing jazz. It didn't bother her a bit she was a better musician than me. "Music isn't a competition," she'd say.

Sophie got as much pleasure out of keeping time on a garbage can with a wino on his jug as she would jamming with Sonny Rollins at a Greenwich Village jazz club—which she actually did on one memorable occasion, although he was not then as famous as he would become.

I think if I'd been able to capture that spirit, I might've ended up being a musician after all.

***

We hugged like long-lost lovers.

"Emmett, my God, I'm so glad to see you," she said with tears in her eyes. Sophie's tough but emotional.

"I almost didn't recognize you," I said, frowning. "There's something different about you. I'm not sure what it is—"

She pushed me playfully. "Perhaps you remember me as a brunette?"

"A brunette with hair all the way down her back."

"Yeh, well, I always hated getting it in my face when I was playing."

"It looks good," I said. I meant it. She looked like Jean Seberg.

Hary broke in. "Hey man, I forgot to tell you. Sophie's my drummer. This here is my guitarist, Florine. By day, Florine's my assistant investigator."

She shook my hand glumly.

"I see you've brought your alto," said Sophie. "Are you planning to sit in?"

"That's Hary's horn, not mine. I think his evil plan was to get me to come up, but I'm afraid I'm going to have to resist. I'm sure y'all left me behind a long time ago. Don't want to embarrass myself."

"Oh, don't be silly," said Sophie. "There's hardly anybody here. And I'd love to play with you again."

"How 'bout if I sit and listen awhile and see how I feel?"

"Hey Emmett," Hary interjected, "did you see a tall skinny black guy out front when you came in?"

"I saw a couple of them."

"One of them had better be my bass player," he mumbled. "Florine, why don't you come with me. I want to go over that new tune with you and Horace."

Florine went to the stage and picked up her guitar. Hary went outside and retrieved his bassist. He introduced us on the way to the bandstand. "Hary's told me a lot about you," said Horace. "Uh-oh," I said. "All good, man, all good!" he said with a laugh.

Sophie grinned awkwardly. "It's nice of Hary to give us some time alone," she said.

I nodded, overcome by inexplicable shyness. "So, what's new?" I said. We laughed nervously.

"Oh, not much. You?"

"You know. Same old thing."

Neither of us could decide whether to make eye contact. I'd catch her looking at me; she'd avert her eyes. She'd catch me looking at her; I'd find something fascinating on the other side of the room.

"How's the newspaper business?" I asked.

To pay the rent, Sophie works as a journalist.

"Up and down. Mostly down, unfortunately, but I have reason to hope it may get better. I'd just gotten a job writing for the *Herald-Tribune* when the unions went out on strike. I went months without a pay check. I had some money saved and was able make a little bit playing music, but it's been difficult, I must say. After the strike was settled, the *Herald-Tribune* merged with the *World-Telegram and Sun* and the *Journal-American*. It's now called *The New York World Journal Tribune*."

"That's a mouthful."

"Isn't it? They cut staff, naturally, but for some reason they kept me on. I'm not sure why. It's been good and bad for me. Bad, because I'm working twice as hard for only a few extra dollars a week. Good, because at least I have a job and a lot of my former colleagues do not. It's also good because they moved me to the national desk, which means I get to cover stories from all over the United States, which I find fascinating."

"Does that mean you get to travel?"

"I haven't so far. I spend most of my time on the telephone and rewriting wire service copy. But my boss says that once things get back to normal, I'll get to roam the country a bit." She grinned. "Maybe I'll even make it to Oklahoma."

"Don't. You'd hate it."

"You might be surprised." She pointed at my wrists. "What happened there?"

"I didn't try to slit them, in case you're wondering." She gave me a look: *Not funny, Emmett. I know you too well.*

"Seriously, Hary tells me you're here to find your uncle. Did it have something to do with that?"

Before I knew, I'd told her the Younger story, up to and including the part about my abduction and escape. She clasped my hands across the table.

"So you believe your uncle can fill in the missing pieces?" she said.

"I hope so."

On stage, Hary played some rapid-fire scales that sounded like a call to arms. Sophie waved and told him, "I'm coming." She stood and gave me a thoughtful look. "You know, Emmett," she said, "this might be a story for my paper. My editor has been talking about giving the *Times* a run for their money when it comes to national news. The Civil Rights movement is the biggest thing going now, along with Vietnam."

Horace and Florine had joined Hary making warm-up noises. "That's my cue," said Sophie. "Keep me up to date on this, ok?"

"I will. If I'm here long enough, let's have dinner. I'll tell you the whole story."

"That would be lovely." She took a step toward the stage before turning back to me. "Are you going to come up and play?"

"Let me listen first."

"Please play, Emmett," she said warmly. "I always loved making music with you."

I knew it was true. I could tell just sitting there talking to her in person for the first time in 12 years. Our connection was unbroken.

She got behind the drums—a small woman with the build and grace of a ballerina. She picked up a pair of brushes and played light, skittering rhythms across the kit. On bass, Horace bowed long, eerie notes, the vibrations coursing through the room like electricity. Without a word, the performance had begun.

Hary and Florine began playing a sinuous, complex melody in near-perfect unison that seemed to both oppose and synchronize with Horace and Sophie. I closed my eyes, stopped thinking, and lost myself in the music. When they finished some 20 minutes later, the half-dozen folks in the club applauded to fill Carnegie Hall.

I felt like I'd been given a sneak preview of the hereafter.

Hary thanked the audience and said, "For our last piece we may or may not have a special guest." He gave me a questioning look. Part of me thought of reasons I shouldn't, but was shouted down by the part that wanted to play. Almost against my will, my legs carried me to the stage.

"All the way from Oklahoma, ladies and gentlemen," Hary announced. "Emmett Hardy!" A people few clapped, probably thinking they should know who I was.

Were they ever wrong.

"Let your ears guide you, man," whispered Hary. "Play what you feel." Sophie beamed and tapped her sticks together. "Let's make Emmett Hardy music!" she said. "I'm not sure what that that is," I said, "but I'll try."

The band started. I listened. Unlike the prior piece, this one had no specific melody, but seemed organized by a strange, start-and-stop rhythm Sophie played on her tom-toms. I closed my eyes and tried to find a place in the maelstrom. The music seemed to make physical shapes in my mind. Hary's solo was like a hurricane making love to a tornado during an earthquake. The way he wound it down was an unmistakable invitation for me to join in. So I did.

The next few minutes took me someplace I'd never been. I won't describe how it sounded and what it meant, other than to say, I felt like I'd gotten something off my chest that had been there a long time. If I could play music like that every day of my life, I might forget about drinking.

Florine soloed after me. She took what I had done as a starting point and carried it new places.

Afterwards, Horace came up to me, shook my hand and said: "Sounded tremendous, man." Sophie put her face close to mine and cupped my chin in her hands. "That was wonderful, Emmett. I'm so proud of you!" Hary grinned from ear to ear: "Yeh, man. You were born for this!" Florine said, "Nice," straight-faced, but with an air of respect.

I might never have another night like this for the rest of my life, but at least I had this one.

My life's full of ifs and mights and wouldas and shouldas, isn't it?

The musicians started putting away their instruments. Hary suggested we all go out for breakfast. That sounded fine to me. I was too wound up to sleep.

Horace and I were talking when the bartender asked if we'd seen Hary. Horace said he'd gone outside. The bartender went outside to look. Seconds later, the door burst open and he ran back inside. "Your sax player's getting mugged," he said, dialing the telephone. "I'm calling the cops."

I rushed out. A trash can overturned across the street. A tall, muscular-looking fella in a ski mask had pushed Hary into a dark doorway. The guy lifted Hary off the ground, slammed him against the door, and held him there with his forearm.

In his other hand, he held a knife to Hary's throat.

Hary wore the same expression he used to get when we were in a tough spot in Korea—unruffled, calculating, weighing his options. I'm sure he could've gotten out of it by himself.

But hell, as long as I was there.

I pulled Numb Nuts' Charter Arms Undercover .38 Special from the holster in the small of my back, walked across the street, and shot Mr. Ski Mask in the knee.

CHAPTER TWENTY SEVEN

Alright. I lied.

It wasn't his knee. It was his foot. His right heel, to be specific. I said 'knee' because I thought it sounded more dramatic.

"Emmett! Jesus Christ, what are you doing?" He pulled out a small semi-automatic and held it on Mr. Ski Mask, whose right leg had collapsed under him, causing him to fall flat on his back.

"You shouldn't be carrying a gun!" said Hary.

"You've got one," I said.

"I've got a license! Do you?"

"I need a license?"

"Hell, yes! In New York you do!"

"Excuse me," I said. "I thought I was still in America."

Florine, Horace, and Sophie burst through the door of Slugs' and ran across the street. "What happened?" said Horace. "This guy tried to rob me," Hary said. "Emmett shot him." Mr. Ski Mask rolled back and forth on the slush-covered sidewalk, holding his bloody combat-boot-encased foot with both hands, yelling "Shit" and "F***" over and over.

Everyone looked at me. "Hey, he was holding a knife to Hary's throat," I said by way of explanation. "Damn," said Horace said with a half-smile. Sophie rubbed her bare arms trying to warm herself. Her eyes crinkled at the corners, like she couldn't decide whether to laugh or cry.

Florine kept her cool. "Get him out of here," she said, meaning me. Hary picked up the mugger's switchblade and nudged him with his toe. "You too, asshole. Today's your lucky day. Time to split." The guy struggled to his feet and hopped toward Avenue C, chanting his two-word curse.

Hary removed the magazine from his gun and took out a bullet. He dropped it down a storm drain. "I'll tell the cops it was me," he said. "I've got papers for the gun and a P.I. license. Hopefully, they won't do a ballistics test." He saw that I was still holding the .38. "You need to put that away," he said, looking around to make sure nobody was watching.

A yellow cab approached. Florine flagged it down. "Go straight to Hary's," she said to me. "Lock yourself in and don't come out."

Sophie drew close. "Will I see you before you leave?"

"I hope so," I said, then whispered in her ear: "I better ask this now; would it be alright if we got a divorce?"

She was silent for a second, looked at the sky and laughed. "Of course, my dear Emmett. Whatever your heart desires!" She kissed me on the cheek. "Now go!" She pushed me toward the cab. I got in. Hary herded the others back to Slugs'.

The driver had a face like a clenched fist. I gave him Hary's address. He turned around. "You ain't from around here, are ya?" he said.

"I know. It's on the next block. Let's go. I'm in a hurry."

He rolled his eyes. "You'd get there faster walkin'," he said and pulled away from the curb.

He didn't need to know I was trying to avoid the cop car that by now was rolling up the street.

The cabbie dropped me off in front of Hary's building. I must've over-tipped by a considerable amount, judging by how friendly he got all of a sudden. I didn't care. I took the stairs to the fourth floor, two-at-a-time. Nobody saw me as far as I could tell.

Sleep was out of the question. I turned on the TV. All I got was snow and static. I went through Hary's record collection but couldn't figure out how to use his space-age hi-fi. I found a bottle of Coca Cola in the refrigerator and drank that. I noticed his bookcase included an inordinate number of volumes about World War II. I pulled out the thickest and sat down on the couch to read.

I was still reading three hours later when Hary came through the door.

"Oh man, what a night," he said wearily. The pocket of his suit jacket was torn. The cuffs of his trousers were muddy and wet. His collar was open and turned up in the back. He stood by the bathroom and began unbuttoning his shirt.

"You missed all the fun, man," he said. His smile suggested that whatever it was I'd missed, it had been anything but fun.

"I'm sorry if I gave you a hard time," he said. "I should've gotten down on the ground and kissed your feet, man. That guy was going to cut me and I'm not sure I could've pulled my own gun in time."

"You would've done the same," I said. "What happened after I left?"

He tossed his shirt in a hamper sitting by the bathroom door. "A couple uniformed NYPD showed before you were out of sight," he said. "I'd gotten everybody else back into Slugs', so it was just me. They said they'd received an anonymous report of a mugging."

"The bartender called it in."

"I know, but this is New York, man. Nobody wants to get involved. Least of all, an actual witness." He dropped his pants in the hamper, then stood in the door to the kitchen in his BVDs, with his hands on his hips and a sardonic smile on his face.

"Anyway, I told them I was the cat who'd been mugged. They asked me why I was there and I told them the truth: that I was a musician, and I was playing a gig at the joint across the street. I showed 'em my gun permit and P.I. license, which knocked 'em on their ass. I guess they'd never heard of a private cop who plays the saxophone."

He closed the door to the bathroom and turned on the shower. "Turns out they knew where my office was and everything," he yelled over the rushing water, "so we got that squared away. I told 'em I'd shot the guy in the foot and that he'd run off. They were sympathetic and asked which direction he went. The cat left a trail of blood, so I couldn't have lied about that part if I wanted to." He giggled. "I told them he went over to Avenue C and turned right. They argued with each other about whether to call a detective and decided not to. They wanted to follow the blood and see if they could track the guy down, so they made me come with them. Me and one of the cops followed the blood while the other one drove alongside us." He paused. "Hey, let me do this and I'll tell you the rest when I'm done."

I sat on the couch reading the same sentence about Hitler fifteen times, waiting for Hary to finish his shower. After a few minutes he shut off the water and brushed his teeth.

He came out in a terrycloth bathrobe, toweling his hair dry. He picked up the story.

"I didn't want to bring Horace or Florine or Sophie into it, anyway. I just went along with the cops and froze my ass off. We lost the trail on the steps going down into the Delancey Street subway station. I figured the guy went to Brooklyn. They needed to file a report, so they dragged me to the Ninth Precinct over on 5th Street. That's what took so long. They took their sweet time taking my statement. Probably didn't want to go back out in the cold if they didn't have to. We only finished about fifteen minutes ago. I'll have to go by Slugs' tonight to pick up my horns and coat. Jesus H. Christ, what a night."

"Other than that, Mrs. Lincoln, how'd you like the play?"

"Hah!" he said. "That's right, man, it was actually a hell of a night, musically. Except for the fact I might never get another gig at Slugs', since the crowd was so small." He walked past me to the bedroom. "You played great, man. I knew you were cut out for that kind of music. You and me, we're not exactly rules-followers, are we?"

I chuckled. "I try to be, but something always gets in the way. It used to be alcohol, but I haven't had a drink in months, so I don't know what to blame last night on."

"Blame it on having a deeply human soul, my brother." He came back out wearing a pair of blue gym shorts and a red polo shirt. "You don't have the chops I do, but the passion and intensity, man ... it brought tears to my eyes. And I'm not blowing smoke, my friend. It was beautiful."

I said, "Well thanks, bud," and changed the subject.

"You said you know where to find my uncle. Where might that be?"

"Ever heard of the Ravenite Social Club?"

"Does not ring a bell."

"It's like a five-minute walk from here. Over on Mulberry Street, in Little Italy. It's Neil Dellacroce's headquarters. Your uncle's boss."

"Think we could go over there later today?"

"We can, but it's not as simple as just knocking on the door and inviting ourselves in. The Ravenite's been a mob hangout for years. Ever heard of

Charlie Luciano? Better known as 'Lucky'?" I nodded. "He hung out there during prohibition. Carlo Gambino took it over in the '50s. Now it's Dellacroce's place."

"So what'll we do?"

"We'll go over there and knock on the door."

"I thought you said it wasn't that easy."

"You got to start somewhere." He paused. "When's your return flight?"

"I've got an open ticket. I just have to call the airline and make a reservation."

"Let me suggest you book a plane out of here tonight. Those cops pretended to buy my story, but if that clown you shot gets braced by a detective and tells what really happened ... well, it might be better if you were impossible to find, you dig?"

"I reckon I do."

"Crazy," he said with a crooked grin. "Let's crash for a few hours, then go and say hi to our pals at the Ravenite. Worst they can do is shoot us."

"They can try."

He chuckled. "No guns this time, Marshal Dillon. You ever hear the saying, 'shoot first and ask questions later?' With these guys, it's 'shoot first, chop your body into little pieces, stuff it into a suitcase loaded down with bricks and dump it in the East River.' You dig?"

"Oh, I dig, partner. I most definitely dig."

CHAPTER TWENTY EIGHT

It was a little after one o'clock before we got up and around. I dug out a fresh flannel shirt, underwear and Levi's from my satchel. In this weather, I'd have been as warm if I'd wrapped myself in paper towels, but it was all I had. I was too big to borrow anything of Hary's, and he'd given my old clothes away years ago.

Hary dressed like Phillip Marlowe in *The Big Sleep*: dark wool suit with a white handkerchief poking carelessly out of the front pocket; white shirt, skinny tie, black Florsheims, and a tweed overcoat. His grey fedora had a wider band and narrower brim than mine. He wore it tilted slightly to one side.

He looked me over before we left, trying to decide whether he should get me a suit before we went on our errand. He shook his head. "Nah, I'm thinking the mafia cats might dig the whole cowboy look."

"Great," I said in a flat voice. "Can I at least buy an overcoat?"

"No, man, can't lose the denim jacket, it's part of the overall vibe."

Overall vibe. Huh.

We stopped at the corner deli and picked up some coffee and bagels. Hary ordered sesame with cream cheese and lox. I had garlic, buttered and toasted. I'd always loved New York bagels.

"Hey, Jock," Hary said to the sad-sack fella who ran the bicycle messenger service. "Did I introduce you two yesterday? Jock Bernstein, this is Emmett Hardy, an old Marine buddy of mine. Emmett, this is Jock." He slapped Jock on the back. "How's business, Jock-o?"

Jock looked like Fred Mertz in *I Love Lucy*—one of those faces that could sink a thousand ships. "Business?" he growled. "What business? It's the week before Christmas. The weather is shit. Nobody's working. The offices are closed. Even if anyone needed a messenger, my guys are calling in sick. I'll be lucky if I'm not bankrupt before spring." He snorted and blew something wet into a handkerchief. "That's 'how's business'."

Hary slapped him on the back. "C'mon, man! You know things pick up after the holidays."

"What if they don't?"

"They will."

"But what if they don't?"

Hary laughed. "You go through this every year, man. Be cool. Things'll get better."

We walked back to his desk. Florine was there, sitting at her own, catty-corner to Hary's. He asked her if she made it home ok last night. She gave him an annoyed, "I'm here, aren't I?" look. "Mrs. Greenaway called," she said. "Apparently, Mr. Greenaway is going to be on Fire Island this weekend if you want to check on him out there. Otherwise, you can wait until Monday."

"You want to go?"

"In this weather? No thanks."

"Then we'll catch up with him on Monday." He gave me a pained look and said, "Don't even ask."

He unfolded a wooden folding chair for me. We ate our bagels and drank our coffee. Hary made some calls. Florine wrote in a notebook. After a while, she said without looking up: "You played great last night." I said thanks and told her she played great, too. She grunted. I meant it. That girl's a player.

Hary finished with the phone. "You ready, cowboy?" he asked.

I said in the thickest Okie accent I could muster: "I was born ready."

"Alright then, let's blow this pop stand."

He said to Florine, "If we're not back in a couple of hours, call Bobby Kennedy."

I assumed he was kidding.

The wind slapped my face like a jealous girlfriend. As much as I hate the cold weather back home, here, it's a million times worse. You take your life in your hands just trying to navigate the icy sidewalks. The weatherman said to expect temperatures below zero. He got it right this time. Nobody with half a brain in their head would go out if they didn't have to.

What in hell was I getting into? Knock, knock, knock. "Excuse me, Mr. Dellacroce, can Uncle Ernie come out to play?" For all I knew, Ernie had changed jobs years ago. Hell, for all knew, the Youngers were alive and well. This whole thing was crazy. Checking into the VA had been a mistake. I should've checked into a motel, curled up into a little ball and drank formaldehyde until I embalmed myself.

Christ, I missed Red.

All New York neighborhoods look more or less the same after a big snowstorm. A car covered by a mountain of dirty snow in Chinatown looks no different than a car covered by a mountain of dirty snow in the East Village.

We turned left on Avenue A and headed west on Houston. A gust of wind almost blew off my hat. "Don't you ever drive anywhere?" I asked.

"Hey man, my car's under six feet of snow like everybody else's. You want to spend all day digging it out, so we don't have to walk a few blocks, be my guest."

"No thanks."

We stopped and waited for the light to change. "Do the cops know about this place?" I asked.

"Sure they do," he yelled to be heard over the traffic. "The mafia cats don't even try to keep it a secret. Everyone knows the Ravenite used to be Carlo Gambino's joint. Now it's Dellacroce's, and it's where half the made guys in New York hang out."

The light changed. We crossed Houston. "If everybody knows, why don't they shut it down?"

Hary laughed and yelled over the traffic: "Man, wouldn't life be beautiful if things were that simple?"

On Bowery we passed a group of disheveled-looking gentlemen waiting outside a soup kitchen. The line stretched out the door and halfway down the block. I almost asked one of them if he wanted to swap his smelly overcoat for my clean denim jacket. I decided it would be ill-advised. Didn't want to spoil "the vibe."

Also, just because those fellas were poor didn't mean they're stupid.

We turned west onto Prince Street where it T-bones Bowery and crossed the invisible border into Little Italy.

The last time I'd been there was for the Feast of San Gennaro in the late summer of 1954, right before I returned to Oklahoma. That was the day I got the phone call asking me to be the Burr police chief. I told them I needed to give it some thought.

That evening I went to the festival. By then, Sophie and I were a couple in name only, so I went unaccompanied.

I remember the decorative lamps forming a tunnel of light over the street, and the smell of grilled sausages. I remember the heat. I remember the thousands of people milling around having the time of their lives, and I remember feeling as out of place as an ostrich in a chicken coop. The next day I called Burr and accepted the job.

This time, except for the Christmas lights draped over the street and the decorated shop windows, this piece of Mulberry Street could've been almost any block in the city.

We started toward the Ravenite. A few doors down, Hary grabbed my arm and pulled me into a doorway. "Listen, Emmett," he said, his lips hardly moving, like he was afraid of having them read. "Let me do the talking."

"Nah, don't be silly Hary. This is my problem. I can handle it myself."

"Man, you don't know these guys—"

"And you do?"

"Yeh, actually I do." He pulled down his hat and raised his lapels to obscure his face. "I'm tight with some low-level guys in the Gambinos."

"I'll make you a deal," I said. "If someone you know answers the door, take the lead. If not, let me handle it."

He shook his head slowly. "Alright, man, if that's the way you want it. One more thing. From this point forward, assume you're being watched."

"Watched? By who?"

"By the mob, by the feds, by the NYPD. Take your pick. Neil Dellacroce lives in the building across from the Ravenite. The Genovese family might have a bigger claim to this block than the Gambinos. I'd be shocked if the FBI doesn't have the whole damn street under 24-hour surveillance. Just take it for granted." He elbowed me in the ribs. "Smile. You're on *Candid Camera*. Dig?"

"Dug. Let them watch. I got nothing to hide."

"Except you shot a guy with an unlicensed firearm last night."

"Yeh, except for that. You coming?"

He smiled. "Let's do it, man."

The Ravenite Social Club looked like the kind of storefront you see on the first floor of tenement buildings all over the city. In a former life it might've been a barbershop, a restaurant, a clothing store. The front had two big fat and wide windows rising from about two feet off the ground all the way up to where a fire escape ladder hung over the recessed door, ten- or twelve-feet above the sidewalk.

Curtains obscured the view from the outside. Ornamented ironwork ran the width of the building. Christmas lights twinkled from within. There was no sign that said, "Ravenite Social Club, Home of the Gambino Organized Crime Family," or anything like that. Just two words—"Members Only"—painted in small cursive letters on one window.

"In the summer there's always a bunch of old cats out here smoking cigars and playing dominos," Hary said.

"Not domino-playing season, I guess."

"Nope," he said. There was a buzzer by the door. Hary made a "be my guest" motion. I buzzed.

A scratchy voice came out of a small speaker: "What?"

"Uh, yeh, my name is Hardy. I'm looking for my uncle Ernest Hardy. I understand he works for Mr. Dellacroce."

A pause, then the same scratchy voice: "Members only. Get the f*** out of here."

I tried again. "Ernest Hardy? Y'all heard of him?"

Nothing. I re-pressed the button.

The voice, annoyed: "I said, get the f*** out of here."

"You sure there's no one in there who knows Ernest Hardy?"

The voice said: "This is a member's only club ..." Faintly I could hear a voice in the background say: "Hey John, I bet the guy's talkin' about Ernie Cowboy." The tiny speaker died. I started to buzz again. Hary grabbed my arm and stopped me. The door opened a crack. A chubby-faced guy with a small growth of stubble and black hair greased into a ducktail stuck his head out. "You say your name's Hardy?"

"That's right. Emmett Hardy."

"Let me see some ID."

I pulled out my driver's license.

He looked at it and snickered. "Oklahoma, huh? Shit. Alright, wait here."

He came back a minute later.

"Follow me," he said. I stepped forward. Hary followed. Chubby-Faced Guy put a hand on Hary's chest. "Not you, cop. Just this guy."

"He's not a cop—"

Hary interrupted. "That's cool, Emmett, I'll wait out here."

Chubby-Faced Guy pointed to the building next door and said, "You'll wait over *there*."

"That's cool," Hary said again, and walked away.

Leaving me alone in the hands of murderous thugs.

What am I doing? I thought.

The right thing, I hoped.

CHAPTER TWENTY NINE

No sooner had we stepped inside than Chubby-Faced Guy shoved me face-first against the nearest wall and said, "Spread 'em." I could hardly believe an actual gangster would talk like that, but I obliged. He frisked me. Fortunately, I'd left Numb Nuts' .38 in my satchel back at Hary's.

The interior of the Ravenite gave no clues about what sort of business it may have once been. A threadbare couch took up one side of the room. Opposite that was a table and a few cheap wooden chairs. In one corner slanted diagonally was a leather recliner. A television mounted on a rack hung from the ceiling.

Chubby-Face led me to the back of the room. A trio of heavy-set guys in polo shirts playing cards regarded me like I was some odd species of fish. We cam to a door marked "Private." Chubby-Face knocked. A voice side said, "Come in."

Chubby-Face opened the door, poked his head in and said, "Here he is, Mr. Dellacroce." He stepped aside and let me enter, then shut the door behind me.

Behind the desk was a man in his early 50s, wearing a dark suit, white dress shirt with a blue and white checked tie. His gray, brilliantined hair was thinning, but still wavy. His jowls were starting to sag and you could lug groceries in the bags under his eyes. I thought he looked like the Cowardly Lion. I suspect no one ever told him that.

On the other side of the desk was another man, quite a bit older than the first but somehow more youthful. He had on tan slacks and an orange and brown sweater zipped halfway up his chest, open at the throat. Underneath he wore a white sports shirt with tiny blue crosshatchings. His hair was thick and black, without a speck of gray, parted to one side. His eyes were the same color of blue as my father's. The same color as mine.

The second man stood, hitched up his pants and looked in my eyes. "Emmett?" he said. I nodded. He smiled and offered his hand. As I took it, he pulled me close for a bearhug that probably broke several ribs.

"You look just like your grandfather. I'll be damned."

"Good to see you, Uncle Ernie."

He said to the man behind the desk, "Neil, this is my nephew Emmett. The Marine. Emmett, this is my boss, Mr. Dellacroce."

Shaking Mr. Dellacroce's hand was like squeezing a peeled banana.

"So this is the black sheep of the family?" Mr. Dellacroce said.

Ernie laughed. "Yeh, the cop. We like him anyway."

Mr. Dellacroce gave me a funny look and said, "Were you brought up in a barn?" Confused, I looked at Ernie. He nodded at my hat. I'd forgotten to take it off.

I snatched it off my head and said, "Sorry about that, Mr. Dellacroce."

He smiled and said, "I'm just bustin' your balls, kid," which was probably meant to be good-natured but gave me goose-bumps.

Ernie reached behind me and opened the door. "Neil, I know you got work to do, so if you don't mind, I'm going to take Emmett down to Emilio's for a cup of coffee, so we can catch up. That ok?"

"Go ahead," he said in voice that sounded like the Cowardly Lion's. "I won't need you for a couple of hours. Don't forget there's that thing we got to do tonight."

He seemed friendly enough, but behind that smile, his eyes made you feel like he was sizing you up for a pair of cement shoes.

Uncle Ernie introduced me to the other fellas on the way out. Chubby-Faced Guy was called John. He asked me if I'd ever had physical relations with a sheep and got some laughs. My similarly lewd response got more. John took a couple of threatening steps toward me. Ernie told him to cool off and hustled me out.

Hary was waiting in front of the building next door, as ordered. I introduced him to Ernie. He thought Hary looked familiar. "Have we met before?" he asked.

"It's possible," Hary said. "It's a big city but a little town."

Harry hopped up and down with his shoulders hunched and hands jammed into his overcoat pockets, trying to keep warm. "You ok getting back on your own? I should probably go back to the office and take care of a few things."

"I'll make sure he gets back," said Ernie.

"Don't worry about me, either of y'all. I can handle myself."

"I guess he can," said Hary knowingly. "Tell your uncle about that guy you shot."

Ernie's eyes bugged out. "What the—? You shot a guy?"

Hary grinned and said, "Yeh. Yesterday, over on East 3rd Street. It's a great story. Tell him, country mouse." He winked, turned, and walked away.

Emilio's was a pastry shop. Like bagels, Italian pastries aren't something you can find in Burr, or anyplace else in Oklahoma, as far as I know. Ernie apologized in advance ("It's not fancy, but the cannoli is the best in the city"), but it seemed plenty nice to me. The lady behind the counter treated Ernie like a celebrity. They made small talk in Italian. Ernie ordered coffee and cannoli for the both of us, and we sat at one of the six or seven small circular tables scattered about the room.

First thing he did was insist I tell him about the events in front of Slugs'.

"What if one of these folks hear?" I said, pointing out the woman who waited on us and a couple of old men sitting at separate tables by the window. Ernie made waved away my concern. "They don't even speak English," he said.

I lowered my voice anyway.

"Oh brother, I wish could've seen that!" he said when I'd finished, barely able to contain his laughter.

The lady brought us our coffee and pastry. Ernie took a bite and looked delighted. Mine was as tasty as advertised. I nodded my approval, then washed it down with a sip of the strongest coffee I'd ever had.

"So how long has it been, nephew? Last time I saw you, you were just a kid."

"Last time I saw you was the first week of August in 1940," I said. "I was 13."

He sipped his coffee. "You remember the date, huh?"

"A lot of things were happening around that time."

"You know, you should've called before you came."

"I would've called, but the number Dad had for you was disconnected."

"How'd you find me?"

I told him about Hary being a private detective. I didn't tell him how easy it had been. "How is Everett, anyway?" he asked.

I took a bite, swallowed and asked, "When was the last time you talked to him?"

"Last time I called him was right after you'd busted Edgar Bixby's kid for killing some colored whore. He was real proud of you for that."

"That was about a year-and-a-half ago. He's gone downhill quite a bit since then." I described his mental decline.

Ernie sighed. "Believe it or not, I always felt bad about leaving Everett behind to cope with your grandfather all by himself. Dad wanted both of us to be farmers. There wasn't no way I was going to do that." He took the last bite of his cannoli, then wiped his mouth with a paper napkin.

"I felt like I was living in a box the whole time I was growing up," he continued. "I couldn't stand all that shit—cows, horses, hay, wheat. I even hated the goddam smell. The more I tried to tell him it wasn't for me, the more he insisted I do it. Everett was better-suited to that life. When Wilson got us into the war, I saw a chance to get out and I took it."

His voice trailed off and he started shredding the napkin distractedly.

"I didn't exactly come here to talk about dad," I said. "There's something else I'm hoping you can help me with."

I began by telling him about my visit to Rufus Kenworthy, in particular the part about the night Rufus went drinking with some fellas at that Butcherville bar and how he thought my dad had been there.

"Oh, I remember that night," said Ernie. "That wasn't your dad. That was me."

"I figured," I said. "You two looked so much alike."

I told him what I knew about the firebombing, and said I reckoned Vernon Raymer was behind it, along with Harold Prentiss and other members of The Sons of Aaron Burr Society. I told him I suspected the

Youngers had probably been killed by the same men. I showed him the picture of him with the smiling fellas in the drugstore, proud to be members of The Sons of Aaron Burr Society, a club whose sole reason for existing was to make sure Burr was a whites-only town.

He looked at it, smiled faintly, then looked out the window. I followed his gaze. People walked quickly past the café, their heads down to avoid the wind. Trucks with "New York Daily News" and "Rheingold Beer" written on their sides threw slush into the sidewalk. Snow was starting to fall again.

"This f***ing city," he said in a subdued voice. "Sometimes I wonder how in hell I got here." He shook his head sadly. "I've f***ing wasted my life. My dad—your granddad—was a hard-ass, but he was a good man. My mom was a kind woman. Everett was the best brother a guy could have. No matter what trouble I got into, he was always there to pull me out of it. Yet here the hell I am."

He rolled a piece of torn napkin into a little ball and flicked it into the ashtray.

"I remember how you used to look at me," he said with a wan smile. "A man can tell when he's being hero-worshiped. You thought my shit didn't stink. Sometimes it even mattered to me. I'd do something stupid and think, 'What if Emmett saw me doing this, would I want him to think it was an ok thing to do?' And I'd stop. Not always, but once in a while I did."

He sighed and looked out the window again. "I've done some lousy things, nephew," he said, his voice fading to almost nothing.

"You were a war hero," I said, wanting to help.

"Yeh," he chuckled mirthlessly. "A war hero." He looked at a spot over my head and sighed. "That was a long time ago." He paused. "I could've been like your dad. Not a farmer, but someone who maybe had a family, a son like you I could be proud of. Now I'm 65."

"That's not that old."

He smirked. "It is in my business. And there's no retirement age. You're in it until someone decides you're not."

Not much I could say to that.

He took a deep breath. "Ok, it's like this," he said. Suddenly his voice was strong and professional. "I wasn't an official member of Vernon Raymer's little club, although I might as well have been. They would've been just as happy to run off Jews or Catholics if there'd been any living in Burr. There weren't, so they settled for spades. I didn't have the patience for their dumb-ass meetings and secret handshakes and shit, but when it came time for action, I was all in, You probably remember that my bar got burned down." I nodded. "We never found out who was burning down all the bars in Butcherville, but it wasn't those Aaron Burr Society assholes. Hell, most of them had a financial interest in a bar or two. But when mine got burnt, it pissed me off. Made me want to kick some ass. So when Vernon came to me and said, 'Hey, we're going to burn this house down and we'd like you to help,' I was like, sure, why the hell not?"

"So it was Vernon's idea."

"Oh, hell yeh, it was his idea alright. He asked me and Harold to take his son Clyde along. Another fella went with us, too. I didn't know him, but I got the impression he was from out of town. From Temple City or Alva. Something like that."

"Did you hear anyone call him Smiley?"

"Hah," he said in recognition. "Smiley. I'd forgotten about that. I remember him because after we'd set the house on fire, he made me stop—I was driving—so he could get out of the car and get something off the front porch. I'm not sure what."

"Could it have been a badge of some kind?" I thought it might have been that Bill Pickett 101 Ranch badge Gabe showed me that time. Clarence's good-luck piece.

Ernie shrugged. "Maybe. I don't know. I didn't ask. Anyway, those other fellas did all the burning. I stayed in the car and drove. You remember that little car of mine?"

I smiled at the memory. "1937 Frazer Nash BMW."

"You remember that? Beautiful car," he said wistfully. "Too slick for those crummy county roads, that's for sure. Wish I still had it, although I don't know where I'd park it."

"I reckon that was the first car I ever loved," I said. "Maybe the only one."

"It was something else, that's for sure."

I gestured at the photograph laying on the table between us. "Was that Smiley fella in this picture?"

"No, I don't think so. If he is, I don't recognize him." He scanned it one more time to make sure. "Nah. Don't see him." He shook his head. "I was such a stupid shit back then. I didn't have nothing against colored people.

None of the Hardys did. Did you know my grandfather's father was some famous abolitionist in New York before the Civil War?" I shook my head. "It's true. That's probably why I did what I did. Piss everyone off. Embarrass the family. It's the only thing I was any goddam good at."

I started to say something comforting but he cut me off. "No excuses, Emmett. I f***ed up. But one thing I *didn't* do was kill those people."

"I never thought you did," I said, which wasn't as true as I would have liked it to be.

"I wouldn't have blamed you," he said. "But I promise, I didn't have a hand in it. You're right about them being killed, though. I didn't do it, but I know who did."

He took a deep breath. "And I know why."

CHAPTER THIRTY

"There were four of us," he began. "Harold Prentiss was one. You remember Harold? He was that stupid bastard who did Vernon Raymer's dirty work."

I'd recently discovered any mention of Mr. Prentiss' name was invariably followed by a slur on his intelligence and parentage.

"Clyde Raymer was there because his old man wanted him to grow some hair on his balls. The third guy was that Smiley fella. I remember he was all dressed up like a movie cowboy. More like Gene Autry than John Wayne, if you get my drift. I got the feeling he was new to town, because Harold kept explaining things to him."

"What things?" I asked.

"Oh, I don't remember exactly. Stupid-ass things he should've known if he'd lived there. If you got to ask Harold Prentiss about anything, you're in f***ing trouble, I'll tell you that."

"Did this Smiley know the Youngers?"

"Beats me. I mostly remember how excited he was by the whole thing. It was like he was trying to impress everybody by showing how gung-ho he was."

"What about Clyde and Harold?"

"What? You mean were they excited?"

"Yeh."

He thought about it. "Well, a lot of times I've seen guys act like they're all jazzed when they're really scared shitless. Trying to build themselves up, so they can do whatever it is they want to do. Harold and Clyde were like that. The other guy wasn't trying to convince himself, though. He was enjoying it. He couldn't wait to burn down that damn house and didn't care who knew it."

"Tough guy, huh?"

Ernie chuckled. "Nah. He was a pussy. It doesn't take any guts to set someone's house on fire and run off." He paused. "You know what he reminded me of? In my line of business, we meet all these so-called respectable guys—politicians, business men, guys like that—who worship gangsters." He smiled ruefully. "They meet someone like me, and all of a sudden start talking tough and ask stupid-ass questions. I just answer them all mysterious-like, which makes 'em drool even more. They f***ing love us, treat us like movie stars. Then they go tell their friends, 'Hey, guess who I just played golf with? Neil Dellacroce!' They think it makes them look tough. Tough by association." He laughed. "Neil eats that shit up. Those important bastards treat him like he's one of them. Or better, even. Anyway, I lost track of what I was saying. Oh, yeh. About that guy. Smiley. He was like one of them. A tough-by-association type."

Sounded like Clyde to me, although it obviously wasn't—unless, of course, Ernie had gotten his wires crossed. Couldn't have been one of the Bixbys. Too young.

"Anyway, about that night," Ernie continued. "We met at this bar in Butcherville. I don't think it even had a name. It was a plain wood building with a pool table and a juke box. I think later it became a strip club, but I could be wrong. Anyway, we got juiced and piled into my car. I drove to the little gas station and store out on Butcherville Road. What in hell was that called?"

"Butcherville Store."

"That's right, Butcherville Store. What in f*** else would it be called? It was closed, but we filled up some empty whiskey bottles with what was left in the hoses."

He wagged his finger like a schoolteacher. "Remember, nephew: If you ever need to make a Molotov cocktail and all the gas stations are closed, you can get all the gas you need by draining what's left in the hoses."

"I'll remember that," I said.

He grinned. "Don't say I never taught you anything. So after we filled the bottles, we drove out to that little street where all the coloreds used to live."

"Jackson Corners."

"Yeh, Jackson Corners. We went out there and lit up that little house. If you want to call it that. Just a shack, really. I remember thinking we were probably doing them a favor." He spread his arms. "That's all there was to it. I got to admit, I thought it was exciting. I didn't think about what we was doin' to the people living there. I did feel bad about it later, after I heard what happened to them. I mean, it's one thing to burn down their house. Hearing about them getting killed was something else."

He didn't seem to be in any hurry to tell the rest. After a few moments, I had to ask.

"Who killed them?"

His face tensed. "I didn't have nothing to do with killing them, ok? Neither did Harold or Clyde. Not directly, at least. Nah, it was someone else."

That's not exactly what I'd expected to hear.

"If not Clyde and Harold, who did it? Smiley?"

He slouched and tapped his fingers on the table. "Nephew," he said, "I know what you must think. You haven't seen me for 25 years. You come to New York and find me working for the people I do. You hear stories about people like them. Hell, they make movies about people like them. Jimmy Cagney and Edward G. Robinson. Most of that stuff is bullshit. I'm not saying they're angels. This thing of theirs is a hard business."

"Isn't it your thing, too?

His face darkened. "Uh-uh. I'm not Italian. I work for them, but I can never *be* one of them. Not really. Anyway, listen to what I'm telling you. These guys don't put up with any shit. You cheat or lie, you're going to pay a heavy price. But they don't cheat or lie to each other. They have a sense of honor. They don't call them 'families' for nothing. Do they do bad things? To you, it might seem so. But their word means something. They live by a code. You break it, like I said, you're going to pay. People get hurt, no question. But it's always business. Never personal."

For someone who said 'no excuses,' it sure sounded like he was making one.

"You're a small-town cop," he said. "You probably think of yourself as some Lone Ranger-type making the world safe for truth, justice and the American Way. I know your folks believed in all that crap. But let me tell you this, Emmett. Some cops and politicians my boss deals with make him look like George f***ing Washington, ok? If Neil Dellacroce is such a bad guy, what does that make the guys on his payroll—guys way up in the police department and city government and state government? What does that make them?"

Just as bad. No. Worse.

"Neil can get at least one well-known United States senator on the phone any time of the day or night," he said animatedly. "He tells all these big shots—these honorable people—he tells them he needs something, and they make sure he gets it." He made a dismissive noise. "No offense, nephew, but cops are the worst. The cheapest goddam thing in the world is to pay a New York City cop to look the other way. These are the 'good guys' I'm talking about. You understand?"

What could I say?

"Sure, I understand."

"I'm not sure you do," he said grimly, "so let me spell it out for you. I'm saying: That colored family wasn't killed by some rednecks from Vernon Raymer's little club. They were killed by cops."

***

"The next night around ten o'clock I got a call from Harold. He said he needed to talk to me. He didn't say why, but it didn't take a shitload of imagination to figure it out. You get me?" I nodded. "We met at that same bar in Butcherville. Kenworthy came later, but when I got there, it was just Prentiss and Clyde. Harold said the Gene Autry guy wasn't comin'.""

"Smiley?"

He nodded. "Yeh. Smiley. He didn't say why. Anyway, Clyde told me Clarence Younger was dead, and so was his family."

So Clyde knew.

"How'd he know unless he was the one who killed them?"

"He saw who did it, or at least he claimed to, and I believed him. He'd heard around town the Youngers hadn't left like they were supposed to. They'd camped out by Burr Lake instead, which made Clyde nervous. After it got dark, he went out to check. He saw a couple of sheriff's deputies giving Clarence Younger a hard time, yelling at him and threatening him. Clarence yelled right back, standing up for himself. Suddenly, one cop pulled out a gun and shot Clarence in the head, then shot the wife and the little girl. The boy made a run for it. Clyde heard a gunshot and thought they'd gotten him, too, but wasn't sure. He watched the cops stuff the bodies into Clarence's car, roll it out onto the pier and push it into the water. I asked Clyde if he knew the cops. He said he did, but he wouldn't tell us who they were. He said that information might come in handy someday and he was going to hold on to it."

"He could've been lying," I said. "Making up a story to cover his own rear end."

"No f***ing way, nephew. Clyde didn't have it in him to kill those people. Trust me. When he told us, the little chickenshit bastard was shaking like a leaf."

As someone who'd recently been abducted by an Oklahoma state trooper working in cahoots with at least one Texas Ranger, the story seemed all too plausible.

"Is that why you skipped town?"

"A cop who commits a murder won't think twice about framing someone for the crime. I'd have been a prime suspect. Probably *the* prime suspect. It didn't occur to me they'd be able to cover the whole thing up."

"Did Clyde have any idea why the sheriff's deputies would've done something like that?"

"He thought his father must've put them up to it. Vernon wanted them gone. By staying, Clarence was flipping him the bird. Vernon couldn't stand that, so he had them whacked. It surprised me back then. It doesn't now. You wouldn't believe some things Neil pays cops to do."

"Yeh, but this is New York."

He gave me a pitying look. "Are you not listening to what I'm saying, nephew? Cops are the same everywhere. I guess some of them are Boy Scouts and help little old ladies cross the street and all that horseshit. But for the right price, plenty of them will work for either side of the law. Cops are like anyone else. They're out for themselves."

I looked out the window. Snow fell. A line of cars shining headlights in the daytime following a black hearse drove by. New York and Oklahoma have funerals in common, too.

I took a sip of my coffee. It had gone cold.

"You could've stayed," I said. "Nothing came of it. Anyone who knew the Youngers had been killed kept it to themselves. If it wasn't for Rufus Kenworthy getting sick and trying to get into heaven, no one would have ever known."

Ernie sighed. "Probably so, but I'd already stayed as long as I wanted. These boots were made for walking. Just like the song." His face brightened. "You know, that Nancy Sinatra sure is a hot little piece. Did I ever tell you I met her dad?"

"Frank? You met Frank Sinatra?"

I love Frank Sinatra.

"Yeh, I drove Neil and Mr. Gambino to Atlantic City one time to see him sing. Afterwards, Mr. Gambino said, 'Let's go say hi to Frank.' I had my picture taken with him. I'll show it to you one of these days."

He looked at his watch, one of those expensive Rolex jobs. "Nephew," he said. "This has been great, but I'd better get back. How long you going to be in town?"

"I'm not sure yet. Not long, though."

He got up and borrowed a pen from the lady behind the register. "Here," he said, scribbling on a napkin. "This is my phone number. For now, at least. Call me if you're going to be around. I promise, I can show you a real good time."

"I'll bet you can."

"Anyway, I want to hear what's going on with you. Did you ever marry that cute little gal? What was her name? Benny?"

"Denny. Denny Kinney. No. She married Edgar Bixby."

"She married that piece of shit? When she could've had you?"

"It all worked out. I ended up with someone better."

"Glad to hear it, buddy. You'll have to tell me about her some time."

We paid our bill and walked out into the cold and wet.

"You ok finding your way back?" he asked.

I couldn't remember if he knew I'd once lived in the city. I decided not to mention it. "Yeh, I'll be fine," I said and held out my hand. He grabbed it, pulled me close, kissed me on the cheek and gave me another bearhug. "You take care of yourself," he said, holding my face between his meaty hands. "And take care of my little brother, ok?"

"I will," I said. "Hey, that wasn't one of those 'kisses of death,' was it?"

He laughed. "You watch too many movies, kid."

CHAPTER THIRTY ONE

The slate-gray sky was getting darker. It gets late early around here. I stopped at a phone booth on Houston Street. It was a relief not having snow pelt my face.

I dialed Hary's office. "I'm finished talking to Ernie," I said.

"Did he tell you what you needed to know?"

"Not everything, but I know more than I did."

"That's cool," he said quickly. "Hey, man, you need to move your ass over here fast."

"What's going on?"

"I'll tell you when you get here. Just make tracks, baby."

In that snow making tracks was easy. Making good time wasn't. The soles of those goddam cowboy boots felt like they were coated in motor oil. The temperature was colder than a witch's you-know-what, too. I passed by a second-hand clothing store on 1st Avenue. I went in and bought a Brooks Brothers overcoat for five dollars. I reckon I got a pretty fair deal. I put it on over the denim jacket.

The streetlights had switched on by the time I got to Hary's office. There were no bicycle messengers in sight. I asked Hary where Florine was. "She has a gig tonight out on Long Island, so I let her go early." He looked me over. "Nice coat, man."

"Brooks Brothers," I said. "Five dollars at that Goodwill Store over on 1st Avenue."

"Smart, man. No one this side of 14th Street pays full price."

"So what's going on?"

"We need to get you on a plane out of here, buddy."

"Uh-oh."

"Uh-oh is right," he said. "I got a call from the 9th Precinct from a Detective—" he looked down at some notes written on a piece of paper. "A Detective Miller. Our friend from last night tried to check himself into a hospital. They called the cops. This detective braced the punk. The kid gave it up easy. Told him what happened and where. This Miller cat matched it to my story, except the kid said the guy who shot him wasn't the guy he mugged. You dig where I'm going with this?"

"The detective wants to talk to you about this other guy."

"The other guy being you."

"Me."

"Exactly. I'm going to tell him it was just a Good Samaritan who rode off into the sunset." He smiled. "That's almost the truth, anyway."

He pushed his phone across the desk. "Call your airline and book the first available flight back home."

I took out my wallet to make sure my ticket was still there. It was. "I don't want to leave you facing this all yourself."

"Ah, don't worry, man," he said. "This is nothing. But it's best to get you as far away from here as possible, as soon as we can."

I called the airline. The lady on the phone told me there was a plane to Chicago out of JFK at seven-fifteen, but the connecting flight to Oklahoma City wouldn't take off until the next morning. I said that would be ok. I've slept in plenty worse places than airports.

"Alright," said Hary. "You're going to have hustle if you're going to make it on time. Take a cab." He reached for his wallet. "You ok, bread-wise?"

"I'm not taking your money," I said. "I'm fine. In fact, I owe you for your services."

"Are you kidding, man?" he said. "This might be the easiest case I've ever had. As soon as you told me who your uncle worked for, I knew exactly where to go. Anyway, we saved each other's asses many times in Korea. Who knows who owes who?"

Hary was waiting for an important phone call, so he couldn't leave, and I had to drop by his apartment to get my stuff. "Let yourself in and keep that spare key. You might need it again someday."

We shook. "This has been a memorable 24 hours," I said. "I owe you one"

"Hey, no problem, man. It was a gas seeing you again. Do me a favor and keep playing your horn. You got something inside that needs to come out, brother."

"Thanks for helping me find that out," I said.

"Alright man, later," he said.

"Later, buddy." I moved toward the door, then remembered something. "You expect to see Sophie any time soon?" I asked.

"Yeh, we're rehearsing tomorrow."

"Tell her I said goodbye, and that I'm sorry we can't have dinner. Tell her I'll be calling her about that thing were talking about. She'll know what it means."

He smiled. "You mean the divorce?"

I laughed. "Yup."

"Will do, man. Now split or you're going to miss your plane and you'll have to stay here and work for me."

"Playing saxophone or being a private eye?"

"Both," he said. "You got skills, man. I could use you."

"I'll think about it."

"You should."

***

I picked up my satchel and caught a cab to the airport. The roads were a mess and the traffic was terrible. After all that rushing around, there was a delay because of the weather. We sat at the gate a long while before we finally were given clearance to take off.

We landed in Chicago after midnight. I was hungry, but the only thing open was a bar, and I didn't want to tempt fate. I stretched out across several seats in the waiting area and used my satchel as a pillow. I slept as well as I ever do.

The next morning, I ate breakfast in an airport diner. I read that morning's *Chicago Tribune*. Lots of crime in Chicago. Dangerous place to live,

I guess. Worse than Burr? Hard to know. Crimes in Burr don't always get written about in the newspaper. You can read an article about some old boy who found a family of possums living in his car 40 years after it happened, but stories about a black family's house being burnt down get erased from history by someone with a pair of scissors.

This time I didn't have to rush to make my plane. I called Karen collect and told her I was on my way home. The flight was uneventful. Once I landed in Oklahoma City, it took almost as long to find Red's car as it took to fly from Chicago to Oklahoma. I had to spend half my life's savings to get out of the lot. I wondered if Neil Dellacroce had ever considered getting into the airport parking racket.

The weather in Oklahoma City was sunny and mild. Compared to how it had been in New York, it almost felt like summer. I stopped at a Burger Chef in Mustang on the way home. My meal was a disappointment. Drive-in hamburgers were all starting to taste the same.

The drive home gave me time to think and plan. If my uncle was right, the Youngers and their car were somewhere on the bottom of Burr Lake. The old pier rotted away years ago, but those few stumps still stuck up out of the water where it used to be. I'd have to find a decent swimmer willing to dive and see if there's a car down there. Maybe one of those crazy bastards who catch catfish with their bare hands.

I could be wanted by the law for what had transpired with Leander McNelly and his Texas Ranger friend, although I thought that unlikely, since what they'd done was clearly a rogue operation.

The two people in the best position to help me were Rex McKinnis, the Tilghman County District Attorney, and Sheriff Burton Murray. Rex is honest. Burt can be, but it's always a roll of the dice. I reckoned they'd both have to be brought into the loop, eventually. I'd start with Rex.

It was mid-afternoon when I hit the Burr city limits. I couldn't resist taking the turnoff to the lake again, now that I knew for sure the Youngers had been killed and dumped there.

I'd been thinking about things, and I reckoned the lake might have filled up quite a bit since 1940. I looked out to where the pier once stood. The nearest visible piling was about 100 yards from the water's edge. The pier had extended even further than that, over the section of shore where the water was deepest.

If the Youngers were out there, I hoped Rex or Burt could marshal enough resources to recover the remains. Rufus Kenworthy's wish might come true: The Youngers could finally get their Christian burial, after all.

As I got to town, I ran into Kenny Harjo, on patrol in the Galaxie. We stopped in the middle of the street and rolled down our windows. "The return of Peter Gunn!" he said. Kenny likes those old detective shows. "How was New York?" he said.

"Big," I said. "What'd I miss?"

"About what you'd expect."

"That much?" I said.

He grinned. "I caught Dizzy getting in Mrs. Hughes' trash, but that's about it."

"You didn't run her in, did you?"

"Mrs. Hughes? Nah, but I took Dizzy back to the station. Karen's got him. She's at the station now. She'll give you the scoop."

A fella behind me in a blue Ford tapped his horn. I told Kenny I'd see him later.

The Fury was parked in the "Reserved for Chief Hardy" parking spot, meaning that, unless it had broken down again, Bernard was there, too.

I received a warm welcome.

Bernard said, "Welcome back, Chief."

I'd given up reminding him that until January 1st, 1967, he was the chief.

I said, "Thanks, buddy," and looked around. "Where's Dizzy?"

Karen said, "She's at my house," then scooted out from behind her desk and gave me a hug. "You ok?" she asked.

I said, "Yeh, I'm ok, considering I'm wanted in two states. Or maybe three, I don't know."

They already knew about Oklahoma and Texas, but throwing New York into the mix required an explanation. I swore them to secrecy and told them about my Manhattan adventure. I left out the part about seeing my ex-wife, but I included the episode where I shot a genuine New York street punk. Not everyone gets to do that.

"Just another day at the office, then," said Bernard.

"Yeh, pretty much."

"I'm going with you next time," said Karen.

"Not going to be a next time."

"Well, I'm going anyway" she said. "Someone's got to be there to keep you out of trouble."

"Hary did an ok job."

"Doesn't sound like it to me."

She had a point.

"Has there been any blowback from my joy ride in Leander McNelly's trunk?"

"That reminds me," said Karen. "Let me see those wrists." I rolled up my sleeves. I unwrapped the bandages I'd changed in the men's room at Will Rogers before I left the airport. I thought my wounds looked better, but she didn't agree.

"Did you go to a doctor?" she asked sternly.

"Didn't have time."

"You're going today." She picked up the phone, called Dr. Pepper—yes, the town doctor's last name is Pepper—and made me an appointment. "He'll see you at 3:00," she said.

"You didn't answer my question."

Bernard answered for her. "I called Sheriff Murray right after you got hauled off. He said he'd look into it. I called Rex McKinnis, who, to tell you the truth, sounded more concerned than Burt. Then I called the Highway Patrol headquarters in Oklahoma City. They said they had no record of a trooper being in Burr at that time. They said they'd investigate and get back to us, but they never did. This was all on ... what, Tuesday? Wednesday? The days are all running together. Anyway, I've called Burt several times today but haven't been able to get through to him. I don't know if he wasn't there or if he doesn't want to talk to me. I did get through to Rex. He basically says he's asking everybody questions, but he's not getting any answers."

"What about this Leander McNelly?"

Karen asked, "You mean the trooper who picked you up?"

"Yup."

"The Highway Patrol claims they don't have a trooper by that name," said Bernard. "I thought it sounded familiar, so I asked Kate over at the library if she'd ever heard it. She tells me the real Leander McNelly was a Confederate war hero during the Civil War. Later on, he became a big shot in the Texas Rangers."

Karen added, "... who died in 1877."

"So you're saying this is a different fella?" I said.

"I'd say it's likely," she said blandly, "although some crazy 'south-will-rise-again' yahoo could've named his son after him."

"Well, whoever it was, I got his badge, so we should be able to find him. Any word on what happened to him after I left him in front of the whorehouse?"

"I drove out after things calmed down, Wednesday morning," said Bernard. "The car was gone. The diner and the girls had closed up. I went back yesterday. Nobody in the diner saw anything, but Yvette says someone in a dark sedan came by about an hour after you left. Both cars left without bothering anybody."

"Nobody's come around asking for me?"

Karen nodded. "Keith called me at home the day after it happened." Keith Belcher is the only Tilghman County sheriff's deputy worth a damn, in my opinion, and I'm not saying that just because we're friends. "I didn't tell him anything," she added, "just said you were fine, and I'd have you call him when you got back."

I asked Bernard where they'd stashed Yvette's VW.

"My Aunt Hannah's barn, like you said."

"Think you could help me get it back to Yvette?"

"I'll have Kenny or Jeff do it."

"Jeff still works here?" I said. "I can't remember the last time I saw that boy."

"He's still on the payroll," said Karen. "Whether he works is another question."

I had more to tell and questions to ask, but apparently at the moment I had a doctor's appointment. Red and I made arrangements to meet at Dad's house after work. In my absence, she'd hired Peggy Miller, who was already a hit with Dad. Peggy seemed to think Dad had improved just in the short time she'd been there.

"I'm sure having a cute girl around cheers him up," I said.

Bernard said, "Everett definitely likes the ladies, don't he?"

"Everett doesn't only like the ladies," said Karen archly, "he respects the ladies. If more men were like Everett Hardy, there'd be a lot fewer bachelors in this world."

I hope that part of my dad rubbed off on me. I think it did.

CHAPTER THIRTY TWO

Old Dr. Pepper has a face like a rhubarb pie left out in the rain, then stuffed into the rear end of a turkey that's been burnt to a crisp by a newlywed bride preparing her first Thanksgiving dinner. But he's delivered half the babies born in Burr after World War II and sincerely cares about his patients, which is what people expect from a country doctor.

I hadn't seen him since I'd been in the hospital, so I was forced to endure a several-minutes-long lecture on the evils of strong drink before he got down to examining my wrists. He unrolled my improvised bandages, made a face like I was trying to shove his head into a toilet, then wrote me a prescription for penicillin. His nurse showed me the correct way to apply the gauze. Apparently, I'd been doing it wrong.

I drove over to Miller's Drug. Everyone there seemed to have gotten news of my arrest. A couple of women asked me about it while I waited for the pharmacist to fill my prescription. I thanked them for their concern but said I couldn't tell them much; I was still in the dark about why it happened. They acted skeptical but didn't press the matter.

When I got to Dad's, he was sitting on the couch in instead of the easy chair, eating popcorn and watching television with Peggy Miller. She jumped up when she saw me and cried, "Chief Hardy, you're back!" Pieces of popcorn flew out of her mouth. "Whoops, sorry," she said and giggled. Dad laughed. I couldn't believe my ears.

"You remember me?" she said. Before I could say "yes," she added, "Miss Dean hired me while you were gone. I'm not just some crazy person who broke into your father's house."

I assured her I remembered her and that I'd been apprised of the situation.

"Good!" she said. "We're watching Match Game. Everett's real good at it. He guesses right almost every time." She picked up an empty glass from the end table and asked him if he wanted more iced tea. He said, "Ok." She said, "I'll be right back."

"How are you doing, Dad?" I asked.

He said, "Oh, I'm doing alright, I guess."

"This gal treating you right?"

He smiled and nodded. "Oh, I reckon she is."

I followed Peggy out to the kitchen.

"How'd you get him out of the chair?" I asked.

"I just said he was going to get saddle sores if he didn't get out of that chair once in a while. He thought that was funny and got right up, moved over to the couch." She filled the glass with water and ice and spooned in some instant tea. "Really, he's doing fine. He's telling jokes and everything."

"Telling jokes? My dad?"

She giggled. "Oh, sure! He's real funny. 'What do you call someone with no body and no nose?'"

I shrugged. "I don't know."

"Nobody knows!" she said and laughed so hard she almost spilled the tea.

We walked back out to the living room. "Hey Dad, how 'bout if we go out this weekend and shoot at some tin cans? Haven't done that in a while."

He nodded. "That'd be good," he said. His voice was hoarse but stronger than it had recently been. "You still got that .22 I got you for your birthday?"

"Yeh, I do dad, I've had it since I was a kid. I'll bring it along."

He looked at Peggy. "You shoot?" he asked.

"I got me a little gallery gun that only shoots .22 shorts, but I think that's something you two should do by yourselves."

He nodded. "Suit yourself."

Red came in the front door and kissed Dad on the cheek. Both women pretended to flirt with him, and he pretended not to realize they were pretending.

I asked Peggy about his appetite. She said she'd cooked him tuna casserole last night. "You should learn to make something besides fried chicken," he said.

We exchanged ornery looks.

It was clear Peggy had things under control, so Karen and I left.

Diz jumped all over Karen when we walked into her house, then saw me and went even crazier, jumping for joy at seeing me for the first time in a couple of days. We both petted him and Red laid out a bowl of dog food. Diz gorged.

I sat down on Karen's puffy couch and pronounced, "I'm tired."

She said, "I'll bet you won't have any trouble sleeping tonight."

I wouldn't take that bet.

She plopped down next to me. "I'm going to rest a minute before I cook," she said. "That's fine," I said.

We small-talked about my dad and how preliminary evidence seemed to show Peggy was a big help. I told Red that he and I were going shooting over the weekend. She thought it was a fine idea.

Before long, the conversation turned to the target on my back.

"The way I see it," Karen began, "we have different but related concerns here. What I'm most worried about is you. By digging around, you made some people nervous. We don't know if that trooper was part of a plan to kill you or scare the heck out of you. Whatever it was, it isn't good."

"I'd like to know who that fella was." I pulled his badge from the pocket where I'd been carrying it for several days, looked at it hard—willing it to reveal its secrets—then tossed it on the coffee table. "This could tell us, if we ask the right people."

"You want me to make some calls?"

"Probably not," I said. "A call from our department might set off some alarms. Better if we did it through someone not connected to the case."

"Rex McKinnis?" she said.

"I was thinking Keith Belcher."

"What about Burt?" Red asked. "You going to keep him up to date?"

"I'll go to Burt when I get my ducks in a row and not before. He likes to talk too much."

"What about the state?" she said. "A trooper involved in a scheme to kidnap a private citizen is a case for the Attorney General, if you ask me."

I nodded. "True. The problem is who to trust. Even going through Rex might not be the best idea. Much as I like him, he's a politician. For another, he has to work with Burt, who I kind of trust, but mostly don't, if you get my meaning."

"He also has dealings with the Highway Patrol."

"Yep, he works with them, too." I paused. "I think I'll go to Keith first, ask him to dig around. Except for my own people, he's the only one I'm sure will do the right thing."

Red popped a piece of Dentyne into her mouth. "Let's move on to issue number two: Who did what to the Younger family? The way you tell it, the only fella who knows everything that happened is Clyde Raymer."

"He's not going to give us anything."

"No, he's not." She snapped her gum. "He almost has to be behind your fake arrest and the other delightful things they'd planned for you."

"I agree," I said. "Which means there's some connection between him and Leander McNelly, or whatever his name is. Not to mention Frank Sallee."

She arched her eyebrows. "Who's Frank Sallee?"

"I have no idea. Frank Sallee was the name on the ID card in the Ranger car. Whoever he is, maybe he's involved with this."

She nodded and chewed her gum. "It's a place to start."

"Exactly."

We sat quietly for a minute.

"If Clyde wasn't lying to your uncle and there really were two county deputies who killed the Youngers, who were they? They could still be around here somewhere." She shuddered. "Heck, it could even be Burt Murray. Wasn't he a sheriff's deputy back then?"

"He says he wasn't hired until '41."

She looked doubtful. "You believe him?" she said.

I chuckled. "Burt's a talker and a hustler and the type of person who'll smile to your face while he's picking your pocket, but he's no killer."

Karen nodded. "You're probably right. I've always liked the old fart."

"Me too, although for the life of me, I'm not sure why."

A cricket chirped inside one of the living room walls.

"I think you should tell Rex what your uncle told you," Karen said. "Let him decide what to do about Clyde Raymer and whether he should drag the bottom of the lake and whatever other steps to take. But keep quiet about that badge until you find out who it belongs to. Keith should be able to help you with that." She paused. "That's what I think, anyway. For what it's worth."

"It's worth a lot. Food on the table would also be worth a lot, too. What's for dinner?"

"I thought I'd whip up a batch of goop."

Oh boy.

***

I was glad to be back, but I couldn't relax. Nothing seemed right. My worst fears about the Youngers had been confirmed. Clarence, his wife and daughter were dead. Gabe tried to get away, but the killers probably got him, too.

There's no way around it. My dad's reluctance to help the Youngers cost them their lives.

In his defense, he couldn't have known what was to happen. The fact remained, however: If he'd just let his family use our old bunkhouse that day, they might still be around.

Now, 26 years later, there I was, conducting a one-man, off-the-record investigation into the crimes, with the as-yet-unknown (or at the very least, unconfirmed) perpetrators trying to shut me up or kill me or both.

On top of everything, the killers were apparently cops.

Nah, relaxing wasn't in the cards.

We watched some television and went to bed before Carson's monologue. I tossed and turned. The cricket chirping in the wall didn't exactly help. A glass of bourbon would've helped, but falling off the wagon would've been the same as flushing the last three months of my life down the toilet. I wasn't ready to do that.

Karen huffed and puffed and eventually raised up on her elbows and said: "Darlin', I know you got a lot on your mind, but one of us is going to have to sleep on the couch. I got a long day tomorrow."

I said "I'm sorry. You go back to sleep." She covered her head with a pillow and muttered something about not being asleep to begin with. Diz was dead to the world at the foot of the bed. I asked Red if it she could stay. I heard a muffled "uh-huh" from underneath the pillow.

I got dressed and drove home, which was probably for the best. I'd parked in Red's driveway and I didn't want it sitting there the next morning for Reverend Hankins to cluck over.

Once home, since there was no possibility of sleep, I made myself a cup of coffee, sat at the kitchen table and planned out the next day. I reckoned I'd talk to Rex and Burt separately about the two different sides of the case. I'd talk to Rex about prosecuting the murders and Burt about hunting down whoever was out to get me.

And I'd ask Keith to find the owner of that badge.

Once everything was sketched out, I did what I usually do when I'm up all night: took my saxophone out of the case and blew.

After playing Hary's alto, I realized right way my own horn was in dire need of repair. I normally play along with a Charlie Parker record, but this time I closed my eyes and imagined I was back at Slugs', with Sophie and Horace and Florine behind me and Hary urging me on.

I played whatever came to mind. It didn't sound much like Charlie Parker.

It did sound like Emmett Hardy, for whatever that's worth.

CHAPTER THIRTY THREE

I called the sheriff's department dispatcher first thing in the morning and asked if Keith Belcher was on duty. She said he was due to report for his shift any minute and she'd have him return my call.

The phone rang five minutes later.

"Is this the fella who got abducted by the state trooper from outer space?"

"I'm of the opinion that it was a ghost, but you could be right. He was an ugly bastard."

Keith laughed. "Seriously, bud, how're you doing?"

"I'm fine, all things considering."

"I called Karen a couple of days ago, but she couldn't tell me much. What in hell happened?"

"You calling on an official line?"

"Kind of. I'm calling from the locker room."

"How 'bout we grab some coffee and I'll tell you all about it?"

"Cup O'Joe's?"

"I was thinking Mickey Pete's in Watie Junction."

"Mickey Pete's, huh?" he said, sounding puzzled, probably because nothing about Mickey Pete's is as good as Cup O'Joe's. Its only advantage was Burt Murray and his posse were much less likely to pop in.

"Alright," he said. "I'll see you in half an hour."

With at least one Oklahoma state trooper and a Texas Ranger out to get me, I was not about to go out into the world unarmed. I dug out a little clip-on holster I'd had lying around for years, stuffed Numb Nuts' .38 in it, and clipped the holster on the inside of my right boot.

Within thirty minutes, Keith and I were sitting cross from each other. Mickey Pete's does the term "greasy spoon" an injustice. The vinyl seat coverings in our booth were worn down to the foam rubber. Pretty near all diners have chunks of old, chewed bubble gum stuck underneath the table. The tables at Mickey Pete's have them on top. There were a couple of patches that would've taken a jackhammer to dislodge.

An indifferent waitress poured coffee and took our orders. Keith ordered bacon and eggs. I ordered sausage and toast.

Keith took a large swallow of coffee. "So I gather someone don't exactly like your looks," he said.

"Hard to imagine, I know," I said, then recounted the details of my abduction, along with an outline of the Younger case.

He whistled silently. "Holy Christ. Yeh, everybody at work's been talking about you being snatched. I thought the part about it being a state trooper might just be a rumor."

"Not a rumor, my friend," I said with a bitter laugh.

"And you didn't recognize the guy?"

"Come to think of it, he had a familiar look, but maybe that's just my imagination. I couldn't tell you who he was."

Keith nodded slowly. "I can tell you this much," he said, downing the rest of his coffee. "No one I talked to knows anything. Or if they do, they're not telling. Burt told me he's looking into it, but I got the feeling he'd rather not. This is the first I've heard about that Younger thing."

"I told Burt about it just before I this happened. He didn't seem interested then. Hopefully, he will be now."

"I wouldn't count on it. Sorting this out might require actual police work." The waitress topped off Keith's cup. I'd taken one sip and that was enough.

"What can I do to help?" he asked.

I pulled Leander McNelly's badge from my shirt pocket and pushed it across the table. "I was hoping you might find out who this belongs to."

Keith laughed. "Beat the shit out of him with handcuffs on, *and* you got his badge. Batman don't got nothing on you, does he?"

"Yeh, well, Batman probably would've remembered to write down the license plate number."

"Ah, yes," he said with a nod, "that would've been helpful. In fact, speaking of writing stuff down—" He took a pen from his pocket and wrote the badge number in his black notebook.

The waitress came our way, juggling enough plates to make an octopus jealous. She dropped ours off and moved on to the next table.

"I got a friend in the Highway Patrol who works out of Guymon," Keith said after a mouthful of cold scrambled eggs. "I was just asking him the other day if he'd heard anything about your situation. He said no one there has any idea who did it. The brass is keeping a lid on it." He examined the badge. "I'll bet he'd be more than willing to help us solve the mystery."

"Maybe, but I'd rather he not know that it was connected to what happened to me."

"Ah," he said, nodding. "That's probably a good idea. Don't worry, I'll make something up."

"Thanks, bud."

We finished as much of our food as we could stand.

Keith looked around to see if anyone was listening. "What do you think of this place?" he said in a low voice.

I summed it up simply: "Bad."

"Mmm-hmm," he said. "Cup O'Joe's is better."

"It is," I said, "but Cup O'Joe's has Burt Murray."

"Got ya," he said.

He pulled out the last paper napkin from the dispenser and wiped his mouth. I leaned over to the next empty booth and grabbed one for myself.

We paid the cashier and walked out to our vehicles parked side by side. The sky was overcast. The bank sign across the road said it was 32 degrees. After New York, I'll never complain about the cold again.

"Any idea when your friend might check that badge number?"

"I should have something for you tomorrow," he said, unlocking the door of his county cruiser. "Maybe tonight if we're lucky"

"That'll have to do," I said. "I appreciate it, bud."

"Glad to help. Have a good one. And watch your back."

I chuckled. "I'd grow a new set of eyes back there, if I could."

***

Rex McKinnis' predecessor as District Attorney would've sold out his mama for a box of animal crackers. Rex ran against him, promising to clean house, and won. He was as good as his word. Rex wasn't for sale.

As far as he's concerned, it doesn't matter who you are or how much money you have; if you do the crime, you'll do the time. Rex showed that when he sent Edgar and EJ Bixby to jail.

He would've gone after Clyde Raymer hammer and tongs, too, but the evidence just wasn't there.

On the other hand, he still has to work with the same sheriff and the same sheriff's department. His cases are only as strong as their investigations. Rex does the best he can, but with Burt in charge and a posse of redneck lackeys working under him—excluding Keith, of course—the quality of justice in Tilghman County remains uneven.

Like with Keith, I wanted to talk to Rex in private, which ruled out his office. I stopped at a 7-11 on my way out of Watie Junction and called him on a pay phone.

He asked how I was doing. I said that apart from the bandages on my wrists and my bruised pride, I was doing fine. I then asked if he had time to get together and talk. He suggested I come to his office. I said I'd rather avoid the courthouse and suggested Mickey Pete's.

"Mickey Pete's?" he said. "You realize the food there's pretty bad, right?"

"Yeh, I know. I'll just have a cup of coffee," I said without mentioning that it was as bad as the food.

He sighed. "Alright, then. Mickey Pete's it is. I'll see you there in a half-hour."

***

I sat in my truck in front of Mickey Pete's and waited for Rex. I'd decided to share details on a need-to-know basis. Given what had happened so far, a certain measure of stealth was justified when dealing with my law enforcement brethren. Even Rex.

I was a little hesitant to tell him about the part my uncle played in all this, although Ernie was so far away and his role so limited, I doubted it would matter. Arson was the extent of his involvement, and the statute of limitations on that had run out long ago. I was after whoever killed the Youngers, and there's no statute of limitations on murder.

Rex pulled up next to me in a cream-colored Ford Thunderbird. The hairs on my necked usually stand up when I see a county official driving a fancy car, but I figure Rex must've come by it honestly. Even honest lawyers make good money.

We sat in the same booth I'd shared with Keith. The same waitress poured our coffee and gave us menus. "I'm back," I said with a smile. She gave me a dirty look and walked away.

"I was just here," I explained to Rex.

"Did you tip her?"

"Not enough, I guess."

We watched her walk away. "Something's got her goat," he said, then turned back to me. "So tell me what happened."

I could tell the story in my sleep by now, although I had to take care to exclude certain things.

He shook his head when I'd finished. "I'm going to find out what's going on with this, Emmett. Burt seems to want to slow-walk it, and the Highway Patrol hasn't been cooperative at all. I called your friend at the OSBI, what's his name—"

"Agent Jones?"

"Right, Ovell Jones, the one we worked with on the Cheryl Foster case. He seemed genuinely angry about it and said he's going to investigate it, too, so we've got him on our side." He tapped on the underside of the table. "Knock on wood."

"To tell the truth, there's something else I wanted to talk to you about," I said.

The waitress interrupted. Rex ordered a club sandwich. I ordered a Coca Cola. She walked away, no happier than before.

"Anyway," I said, "what I really wanted to talk to you about was an unsolved case we have in Burr dating back to 1940. You ever heard of an organization called The Sons of Aaron Burr Society?"

He shook his head.

"I hadn't either until recently. It was a social club in Burr back in the late '30s, early '40s. Supposedly, they modelled themselves on the Masons, but I got hold of a copy of their rule book, and it's copied almost word for word from the Klan's."

"Not good," said Rex. "Are they still around?"

"I don't think so. I suspect they more or less disbanded after they accomplished their primary goal."

"Which was?"

"Running all the black folks out of Burr."

"Hmmph," he said. "I didn't know Burr ever had a negro population."

"Hard to believe, I know, but we did. From what I gather, members of this club hounded all the black people out of town. The Youngers were the last to go."

His made a thinking face. "Why does that name sound familiar?"

"You could've seen it reading through old case files. Their house was burnt down in the summer of '40."

He nodded slowly. "That's right. I remember. No one was ever prosecuted for it, were they?"

"White folks didn't get prosecuted for burning down black folks' houses back then."

"Yeh, I'm sure you're right. More likely they'd get a medal for it."

"I knew about it when it happened, but not who did it. When it was over people hardly ever talked about it. I always thought it was because they were ashamed, but I few days ago I was told a story that makes me think there's more to it than that."

I then recited another story I now knew by heart: the Younger tragedy, including their deaths at the hands of sheriff's deputies as witnessed by Clyde Raymer, who told my uncle what he'd seen.

"Ernie admits he helped burn the place, but says he had nothing to do with their deaths. No one can touch him now, anyway. He knows that.

Everything he said lines-up with what Harold Prentiss told Rufus Kenworthy, plus the part about this Smiley being involved."

The waitress served our food.

"It's all hearsay, though," Rex said, then took a bite out of his sandwich. "Is there any hard evidence?" he said with his mouth half full.

"I reckon there might be some sitting at the bottom of Burr Lake."

He nodded and ate.

"I don't know about forensic evidence," he said, "since there wouldn't be much left of them after all these years. But you never know. At least finding the actual bodies would give me a reason to investigate further. I imagine it would be enough to interest the OSBI, too."

"I can show you where it occurred. I was just out there the other day. You can still see the pilings sticking up out of the water where the pier used to be."

Rex munched some potato chips. "Well," he said, "it's likely what happened to you is related to this. Unless you have some skeletons in your closet I don't know about."

"I probably do, but nothing that would cause something like that to happen."

He looked at his watch and scarfed down what was left of his sandwich. "My Lord," he said with a sardonic smile and stifling a belch. "That was the worst sandwich I've ever had. Alright, I got to get going. Let me look into this, and we'll see where it leads. With Clyde Raymer in the picture, this could be a big deal." He lowered his voice. "Keep it to yourself, but he's still officially under investigation for the Collins murder."

That little piece of news turned the contents of my stomach upside down.

"How would that affect this?" I asked.

"Let's keep the two things separate for now," he said. "Don't share this with anybody."

He handed me a five and asked if I'd mind paying, since he was in a rush to get back to the courthouse. I said that'd be fine. On his way out he said, "You should probably go to the sheriff about this, too. You know the history of this better than I do. I think you could bring home the importance of this in a way he'd understand."

I had my doubts, but he was the lawyer. "Ok, if that's what you think I should do."

He winked. "Don't worry, we'll figure this out."

I promised him I wouldn't give it a second thought.

CHAPTER THIRTY FOUR

Kate Hennessey was checking out a book to a little girl about three-feet tall wearing a plaid jumper and a dark pink wool coat roomy enough to accommodate a twin sister if she had one. Kate saw me and smiled.

Pinky scooted past me out the door.

Kate said, "Back from the big city?"

"You heard about that, huh? You miss me while I'm gone?"

Her face turned a shade darker than the little girl's coat. "What can I do for you today, Chief?"

"I was going to ask you another favor."

"Does it involve the microfilm machine?"

"Sorry, but it does."

She chuckled. "That's fine. What do you need?"

"I'm trying to find out the identities of any Tilghman County Sheriff deputies from around the time the Youngers were run out of town. I was thinking there might be mention of them in the newspapers from around that time. Or do you have records of some sort that would have those names? I reckon I could probably ask around the courthouse, but I'm trying to steer clear of it for the time being."

"Sounds a little like looking for a needle in a haystack, to be honest."

"I know, and I hate to ask you to spend time on it. I wouldn't if it wasn't important."

She brushed a strand of hair out of her face. "Does it involve catching bad guys?"

"It most surely does."

"Well then, I'm glad to do it," she said. "I believe you owe me a dinner, anyway. If I find what you're looking for, I'll order steak."

"Sounds like the deal of the century."

***

I went to the station to use the telephone and check in with Red, who was tending the store. I asked her what she'd done with Dizzy. She'd fed him and sent her on her rounds.

I thanked her and told her I needed to make a call.

She asked, "Is it local?"

"Is Butcherville local?"

She pushed the phone where I could reach it. "Go on, then," she said.

"Would you mind looking up Clyde's number?" I asked.

She opened her side drawer, dug out the directory and tossed it down on the desk. "You got eyes."

"So that's how it's going to be," I muttered and thumbed through the pages until I got to the R's. No luck. "Unlisted," I said.

"Alright, hold on," she said irritably.

She sighed and scrolled through her Rolodex.

"You could've done that in the first place," I said.

She gave me a look. I smiled sweetly.

She found the card and handed it to me.

"Much obliged," I said.

Clyde's wife, Clara, answered after five rings. I asked for her husband. She said he left early in the morning for the construction site and I could probably reach him there. I thanked her and said goodbye.

"I'm heading out to WestOK and try to track down Clyde."

"Alert the media," she said.

"What's the matter with you?" I asked. "You mad because you didn't get to wake up to my handsome face?"

"Oh, I'm sorry," she said, her eyes coming to rest on the six-inch-tall stack of papers clogging her 'In' basket. "Bernard gave me a bunch of reports to type up." She's been itching to get out from behind the desk and do come real policing.

"You want me to talk to him?" I asked.

"Nah, don't worry about it. Someone's got to do it. I'd just like us to take turns, is all— either that or hire someone whose job it is." She tried on a more pleasant expression. "You intend to ask Clyde about the Youngers?"

I nodded. "I don't expect him to give me a straight answer, but I've got to ask."

Red said, "You watch yourself."

I said, "I always do."

She groaned and slapped her forehead. "No," she said exasperatedly. "You never do."

***

Clyde wasn't at the plant. I tracked down the foreman, who told me he'd been there for an hour but left before lunch. It was now well past lunch. I asked him if he had any idea where Clyde had gone off to. He said 'no,' in so many very colorful words.

As I was leaving, the contents of a truck being unloaded caught on fire. I stayed for a couple of minutes and watched. Nobody got hurt and I don't imagine it burned for too much longer after I left, but I reckoned anything that set back the project was a positive development for the community. In other words, the trip wasn't a total waste.

I started to go to Dad's place, but before I got there, I ran across him and Peggy taking a walk.

I slowed, rolled down my window and inched along with them. "What're y'all up to?" I asked.

"Just getting' some air," said Peggy.

"Yup, just getting' some air," said Dad.

"I was thinking we'd go out shooting on Sunday, Dad. I got this little gun I've been wanting to show you."

He stopped walking . "What do you got?"

I pulled over, reached down and took Numb Nuts' gun out of my boot. Dad walked over from the sidewalk to take a look. I handed it to him. "It's a little private eye-type of gun. A Charter Arms Undercover .38 Special snub-nosed revolver."

He swung open the cylinder to see if it was loaded. It was. He snapped it shut.

"You ain't going to hit much with that short little barrel," he scoffed.

I grinned. "Well, Dad, you know me and handguns."

He nodded. "Yeh, I reckon I do. You're a hell of a shot. Never seen better."

He'd never said that to me before.

"How 'bout I come get you tomorrow after lunch?"

"Ok," he said and turned to Peggy. "You want to come along?"

Peggy shook her head and smiled. "Y'all go on."

Dad said, "Suit yourself."

I left them and headed for home. I came across Dizzy running with some of her dog buddies, so I stopped and opened the passenger door so she could jump in. I believe she may have stuck out her tongue to her friends as we drove away.

I treated Diz to an early dinner of Gravy Train when we got home, then undid any of the messes I might have made since I'd last cleaned house. If I was going to turn over a new leaf, I aimed to keep it turned over. This place had originally belonged to my grandparents, Pearl and Bunk Hardy. It's a nice little house. They left it to me when they died. The least I could do is to take better care of it.

I'd recently hired a stone mason to refurbish my grandfather's old fire pit in the back yard and was planning on unveiling it to Red over the holidays. The rest of the backyard still needed work, but the fire pit looked great. I'm not handy at anything, and I'm terrible at planting flowers and trees and such. I manage to keep the weeds mowed but that's about it. Lately, I've been remembering the good times I had in this backyard when I was little. I've often wondered what it would be like to have my own kids playing in the same back yard. Maybe I'll find out one of these days.

Given that my investigation had stalled for the time being, I thought I'd call the sheriff and rattle his cage. I didn't expect to get through but I hoped to at least get him a message. To my shock, his secretary put me straight though to him like they expected me to call.

"Emmett, is that you?" Burt said, his voice slightly garbled. Probably chewing on those sunflower seeds.

"Yeh, Burt, hey, I was wondering if I could come in to talk to you this afternoon. I got something important I think you need to know about, and it's not something we should be talking about on the phone."

"Yeh, I got a pretty good idea what it is," he said. "I'm running around like a chicken with my head cut off today. How 'bout you came out to my place tonight around nine o'clock? Give us more time to talk."

I'd only seen Burt's house from the outside. I was curious to see what it looked like on the inside.

I told him I'd see him at nine.

As soon as I hung up, a wave of exhaustion swept over me. I called Karen at the station and asked if she'd mind checking on my dad after work. I told her I was going out visit Burt at nine o'clock and I was tired and needed to take a nap. She was in a better mood than when I'd left and said she'd be glad to. I thanked her and said I'd come by her place when I was done at Burt's.

I then collapsed in my La-Z-Boy and slept for four hours.

CHAPTER THIRTY FIVE

The house was dark when I awoke and for just a second I thought I was back at Hary's apartment. I soon got my bearings, and, as a reflex, reached down beside me on the floor where I used to keep a bottle of Old Grand Dad.

Nope, I said to myself, I don't do that anymore.

I turned on the lights and looked at the clock. It was a little after eight. If I was going to meet Burt at 9:00, I needed to get a move on.

My wrists were feeling better—not great, but I could tie my shoes and scratch my elbow and perform most basic functions without experiencing too much discomfort. I took some of the penicillin Dr. Pepper had prescribed, which I'd neglected to do earlier. I peeled off the bandages and applied the salve he'd given me.

It stunk like rotten cabbage, and since I wasn't exactly smelling like a bouquet of roses, anyway, I decided to take a quick shower first. I got out, towelled off and applied the salve. The smell wasn't quite as strong once I covered it with bandages.

I took a peek outside to gauge the temperature. The water in Dizzy's drinking bowl was frozen over. That told me what I needed to know.

I put on a pair of jeans and a flannel shirt, wool socks, and boots. I reached into the bedroom closet for the Brooks Brothers overcoat I bought in New York. I changed my mind and grabbed my insulated Marine field jacket, instead. I tossed it on my bed and strapped-on the shoulder holster for my Colt .45 semi-auto.

Numb Nuts' little Charter Arms was fine for what it was, but until this situation was resolved, I wasn't about to leave the house unless I was armed to the teeth.

I put my denim jacket on over the .45, and the field coat over that. I grabbed my keys, said goodbye to Dizzy, and started for the door.

The phone rang. I picked up.

"Chief, this is Kate down at the library."

"Hey, Kate, I'm on my way out. Could I call you tomorrow?"

"I just wanted to tell you, I found a picture of a Tilghman County deputy from January 1940 in the Temple City paper."

"You're working late." I said.

"Yeh, I lost track of time," she said hurriedly. "Anyway, it's a photograph of a young man alongside a police car with a 1939 license plate."

"What's his name?"

"Frank Sallee."

What a tangled goddam web we weave.

I thanked her and rushed out to my truck. My tires spewed gravel. Frank Sallee was a Tilghman County sheriff's deputy when the Youngers were killed.

Now he's a Texas Ranger and coming after me.

That must mean he was the fourth man in the car with my uncle that night.

Frank Sallee was Smiley. Had to be.

Two deputies murdered the Youngers. Now I knew one.

One down, one to go. Shouldn't be too hard to find the other.

***

I've always associated multi-storied mansions with millionaires. When I was a kid, I saw a movie called *The Magnificent Ambersons* about a family that use to be rich but ended up losing everything. Their mansion had more rooms than a possum has tits and enough stairs to take you to heaven if you lined them all up in a row. The two richest SOBs in Tilghman County, Edgar Bixby and Clyde Raymer, built themselves houses like that.

Maybe Burt Murray wasn't as wealthy as those two. Maybe he was but didn't want to call attention to the fact. For whatever reason, his house was enormous but close to the ground, stretching across his property like a skyscraper laid on its side.

Maybe he just doesn't like to climb stairs.

His house was set a couple of hundred yards from the road. It was built to resemble an old-fashioned log cabin, although I reckoned there's some fakery going on somewhere.

Burt probably built it like that so regular people will see it and think he's just like them—a hard-workin' good ol' boy unafraid of getting his hands dirty. Like the founders of Tilghman County, although, in point of fact, the men and women who founded this county might've had trouble building even a regular-sized log cabin even if they'd wanted to, never mind one the size of Burt's. In those days, there wasn't hardly enough timber in these parts to build a pig pen.

If Burt really wanted to be authentic he would've built his house out of sod.

The house was dark except for a light in a window at the far east end. I eased into the driveway, which accommodated four separate garage doors. The only vehicle visible was a county cruiser. Clyde's personal cars would've been parked inside.

It was quiet except for the sound of an occasional passing truck in the distance. The chirring of bugs that dominates the soundscape of spring and summer was absent.

My boots clicked on the glazed concrete. The sound seemed amplified, somehow.

The doorbell played the first few notes of "Boomer Sooner."

A small plastic speaker above the doorbell—not unlike the one at the Ravenite Social Club—emitted a burst of static. A tinny voice spoke, not with a New York accent, but with an Okie twang.

"Who's there?" I announced myself. "Come on in, Emmett," Burt said in a sing-song rhythm. "I'm in my office in the back." The door buzzed and unlocked itself.

I opened it and went inside. It was darker indoors than it was out, but I decided it wasn't my place to switch on the light. As well as I could make out, the front room was about the size of a basketball court. I put my hand on the wall. It was indeed made of logs.

The floor was covered wall to wall in green shag carpet split down the middle by a walkway made of polished stone tiles. It stopped after about thirty feet and branched off into two long hallways. A light shined under a door at the end of the one on my left. I walked toward it.

The door was slightly ajar. I knocked lightly. Burt said, "Come in." I pushed open the door. Burt was sitting behind a heavy oak desk at the wall opposite from where I stood. Mounted above him was an eight-point bull elk's head. He wore a light-blue western suit. Either he'd had it for a while or was unduly optimistic about slimming-down when he bought it. His white dress shirt was unbuttoned at the collar, adorned by a leather bolo tie with a silver and turquoise clasp.

Burt's office or den or whatever it was may have been bigger than my entire house. On one side was a huge gas- or electric-powered fireplace with fake logs glowing bright orange. Venetian blinds were drawn on all the windows. Two small couches sat across from each other in the middle of the room. A coffee table sat in-between.

On the walls were hung photographs of Burt posing with fish he'd caught, game he'd shot, and famous people he'd sucked up to. Certificates and plaques attested to his boundless generosity and selflessness. In front of the desk was a plush armchair that matched the couches.

I was once again reminded of the Ravenite Social Club. "Members Only," the sign had said. Burt's room was fancier, but the motto—or warning— might well have been the same.

I sure as hell didn't belong here any more than I did there.

"Hey, Burt," I said.

He stood and waved me over. I made the long walk. We shook hands.

"Take a load off your feet," he said.

"You mind if I look around a little bit first? This place is like a museum."

"Sure, take your time," he said, obviously proud I'd been impressed. "Sorry I couldn't see you earlier, but things were crazy around the office. Could I get you something to drink?"

"Coca-Cola?"

"Comin' right up." He opened a door in a cabinet behind his desk, pulled out a Coke and a Lone Star beer. "I got this little refrigerator so I don't have to run out to the kitchen every time I want something cold." He opened both bottles with a church key, handed me the Coke and took a long swig of beer.

"Hell, this is the only part of the house that's mine. The rest belongs to my wife."

The room did bear his imprint. And then some. There was a picture of him shaking hands with Bud Wilkinson, another of him holding up a giant fish alongside Ted Williams. In one, a much-younger and beaming Burt stood with his arm draped around a smiling but confused-looking Kitty Wells. Behind them was a bus with "The Kitty Wells Show" painted on the side in big letters.

"*It wasn't God who made Honk-ee-tonk, A-a-ngels,*" Burt sang in a voice like a cross between Alfalfa's from *Our Gang* and a chicken that knows it's about to get its neck wrung. "That Kitty sure is a sweet lady," he said. "She asked me work for her as director of security. I'd just been elected sheriff for the first time, so I had to say no."

A plaque caught my eye: "The Vernon Raymer Award, given on this day, May 31st, 1959, by the citizens of Burr, Oklahoma to Sheriff Burton Murray, in appreciation for his lifetime of service to the Town of Burr and the citizens of Tilghman County."

Burt lowered himself into his chair. "Take a seat, Emmett, and tell me what's on your mind."

I took off my field jacket, draped it over the back of one of the couches, removed my hat and laid it on top of the jacket. I sat down and nearly disappeared into the cushions of the overstuffed chair in front of the desk.

"To be honest, Burt, I hardly know where to begin. I reckon you know what happened after I talked to you the other day."

He clasped his hands behind his had and leaned back. "I sure do," he said like he found it funny, somehow. "You're doing alright after all that, are ya?"

"Not as good as new yet, but I'm getting there."

"So fill me in," he said.

I don't know if it was the surroundings, or his skeptical attitude, but I got a sudden a case of stage fright and couldn't remember a word of what I'd been prepared to say.

Burt sensed my discomfort. "Let me ask you something, Emmett," he said. "Have you ever done anything you were ashamed of?"

"Of course I have. Everyone has."

"That's right. Everyone has," he said like he was talking to a child. "And wouldn't you agree what's done is done and can't be changed?"

"I'd have to say yes. Up to a point."

"And what point is that?"

"Well, look at what we do for a living, Burt. We aren't exactly in the forgiving business, are we? We're in the 'putting-bad-guys-in-jail' business. We can't throw our arms up and say, 'Oh well, what's done is done.' Actions have consequences. If they didn't, we'd be out of a job. It'd be every man for himself. I don't want to live in that world, do you?"

He gave me the kind of look a cat gives a mouse he's got trapped in a bathtub. "Well, I sure as heck wouldn't appreciate being out of a job, that's for sure," he drawled. "But my job, as I see it, is to make sure good people don't get hurt. The way you've been sniffin' around, lookin' for someone to blame for a fire 25 years after the fact—and now you're saying the family was murdered, without a bit of evidence—well, Emmett, it seems misguided, if you understand my meaning."

He rubbed his stubble-covered cheeks and smiled patronizingly. His head revealed the greasy remains of a comb-over. I realized it had been a long time since I'd seen him without his hat. He'd lost a lot of hair in the interim. A businessman's Stetson hung on a hook behind his desk, next to an old badge mounted in a frame. Probably one of his from a long time ago.

"Actually, Burt ... yeh, I know what you mean, but I guess I'm not expressing myself very well. I didn't come here to talk about that. I wanted to fill you in on what happened to me the other day."

"So we're back to that, are we?" he said in an amused voice. "Wasn't that the darnedest thing?"

I laughed, not because it was funny, but because he seemed to regard it as no more serious than losing a sock in the dryer.

"I guess. I reckon I'd use harsher language to describe it."

"So does that mean you're giving up on this nonsense about the Youngers?"

"No, not exactly, but we can talk about that later. I talked to Rex this afternoon, and he thought I should tell you about—"

The phone on his desk rang. He picked it up.

"Hello," he said in a jovial voice.

Even from where I sat, I could hear who it was. "Sheriff Murray, this is Karen Dean from over in Burr." I swear, she might've been in the room with us. "I'm looking for Emmett. Is he there?"

"Yeh, he is, sweetheart, hold on a second." He held his hand over the mouthpiece and winked. "It's your lady friend." The cord didn't reach so I had to get up and stand by the desk to take the phone.

My eyes drifted to the mounted badge on the wall. Up close, I could read what it said: *101 Ranch Show, No. 7, Bill Pickett.*

I forced myself to keep a straight face and put the phone to my ear."What's up, Red?"

Shew said, "Emmett, just nod and pretend we're having a nice conversation."

Burt heard her, of course. Suddenly his smile seemed painted on.

"Ok," I said, pressing the phone to my ear tighter, trying to make it harder for him to eavesdrop.

"Keith just called. The trooper who abducted you is Joe Guthmiller, Jr."

It took me a second to process the name. Joe Guthmiller, Sr. had gone to school in Burr a few years behind me. His older sister was in my class. Her name was Katharina.

She got married after high school and became Mrs. Burton Murray.

I couldn't think what to say. She interpreted my silence to mean I didn't understand, and said, "Joe Guthmiller, Jr. is Burt's nephew."

Burt looked around as if he was expecting the cavalry to swoop in, then jerked open his desk drawer and fumbled with an ivory-handled Colt Peacemaker. I reached inside my denim jacket and pulled my .45.

Burt never had a chance.

CHAPTER THIRTY SIX

"*You're* Smiley," I said, thinking, in terms of stupidity, Harold Prentiss had nothing on me.

I edged behind the desk and put my gun to the side of Burt's head. His knuckles were white as he gripped the drawer handle. I told him to raise his hands. He complied.

I picked up his ivory-handled Colt and gave it a once-over. It was elaborately engraved, like one of those fancy guns Colts makes special for movie stars like John Wayne or Randolph Scott.

"You ever fire this thing?" I asked.

"Oh, it's been shot," he said wryly.

I was surprised at how calm he was—more like a fella who'd lost a hand of Crazy Eights than someone about to go to jail for a very long time, although he winced when I tossed his fancy pistol on the floor out of his reach.

Karen was still on the line, asking what was going on. I explained what had happened and told her I trusted her to do what needed to be done. She said she would. I hung up and walked back around to the front of the desk.

"I had the dang phone turned up extra loud for Kath," Burt said, still sounding amused. "She's been goin' deaf for years. Won't get a hearing aid, though. Too vain."

He tilted back his chair and banged against the log wall hard enough to jiggle the stuffed elk's head. "How are we going to handle this, Emmett? I reckon you aim to call Rex McKinnis and tell him what you think you know. Or maybe one of your buddies at the OSBI. Is that what you got planned?"

I didn't respond.

He reached slowly for the beer on his desk. "I'm just a little thirsty, alright?" I nodded. He drained it.

"Because if it is," he said, wiping his mouth with his shirtsleeve, "you're in for a surprise."

I spun around and looked behind me, in case the surprise he was talking about was about to whack me on the head. There was nobody. I kept my gun pointed at the clasp on his bolo.

"Rex'll do what's right," I said.

Burt waved his hand dismissively. "You wouldn't believe all the dirt I got on Saint Rex. He likes for folks to think he's the last honest man. Let me tell you, he's got plenty of snakes under his bed. Unless he wants his next job to be scrubbing toilets, he'll do what I tell him."

He looked at his watch. "What is it your lady friend is going to do?" he said with a leer. "Boy, I'll tell you, I have always admired the way she fills out a pair of jeans."

I didn't rise to the bait.

"We'll let that be a surprise," I said.

He grinned, exposing a gold tooth I'd never noticed before.

"Oh, I like surprises," he said, as something cold and hard pushed against the back of my neck.

I heard a gun being cocked and a familiar voice saying: "Remember me?"

***

Burt roared with laughter. "He's been in the bathroom this whole time, goddammit," he said. "Hell, he took so long, I was worried he'd fallen in. I don't know if you two have properly been introduced. Joe this is Emmett. Emmett, this is my nephew Joe."

I carefully placed my .45 on the floor next to the chair. Numb Nuts kicked it under one of the couches. Burt wrapped the telephone cord around his hand and ripped it from the wall.

"First time we met he was calling himself Leander McNelly."

Burt slapped his thigh. "My goodness, is that what you called yourself?"

Numb Nuts jammed his gun harder against my head and grinned. "Yup," he said in a self-satisfied tone of voice.

"Well, good for you, son. Good for you," said Burt. "Leander McNelly was a Confederate officer during the Civil War. 40 troops under his command captured a Union force of over 800 men, without firing a shot. Later on, he joined the Texas Rangers and cleared south Texas of banditos." He drew out each syllable: 'ban-dee-toes.' "Those he didn't kill, he chased across the Rio Grande and killed 'em there."

He looked proudly at his nephew. "Joe, dadgummit, I'm impressed you remembered."

"I remember everything you ever taught me, Uncle Burt," said Numb Nuts. The vibrations of his voice traveled through the gun barrel still jammed against my head.

"Well, I ain't going to give you a written test on it now, boy," said Burt. "Why don't you let Emmett sit down while we're gettin' ready. I doubt Miss Dean will have much luck rousing anyone to come out here and arrest me, but that's no reason to dawdle."

Numb Nuts removed the gun from my skull. I settled back into the overstuffed chair. He sat next to his uncle in a little bitty wooden step stool, like a little boy on his potty chair. I finally got a clear look at the damage I'd inflicted upon him.

A white bandage the size of a baseball covered his nose. Both eyes were as black as burnt sirloin. There was a cast on his right forearm where the trunk lid had come down on it; he had to hold the revolver in his left hand. The gun was a Smith & Wesson .357 magnum. He sat leaning forward, and rested it on the desk, pointed at me.

I said to Burt: "So you're Smiley."

"I haven't been called that in a long time," he said, his voice almost tender. "People used to say Sheriff DeLong looked like Gene Autry. When he hired me and I started sticking to him like shit on a shovel, they took to calling me Smiley, after Gene's sidekick, Smiley Burnette."

"You said you were hired as a deputy in '41," I said, knowing how weak that sounded.

"Did I?" he said and popped the top of another Lone Star from his miniature refrigerator. "You must've misheard. I was hired in January 1938."

In all the time I'd known him, I'd hardly ever trusted the slimy bastard about anything. Why in hell had I trusted him about this? My problem is that despite him being the way he is, I liked him. I wouldn't make that mistake again. If I ever got another chance.

"Why'd you do it, Burt? You didn't even live in Burr. Why'd you care if black folks lived there or not?"

"Hah!" he exclaimed. "I didn't care. That's the point. I did what I had to do to get ahead. I thought that was clear. Sheriff DeLong wasn't going to be in office much longer. I was too young to run for the office myself, but I wanted the new fella—whoever he was—to make me his top deputy. That way, when the time came for me to run for the top job, I'd be ready. So I kissed every butt cheek in sight. I cozied up to Vernon Raymer and Tom Bixby because they called the shots in this county. They wanted the coloreds out of town? I helped 'em run the coloreds out of town. They wanted Clarence's house burned down? I helped burn it down. When Vernon got cold feet, worried Clarence might identify Clyde as one of the arsonists, I did what I had to do. I didn't like it, but I did it. When something needs doing, I don't get all wishy-washy about it. I get the son of a bitch done. That's why I'm me and you're you."

Numb Nuts took in every word, awestruck. He kept the gun pointed at me.

"How'd Frank Sallee fit into this?" I asked.

Burt snorted contemptuously. "Oh hell, Frank was just a snot-nose, younger than me even. He wasn't no Einstein, but could see which way the wind was blowing in this department. He attached himself to me like I attached myself to Elton DeLong. Stupid son of a bitch didn't even know where I was taking him that night."

"That's the night you killed the Youngers?"

He nodded. "That's right," he said, frowning. "Frank didn't have nothing to do with burning their house. That was me, Harold Prentiss, Clyde and your uncle. Frank didn't even know about it." He paused. "I reckon your uncle must've told you all about this. That's what your trip to New York was for, am I right?"

A chill ran up my back. "How'd you know about that?"

"Ain't nothing in this county goes on I don't know about," he said dryly. "You should know that by now."

I did, but I guess I forgot.

"All my uncle remembered about you was that everyone called you Smiley. He didn't know who you were and that you were a deputy."

"No reason why he would. We'd never met. I sure as hell would never have mentioned it in his presence."

"Clyde told my uncle that on the night after the arson, he saw a couple of sheriff's deputies kill the family. He didn't tell him one of them was you, though. He just said that information was valuable and he'd save it for when he needed it."

He scratched his head. "Yeh well, he put it to use soon enough. How in hell he drove up without Frank and me seeing him, I'll never know. Clyde's always been a sneaky bastard. He's been holding that over my head ever since—especially after I got elected sheriff. If all he'd seen is me pull the trigger, it would've just been my and Frank's word against his. But he saw us dispose of the bodies. I had to be careful, with the whole family out there under a few feet of water, just waiting to be found."

"Clyde's been blackmailing you all this time."

"Let's just say: Clyde ain't exactly the genius businessman he makes himself out to be. Most of what he's gotten done has been because I greased the skids for him. Had to, with a murder charge hanging over my head." His smile returned full-bore. "Of course, things have changed a great deal over the last few months, with the killing of that Collins boy."

I felt a knot forming in my throat.

"What does that have to do with this?"

He looked like he was trying to decide whether to tell me.

"How 'bout I show you?" he said finally. He pulled an envelope out from under the blotter on his desk and waved it in the air. "This serves notice to Clyde Raymer that my days of licking his boots are over." He tossed it on the desk to where I could pick it up. "Go ahead. Read it."

In the open envelope was a letter, hand-written on WestOK stationery.

"*To whom it may concern: I, Dennis Tyler, confess to the kidnapping of Earl Collins. I didn't want to do it but was ordered to by my boss, Clyde Raymer of WestOK, Inc. If you're reading this, it's because I'm dead.*"

It went on to describe the plan, dates and locations of meetings where it was discussed, names of those involved—Darryl Martin, Tommy Drury, Elmer Kepley and of course Clyde—their roles, and why it was done: namely, to force Merle Collins to sell the land his house stood on, so Clyde could go forward with his plant expansion.

"Mr. Raymer said to me and Tommy, 'If threatening to kill his son won't make the stupid bastard sell, nothing will.' He told us his plan and said if I didn't do it I'd be fired. So me and Tommy and Darryl did it. I'm writing this letter and mailing it to myself so if something goes wrong and I get killed my wife can take it to the sheriff, and he can arrest Mr. Raymer. Because what we're about to do is wrong and I know it. I won't turn myself in because I don't want to go to jail, but I told my wife to give this to whoever the sheriff is after I die, no matter when it is."

In other circumstances, the letter would've seemed like an early Christmas present. As it was, there seemed little chance I'd live to see Clyde prosecuted.

Still, if this was the end, at least I would die with the knowledge Clyde might someday get what's coming to him.

"That's something else, huh?" Burt said. He held out his open hand. "I'm going to need that back."

I gave it to him and muttered, "I'm going to put that son of a bitch away for the rest of his life."

He slipped the letter back under the blotter. "Maybe you would," he said, "if I gave you the letter—which I'm not—or if I was going to let you live— which I'm probably not, either." He made a quizzical face. "Does that make any sense?"

Evidently, Numb Nuts took that as his cue. He got up from his little stool and leveled his revolver at my head.

Burt grabbed his arm. "No, goddammit, not here, dumb ass. That's all I need, a bunch of blood all over the carpet. We'll do this out back."

He tried to push himself up using the arms of his chair but his knees rebelled. He stumbled. Numb Nuts tried to break his fall. Just then, a voice called out from the doorway behind me: "What in the hell is going on here?"

Numb Nuts raised his gun and fired wildly. Burt ducked behind the desk. "Stop shooting, you goddam moron!" he yelled too late. Someone—Keith, it was—hollered: "Get down, Emmett!" I got down. Bullets whizzed back and forth over my head. Numb Nuts stopped to reload. In one motion, I pulled the Charter Arms .38 out of my boot, rose to a half-crouch and emptied five slugs into Joe Guthmiller, Jr.'s chest.

He was dead before he hit the floor.

CHAPTER THIRTY SEVEN

I looked from the desk to the doorway and back again. I couldn't see either Burt or Keith, but I could hear both breathing heavy.

I shouted, "Keith, are you ok?"

His head peeked out waist-high from behind the splintered door frame.

"No need to yell. I'm right here."

"You all right?"

"My right arm's shot to shit, but I'll live."

Burt's head emerged from behind his desk.

"Burt, don't you even think of crawling after that fancy-ass gun of yours. I saved a one for you." That was a lie. The Charter Arms only holds five shots, not the usual six, and I used them all on Joe, Jr. I counted on Burt not knowing that. Fortunately, I didn't click on an empty chamber.

Joe, Jr. had slid down and landed flat on his behind, arms slack, legs spread, feet splayed, like a puppet with its strings slashed. The wall behind him was streaked with blood and marred by bullet holes. The carpet was stained red.

Good luck explaining that to your wife, Sheriff Murray.

I stepped past Joe, Jr. and stood over Burt. I caught him in mid-crawl, on all fours, cringing in the expectation that I was about to do to him what he'd planned on doing to me. "Oh hell, Emmett, I surrender, I surrender."

"Get up."

He shook like a leaf but with some effort he managed to stand under his own power. I gestured for him to move from behind the desk. He tottered sideways like a crab, hands over his head, saying, "Don't shoot!"

I forced him down on the floor next to a huge trophy case that had somehow had escaped the hail of bullets unscathed. I borrowed Keith's handcuffs and locked Burt by one of his fat wrists to a leg of the trophy case, forcing him to lie awkwardly on his side. He bitched that it hurt. I pulled up my sleeve, ripped off the bandage and showed him my wrists. "Welcome to my world," I said.

He quieted down.

I picked up my own .45 from the floor where I'd dropped it and put it back in my shoulder holster. I carried Burt's Peacemaker over to Keith, who was sprawled on his butt in the hallway outside the door.

I held out the Peacemaker, grip-first. "Happy birthday," I said.

"Hell, I don't want it," he said. "That's a ladies' gun."

"A gal'd have to be mighty big to handle this thing," I said. "You don't want Karen to hear you say that. She should be here any minute."

I pulled a handful of shells out of my pocket and reloaded the .38. I already had my .45 and Burt's gun, but there's no such thing as being over-prepared. You never know who might come through that door.

I squatted on the floor next to Keith and examined his wound. "The shoulder, huh?" I said.

"You're a hell of a detective," he said

"Sam Spade, I ain't."

He laughed, then gasped. "More like Doc Holliday," he said through gritted teeth.

"Last time this happened, you called me Wyatt Earp."

"Yeh, well, consider it a promotion."

"That's no promotion. Doc was a consumptive and an alcoholic and a terrible dentist."

"Oh hell, all those gunfighters were alcoholics."

"Must be why I'm so good at it."

"Humph," he said, careful not to laugh this time.

I asked what brought him out.

"The guy who was helping me with that badge number called an hour ago. Told me it belonged to a fella named Joe Guthmiller, Jr. I tried to get you at home but you weren't there. I called Karen. When I mentioned Guthmiller's name, she said a cuss word I've never heard her use before and told me Joe, Jr. was Burt's nephew. We put two and two together. She told me where you were. I said I'd meet her here. So here I am."

"In the nick of goddam time, I'd say. They were about to take me outside to finish me off."

He shrugged then winced. "Just doing my job," he said, his voice strained.

I patted him lightly on the shoulder that hadn't been shot. "Would it be ok if I use your radio to give her a call?"

"I don't mind, as long as you call an ambulance while you're at it."

"I guess I'd better do that, huh?"

"If it's not too much trouble."

Given the condition of his right arm and shoulder, I had to fish his car keys out of his pocket myself. I picked up his revolver, reloaded it, and handed it to him. "Shoot him if you have to," I said, meaning Burt.

He looked over his shoulder at his thoroughly dishevelled and humiliated boss lying on the floor chained to a trophy case.

"I don't think that'll be necessary," he said.

I went into the bathroom in which Joe, Jr. had apparently spent so much time and grabbed some clean towels. I gave them to Keith to stanch the bleeding and went outside.

I fiddled with the radio in his cruiser until I got through to Bernard. He and Karen were on their way. I explained what had happened and told them to get the word out to Rex McKinnis and our friend at the OSBI, Agent Ovell Jones.

Calling a Temple City ambulance would've brought the sheriff's department. I radioed Pate's Funeral Home in Burr, instead. They were confused by the request, but agreed to send their ambulance

Back inside, I left the door open and turned on every light switch I could find, including a dozen or more spotlights aimed at the front of the house from every angle. Back in Burt's den, Keith had gotten up and moved to one of the couches. He held the now-bloody towels to his shoulder, careful not to make a mess of Kath Murray's furniture.

"He behaving himself?" I asked.

He shook his head. "Burt here's been trying to convince me you broke into his house and killed his nephew in cold blood. I had to remind him that his nephew was holding a gun on you when I got here and tried to blow my head off just as soon as I stuck it in the door."

"Well, you can't blame a guy for tryin', can you?" Burt chortled. "Just so you know, that's exactly the story I intend to tell Rex McKinnis and whoever else gets involved."

"Good luck with that one," Keith said.

A siren sounded in the distance.

"You don't seem too broken up about your nephew, Burt."

Joe, Jr.'s dead face seemed to register acknowledgment of his final screw-up, as if his last thought had been, "Oh yeh, I should've frisked that guy when I had the chance."

His highway patrol uniform shirt had no insignia or badge. His chest was a mass of blood and gore.

Burt sighed. "Oh well, you sign up for this business we're in, you got to know there's always the chance something like this will happen."

"Which business are you talking about?" I said. "Law enforcement or organized crime?"

His smile turned mean but he said nothing.

The siren was now sounding right outside the house. The blinds were closed but blinking red lights still cast a fiery, pulsing glow. Someone came in the front door.

"Did someone call for an ambulance?"

"Back here!" I yelled.

Two men rolled one of those portable gurneys through the door to Burt's office. They surveyed the scene, registering some amazement. I nodded toward Joe, Jr. "That one there's dead. The fella on the couch is the one needs help."

They got to work on Keith. I said, "Burt, let's you and I leave them in peace."

I took the Charter Arms out of my boot and stuffed it into the front of my pants. I unlocked the cuff holding him to the trophy case and helped him to his feet. "You need to lay off the chicken-fried steak, Burt." He didn't laugh. I cuffed his hands behind his back and marched him outside. He did not resist. I stuffed him into the back seat of Keith's cruiser, got in the back, and watched him in the rear-view mirror.

"Burt, I always knew you were out for yourself, but I thought for sure there was a conscience in there somewhere."

"Conscience!" he spat. "A conscience is like a soul—another one of them things people pretend to have to keep from bein' scared to die. Something that gives them comfort."

You can't argue with someone like that.

"I will say this, Emmett: I always liked you, even if you were weak."

"How was I weak, Burt?

"Ain't it obvious? You're the type who helps old ladies across the street. You never learned how to go through their purses when they weren't looking. People don't expect to get something for nothing. They expect you to take something extra for your hard work. People respect you for it. You always did what you did because you thought it was 'the right thing to do,' or some other horseshit." He paused. "I will say, I was tickled to see how close you got to putting Clyde away. Now that you and Rex got that letter, he should finally get what's coming to him."

"So you knew Clyde was behind the Collins kidnapping all along?"

"Who the hell didn't know?" he said. "I just didn't have any proof until I got that letter. Now you got it." He settled back in the seat. "At least I'll get a laugh when Clyde ends up in McAlester," he said dreamily. "After all these years of him holding this thing over my head—" His voice trailed off. More highway patrol cars pulled into the driveway. The place was getting crowded.

"Anyway, Emmett," he said. "This thing between you and me: It ain't nothin' personal. It's just business, is all."

I thought that was bullshit the first time I heard it. Still did.

Karen and Bernard drove up in the Fury. I left Burt locked in the car, got out and greeted them. They were naturally glad to see was I was ok. I explained what had happened. They didn't ask a lot of questions, which I appreciated. The folks with questions would be there soon enough.

The ambulance attendants wheeled out Keith. They'd given him a shot for the pain but said his injuries were not life-threatening. I asked him how he felt. He smiled dreamily. "Great, buddy. Top of the gol' dang world." His eyelids fluttered and closed. I asked the medics if it would be safe for Keith if waited for the investigating officers to arrive. They said it would, if they didn't take too long.

Agent Ovell Jones arrived a minute later. He introduced me to his new partner, a young blond woman by the name of Isabel Cruickshank. I told him what had transpired and gave him the .38 I'd used to shoot Joe, Jr. I asked if he wanted my .45, too.

"Did you use it?" he asked.

"Nah, never got a chance."

"Then keep it. I don't want you going around unarmed."

The medics had placed Keith in the ambulance. Agents Jones and Cruickshank stood outside the open rear door and questioned him. I doubt they got too much out of him. He was as high as a kite.

They then went inside to examine the crime scene. By now, cops from various jurisdictions had appeared. There was some wrestling for control until eventually Ovell shamed or otherwise intimidated the lot into accepting his overall command.

He issued a series of orders, then sat me down on a couch in Burt's living room. He grilled me for what seemed like an hour but probably wasn't that long. Rex arrived and sat in on some of it. I'd told him the background story earlier that day, but Agent Jones was hearing it all for the first time, so I had to start from the beginning.

When we were finished, Ovell and Agent Cruickshank went outside to question Burt, still cuffed in the back seat of Keith's cruiser. The back door was open and two state troopers stood laughing and carrying on with Burt like it was a normal weekday lunch at Cup O'Joe's. Ovell chewed them out ordered them to vacate. They slunk off.

Agent Cruickshank had requested I stay in the living room, but I was stir crazy and followed her down the hall back to Burt's office. She saw me step through the doorway, physically turned me around, and pushed me back in the direction of the living room. I ended up outside, standing in the driveway, which was now crowded with official vehicles and lit up like Yankee Stadium for a night game.

Ovell was huddled with Rex in a dark corner. Rex seemed to be doing most of the talking. They separated and approached a pair of Temple City policemen, who pulled Burt out of Keith's car, loaded him into their cruiser, and drove off, lights flashing. I noticed they didn't remove the handcuffs.

Rex came over to where I stood. "Agent Jones and I don't want the patrol involved any more than necessary," he said.

"Sounds wise, given the circumstances."

"Listen, Emmett, by the looks of things, you should be in the clear, but I'm going to need time to sort things out. Maybe a day or two. Something else happened today I'm not at liberty to talk about. It complicates things even more." I must've looked concerned, because he added, "Don't worry. It should work to your benefit."

"Can't you give me a hint?"

He gave me a grim smile. "Let's just say you were on the right track about a few things. We'll let it go at that. For now."

CHAPTER THIRTY EIGHT

Karen and I decided it would be best for me to sleep in my own bed. Or at least my own La-Z-Boy. I got home around 4:30 and lay awake for an hour before finally falling asleep. I slept until just after 11:00, when it became impossible to ignore Dizzy's increasingly frantic requests to eat, play and whatnot.

After a much-needed shower, I sat at on my couch in my underwear, drank coffee, and watched the noon news. I switched it off during the farm report and got dressed. I had an early afternoon appointment with Agent Jones to give my formal statement. Happily, I'd be doing so at our own station instead of OSBI headquarters in Oklahoma City.

When I walked in there were a half-dozen people jammed into our cramped cinder block cube. Agents Jones and Cruickshank were in deep conversation with Bernard. Karen was typing up the last of those documents from the other day. Kenny was talking on the phone and Jeff was losing a wrestling match with our electric coffee pot. Everyone was glad to see me and I was glad to see them.

Ovell was wearing the same dirty red tie as when we met for the first time. In the light of day, his saggy jowls, bloodshot eyes, and five o'clock shadow made him look like Fred Flintstone, if Fred laced his oatmeal with rubbing alcohol. He asked me how I was feeling.

"Better than I have any right to," I said.

He looked at Agent Cruickshank and me. "Y'all ready?"

She nodded.

I said, "I reckon so."

We went back to my former office, which for the time being was still Bernard's.

Ovell said, "You can have a lawyer present if you want one, but I'd advise you to save your money."

"No need," I said. "Let's get it done."

The agents were kind enough to let me sit behind my old desk. Ovell sat in a folding chair across from me. Due to the cramped conditions, Agent Cruickshank had to sit on the cot in the holding cell. I made my statement, which remained unchanged from what I'd said the night before, except it took longer because I added more detail. Agent Cruickshank recorded my words in shorthand. I'd still barely heard her speak.

Ovell appeared satisfied when it was over. "Just a matter of crossing the i's and dotting the t's," he said.

"I appreciate your consideration, Agent Jones."

"Yeh, well, we've got witnesses who can confirm almost everything you say. In fact, not only did you did nail Murray and this Sallee character, apparently your D.A. might also charge Clyde Raymer for conspiracy in the Collins case. That's some pretty fancy police work for someone who ain't even officially a cop. Not for another week, anyway."

"I'd say I was just doing my job, but that wouldn't be true, I guess," I said. "I'll be glad just to get cleared to go back to work."

He winked. "You ain't in a bit of trouble. In fact, I wouldn't be surprised if you got a medal."

He was half right. I wasn't in trouble. But I sure as hell wasn't getting a medal.

***

I made the drive to Temple City to see Rex at his request. He met me at his office door offered his hand.

"Thanks for coming, Emmett. First of all, I want to tell you what a fine job you did on this. Your town's lucky to have you."

Him saying 'first of all' meant there'd be a 'second of all,' which made me nervous. We sat across from each other around a low glass-topped table. A grandfather clock next to door kept time. Charlie Parker's song "Confirmation" ran over and over in my head. "Yesterday morning," he began, "I got an anonymous phone call from someone who said Sheriff Murray was concealing evidence that Clyde Raymer had conspired in the kidnapping and murder of Earl Collins."

He lit a cigarette, thought better of it and crushed it out in an ashtray on the glass tabletop. "I walked downstairs to Burt's office to ask him about it. He wasn't there, which was unusual. Nobody knew where he was. I drove out to his house. No one was home, not even his wife. Later on, someone told me she was in Arizona. I left a note on the door asking him to contact me as soon as possible. He never did. I called his office again. His secretary said he was there briefly, took a call from you, then went out again."

I nodded. "I wanted to make an appointment to talk about the things you and I discussed."

"I guessed as much. Presumably, he invited you to his house."

"He said he had a lot on his plate and couldn't fit me in during the day time and asked if we could meet at 9:00."

"Well, he left right after that, and didn't tell his secretary where he was going. She assumed that he was just getting an early start on the weekend. Clyde Raymer's wife had phoned a couple of times. She wanted to know if Burt had seen him. He'd left for the construction site that morning, saying he'd be home for lunch, but he didn't show. She called the site. The foreman said he left before lunch and never came back."

"He told me the same thing when I went out there looking for him."

"Why were you looking for him?"

"My uncle told me he'd confessed to witnessing the Younger murders, and I wanted to ask him about it."

He nodded. "Yeh, Clyde was in demand yesterday." He covered his mouth and yawned. "Sorry," he said wearily. "Late night."

"Sure was."

He stifled another yawn. "Anyway," he said, "the foreman told me Burt showed up looking for Clyde right after you left."

"Doesn't surprise me."

"Why is that?"

"Oh hell, last night Burt told me a story about how Clyde had been holding the Younger murders over his head all these years. He showed me that letter and said he was done having Clyde lord it over him."

Rex nodded thoughtfully. "Perhaps. Right now, we don't know if Clyde was in on the plot to abduct you."

"Any idea who called you about that letter?"

"Well, it's a funny thing," he said. "When you were, uh, out of commission—"

"You mean when I was drying out?"

He looked at his shoes and nodded. "Yeh. In the two or three weeks after the Collins kidnapping, I questioned several people who I thought might be able to shed light on it. One of them was Lorena Tyler, Dennis Tyler's ex-wife. She insisted she didn't know anything about the crime, that she'd cut all ties with him. She was easy to believe, but I still got the feeling she was holding something back."

"You think she was the one who called you yesterday?"

"Yeh, well, I'll get to that in a minute," he said. "The first time I talked to her, she told me she'd divorced Tyler on grounds of physical abuse. She swore she hadn't had anything to do with him since, but the way she said it made me suspect she wasn't being completely honest."

"You get a sense of those things in this business," I said.

"You do," he said with a nod. "So anyway, the woman on the phone yesterday tried to disguise her voice, but I was 99-percent sure it was Lorena Tyler. I stopped by her house last night on my way home. She held out for maybe five minutes before admitting she made the call. She told me what I imagine Burt told you—that Dennis had written himself a letter confessing to the crimes, and telling who else was in on the deal, including Clyde. He mailed it to himself and gave it to her for safe-keeping. She was supposed to keep it sealed and turn it over to law enforcement if something happened to him. Initially she thought he was just being paranoid. Apparently, he's inclined to think folks are out to get him, so she didn't give it much thought, just put the letter aside. Unopened."

"Until the shit hit the fan," I said.

"Exactly."

"At which point she must've gotten curious as to what was in that letter."

Rex nodded. "She insists she didn't open it until Tyler was killed. That's what's keeping her out of jail, for the time-being, at least. If he'd told her about the scheme before the crimes were committed—or if she'd read the letter beforehand—then she'd be an accessory. But she claims not to have known. She says only found out when she read the letter."

"Which was afterwards."

He nodded.

"You believe her?" I asked.

He see-sawed his hand in a maybe-maybe-not gesture. "I'm deciding I do, until I decide I don't."

"I see," I said. "What else'd she say?"

"Even after Tyler died, she claims she didn't open it. Not at first. She left it sealed, not sure of what to do. She claimed she didn't tell me about it when I questioned her because she didn't want to get in trouble. It sounds fishy and probably is. She claims to have thought about burning it without reading it, but says her curiosity got the best of her. She steamed it open. It scared the bejeesus out of her, so she resealed it, put it in a manila envelope, and mailed it to Burt. She says she waited and waited for someone to do something. When nobody did, she called me. Yesterday."

Her story had gaps big enough for an elephant to waltz through sideways. I said as much.

"I know," Rex said. "There's a lot wrong with it. But hear me out. Believing her is to our benefit. Lorena Tyler's not who we want. Anyway, it'd be hard to prove she's lying. Of course, if you hadn't nailed Burt and discovered the letter, we wouldn't have any ammunition against Clyde at all."

"Except my uncle's testimony."

He made a skeptical face. "You think he'd testify?"

"Maybe," I said. "If he doesn't, would that letter be enough to convict?"

He hesitated. "The short answer to that is 'no,' Emmett. But there's more to it."

He got up, walked over to the water cooler, and took a drink. He asked if I wanted one. I said no. He sat back down.

"Ok," he said. "By late yesterday afternoon both Clyde and Burt were missing. Something was up. I drove around looking for them. No luck. While I was out my secretary got more calls from Clara Raymer, who was frantic. I was getting concerned, myself. I issued a BOLO for Clyde—not because I was worried for his safety, necessarily, but because I wanted to question him about his involvement in the Collins case and thought he might be on the run."

"So last night when you read Dennis Tyler's letter, you realized you had Clyde nailed."

"I thought it was possible," he said cautiously. "I had evidence of his participation. Enough to arrest, definitely. Enough to convict? Maybe not." He paused. "Probably not."

My heart sank.

"You're not going after him?"

"I'm not saying that. Heck yeh, we're going after him. I woke a judge in the middle of the night and got him to issue an arrest warrant. The Highway Patrol picked him up in Durant at three o'clock this morning, about to cross the river into Texas. No, I guess what I'm saying is: I'm going to leave it up to you whether to prosecute."

"Me?" I said incredulously. "Hell yeh! Put him on trial and see how it shakes out. The worst that could happen is he gets off. He wouldn't be the first guilty man to walk free."

Rex sighed.

"No, Emmett, there's something else to consider," he said in a sorrowful voice, "which is why I asked you here today. We've got some decisions to make."

CHAPTER THIRTY NINE

It might be nice if once in a while we got a decent snowfall.

Not like in New York City last week, necessarily, or in Korea, where the first thing I did every morning was disinter myself from the coffin of ice that enveloped me on the rare winter nights I could sleep.

Still, I wouldn't mind if, during the holiday season, at least, we got something white and fluffy, instead of the mean and stingy little grains of ice that we usually get.

It was the day before Christmas, 1966. I was standing on the shore of Burr Lake with a small assembly of law enforcement agents and curious onlookers. Except for Karen and Bernard on either side of me, everyone spaced themselves wide-apart from one another, like they were scared of catching some contagious disease.

The snow was slow and sparse. The temperature hovered around freezing. Flakes hit the ground not knowing whether to live or die. The water was dull brown, the sky gray and without distinguishing features. I felt like a plastic figure in a leaky snow globe.

The OSBI had borrowed a boat from a state park ranger and used sonar to locate Clarence's car. It didn't take long to find. It was a few feet past the last piling, where the end of the old pier once rose above the water.

Someone found a qualified diver, so we gathered in the cold and wet and watched, as a guy dressed up like Lloyd Bridges in *Sea Hunt* attached a cable to a submerged Model T for the purpose of raising it and poking around in it looking for dead bodies.

The diver trudged into the water carrying a hook at the end of a long cable attached to the winch on Wes Harmon's green Sinclair tow truck.

When the water got deep enough, he dove. For a couple of minutes, all we saw were bubbles from his air tank rising to the surface. The cable danced. He continued to tug. Wes let out more slack.

The diver reappeared and gave us a thumbs-up.

"Here we go," I said under my breath to nobody in particular. Red took my hand and squeezed.

Wes started the winch's motor. It lurched and squealed and pulled. After a few seconds, the square rear end of an antique automobile rose above the surface.

"Hello, Lizzie," Bernard said quietly.

"Lizzie?" asked Karen.

"Tin Lizzie," I said. "That's what they used to call Model T's, back in the day."

"Looks like this one was a hard top," added Bernard. "Most of 'em were rag tops."

The car was the same reddish-brown color as the water in which it had been submerged for 26 years. At first, I thought it was because of the mud, but upon closer inspection I realized it was mostly because of rust. Big jagged gaps were visible where the metal had been eaten away. Pieces of the body as big as my fist flaked off into the water as they pulled it ashore.

The roof was only a decomposed metal frame. The tires were misshapen and falling off the wheels. The glass in the rear window was partially intact, although the surrounding metal had largely rotted away. It had spider-web cracks, like it had been struck by a rock or maybe a small-caliber bullet.

The process was slow but sure. Lloyd Bridges talked quietly with Ovell Jones. A few men—Bernard among them—waded into the shallow water and tried to help, but the winch did most of the work. The axles were rusted solid. The wheels cut deep ruts into the mud.

The car cleared the water. Wes shut off the winch.

Ovell and Agent Cruickshank approached the car, accompanied by a youngish-looking man man in gray coveralls who I took to be the OSBI's forensic sciences expert. Ovell tugged gently on the driver's side door. He let go when it threatened to come off on his hand. The three looked inside, dour looks on their faces. They talked among themselves. Jones peered inside one more time, shook his head, and walked over to me.

"Emmett," he said.

"Ovell."

"I believe we've found who we're looking for."

I looked past the derelict car and out at the water. A seagull landed on one of the pilings. Must've come from the Salt Flats over by Rose Crest.

I nodded. "I'll take your word for it."

"You don't want to look?"

I sighed. "No, but I guess I should."

"It's up to you."

"Let's get it over with."

We walked over and I looked inside.

The interior was distorted by mud and rust. It looked like it had been formed out of modelling clay and fence wire by an untalented six-year-old. The metal parts were corroded beyond recognition. The seat fabric had disintegrated, leaving the springs exposed. At first, I didn't see any traces of human remains.

No doubt because I didn't want to.

I took a deep breath and looked harder. There they were. Three human skulls, covered in layers of mud but easily identifiable as being what they were. Two were adult—presumably Clarence and his wife Eunice. The third was a child's—the couple's daughter, Ethyl. I looked for a fourth but didn't see one.

I remembered how they all looked when I saw them last, sitting dejectedly in this same car, as Clarence came to our front door and asked my daddy for help. I remembered waving to my friend Gabe. I remember him waving back and saying, "Hey, Emmett."

For a split-second I felt a blind rage toward my father, but I fought it off the way I always do.

Everett Hardy didn't kill the Youngers, I told myself. Sure, he could've helped them, but things were different back them. It's not fair to judge him using the standards we use today. He did what he had to do to protect his family.

I let that voice have its say, then chased it back to where it came from—
that dark place where we lock up the lies we tell our heart.

Of course, believing we can imprison them forever is just another lie.
They metastasize, consume us, like the rust that ate away that old Tin Lizzie,
until, finally, there's nothing left.

But meanwhile, you've got to live your life.

Ovell jolted me back to the present. "This the car you remember?" he
said.

"It is," I said, and walked away.

CHAPTER FORTY

With everything that was going on, I forgot about Christmas until it was almost too late. I never did visit Tiffany's when I was in New York—I doubt I could've afforded anything there, anyway—so I needed to buy Karen something nice.

On Christmas Eve afternoon, after the unfortunate business at the lake, I took a trip to the fancy ladies' underthings store in Temple City and bought Karen a set of blue silk pyjamas.

The next morning, my losing streak of unsuitable gifts to my beloved ended. She liked them. I liked how she looked in them. A good time was had by all.

I spent the week before New Year's preparing to re-take the reins of the department. The transition promised to be seamless. Bernard did a terrific job while I was gone, and I'm not saying that because he did everything the same as I would have. But he did.

Usually on New Year's Eve, Karen and I attend the party at the Moose Lodge in Alva. This year we spent a quiet evening at Dad's with him and Peggy. Dad's friends Jerry and Becky Fuller joined us, as well.

Peggy cooked a terrific meal—roast beef with carrots and onions, mashed potatoes and gravy on the side. Dad was at his best, almost like his old self. He and Jerry told stories I'd heard a million times. I don't think I ever enjoyed them more. Red and Becky pretended to complain about what lunkheads their men were. In deference to my father, talk of recent events was avoided. All the while, Peggy kept a close eye on Dad.

I pulled her aside and thanked her for what she was doing to help him. "I should thank you!" she said in that bubbly way she has. "I couldn't ask for a better job!" Around 10:00 she made it known that Dad was getting tired and should probably go to bed.

"We've got a long drive ahead of us, anyway," said Becky graciously. We all said our farewells and drove into the frigid night.

When Karen realized we were headed to my place instead of hers, she tensed up like Dizzy when I take her to the vet.

"What's goin' on?"

"Don't worry, I've got a surprise," I said. "More than one, in fact."

"One of them had best involve a clean house," she said warily.

"Funny you should say that."

The time and effort I'd spent cleaning paid off. "There may be hope for you yet," Karen said.

"There's something else, too." I handed her a gift-wrapped box. Inside was another pair of silk pyjamas—black this time, instead of blue. Now that I'd gotten my gift-giving right, I intended to ride the streak as long as I could.

"Now what am I going to do with two sets of fancy pyjamas?" she said coyly.

"One for your place and one for mine."

I expected her to say something sassy, but instead, she said, "Ah, that makes sense," which I took as a hopeful sign.

She changed in the bathroom. We sat close on the couch and looked for something worth watching on the TV. Lawrence Welk introduced the Lennon Sisters (recently, Bernard asked me if they were related to the fella in the Beatles; I told him if I had to bet, I'd say no). I changed the channel before they could do much damage.

We settled on Johnny Carson, same as we do most nights. By 11:30 Red was starting to nod off. I extricated myself from her embrace and went out in the back yard. Karen hadn't seen the fire pit since I'd had it refurbished. I built a fire and went back into the house to get her. She bundled up in a heavy blanket and I led her out with my hands over her eyes.

"Ready?" I said.

"I was born ready, pardner."

"Surprise!" I took my hands away.

Her eyes lit up before she remembered it was her job to act blasé.

"Not bad," she said coolly. "Not bad at all."

We sat around the fire in a couple of new cushioned lawn chairs I'd purchased for the occasion. The temperature was well below freezing, but we had a fire to keep us warm.

We didn't say much, just enjoyed each other's company. I could hardly take my eyes off her. She looked, I don't know ... I guess *radiant* might best describe it. The way the light bounced shadows across her face. The glint in her green eyes, the shine of her auburn hair. At that moment I considered myself a very lucky man.

I realized I couldn't recall when I'd last craved a drink. It was earlier in the day, I was sure, but I couldn't remember exactly when. I reckoned that was a good omen.

I checked the new Timex Red had given me for Christmas. My wrists had mostly healed. This had been the first day I could wear it without pain.

"11:49," I said.

"Eleven more minutes and we can put this terrible year to bed," she said.

"I will be glad to get 1966 behind us."

I watched her watch the fire for a minute.

"I hate to break the mood," she said, "but I just want to get something straight."

I had an idea what was coming. "Rex swore me to secrecy about the case," I warned.

"Oh, come on, now, don't be ridiculous. He wasn't talking about me."

I had to admit she was probably right.

"Alright," I said. "What do you want to know?"

"Ok," she said, and took a deep breath. "You've given Rex evidence of two very serious crimes, but now he's saying he can only prosecute one? And he's going to leave it up to you to decide which?"

I stared into the fire and let it blur my vision. "Yeh," I said. "That's about the size of it."

"Why?"

I shrugged. "He has a lot more on Burt than he does Clyde. All he has on Clyde is Dennis Tyler's letter accusing him of being behind the abduction and death of Earl Collins. He also has Burt saying Clyde confessed to him, but under the circumstances, nothing Burt says is worth much."

She nodded. "I see. One son of a gun's word against another."

"Yeh, you could say that."

"On the other hand," she countered, "Clyde actually saw Burt kill the Youngers, stuff their bodies in the that old Model-T, with Frank Sallee's help, and push it in the lake."

"That's right," I said, "and now we have their remains and—hopefully—Sallee's testimony to back it up."

"Have you heard from the coroner yet?"

"I talked to him yesterday. He confirmed what Ovell said. Three people. One adult male, one adult female, one minor female. All shot in the head."

The flames crackled. She said, "That means your friend Gabe must've gotten away."

"That's what Sallee will say if we can get him to testify."

"What's the hold up?"

"It's complicated. Clyde witnessed the killings, but won't testify unless Rex drops the charges against him in the Collins case. Sallee will testify against Burt if he gets a reduced sentence, but only if Clyde testifies."

"What's Sallee got to say?"

"He'll say Burt took him out there under false pretenses and did all the shooting."

"Is that true?"

"No question about it. The OSBI found the slugs on the floor of the car. They're 90-percent sure it's a match with that fancy-assed nickel-plated Peacemaker Burt tried to use on me."

"Why do you need Clyde if you have the ballistic evidence?"

"The bullets are pretty degraded after all that time under water, which is why they say they're only 90-percent sure and not 100. Also, Burt's lawyer could claim the gun belonged to someone else and that Burt acquired it later, or some other bullshit. Rex believes he needs Clyde to back up Sallee's story that Burt did the shooting."

A gust of icy wind blew over us. Karen pulled her blanket tighter. "Why is it that Sallee won't testify unless Clyde does?

"It makes sense when you think about it," I said. "Clyde's the only one other than Burt who can place Sallee at the scene of the crime. If Rex doesn't give Clyde what he wants, he'll refuse to testify. If Clyde doesn't testify, Sallee won't testify. The whole damn thing falls apart."

"Well, you have that letter from Dennis Tyler," she said. "Rex could still go after Clyde."

"Rex says it's a pretty flimsy case. He doesn't doubt for a minute that Clyde's guilty, but it would be hard to prove. He'll take it to court if I want him to, but he doubts a jury will convict based almost entirely on that letter. On the other hand, there's at least the possibility Clyde would be convicted, which is why he's willing to testify against Burt—"

"—in exchange for dropping all charges against him for the Collins case."

"Exactly," I said. "I assume it's also because he hates Burt's guts."

"So prosecuting Burt is close to a sure thing, while going after Clyde is a coin flip."

"It's not fair, but that's the way it is." I picked up a rock off the ground and tossed it into the fire. Embers floated onto my boots.

"Brrr," she said. "How long 'til midnight?"

I checked my watch. "Two minutes."

"I don't suppose you'd go inside and get my stocking cap?" she said, as sweet as a New York cannoli.

"Come on, girl, you can wait two minutes," I said.

"Grrr," she snarled and wrapped the top of the blanket around her head, leaving just her eyes exposed.

A minute passed.

"Emmett, I'm sorry," she said. "I know how much all this has taken out of you. I know you want to see Clyde pay for what he did. But you did a wonderful thing, getting to the bottom of the Younger case after all these years. Who knows? Gabe might be out there somewhere. Maybe you can track him down and let him know you've gotten justice for his family."

"Stranger things have happened," I said.

I checked my watch again. "Uh-oh, here we go ... five, four, three, two, one ... Happy 1967, beautiful." Across town, folks cheered and shot off firecrackers. We leaned close and kissed.

I'd been keeping an important piece of news to myself.

"There *is* one other thing I can do about Clyde," I said. "In fact, I've already done it."

She pulled the blanket off her head. Mussed hair fell across her forehead. I love that look.

"What did you do?" she asked.

I waited for the drama to build.

"Did I tell you I saw my wife when I was in New York?"

Her jaw dropped. "I believe I would've remembered it if you did," she said dryly. "Did you behave yourself?"

"Of course," I said. "We were just friends." That wasn't exactly true, but it wasn't exactly a lie either. "Anyhow," I continued, "I don't know if I ever told you, but she's a journalist. She writes about national news for a big New York City newspaper. I told her about the Collins and Younger cases. She thinks it's an important story."

"She's going to write for a New York paper about something that happened in little old Burr?"

"That's right."

"Including what Clyde did?"

"Including Clyde's part in both the Younger and Collins cases," I said. "It all ties in. She thinks a story might even draw enough attention to get the U.S. Attorney's office involved. She says these days LBJ's boys are more and more inclined to prosecute civil rights violations."

"Hah!" she said. "If what happened to that poor family isn't a civil rights violation, I don't know what is."

"True enough," I said. "In any case, you might want to get ready for a visit from her."

She looked at me blankly. "She's coming here?"

"Last I heard."

"What was her name again?"

She knows, but I played along.

"Sofie."

She wavered. "I guess that would be ok."

"I also talked to her about something else."

"What?" she said glumly.

"I asked her for a divorce."

Her eyes brightened. "What'd she say?"

"What else would she say? She said yes."

She got a mischievous look. "Doesn't need you anymore, huh?"

"If you're asking if she's a legal resident, I didn't ask," I said. "But she said yes, so I guess she's not worried about getting deported anymore."

"Did it break her heart?"

"I think she forgot we were still married, to be honest. Anyway, I got some papers in the mail the other day. I just need to sign them."

"Then you'll be a single man, huh?"

"Not for long, I hope."

She gave me a sideways look. "Is that your way of proposing, or is there someone else I don't know about?"

"No one else. Just you."

A smile spread across her face. "So that's what all this fixing up your house was about? Trying to butter me up?"

"I reckon if we get married, we should probably live under the same roof."

"Yours?"

"This was my grandparents' house before it was mine. Just the other day, I was thinking about how I used to play in this yard, and how it might be nice to watch my own kids do the same thing."

"Kids, as in, more than one?"

"I reckon we'll start with one and see how it goes."

Her smile dimmed. "Promise you'll take care of yourself?"

"I promise."

She scanned my face as if trying to scientifically measure the likelihood I'd keep my word. After several uncomfortably long seconds, she nodded and stood. "Alright then, we'd best be getting to bed."

I stayed put. "I'm not sleepy."

There was a naughty twinkle in those green eyes. "Neither am I."

The spitting image of Susan Hayward. That's what I've always thought.

A combination of unexpected lust and bitter cold froze me in my seat.

"Come on, tall, dark, and handsome," she said in a throaty voice. "Don't make me start without you."

I jumped right up. Funny how nimble I can be when properly motivated.

She offered her hand. I took it. We walked toward the house.

She gave me a playful elbow to the ribs. "Your bed *is* made, right?"

"I haven't slept in it much lately, but it was the last time I checked."

"It'd sure better be," she warned, then glanced over her shoulder. "You going take care of that?" she asked.

"The fire? It'll burn itself out."

"Hmmm," she said, nuzzling my cheek. "We'll see about that."

"Oh, *that* fire'll never go out," I said. "It's the eternal flame."

ABOUT THE AUTHOR

Chris Kelsey is a native Oklahoman now living in Dutchess County, New York. In addition to being the award-winning author of the Emmett Hardy series, Chris is also an accomplished jazz saxophonist. He is currently Director of Instrumental Music at Trinity-Pawling School in Pawling, NY.

NOTE FROM THE AUTHOR

Word-of-mouth is crucial for any author to succeed. If you enjoyed *Ain't Nothin' Personal*, please leave a review online—anywhere you are able. Even if it's just a sentence or two. It would make all the difference and would be very much appreciated.

Thanks!
Chris Kelsey